*For my sisters, Laura Ly and Alyssa Cheng,
and all the other fierce women who hold up the sky.*

★ "This captivating novel explores intersectionality, conveys the effects of restrictions placed on women and people of color, and celebrates the strengths and talents of marginalized people struggling to break society's barriers in any age."
—PUBLISHERS WEEKLY, starred review

★ "A compelling domestic drama with a winning heroine."
—THE BULLETIN OF THE CENTER FOR CHILDREN'S BOOKS, starred review

"A triumph of storytelling. *The Downstairs Girl* is a bold portrait of this country's past, brilliantly painted with wit, heartbreak, and unflinching honesty. Everyone needs to read this book."
—STEPHANIE GARBER, bestselling author of *Caraval*

"A gorgeous tale that will steal your heart. This is not only a keeper, but a classic!"
—ROBIN LAFEVERS, bestselling author of the His Fair Assassin trilogy

"A jewel of a story. By shining a light on the lives of those whom history usually ignores, Stacey Lee gives us a marvelous gift: An entirely new and riveting look at our past."
—CANDACE FLEMING, award-winning author of *The Family Romanov*

"Clever, funny, and poignant, *The Downstairs Girl* is Stacey Lee at her best."
—EVELYN SKYE, bestselling author of *The Crown's Game*

"Immersive, important, and thoroughly entertaining, *The Downstairs Girl* sparkles with all of Stacey Lee's signature humor, charm, warmth, and wisdom."
—KELLY LOY GILBERT, Morris Award Finalist for *Conviction*

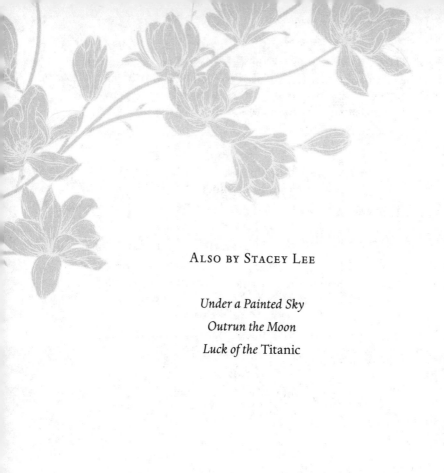

ALSO BY STACEY LEE

Under a Painted Sky
Outrun the Moon
Luck of the Titanic

THE DOWNSTAIRS GIRL

Stacey Lee

PENGUIN BOOKS

PENGUIN BOOKS
An imprint of Penguin Random House LLC, New York

First published in the United States of America by G. P. Putnam's Sons, 2019
Published by Penguin Books, an imprint of Penguin Random House LLC, 2021

Visit us online at penguinrandomhouse.com

THE LIBRARY OF CONGRESS HAS CATALOGED THE G. P. PUTNAM'S SONS EDITION AS FOLLOWS:
Names: Lee, Stacey, author.
Title: The downstairs girl / Stacey Lee.
Description: New York, NY: G. P. Putnam's Sons, [2019]
Summary: "1890, Atlanta. By day, seventeen-year-old Jo Kuan works as a lady's maid for the cruel Caroline Payne, the daughter of one of the wealthiest men in Atlanta. But by night, Jo moonlights as the pseudonymous author of a newspaper advice column for 'the genteel Southern lady.' "—Provided by publisher.
Identifiers: LCCN 2018018881 | ISBN 9781524740955 (hardback) |
ISBN 9781524740962 (ebook)
Subjects: | CYAC: Household employees—Fiction. | Wealth—Fiction. | Advice columns—Fiction. | Authorship—Fiction. | Chinese Americans—Fiction. | Atlanta (Ga.)—History—19th century—Fiction.
Classification: LCC PZ7.1.L43 Dow 2019 | DDC [Fic]—dc23
LC record available at https://lccn.loc.gov/2018018881

Penguin Books ISBN 9781524740979

10 9 8 7 6 5 4

Printed in the United States of America

Design by Kirin Diemont and Eileen Savage
Text set in Dante MT Pro

One

Being nice is like leaving your door wide-open. Eventually, someone's going to mosey in and steal your best hat. Me, I have only one hat and it is uglier than a smashed crow, so if someone stole it, the joke would be on their head, literally. Still, boundaries must be set. Especially boundaries over one's worth.

Today I will demand a raise.

"You're making that pavement twitchy the way you're staring at it." Robby Withers shines his smile on me. Ever since the traveling dentist who pulled Robby's rotting molar told him he would lose more if he didn't scrub his teeth regularly, he has brushed twice daily, and he expects me to do it, too.

"Pavement is underappreciated for all it does to smooth the way," I tell his laughing eyes, which are brown like eagle's feathers, same as his skin. "We should be more grateful."

Robby gestures grandly at the ground. "Pavement, we're much obliged, despite all the patty cakes we dump on you." He pulls me away from a pile of manure. It was Robby's mother who nursed me when I was a baby, God rest her soul. And it was she who told Old Gin about the secret basement under the print shop.

Whitehall Street, the "spine" of Atlanta, rises well above the treetops with her stately brick and imposing stone buildings— along with the occasional Victorian house that refuses to give up her seat at the table. Business is good here, and like the long-leaf pine forests, being burned by Sherman's troops a quarter century ago only made the city grow back stronger.

"You look different today." I pretend to appraise him from his cap to his tan trousers. "You forget something?" It is rare to see him without the mule and cart he uses as a deliveryman for Buxbaum's Department Store.

"They're down a clerk. Mr. Buxbaum's letting me fill in until they find someone new." He straightens his pin-striped jacket, though it's already straight enough to measure with.

"You don't say." Mr. Buxbaum is popular among whites and colored alike, but hiring a colored clerk isn't done in these parts.

"If I do a good job, maybe he'll let me fill in on a more permanent basis." He gives me a tight smile.

"If you don't stick your foot out, you'll never advance. You'd be perfect for the job. I myself am fixing to ask Mrs. English for a raise."

He whistles, a short low sound. "If Mrs. English had any sense, she'd give it to you. Of course, common sense was never very common in these parts."

I nod, a surge of righteous blood flooding my veins. Two years I have worked as a milliner's assistant at the same wage of fifty cents a day. Measly. It is already 1890. Plus, Old Gin has lost too much weight, and I need to buy him medicine—not a booty ball or buckeye powder, but something legitimate. And legitimate costs money.

One of the newly electric streetcars approaches, bringing by an audience of Southerners in various stages of confusion at the sight of me. An Eastern face in Western clothes always sets the game wheels to spinning between curiosity and disapproval. Most of the time, the pointer lands on disapproval. I should charge them for the privilege of ogling me. Of course, I'd have to split the fee with Robby, whose six-foot height also draws attention, even as he keeps his eyes on the sidewalk.

He stops walking and squares his cap so that it's flat enough to play chess on. "Here's my stop. Good luck, Jo."

"Thanks, but keep some for yourself."

He winks, then slips down a narrow alley to use the back door to Buxbaum's. Old Gin tells me things have changed for the worse since I was born. After good ol' President Hayes returned the South to "home rule," Dems told colored people they should use the back alleys from then on, which pretty much sums up everything.

Fluffing the sleeves of my russet dress, which have lost their puff and hang like a pair of deflated lungs, I carry myself a block farther to English's Millinery. The shop stands between a candle maker and a seed store, meaning it can smell like a Catholic church or alfalfa, depending on which way the wind blows. This morning, however, the air is still too crisp to hold a scent. The picture windows are as clear as our Lord's eyes— how I left them last night—with several mauve hats displayed. Mauve is having a moment.

Instead of going through the front, I also trek to the back entrance. Folks care less about which door Chinese people use nowadays, compared with when the laborers were shipped in to replace the field slaves after the war. Perhaps whites feel the same way about us as they do about ladybugs: A few are fine, but a swarm turns the stomach.

Three boxes have been left by the back door, and I gather them in my arms, then enter. The sight of Lizzie trying on the nearly finished "sensible" hat I'd been designing stops me in my tracks. What is she doing here so early? She barely traipses in at nine, when the shop opens, and it's not even a quarter past eight.

"Good morning." I set the boxes on our worktable, which is already weighed down with reams of felt. The broadsides for the charity horse race are barely dry, and orders are already flooding in. Fashion is supposed to rest on Lent, but God will surely make an exception for the event of the year. The proprietress will probably want me to stay late again or work during the lunch hour so she can sneak off to nip her coca cordial. Well, not without a raise, I won't.

"Mrs. English wants to speak with you," Lizzie says in her breathy voice. She smooths a hand down the rooster tail I'd pinned to the sensible hat with an eternity knot. Ringlets of strawberry-blond hair play peekaboo under the saucer brim.

I remove my floor-length cloak and black hat, one of the misfits that Mrs. English let me purchase at a discount, this one made possible through Lizzie's clumsy hands. Then I tie on a lace apron.

The velvet curtain separating the store from the workroom

jerks to one side, and Mrs. English bustles in. "There you are," she says in her haughty schoolmarm's voice.

I dust off my drab shop cap. "Good morning, ma'am. I had an idea. What if, instead of wearing these toadstools, we model our latest styles? See how fetching my sensible hat looks on Lizzie—"

Mrs. English frowns. "Put the toadstools on, both of you."

"Yes, ma'am," Lizzie and I say in unison. I slip my cap over my head. I should ask now, *before* she asks me to stay late, so my request does not appear a hair-trigger reaction. I wipe my palms on my skirt. "Mrs. English—"

"Jo, I will no longer be requiring your services."

"I—" I clamp my mouth shut when her words catch up to me. No longer required . . . I'm . . . dismissed?

"I only need one shopgirl, and Lizzie will do."

Lizzie draws in a sharp breath. Her normally sleepy eyes open wide enough to catch gnats.

"Lizzie, open the packages. I hope the new boater block's in one of them." Mrs. English wiggles her fingers.

"Yes, ma'am." Drawers clatter as Lizzie rummages for a knife.

"B-but—" I turn my back on Lizzie and lower my pipes to a whisper. "Mrs. English, I *trained* her. I can felt a block twice as fast as her, I'm never late, and you said I have an eye for color." I can't lose this job. It took me almost two years to find steady work after my last dismissal, and Old Gin's meager wage as a groom isn't enough to sustain us both. We'd be back to living hand to mouth, tiptoeing on the edges of disaster. A bubble of hysteria works up my chest, but I slowly breathe it out.

At least we have a home. It's dry, warm, and rent-free, one of the perks of living secretly in someone else's basement. As long as you have a home, you have a place to plan and dream.

The woman sighs, something she does often. Her great bosom has a personality of its own, at times riding high, and at times twitchy and nervous, like when the mayor's wife pays a visit. Today's gusting tests the iron grip of her corset. Her rheumy eyes squint up at me towering over her. "You make some of the ladies uncomfortable."

Each of the syllables slaps me on the cheeks, *un-com-for-ta-ble*, and mortification pours like molten iron from my face to my toes. But I'm *good* at my job. The solicitor's wife even called the silk knots I tied for her bonnet "extraordinary." So what about me causes such offense? I wash regularly with soap, even the parts that don't show. I keep my black hair neatly braided and routinely scrub my teeth with a licorice root, thanks to Robby. I'm not sluggish like Lizzie or overbearing like Mrs. English. In fact, I'm the least offensive member of our crew.

"It's because I'm . . ." My hand flies to my cheek, dusky and smooth as the Asian steppes.

"I know you can't help it. It's the lot you drew." She matches her round eyes with mine, which are just as round, but taper at the outside corners. "But it's not just that. You're . . . a sauce-box." She squints at my cap, and I regret calling it a toadstool. "You don't know when to keep your opinions to yourself."

She draws back her head, causing her neck to bunch. "Women want to be complimented. They do not want to be told they look washed-out, square in the jaw, or pie-faced."

If a hat made me look pie-faced, I would certainly want to

know before I purchased it. Lizzie routinely gives opinions. Just last week, she told a woman with a lumpy head that maybe she should give up wearing hats entirely. Mrs. English only smiled. I'm about to give my opinion of her opinion, but that would only prove her point. "I only wished to help them find the best fit." I try to keep a tight grip on my indignation, but my voice trembles.

"Well, the simple fact is you are not the best fit here. Today will be your last day. Don't make this harder than it needs to be. I am sure you will have no trouble getting a job as a lady's maid or some such."

A lady's maid? I suck in my breath. Now, that would be a fall backward, not that someone like me can be choosy.

"Not a hatter's apprentice, of course," she jabs the pin in deeper. "I have already talked to the Sixteen, and they will not hire you."

Despite being competitors, the sixteen milliners that dress Atlanta's heads are tight as hatbands. Something bangs on the floor, but Lizzie's apologies for dropping the boater block sound far away. I have been blacklisted. Servants are routinely black-listed when their services come to an end, even when they have done nothing to deserve it, except working their fingers to the breaking point each day, coming in early, leaving late, cleaning up other people's messes, painstakingly redoing their stitches. I can barely breathe. "B-but, I—"

"I can't risk you spilling my secrets."

The door chimes clang, and Mrs. English scurries back to the front.

Tears gather in my eyes, and I press my sleeves to them

before they fall. And I had once thought Mrs. English kind for taking a chance on me.

The proprietress pokes her head back into the workroom. "Jo, a lady is asking for you."

I swallow the lump in my throat. "Me?" No one has ever asked for me. And it's a little early for customers.

"The precise words were 'the Chinese girl,' and so I had to give it my best shot. Don't dawdle."

I dry my face and follow her into the shop. On the other side of the oak counter stands a woman in a gray suit with a modest bustle and a white blouse with a high collar. Narrow shoulders slope into an equally narrow neck, a pointed chin, and high cheekbones. Her prematurely white hair is tied into a practical knot.

I gasp. It's Mrs. Bell, my upstairs neighbor. Though we have kept our existence secret from the printer and his family, I have stolen glances at them through the print shop window. Her flannel-gray eyes spread over me, and I can almost hear the underground walls of our home caving in. Outside, a whip cracks. A mule brays, and the last of my hopes seem to stampede away.

Two

Dear Miss Sweetie,

Six months ago, a Jewish family moved in next door. These people do the oddest things: kissing scrolls in the doorway, building huts in their yards to "camp" in, singing gibberish words, and waving branches. It's enough to shake the powder from my wig. How can we restore the quality of our neighborhood?

Sincerely,
Mr. and Mrs. Respectable

Dear Mr. and Mrs. Respectable,
    You could move.

Sincerely,
Miss Sweetie

"This is Mrs. Bell. Well, don't just stand there. Speak, girl." Mrs. English puts her fists on her hips. Even her bosom seems to glare at me, frozen in front of her. Has the woman come to have me arrested? If it were discovered that two Chinese people were squatting in her basement, we could be imprisoned or worse. In this part of the world, mobs form as easily and violently as cloudbusters.

"Ma'am, how do you do?" I force my face into something pleasant or, at least, less grim. Act natural. If she's looking for the Chinese girl who's been tunneling under her, she's got the wrong one, never mind I'm the only one for miles and miles. My twitchy fingers pluck a fan from a basket. "Nice weather we're having."

Mrs. English snatches the fan and glares at me.

"Er, yes," says Mrs. Bell, despite the gloom outside. Now that I am forced to face the woman, I have to admit, she appears more bemused than angry, her dark eyebrows steepling, her mouth halfway ajar. She unpins her hat from her head—a simple spooner in mourning-dove gray—and sets it on the counter. "I have been admiring the knot embellishment on my friend's hat, and she said it was made by the Chinese girl who works here."

The solicitor's wife? I stop fidgeting. Perhaps our residence is still a secret.

Mrs. Bell gestures at her hat. "I was hoping you could do the same for me."

Mrs. English clears her throat. "Actually, she is busy." Her eyes flit to a familiar folder beside the cash register. "We're taking inventory today."

My jaw grinds. That tedious chore is typically done on Friday, but she's trying to get her money's worth out of my last day. Lizzie never gets the numbers to come out right.

"But," she adds, "I would be happy to assist you myself."

Mrs. Bell's head pulls back a notch as she addresses Mrs. English. *"You* can do the Chinese knots, too?"

"Er, no." The proprietress's mouth draws in like a purse string being cinched. She had thought my knots looked bizarre, but didn't complain when the solicitor's wife paid her handsomely for the work.

"I would be happy to do it," I cautiously pipe up. If Mrs. Bell has come to arrest me, where is the constable? The shock of my dismissal may have dulled my perception, but the woman's behavior doesn't strike me as someone who has smoked out a rat. In addition, the prospect of sticking Lizzie with the inventory makes me positively giddy.

"But the embellishment will take more than a day," Mrs. English says with a meaningful jab of her eyebrow.

Mrs. Bell presses her palms together. "Oh, take your time. I don't need it for a couple of weeks."

"I can do it in a day." I steer a brave smile toward the proprietress, hoping to unearth a pebble of pity in her stony heart.

Mrs. English fans herself. Waves of gardenia crash over us. "If you pay in cash, I would reconsider."

"Ah. I might have something even better than cash." Mrs. Bell fingers the edge of her hat. Her arthritic joints stretch the fabric of her well-worn gloves, and the pads of her fingers are starting to show through. Money is tight in that family. I hold my breath, caught between wondering what she could offer and worrying that there is more to this visit than meets the eye. "You see, my husband runs the *Focus.* In exchange for the work, we could give you a month of advertisement, the equivalent of three dollars. I am told the piece cost a dollar fifty. You'd be getting twice the value."

"Front page," Mrs. English briskly counters. "Plus assurances that you will not run competing advertisements." When Mrs. Bell doesn't answer, the proprietress pours on some charm. "Each piece that leaves our hands is a unique work of art. But don't go to New York, or the Metropolitan Museum might pinch it from you." She bats her fan at Mrs. Bell. No one butters a biscuit like Mrs. English.

Mrs. Bell's genteel smile doesn't falter, but her finger spools a loose thread on her sleeve. "A one-week exclusive is all I can offer."

The two women continue to haggle, though Mrs. Bell's eyes keep wandering to me. I untwist my arms and try not to look like I'm hiding something. Unlike the proprietress, whose speech modulates like a stage actress's, the publisher's wife's voice is as steady as an oak table. It comforts me, even as I worry about the coincidence of her visit. I'm reminded of all those songs she sang to calm Nathan, songs that also soothed me, two years younger than him. Her tales of growing up on her parents' sheep farm enthralled me in ways I never expected sheep could do. And here she stands before me, unaware—at least I hope—of how much she means to me.

Two young women enter the shop dressed in the latest pastels with touches of lace at the collars. Miss Melissa Lee Saltworth and Miss Linette Culpepper, whom I call Salt and Pepper, though never aloud, are the daughters of "merchant aristocrats." Unlike the older cities of Savannah and Charleston, in Atlanta you don't need a family name to boost your social standing. You can climb the ladder by sheer business muscle. Of course, muscles, business or otherwise, never made a difference to how high Chinese could climb.

"Good morning, Miss Saltworth, Miss Culpepper. How are you today?" Mrs. English calls over her shoulder into the back room, "Lizzie?"

Lizzie appears. "Why, good morning, Mrs. Bell. How is Nathan? I haven't seen him delivering the papers at Father's store lately."

"He is well, Lizzie. The reporting keeps him very busy these days. I shall tell him you send your regards."

Lizzie lingers at the counter, a dreamy smile upon her fair face. Mrs. English clears her throat loudly and cocks her head meaningfully toward Salt and Pepper. Lizzie takes languid steps toward the ladies as if the floor were full of horse patties. The building could be burning down and she would still take her time. Salt points to the top shelf, where we display the finest offerings, and with a wooden pole, Lizzie retrieves a straw hat in mauve with a cloud of tulle.

I bite my tongue in frustration. Mauve would definitely clash with Salt's peachy skin.

"A two-week exclusive, then. I hope there will be nothing more," Mrs. Bell adds with more force.

Mrs. English nods at me, a triumphant gleam in her eye. Mrs. Bell's gaze also travels to me. I summon some poise, not wanting her to think me a heathen.

"Did you have a particular event in mind, or is it for everyday wear?" I ask, my tongue strangely thick.

"I would like something unique, a conversation starter. It's for the horse race."

Salt, who's been admiring the straw hat in Lizzie's hands, exclaims, "I'm fizzed about that race. We came as early as we could."

Pepper twirls her parasol with such energy, she might have been divining the ground for water. "I hope your Mr. Q invites you soon."

Salt blushes like a sunset against the white-blond clouds of her locks. According to Pepper, Mr. Quackenbach, the son of a financier who lost his fortune backing Confederate dollars, is "smitten" with Miss Saltworth and seeking her hand. The Quackenbach name still holds currency even if his bank account does not, and Mr. Q has the sort of dreamy face that could ripple even the sourest buttermilk. If I were as wealthy as Salt, the only thing I would give a gold digger like Mr. Q is my foot. Anyway, according to Old Gin, the real looker is his horse, a rare piebald with a white coat offset by a black mane and tail.

Mrs. Bell nods at the newcomers. "Actually, ladies are encouraged to ask the men. We printed the posters ourselves."

"Yes, but no respectable woman would actually do that," says Mrs. English.

Mrs. Bell looses a smile. "The proceeds benefit the Society for the Betterment of Women. Perhaps it is appropriate in this instance."

Salt pushes the mauve hat back at Lizzie, to my relief. "But it's so bold. What if the gentleman refused? I should be humiliated."

"He won't." Pepper tucks a black ringlet back under her crushed-velvet capote, a hat I made just last week.

"It sounds wonderful," Lizzie breathes, squeezing the mauve hat so hard, I think I hear it whimper. I expect Mrs. English to reprimand her, but instead, she's staring at the cash register, a smile fanned across her face. Perhaps she's remembering all the orders the horse race is generating. A tiny bubble of hope rises in my chest, pesky thing.

I SPEND MY last hours as a milliner in the back room, creating Mrs. Bell's embellishment. Lucky Yip, one of the two "uncles" I remember, taught me the folk art of knot-tying one summer when a cloudbuster made it difficult to leave the basement. All you need is silk cord and your fingers.

Mrs. Bell's plain felt sports a duck brim in front and a lifted back for her hair. To wake up its dull planes, I work cord into rose and pansy knots. I add green ribbons to suggest foliage.

The first time I was sacked, I'd been polishing banisters at the prestigious Payne Estate, where Old Gin had worked ever since stepping foot on American soil twenty years earlier. I had grown up on the estate, working first as a stable girl and sometimes playmate to the Paynes' spoiled daughter, until I was promoted to a housemaid. The linseed oil was still slick on my fingers when Mrs. Payne snatched my rag and pointed it toward the door: "Go."

At least Mrs. English had given a reason for dismissing me. Not a good one, but it beat no reason at all.

Lizzie drifts in from the front. Her breathy sighs pelt me from behind. The butterfly I'm knotting slips, and I throw her a wet look. "May I help you?"

"It shoulda been me. I don't love this job like you do."

I deflate, wishing she would make it easier for me to dislike her. "Once you get the hang of things, you'll like it better."

She glances toward the shop, which, judging by the chatter, is full of patrons. Instead of leaving, she drops into a chair. "I bet that horse race will be fine as fox fur." She intertwines her fingers and her shoulders lift.

I cannot help musing that the world would be a happier place if we could all do the things we want to do. I like making hats. I do not want to be a maid to a spoiled Southern miss. Lizzie does not want to make hats. She wants to *be* the spoiled Southern miss. As for Mrs. English, her life would be easier if she just kept me and got rid of Lizzie. At least I would make her profitable.

A few more twists complete my butterfly, its wings spread as if to fly. I am just putting the finishing stitches in my arrangement when Mrs. Bell returns.

"It's lovelier than I could've imagined." Mrs. Bell turns her head from side to side in front of our mirror. "It's a miracle you finished it so fast!"

I resist checking for Mrs. English's reaction as she completes a row of sums next to me.

"Thank you, ma'am. You should always wear a little color, because—"

Mrs. English clears her throat loudly.

I bite my tongue, realizing this is the kind of opining that cooked my goose. "Because, well, we all should."

Mrs. Bell smiles and holds out a nickel to me.

"I—I couldn't," I stammer. I occasionally receive tips, but it doesn't feel right to take money from her when I owe her so much. Her smile wobbles, and I realize I am acting suspicious. I accept the coin. "Thank you."

She says in a low voice, "May God always keep you in His palm."

With that, I am back to worrying that she does know about Old Gin and me. Has she just given her implicit approval that the situation may continue? But why say something so *final* unless she thought we would not meet again? Is she planning to reveal us after all?

Her face betrays nothing. She is back to admiring her hat in the reflection.

Three

Mrs. English drops two Lady Libertys into my palm and snaps the cash register shut.

My tired fingers curl around the coins on their own. "Thank you. Ma'am, won't you reconsider?" I cringe at the desperation in my voice, but I'd hoped millinery held great promise for me. Making hats, you could make statements without saying anything at all. Plus, a hatter can pay her own way without marrying. A good Chinese wife is expected to cook, bear sons, and be willing to "eat bitterness." I have enough of that on my plate right now.

"I'll work twice as hard and try not to have so many opinions and—"

"Jo, you simply do not make economic sense." With a handkerchief, she pats the moisture from her neck, then swabs the space between us, as if to rub away the sight of me. I'm reminded of the dreaded G-word that accompanied my last dismissal. But instead of *go*, Mrs. English says, "Good luck."

Disappointment weighs heavy as a box of blocks on my

heart. My chin quivers, but I hide it under the brim of my hat as I hurry toward Union Station, a brick hangar with a fan-shaped arch. The sooner I get home, the sooner I can eavesdrop on Mrs. Bell to ascertain whether her visit was more than a coincidence.

The Western & Atlantic Railroad was the first of several cuts in the pie that divided Atlanta into six wards. We live near the center of the pie. A uniformed man herds a noisy mass of carriages, carts, and pedestrians through the crossing. I hurry to make it through before it closes. A woman holds a hand-kerchief to her nose and shrinks away from me, and I know it is not the soot she is worried about.

My feet tingle as I cross the tracks and I cast my eyes toward Yankee country. North of the Mason-Dixon Line, even the dogs attend school for manners, and in New York, women are so fashionable, they change hats several times a day. I could've opened my own millinery in Madison Square, had I the right training.

Saucebox, I snort. I barely utter one word to every ten Lizzie speaks, and that's the chattiest I get all day. Chinese people can't afford to be sauceboxes, especially Chinese people who are trying to live undetected.

"Oh!" Past the tracks, I nearly collide with an old man perched upon a crate. He jerks, and a newspaper hat slides off his head. "I am sorry." I pick up the newspaper hat, though he makes no move to take it from me.

"Pa, you a'right?" A young woman with sun-beaten skin snatches the newspaper hat.

The man's yellowing eyes adhere to me like spots of glue. It occurs to me the two might not have a home, given their open rucksacks and dirty fingernails. The woman bends the hat back into shape and sets it gently onto her father's head.

Suddenly, I see Old Gin and myself in these two, reduced to begging, with not even proper hats to shade us. *Please let it not come to that*, I implore both the Christian God and our ancestors. The sky looks coolly down on me. Unlike yesterday, there is no ombré in its sunset or tulle in its clouds. A thin puff of vapor resembles a stuck-out tongue. I'm gripped by the urge to run headlong into the sky and wipe that smug off its face.

Like a common pickpocket, I slip along alleys, keeping myself compact and unnoticeable. A copse of trees lies fifty yards beyond One Luckie Street, the home of the Bells' print shop and attached house. Checking to see that no one is looking, I hasten to the center of the copse, where the heavy skirts of a Virginia cedar conceal a trapdoor. The door does not creak when I open it—we always keep it well-oiled. A rough staircase leads to one of the two tunnels looping to the basement under One Luckie Street.

Old Gin is perched, birdlike, at our spool table, home earlier than usual. Eavesdropping will have to wait. The Bells are probably in their kitchen eating dinner anyway, not in the print shop where I can overhear them.

"Evening, Father." Lately, Old Gin's garments have begun to hang on him, dark trousers and a shirt whose original color is hard to recall. With even strokes, he writes Chinese characters for me to copy. We use English with the uncles gone, but he wants me to keep up the mother tongue for the husband he hopes to find me one day.

His threadbare eyebrows hitch a fraction. Even at the barely audible volume that we use underground, he can tell I'm cross. It heaps insult onto injury that I can't rail about my unjust situation at the volume it deserves. I scrub my hands and face in our wash bucket with more vigor than necessary, soaking my sleeves. Then I seat myself on the upside-down flowerpot I use as a chair, my knees bumping the table.

Old Gin has arranged on my plate two slices of ham, a wedge of cheese, one sesame seed roll, and a dish of peach preserves. Robby's wife, Noemi, the Paynes' cook, always gives Old Gin something extra to take home. We eat simply, avoiding foods that might release suspicious smells into the environment.

"It is better to save anger for tomorrow, hm?"

I sigh. Old Gin knows just how to press the valves that release steam. "Mrs. English dismissed me."

While I pour out my story, he sips hot barley water, peppering my pauses with the musical *hms* that both loosen my speech and rob it of indignation. The *hm* appears so frequently that I forget it's there. I think it comes from spending so much time with horses. "Hm?" is his way of showing them that he values their opinions.

"Guess it's the cotton mills for me," I mutter. The mills will hire anyone willing to work long hours spinning or spooling. Of course, it might cost a finger, or worse, one's life, which is why they're called "widow makers."

Old Gin's horrified gasp sets off another bout of coughing, and I immediately regret my words. It's as if someone had grabbed ahold of his thin shoulders and is shaking him for loose change. It must be the damp. His old corner gets musty when it rains too much.

I travel the two steps to our "kitchen" to fetch the kettle off our coal-burning stove. The stove shares a chimney with the fireplace in the print shop overhead, which means we only use it when that fireplace is lit. Lucky for us, the printer's wife prefers a warm room for her arthritis.

I pour more barley tea. Old Gin nods his thanks, his acorn-shaped face red and grimacing. The spasms have mussed his neatly kept gray hair.

"Robby says some of the new drafts are quite effective for the cough."

"Best draft is time." His gaze strays to an old pair of work boots neatly lined against the wall, where we hide our money. We have always been frugal, but lately Old Gin has become as tightfisted as a man gearing up to throw a punch. Last month, I lost a quarter out of a hole in my pocket, and he didn't sleep well for a week. "We must save for your future."

"Our future." Old Gin is not my real father, and yet I cannot imagine a world without him by my side. Whoever my parents were, they must have known he was the most reliable of the Chinese bachelors in Atlanta when they left me with him. A former schoolteacher in China, Old Gin taught me everything he knew. The handful of "uncles" whom Old Gin permitted to live with us—fieldworkers, ditchdiggers, and rock drillers—took turns watching my infant self, but it was Old Gin who paid Robby's mother to nurse me. It was Old Gin who stayed when the others moved on.

He sips his tea, chest calm once again. "Yes, our future." He inhales a slow breath and sets down the tea. "How would you like to work for the Paynes again?"

I snort too loudly, but his face doesn't alter its expression. "You are serious?"

Old Gin nods. "You could see Noemi every day."

"That would be nice, but—"

"And you will be able to ride Sweet Potato."

Our mare's coal-black face appears in my mind. Old Gin had begged Mr. Payne not to let the head groom, Jed Crycks, shoot her as a foal after a lame leg caused her mother to reject her. Mr. Payne agreed, giving her to Old Gin and even letting him board her at the estate as long as Old Gin paid her keep.

"She has grown into a fine animal," he adds. "Smart, like you."

Aside from the awkwardness of being dismissed, a job at the Payne Estate is nothing to sneer at, with its luxurious surroundings, plentiful food, and a usually fair, albeit distant mistress. Of course, Mrs. Payne's daughter, Caroline, was a horse of a different color altogether, but she was away at finishing school.

Old Gin swirls his cup, gazing at the contents.

Would Mrs. Payne really have me back? "Bad eggs, once tossed out, aren't usually put back in the basket."

Old Gin trains his placid gaze on the kerosene lamp above us, and it's as if my words are standing in line behind another thought. But after a moment, he says, "You were never a bad egg." He sniffs, as though verifying his claim. The sniff sets off a quake in his chest, but he clamps his mouth shut, refusing to let the cough boil over. He lifts himself from his milking stool and takes a moment to scoot it back in place. Instead of saying good night, he nods, then pads creakily toward his "quarters."

After a rushed tidying, I retreat to my own corner under

the print shop, passing through the curtain door Old Gin had embroidered with horses. When the uncles moved away, he suggested I move to a less noisy section under the main house where he lives, but I love my snuggery, softened by a rug I braided out of old flannel. Not to mention, I refuse to be parted from the speaking tube, the only way I can eavesdrop on the Bells.

After slipping into my nightgown and thick socks, I stretch over the raised platform of my bed. From the opening above my pillow, I remove the wool plug that stops sound from traveling up our end of the speaking tube.

A light draft flows in from above, and the flame in my oil lamp wavers from its place on my crate nightstand. Mr. Bell's three-beat pacing echoes down to me. Though I don't know the exact mathematical equation, Old Gin believes the "hearable" space encompasses the area around the Bells' worktable, roughly matching my corner.

They're arguing. I pray it has nothing to do with a discovery of rats in the basement.

"Sixteen hundred subscribers, while that fish wrapper the *Trumpeter* has broken three thousand. Curse that ridiculous Advice from Aunt Edna column," thunders the publisher. "It's embarrassing." His voice only comes in two levels: loud and louder. I imagine his ruddy face with its fleshy eye pads growing bright with indignation.

I release my breath. It pains me to hear Mr. Bell upset, but at least it is not over Old Gin and me.

Circulation for the *Focus* has recently taken a nosedive, after Nathan's risky editorial criticizing a proposal to segregate Atlanta's streetcars, while the similar-size *Trumpeter* has soared, thanks to its new agony aunt column. The family sheepdog, Bear, short for Forbearance, sounds out a hearty *woof*, and her tail begins thumping. Unlike most sheepdogs, Bear's tail was never docked. I like to imagine the Great Shepherd put her heartbeat in her tail and wanted it kept intact.

"We could add more pictures," says Nathan, pronouncing the last word *pitchas*. Unlike his parents, who hail from New England, a light drawl rubs some of the letters from his words. Old Gin says the Georgia accent rubbed off on me, too. "The *Trumpeter* has at least two per page."

"A waste of space. Pictures are for children."

The room falls silent. Even Bear's tail stops thumping. I can almost feel the rise in Nathan's temperature, and my heart reaches for him. Nathan is my oldest friend, even if he doesn't know it. We have much in common, including a love of goobers (what Nathan calls peanuts), a distaste for turnips, and a longing to be heard.

Wood scrapes the floor, probably Nathan pouring himself into one of the worktable chairs. I imagine him sketching out his frustration into one of his political cartoons, art that could easily be featured in *Puck* magazine.

"Where is your article on hickory fungus?" Mr. Bell booms. "Folks want to know why their trees are stunted."

"I'm waiting for it to grow on me," grumbles Nathan. If I had to have a husband one day, I hope he would have a quick wit, like Nathan, minus his grouchiness.

"If it's parasites you want," he adds, "let me write that exposé on Billy Riggs. The *Constitution*'s too gutless to write the real story."

The *Constitution* called Billy a "fixer," but the Bells believe Billy trades in dirty secrets. Last year, the heir to a bourbon fortune hanged himself after a rival revealed the heir preferred the company of men. The Bells suspected the information was bought and sold by Billy Riggs.

Mr. Bell snorts loudly. "The end might be near, but I won't be burnt at the stake of scandal!"

"Yes, yes," Mrs. Bell smooths. My ears perk up. Sometimes it's hard to tell if she's in the room, as she walks with the heft of a mosquito. "Well, there'll be a scandal if you miss the early train. Better turn in now."

Mr. Bell always travels to New York in the spring to meet with the *Focus*'s sponsors. The sound of grumbles is followed by footfalls as the publisher departs.

Eavesdropping is a vile habit. But I have been eavesdropping on the Bells ever since I *had* ears, and I doubt I can change now. Their words comforted me on many a lonely night and made me feel like part of a family. The abolitionists who built this place cleverly disguised the upstairs end of the speaking tube to resemble a vent. Bet they never expected someone like me would be eavesdropping. Who could've anticipated that when the enslaved were freed, Chinese would be shipped in, not just to replace them on the plantations, but to help rebuild the South?

A broom scratches the floor as Mrs. Bell wages her nightly war against carbon soot. I imagine the straw bundle snooping under the worktable, the foot-operated press, and the type case. Bear woofs, chasing the broom.

"Let me do that."

"I *like* sweeping. Please, just humor your father. If things don't go well in New York, it won't matter what we write."

"What do you mean, 'if things don't go well'?"

I hold my breath, my fingers twisted into my flannel nightgown.

"Most of our Northern sponsors have given up floating a paper down here. If we don't return to two thousand subscribers by April, we are done."

"But April's only four weeks away. We'd need a hundred new subscribers a week. Impossible."

"Maybe it's time for us to move to Aunt Susannah's—"

"We're not alfalfa farmers. I don't even like alfalfa. It's a joke of a word. Rearrange the letters and it's a-laf-laf. Those sponsors need to give us more time."

I worry a hole into the toe of my sock. Never did it occur to me that the Bells might move. Is that why she came to Mrs. English's? To give me an implicit goodbye?

"What does the *Trumpeter* have that we lack?" asks Nathan.

Mrs. Bell snorts. "Advice from Aunt Edna." Her broom scratches even harder. "Well, maybe we'll get more subscriptions at that horse race."

The race kicks off debutante season, and everyone who lives on the top branch will want to be seen. Those of us on the bottom branch would be content just to see the horses, but tickets cost two dollars each.

"What did you say?"

I press the right side of my head up against the opening.

"I said, maybe we'll get more—"

"No, before that. Advice from Aunt Edna. If we had an

agony aunt column, we could improve our readership. What do women, er, like? Laundry tips?" He lets out half a grunt. Probably his mother pinched him.

"Sometimes you're as dense as your father." Bear adds a *woof!* "Women get enough household advice from Aunt Edna. Someone should write about meatier topics. Like how to get a bunion of a husband to listen to you. Or what to do if the butcher tries to gull you with an inferior cut of meat."

Gull. Such a great word, though I doubt the seagulls love having their good name tied to trickery. I'll add it to the G-words I chalked on my wall. Mr. Payne gave Old Gin our dictionary, which is intact except for the G section, so I give those words a place here.

"Why don't you write one?" Nathan asks.

"I'd have to run it by your father."

Nathan groans. "Forget I mentioned it."

The upstairs grows silent, and I plug the listening tube. We are careful never to leave the open tube unattended.

If the Bells go out of business, they would leave, and they are like family. Old Gin might even decide it's time to find me a husband with a "fleshy nose," the kind thought to accumulate wealth. Chinese bachelors are so desperate for wives, they spend hundreds of dollars fetching them from China, many younger than my seventeen years. I'd have my pick of noses and all the bitterness I could stomach.

Four

Dear Miss Sweetie,

    I am a young woman with no dowry, and I have enough hair on my upper lip to resemble a dead ferret. Despite this, a certain mister professes he is in love with me. How can I believe him?

Maiden with a
Mustachio

Dear Maiden,

    Sometimes love just stumbles into you, out of the blue, and no amount of facial hair can divert you from its path.

Sincerely yours,
Miss Sweetie

The next morning, I don my russet dress and button my pebbled-goat-leather boots. Then I take the western corridor up to the "tree" exit, assailed by the scent of wet dirt and tree roots. It must have been painstaking work for the abolitionists, digging and reinforcing these passages. But as Old Gin says, great souls have wills, while feeble souls, only wishes.

I swing open the trapdoor and haul myself out.

The heavy skirts of the Virginia cedar spread all around me, a tree as good at hiding secrets as keeping out snow. Foliage blocks the Bell residence fifty yards to the east, the boardinghouse to the north, and the soda factory to the south. Before exiting the copse of trees, I assure myself that no one is looking. A chill picks up the skin of my arms. I scan the area but see no one.

Suddenly, a crow shoots from the bushes with a hard squawk, pulling my heart out of my throat.

"Sneaky old flapper," I mutter as my heart settles back into my chest. Nothing better to do than scare respectable girls hiding in trees. I wish it were a bat, a word that sounds like the Chinese word for "luck." The bats here seem to be waking from their winter slumber later than usual, maybe waiting for the peaches to ripen.

Bending the rim of my misfit hat to shadow my face, I hoof toward the main business district. Had I a mother, she would no doubt be troubled by the ease at which I travel unaccompanied. Thankfully, growing up, Old Gin allowed me to wear trousers, which were more practical for my work as a stable girl. He also allowed me to learn basic self-defense from Hammer Foot, the other uncle I remembered, who had been raised by Shaolin monks. Shaolin requires many years of unerring devotion to master, but my "Hammer Foot" move almost broke Lucky Yip's ankle. May I have a lucky strike today, too.

By three o'clock, I've made over two dozen inquiries. For my troubles, I net seventeen doors and one window closed on my face; two offers of employment as a "chambermaid" that certainly involved chambers, but not the cleaning of them; one twisted ankle from a crone who sicced her dog on me; and one offer to dye cloth, which was revoked as soon as the mistress saw me limping. I count myself fortunate; Lucky Yip once got a dog sicced on him who tore open his knee. Despite his name, he wasn't very lucky.

All the determination I felt earlier bleeds into the sidewalks.

A drunken chorus from somewhere ahead diverts my path onto a narrower street I usually avoid on account of the smell. "Carcass Alley" features both a butchery and a mortuary, though I think the real stench blows in from the courthouse down the street, which has never allowed a Chinese to win a single lawsuit. A sagging dwelling with flaking paint seems to cough with every bang of a woman's hammer as she works to nail a sign into one of its posts. *Room Available.* The iron banisters to the doorway have rusted, and several windows are missing their glass. Who would pay to live in a wreck like that?

I bite my tongue, lest the monkeys of mischief hear my thoughts.

"How much is the room?" I call up to her. Chinese aren't actually allowed to own land or rent—Old Gin and the other bachelors had squatted in a cluster of ramshackle shanties before I was born—but for the right price, folks could be persuaded to look the other way.

The woman twists around, and her eyes clinch at the sight

of me. "Too much for you. Y'ar kind is likely to trek in nits, plus I bet you smoke black tar." She ducks into the house and lets the door swing shut behind her.

My fingernails have lodged themselves in my palms, and I extract them with a slow breath. I don't want to live here, anyway. The only worse abode would be Collins Street, and Old Gin would never let us inhabit that crime pit. I hobble away, my steps tight and quick.

Before the train crossing, people crowd bright food stalls, thick as bees on honeycomb. When the sidewalk grows too crowded, anyone not white takes to the street. Old Gin always instructed the uncles to give way—the river travels the fastest path by moving around the stones—though he never made me walk in the streets.

Leaning against a lamppost, I stretch out my ankle and breathe into it. Hammer Foot said we could move energy through our body through focused breathing. The scent of sausages tempts me into parting with the dime I brought for emergencies. I resist and redirect my nose to a poster on the nearest building, one of the many that has excited a fervor in ladies like Salt and Pepper.

MR. AND MRS. WINSTON PAYNE

invite all Atlantans to attend an eight-furlong race at Piedmont Park Racetrack, a purse of **$300** to be awarded to the winner.

DATE: Saturday, March 22
TICKETS: $2 per person, proceeds to benefit the Society for the Betterment of Women.

SPONSORS: Bids to sponsor one of the twelve contestants will be accepted until March 15. Please
mark your bid "Horse Race" and send to 420
Peachtree Street. Sponsor of the winning horse
will receive a year of free advertising in the
Constitution.

NOTE: In the spirit of the Society for the Betterment
of Women, ladies may ask gentlemen.

FURTHER NOTE: No public drunkenness will be
tolerated.

It is curious that Mrs. Payne chose to make the race a turnaround event where ladies ask men. I never considered her
progressive, even if she did once let a Chinese girl work in her
house. The Payne Estate will be busy. Perhaps that is why Old
Gin believes there may be extra work.

When my ankle stops throbbing, I continue toward the
crossing. Next to Union Station, benches are arranged back to
back for those awaiting the train. My feet slow when I notice a
bundle of white-and-gray fur. It's a sheepdog, its tail thumping
the worn boots of the man on the nearest bench.

Great geese, it's Nathan Bell.

"Keep moving!" barks the crossing guard, gesturing with
his flags.

Instead of crossing the tracks—seven in all—I duck behind
an abandoned dray with a broken wheel and pull my hat low.
Nathan has never seen me, of course, and that is how I want to
keep it. I marvel at the coincidence of seeing him the day after
his mother, though the Chinese believe coincidence is just destiny unfolding.

I should hurry on. Traffic streams by me while the crossing remains open. But curiosity keeps me rooted. I never allowed myself more than a quick glance through the print shop windows. I think he is silently condemning a cigar butt on the pavement, until a breeze blows the nub away, and Nathan's gaze remains fixed. In fact, his ear is cocked in the direction of two ladies seated behind him, their hats bent toward each other.

Nathan is . . . eavesdropping? Not only that, but jotting notes in a journal. Now, that is bold. Of course, I do a little eavesdropping myself, but never mind that now. Perhaps he is writing an article. Certainly not one about hickory fungus.

I maneuver to the front of the dray. Nathan's spindly fingers work his pencil, the dark slashes of his eyebrows crouched low on his face. Hammer Foot, whose own eyebrows were plucked as a boy and never regrew, said folks with crouching eyebrows prefer the comfort of shadows. I always considered Nathan's face unremarkable. But the more I study it, the more interesting it grows: sturdy chin; deep-set eyes in dove gray that take in more than they give away; and a no-nonsense nose that will do a decent job supporting the spectacles he will need one day with all the fine print he sets. A grouchy Homburg in soil brown holds itself stiffly at the brim despite a droopy crown. You can tell a lot about a person by their choice of headgear.

A bark shocks me from my thoughts. To my horror, Bear's head swings toward me, though I can't tell where her eyes are looking, or if the creature even has eyes underneath her mop of a head.

Not two shakes later, Bear bounds over to me, woofing and bellowing like she's discovered the world's largest sheep. It's uncanny that an animal with no eyes could have such accurate aim. Why am I so irresistible to the canine species? My ankle cowers, and I wish I had bought that sausage. Hammer Foot always said *Do not engage an adversary; feed it.*

I dodge one way, then another, but the boot of my injured ankle catches on one of the ties. I fall in a heap right on the tracks. Frantically, I scramble backward, anticipating the teeth that could impale my limb like a drumstick. Something rips! My stockings—they're wet. Dear God, am I bleeding?

No. I am being . . . licked. "Stop! Please," I beg the sheepdog.

"Forbearance! Forbear this instant!" Nathan utters in a voice that could bend grass. The licking stops. I am vaguely aware of him pulling the dog away from me. Traffic carves a path around us with its stamping hooves and squeaking wheels.

"What has gotten into you? I am sorry, miss." Nathan's eyes fasten onto me, and that familiar confused gaze I provoke in others lands squarely on curious.

I pull off a glove and feel for my leg, which, thank the Almighty, is still attached. However, my flaxen stockings have torn. Feeling Nathan's gaze on my exposed limb, I yank my dress back down, and he glances away. Bear, on the other hand, is jumping around as if trying to climb the air, her tongue waving like a pink flag.

Before I can gracefully flee, Nathan pants, "Beg your pardon, miss. She usually only gets this excited with people she knows."

I freeze. Bear *knows* me. She must have smelled me living below her, sure as I recognize the familiar scents of the Bell household on Nathan—lemon laundry soap and printer's ink.

Thank the Lord the beasts don't talk, though it is clear they have opinions.

The crossing guard points his flag at us. "Move along! Next one's in two minutes."

The sheepdog begins circling, as if to herd us off the tracks, and her leash wraps around us, yanking Nathan toward me. Nathan's mouth tucks into a grimace, showing teeth Robby would approve of, teeth I shouldn't be admiring from so close. My skin tingles at the energy surrounding him—warm and vibrant as the tracks, which have started to hum. Before we collide, Nathan releases his end of the leash and grabs the dog by the collar. "Naughty. I should make you into a rug."

I pull free of the slackening rein.

"Clear the track! She's coming through!" The guard clangs a bell, and the last of the traffic scurries across. A plume of smoke drags through the sky.

We hurry off the track, but where is my glove? Dropped between the ties, only ten paces away. What good is one glove? I will need to buy another pair, and I was saving up for a new hat to replace my misfit one. I could make it if I hurry.

A hand stays me. "Is your skull cracked?" Nathan hisses.

I shake my arm free of him.

A train whistle shoots a hole in the air through which all other sound escapes, even the sound of Bear's barking. I chug away as fast as my limbs can carry me.

Five

I return home a quarter of an hour later than usual, owing to a circuitous route I used in case Nathan tried to follow me. If you had tied a string to my ankle, I would've woven an impressive cat's cradle through the neighborhood. It occurs to me that Bear is already on to me, and therefore, whichever route I took matters little. On the other hand, she has smelled me living in her basement for all these years and never spoke up before. Perhaps to the dog, I'm just another scent that makes up home, and we can all carry on as normal.

I attempt to wash the day's filth off my hands, but our soap slips from my grasp. When I pour the rinse water from the pitcher, some of the precious liquid sloshes over the bucket rim onto the concrete.

Old Gin, who goes to the public baths on Tuesday nights, has already set pickled tomatoes and two drumsticks on my chipped plate, covered by a bowl.

I settle onto my bed and remove my ripped stockings. The word *gelogenic*, which means "invoking laughter," catches my eye, and under it, *gigot*, which means "leg of mutton." My wall is mocking me. So is the listening tube, which beckons me to unplug it. I assure myself that everything is normal. Bear doesn't know me from a hole in the wall.

I pinch the wool plug from the tube.

Bear woofs so loudly it seems she is mere inches from my head. I jump back with such force, I tumble off my mattress.

"Bear, get down from that wall—" says Nathan. I stare at the tube in horror, as if the sheepdog might actually jump through the vent and slither out.

Has the creature scented me? She never did that before in the five years she has lived here. I reach for the plug, but then the scrabble of claws fades. Nathan's voice comes back into focus. "Who knew there were so many opinions on how to ask a man to a horse race?"

Bear woofs from farther away.

"My favorite was the chaperone with the chin hairs. 'You must lodge yourself like a poppy seed in his teeth, and he'll be dying to take you out,'" Nathan mimics an impressive Irish accent. In his regular voice, he adds, "What do you think, Bear?"

This time, Bear does not woof.

"You prefer the lady with the birdcage?" Nathan affects a voice that sounds as if its owner is missing teeth. "'Horses stink. I'd rather pick aphids off my azaleas.'" He snorts. "I do like how *azalea* rolls off the tongue. Plus, it gives *z* a chance to get out of the box. Zs have had a hard time ever since Zach Taylor left office."

I stifle a laugh.

"No, I'm going with the poppy seed. That's the kind of thing Aunt Edna would say."

So Nathan was eavesdropping for an advice column. But lodging oneself like a poppy seed? Poppycock. The rules clearly state ladies should ask the men. Why complicate matters? Of course, that's how courtship works. People never come right out and say what's on their minds, preferring a complicated dance to simply walking across the room.

But the Bells need something different from Aunt Edna, something radical, if the *Focus* is to reach two thousand subscribers by April. Why put a second horse in a race when you can put in a dragon, which not only flies but eats horses for breakfast? Atlanta considers itself the capital of the New South, the city that will lead the charge into the twentieth century. Women here, at least white women, are already marching for an amendment that would give them the vote, just like the Fifteenth did for colored men. Surely they are ready for a column that will take on the more serious concerns we face today. Someone needs to blow the trumpets of change. Someone who has viewed society both from the top branch and the bottom, from the inside of the tree and from the outside.

Someone like . . . me. If I am such a *saucebox*, maybe I would make a good agony aunt. I like progress, and I have opinions, just like everyone else. And outside of the Bells, if anyone knows the *Focus*, it's me. Not only would it help keep them in business, but I would be holding a peach to the bats of good fortune to keep us living here. No one would know my identity. The best way to deliver the truth, if not posthumously, is anonymously.

Old Gin would not approve. He required the uncles to

follow a long list of rules to minimize the risk of discovery—no loud talking, no leaving in groups, no dumping of waste into the Bells' incinerator. But this is for us, too. And he need not find out. Old Gin hardly has time to read the news nowadays.

My heart beats to quarters in my chest. I will be the Bells' Aunt Edna.

Six

I alight to Old Gin's side of the house, where a set of drawers holds old fabric and writing supplies. The drawer with the paper fights me, but finally budges. I quickly retrieve a sheet, then steal back to my corner.

The ceiling shakes hardest on Wednesday and Saturday nights for the *Focus*'s biweekly publication on Thursdays and Sundays, but tonight, all is quiet. Instead of switching on my oil lamp, I light a candle, pressing the wax base into a cracked teacup. The light throws my shadow against the concrete walls. I study my darker twin, rolling a pen between her fingers. To whom should I address this letter?

My first thought is Mrs. Bell, but I discard that idea. Her receipt of the mystery letter would come too soon after our encounter at the millinery, one bread crumb away from a trail. That leaves Nathan, who, despite our close encounter, never heard me speak English. It has to be him. Mr. Bell has more than once questioned Nathan's ability to be publisher. Perhaps

I can provide him the chance to show his father some of that forward-thinking spirit for which the *Focus* is known.

Nathan will make a fine publisher one day, maybe not as charismatic as his father, but just as principled. And despite his grouchy disposition, unlike his father, he treads lightly upon the world, as if he knows there is more than one way to make a lasting mark.

Mr. Nathan Bell
Number One Luckie Street
Atlanta, Georgia

Dear Mr. Bell,

I have been a devotee of the Focus for many years. I have especially admired your thoughtful editorials, which demonstrate a commitment to justice as well as a fine-toothed wit (most recently, "Combined Sewer System Stinks: Flush at Your Own Risk" and "Fired Shoe Factory Workers Just Didn't Fit In").

While the quality of your content exceeds that of the larger newspapers, there is one aspect in which the Focus is lacking: women. The Journal features a women's page. The Constitution regularly covers home decoration. Even the Trumpeter runs the popular Advice from Aunt Edna. Magazines such as Ladies' Home Journal are more popular now than ever.

Women demand more content. The Focus can give it to them.

*To this end, I offer up my own pen and heart.
I have lived in Atlanta all of my life, and consider
myself an everyday woman. I do not want payment.
The knowledge that I might have helped my sisters
in Atlanta in some small way is payment enough. To
aid you in your decision, I include a sample of my
writing here.*

———

LADIES ASKING GENTS TO HORSE RACE?
YEA OR NEIGH?

*The propriety of "turnaround" events has reared its
head again due to the upcoming horse race, even though
the sponsors have clearly stated that "ladies may ask
gentlemen."*

*I am of the opinion that there are many occasions
in which the thing said differs greatly from the thing
thought. For example, when one is asked, "Do you like
my cucumber pie?" one might respond, "I do indeed,"
even though one thinks it looks like alligator spit. If later,
the pie eater compliments the fluffiness of said pie, the pie
maker might reply, "It is really nothing," though she be
secretly pleased.*

*However, the horse race is not one of these occasions.
Public invitations do not care what you think of them.
They speak plainly. Why should a lady who chooses to
ask a gent to the race be "ruining her reputation," rather
than simply obliging her hosts' wishes? When deception
is not at issue, words should be taken at their face value,*

*or they are in danger of losing currency. So, ladies, quit
your stalling. Your steed may not be available furlong.*

———

*If my offer interests you, you may simply print
the article, and I will know to deliver a new one. I am
a private person and do not wish to make known my
identity for personal reasons.*

Yours sincerely,

I shake out my hand, wondering what to name myself. It
should be something unique and memorable, a name no one
else has. Our horse comes to mind. I had named her Sweet
Potato because of her gentle and solid nature. Something with
the word *sweet* would be perfect, to temper the more provocative nature of the articles I would pen. *Miss Sweetie,* I write with
a flourish. Then I cautiously uncork the listening tube. A chair
scrapes the floor. Nathan's shoes tap evenly across to the wall
and back again, followed by the scrabble of Bear's paws. She
woofs, but not toward the vent, to my immense relief.

The knowledge that the person to whom I am writing
is also writing just one floor above makes my shadow sit up
straighter, and if shadows had smiles, I might see one reflected
there.

I seal the paper with the candle wax. My legs bounce, itching to deliver it, but I must wait until tonight.

Too fired up to eat, I rummage through the crates Old Gin
keeps in his room, hoping to find another pair of gloves. Most
of the uncles took their scant belongings with them when they
left, but oddments remain, like Lucky Yip's favorite cushion

and Hammer Foot's two-string fiddle, which for obvious reasons he rarely used.

Not finding gloves, I restack the crates, and my eyes catch on a rolled-up rug standing in the corner. It's been there so long, it almost looks like part of the wall. We could use a rug like that under the spool table to cushion Old Gin's creaky ankles.

The rug fights me when I drag it from its corner, spitting dust and making me sneeze. I unroll it, and to my surprise, a set of clothes drops out: a navy suit with fine French seams, a four-ply linen collared shirt, a coat of undyed wool, and one barely scratched pair of black-and-white Balmoral boots. No wonder the rug was so heavy.

Whoever wore the clothes was taller than either Hammer Foot or Lucky Yip and slim in build. He certainly dressed finer than the typical laborer. Maybe he was a gambler. If so, Old Gin would never have allowed him to live with us. But he must have been someone important to Old Gin; otherwise, why not sell the clothes?

I am fitting the rug under our spool table when I hear Old Gin's narrow step approaching. Freshly scrubbed and smelling of cedar, he hangs his coat and cap on a wall hook. He frowns at the mostly blue-speckled rug, then tests the springiness with his toe. "Fits well here, but I see you have been too busy redecorating to eat."

"I wasn't hungry until now." My lowered voice sounds chirpier than normal, and I busy myself working the meat off the drumstick. "Please, I can't finish both." I gesture to the second drumstick with my knife.

"If you only eat one, you will walk lopsided."

I wait for his face to break, but it doesn't. Sometimes it's hard to tell if he's joking.

"I found clothes, too, and a pair of Balmorals. Who did they belong to?"

He doesn't turn around from where he's pouring himself tea at the stove. "One of the uncles. You wouldn't remember him."

"Well, they are fine clothes. The Balmorals alone will fetch ten dollars."

He dries his hands on the towel by the stove, then settles himself on his milking stool. "I will take care of it." Reaching toward me, he pulls something from my ear: a bluebell, one of the deep violet beauties that grow along the Paynes' hedges. A grin spreads across his face. "Mrs. Payne will see you tomorrow about a position."

I take the bluebell and twirl it between my fingers. "What position?"

He pauses, as if readying the words before sending them out. "Weekday maid. For Caroline."

"*Caroline?*" The name of the Paynes' only daughter douses me with cold water.

"She returned from finishing school last month."

I grimace. "You knew."

"I suspected."

"Well, I don't know how to be a lady's maid."

At my dismissive tone, Old Gin's uneven ears twitch. He interlaces his fingers and shakes his hands at the wrist, a "good fortune" gesture to keep away the monkeys of mischief.

I sigh. The wildflower doesn't complain when the horse waters it. It is just thankful for the moisture. I should be grateful for Old Gin's devotion, and willing to do my share. After a day of beating the rug for any paying crumbs that might shake loose, a real job drops in my lap, and I react as if it were a hairy spider. "Forgive me, Father."

He stretches his ankles, and they make cracking sounds. "Caroline is older now. You are older, too, hm?" Despite his mild tone, he sees right through me.

My pickled tomato is so sour, I chase it with water. A long-buried memory of being locked in a rusted bin during hide-and-seek on the Payne Estate bubbles to the surface. When Old Gin finally found me, I had wet myself, and my voice was raw from yelling. Though Caroline was only seven and I was five, and plenty of vile nippers grow into well-mannered adults, I doubt she is one of them. A cockroach will always be a nasty, horrible insect.

I feel Old Gin's eyes on me and try to unbend my frown. "If I get the job, perhaps I'll be able to watch the horse race."

Old Gin's face is as honest as the sun, but for a fleeting second, a cloud passes over it and then burns away. He is hiding something from me, just as I am hiding something from him. The last time I sensed it was when he told me that Lucky Yip had left for a "better home." I only later learned that Lucky Yip had taken a one-way trip back to China. In an urn.

Standing, Old Gin runs his hands over his belly. He hasn't touched the drumstick. "No chess tonight. Turn in early."

"Okay," I say, though it isn't clear whether he is telling me to turn in early or that *he* needs the rest. "I'll clean up."

I watch with concern as Old Gin retreats to his quarters, until dark memories of Caroline muscle out any other thoughts in my head. With bucket and brush, I work out my agitation on the dishes, washing them until they squeak. Then I complete my own toilet in the privacy of my corner. The leftover barley water not only disinfects the skin, but keeps my hair shiny. Finally, I tuck my letter to Nathan in my waistband and carry the wastewater plus my small chamber pot to the eastern corridor.

Like the tree exit, the eastern "barn" exit originates by our stove, but it terminates in the stall of a half-burned barn with a squashed roof. The barn must have provided a handy terminus for the enslaved on their road to freedom, offering not only a lookout but a water source from a well dug deep underground. I can still smell the charred wood from Sherman's infamous march to the sea twenty-five years ago. The barn had been burned beyond repair, yet it persisted.

I will persist, too. Working as Caroline's maid makes good economic sense, as Mrs. English would say. I should be so lucky to get a job right after losing one, especially one with the most influential family in Atlanta.

Maybe finishing school will have snipped off a few of Caroline's more disagreeable threads and stitched a sound hem on her rough edges. I must put my best foot forward.

A cloudless sky has shed its day colors for a robe of dark violet. The scent of sewage, ever present in Atlanta, feels less combative than usual to my nose. Whenever it rains, storm water causes the sewers to overflow into the streets, but thankfully, the weather is finally starting to dry. I make sure no one is looking, and then quickly pour the wastes into the drain by the side of the road.

Leaving the pot and bucket in the barn, I slip around to the Bells' house. A group of men, out for a night of drinking, judging by their boisterous voices, eye me from across the street. One wolf-whistles, starting off a chain of hoots through the pack. A jag of fear streaks through me. I make a show of walking up to the Bells' porch, hoping the men will pass by when they see I have a destination.

The whistling stops and the men move on. Praying the banging of my heart doesn't give me away, I slide my letter into the Bells' mail drop.

My plans are laid.

Seven

Old Gin and I sail up Peachtree Street in Seamus Sullivan's ten-row streetcar, the plodding rhythm of the mule out of sync with the trotting of my heart. Most of the commuters, both black and white, cluster around the coal heater Sully keeps in front. I suggested we sit up front today, though Old Gin refused. It is understood that the warmer rows are reserved for the weakest passengers, which Old Gin insists is not him.

While he exchanges pleasantries with a nanny, Mrs. Washington, I pick at my fraying sleeves and poke my finger through a hole in the seam. I wish I had thought to try on my old maid's uniform last night, when I could've made adjustments.

"Lucy's having a 'first day,' too—at Spelman Seminary. She's a lucky girl," Mrs. Washington says to Old Gin in her slow, lilting voice. All her freckles brighten on her face, which is charmingly set off by a bright yellow bonnet.

A twinge of longing stirs my soul. Only a few years old, Spelman has already established a reputation as a fine school for colored girls. Old Gin has schooled me in mathematics, Chinese, and philosophy since I was five. English and history were more challenging for him, but the Bells' misprint newspapers and conversations stepped in there. When I was twelve, he tried to enroll me at the Girls' High School, but we were told I would have to attend the colored school. Old Gin said I shouldn't take a colored child's seat, given how few seats they had.

He glances at me sitting tight as a new shoe beside him. "I believe Luck rides a workhorse named Joy."

"Luck rides a workhorse named Joy," Mrs. Washington repeats, and she throws back her head. "Ha! That's a good one. She *does* work hard, and she does enjoy it."

One of the colored children rings the bell up front with a *ka-klank! ka-klank!* The kids are always vying for that privilege. The streetcar stops.

"Votes for women!" chants a group from behind us. Heads turn.

A pair of safety bicycles float by, leading a trail of white women wearing sashes of marigold fabric. The women range in age, their faces tight with determination as they chant. A few push baby buggies, and one bangs on a drum to mark the beats.

The matron in front of us mutters to her daughters, "Ain't they got nothing better to do than act like men?"

One of her daughters tugs at her honey-blond braids. "Can we get one of those safeties, Mama? They look like such fun."

Unlike the high-wheeled variety, the chain-driven safeties feature even tires and brakes, so you don't have to jump off to stop. That means women could ride them.

The matron snorts. "Only girls with loose morals ride those. Don't ever let me catch you on one."

Sully transports us past a trim colonial, which looks downright shabby compared to the Greek-looking temple one block up. Peachtree Street is Atlanta's top branch, a stretch so dense with millionaires, you can probably throw a rock and hit three on the way down. A few years back, they carved a special ward out of two neighboring pie slices to separate this wealthy corridor from the rest of northern Atlanta. Not all parts of the pie taste the same.

Ka-klank! ka-klank! The streetcar reaches our stop, a block short of the Payne Estate, and Sully brakes the mule. "Off with you, on with you!" he barks.

Old Gin casually sweeps a foot underneath an empty bench. The man drives through life with one eye on the road and the other on the lookout for fallen coins. Then he offers me his arm, which feels birdlike under his worn coat. Though we stand the same height, today I feel taller than him. The points of his shoulders seem especially sharp, and even his rib cage projects more than usual under his shirt. He is becoming a bag of bones.

As we walk, my gray skirt swings an inch too high over my boots, and my sleeves slowly strangle my armpits. If I need to beat a hasty retreat, it will not be by swinging on trees.

The sight of the crab apple trees that stud the front lawn of the Payne Estate stirs a strange brew of emotions inside me. Looking back, my days working in the stables were mostly carefree, except when Caroline came around, and even then, not all the memories were sour. We played together on occasion—she was the mama, and I, the naughty babe; she captained the ship, while I manned the oars and, too often, walked the plank. But as we grew older, her bossiness crystallized into something sharper, and her pranks would rattle me for days.

My life improved when I was twelve and Caroline was sent to the finishing school in Boston. Mrs. Payne decided I was getting too old to swab stables and put me to work as a housemaid. The winds of change blew a year later when Caroline's brother, Merritt, returned home from Exeter Academy. Abruptly, I was dismissed.

A paved driveway marked with electric lampposts, fancier than the ones on Whitehall Street, leads to the front door. We take a second carriage track to a back courtyard, which houses a white gazebo with red shingles to match the rest of the house. Inside the gazebo, a safety bicycle leans against a post. It looks new, with its pneumatic tires, a polished metal frame, and a red leather seat. Sure, it's a looker, but a pretty horse does not a fair ride make.

My heels drag as I follow Old Gin to the scullery door. He raps on the wood, and not two shakes later, the housekeeper and head of staff, Etta Rae, is grinning her triangle smile at me and clapping me on the back with her wiry arms. The only signs of her age are a few liver spots on her sable skin and the graying of her hair at the temples. "You're growing like a rumor, aren't you?"

"It's good to see you, Etta Rae."

She hauls me past the onion-scented scullery and into the

kitchen, never one to waste movements. Old Gin doffs his hat and follows. He rarely enters the kitchen, and never the rest of the house.

"Watch the shells. Noemi broke her nutcracker and she's had to use a hammer. Makes an awful mess."

The kitchen hasn't changed much. Copper pans and pots hang in neat rows on the wall between a sink on one side and an iron range, where Noemi is stirring oatmeal, on the other. "Good morning, Noemi."

She knocks her spoon against the pot rim. The speckled blue enamel finish contrasts sharply with the cast-iron pots meant for the servants. "Morning, yourself," she speaks in a drawl pleasing to the ear, dropping *r*'s and *g*'s along the way. Those letters don't have much business here in the South for colored and white alike, as worthless as the pecan shells strewn on the floor. A smile animates her handsome features—pointy cheekbones, tawny skin, and bushy eyebrows that hail from her Portuguese ancestry. Smelling like soap, she kisses me on the cheek. "I'm glad to see you, but"—her voice drops—"you sure you want to wrestle a porcupine?" A mischievous coil of springy black hair peeks out from beneath the ruffle of her mobcap, and she pokes it back in place.

"Gin, you've been skipping too many meals!" Etta Rae knocks Old Gin with her elbow.

Old Gin puts up a hand. "Old men don't need much—"

"Take these pecans." With her knobby fingers, Etta Rae scoops a handful of nuts from the piles that cover the farm table where I've taken many meals. "They're like little blobs of fat. You could use a whole tree of 'em."

Old Gin is too polite not to take the pecans, even though pecans make his mouth itch.

The scent of peaches nudges up my pulse. Mrs. Payne appears at the center of a molded doorframe that leads to the dining room, twisting her gold wedding band. It's a bottom fact that if Mrs. Payne had accepted all the proposals of marriage she received, she would have more rings than fingers. "Well, then." Her eyes dribble over me. If she bears me ill will, there is no trace of it on her face. I wonder if she sees any on mine. I was the one dismissed for no reason, after all. "Old Gin, I'm much obliged to you for bringing Jo home to us." Her manners have always been flawless, but if you put a hand to her forehead, I expect she runs cooler than most.

"You're welcome." He bows, then after throwing me a quick smile, leaves.

I curtsy. "Ma'am, I am pleased to see you."

Mrs. Payne glides to me. She stands just a breeze under my height, but I feel like a dandelion in the presence of a rose. By itself, her face is not striking—watery blue eyes and a drawn-out nose that dips toward her too-dainty mouth—but an elegant neck and narrow carriage give her the presence of a queen.

I roll back my shoulders, two bumps that give the illusion of good posture even when I slump. Shoulders are like pavement, underappreciated for the job they do holding one up in the world. Mine have done a decent job.

"Still pretty as a June pay-itch," she says, drawling the word *peach*. Like other ladies of her class, she has a habit of leaning into her words as if to squeeze out all their juice.

She whisks me farther into the house. "You remember where everything is?"

"Yes, ma'am."

The Payne house typifies those of the Southern gentry, with family needs subjugated by the need to entertain, something Southerners consider their God-given duty. In the dining room, black walnut chairs herald from Italy, but they are as difficult to separate from the table as heifers from a trough. The gold-flocked wallpaper attracts dust like a magnet pulls iron. My arms ache just looking at the chandelier, which needs to be taken apart weekly for its routine spit and polish.

From the dining room, we pass into a central hall, to a staircase leading to the private floors. Mrs. Payne lifts her pleated skirts and begins to ascend, hardly making a sound. The daughter of horse breeders, Mrs. Payne was groomed in the Southern tradition of manners and manors, and probably gave up slouching the year she stopped sucking her thumb. "Now, Jo, what is it that separates us from the animals?"

"We know how to open the pickle jar?"

She smiles. "*Religion*, child. Chapel is still nine a.m. on Sunday. You are always welcome."

"Thank you, ma'am." The Paynes invite all the staff to attend Sunday services in their private chapel. When you're as rich as the Paynes, God comes to you. But after the chaplain told me Satan had already hooked one claw into me for being born a heathen and I would have to pray extra hard if I wanted to escape his grasp, I never enjoyed going to the Paynes' services.

Photographs of Caroline and Merritt through the years line

the walls. As a child, Merritt wore frocks, and the two looked like sisters with their soft curls and cherubic gazes. The higher one ascends, the more devilish their gazes become.

"Merritt's in Virginia picking up a new horse," Mrs. Payne continues the pleasantries. "He's engaged, did you hear?"

"You and Mr. Payne must be very pleased."

"It is an exceptional arrangement," she states brightly, though to my thinking, the same could be said of furniture.

Merritt had been standing on this very staircase, a few steps below me, when his mother dismissed me. Only seventeen then, he'd been wearing a ridiculously billowy shirt that spilled out over his tight breeches, as was the style. The air had been so wet, you could drink from it, and I'd rolled my sleeves up as far as they would go.

My legs wobble, and I grip the rail. Was Merritt the reason I was dismissed? Now that he is engaged, it is safe to bring me back. But I had always known my place.

I hurry to catch up with Mrs. Payne. On the third and highest floor, where the women's chambers are located, the scent of the mahogany wood paneling swills acid in my stomach. It's curious how even the faintest smells can inflict injuries. I recall the time Caroline accused me of losing her brooch. I searched on my hands and knees for an hour, before she showed me the brooch on her hat. "I wanted to see how long it took you to notice," she said with a laugh.

Caroline pops her head out of her bedroom, her weasel-brown hair scattered around buttermilk cheeks. The rest of her follows, draped in a gauzy gown. Her body has blossomed— round arms, ample chest, and hips that could stir up hearts and trouble alike. I could never have a body like Caroline's, no matter how many pecans I ate.

Caroline drags her frost-blue eyes down me, eyes that look like they've been pressed too hard into her face. "Your hairstyle is barbaric, take it out. Maids should not try to outshine their mistresses."

Charming as ever. It'd taken me a good part of the morning to plait my locks into a side braid I call "waterfall over rocky ledge." The banister tempts me to hop on and slide away while I still have a chance.

"Now, make yourself useful and bring up a tray. Something robust, as I will be going for a ride this afternoon."

"Caroline," Mrs. Payne interjects, "we have not come to an agreement yet. Please finish sorting through your belongings for castoffs. The Society for the Betterment of Women is sending their wagon tomorrow."

The tip of Caroline's nose draws a checkmark in the air. "I've already sorted my things."

"What about the safety?"

"Bicycles are so vulgar. I don't know why you bought it in the first place."

"Bicycles are quite current. Of course, nothing will ever replace our horses in speed or beauty, but a 'freedom machine' will exercise different parts of you that could use exercising."

Caroline's sharp nostrils flatten, and she makes a vulgar noise at the back of her throat. Snatching her dressing gown around her, she evaporates into her bedroom, the fabric swirling like smoke around her ankles.

Mrs. Payne's movements are jerky as she leads me to a guest bedroom. Her normally controlled expression has come loose, as if her daughter had agitated the water. She closes the door behind us and lets out a controlled breath. "Now, Jo, I do not doubt your ability to handle this job. What concerns me is, well, you and Caroline grew up together here. But you are not equals. You understand that, do you not?"

"Certainly, ma'am," I say, though the words sting like vinegar on a sunburn. "I hope I have never, er, acted above my station?"

"No, you have not. But now that you are both young ladies, I want to be clear on where we all stand."

"Yes, ma'am." I've understood that ever since I *could* stand.

A sigh pulls her shoulders down. "Wonderful. You will work Monday through Friday, with payment on Fridays, five dollars each week. I trust that is acceptable?"

It's much more than Mrs. English paid and includes meals. The Paynes take pride in how well they treat their domestics. Yet, I still prefer my old job, with its promise of a future. "Yes, ma'am. Thank you."

She pulls from a wardrobe a black uniform of thick cotton, and cream-colored stockings. "As before, leave your uniform in the laundry basket for our washerwoman to collect at the end of the week. Your duties are to maintain Caroline's quarters, her wardrobe, and her person, and to accompany her when she goes out. You may use one of my old riding habits. Caroline's might be too big for you."

Back into the wardrobe she goes, selecting a velvet jacket

and matching skirt. A pair of jersey pants with quilted knees hangs next to the other riding clothes.

Noticing my interest, she peers back into the closet. "Is there something there that interests you?"

"I just noticed, er, the riding breeches." As girls, Caroline and I rode horses astride—she in knee-length dresses, and I in boy's overalls—but now that we are older, we are expected to use the sidesaddle. At least, fine ladies are.

"Oh, I thought I had given them away." She brings them out and smooths the fabric under her slender fingers. "I used to show horses on my parents' farm."

Old Gin told me the "farm" spanned more than a hundred acres and produced some of the finest horses in the South. Horses seem to be the only thing that cause her eyes to light, though she had to give up riding them after an injury.

"Would you like to use them?"

"Oh, I couldn't."

"Things are meant to be used."

"Thank you, ma'am. I ride better in the cross saddle."

"As do I. Being packed and twisted into an unnatural side seat is hard on the spine. I swear it's the reason for my bad back, despite what the doctor says. And I daresay it would make keeping up with Caroline easier." Her smooth brow furrows, as if mentioning her daughter's name set off a flurry of thoughts underneath. She digs out a smile. "Of course, they might mistake you for a suffragist."

"Oh, they won't make that mistake," I return brightly. "You have to be a citizen before you can be a suffragist." Without birth records, Old Gin and I couldn't prove to City Hall that I was born here. He suggested there might be an exception for foundlings, but the clerk wheezed in my face, "Not fer you, there ain't."

Mrs. Payne's smile flattens and the beadlike protrusion in the center of her upper lip—same as mine—disappears. Chinese believe a "pearl" lip attracts good fortune. "Well, be that as it may, women have more important worries than the vote. Like raising up our children. Surely you don't disagree?"

"No, ma'am," I demure. If I were truly a saucebox, I would point out that many women are unable to raise their children when factories such as the ones owned by her husband make them early widows.

She snorts. "Those suffragists want equality, but I gave up such romantic notions long ago. One must be careful about what one wishes. Better to be satisfied with one's lot, as there is always someone who is worse off."

Make that a whole lot of someones, in her case. I lower my eyes. "Yes, ma'am."

"I do not want Caroline to go visiting alone." Mrs. Payne's tone crisps. "If I find you have disobeyed me, you will be dismissed. Do I make myself clear?"

"Yes, ma'am."

She breezes away. Quickly, I undo my waterfall braid and finish dressing. But even after every button is fastened and every stray hair is tucked under a mobcap identical to Noemi's, I still feel exposed. Caroline is like spring weather; you know to carry an umbrella in case a cloudbuster comes along. But

Mrs. Payne is winter most days of the year. It was rumored that, when Caroline was still a toddler, Mrs. Payne fell into a year-long melancholic spell during which she lived with her parents in Savannah. There is no understanding her, only the reminder that one should not get too comfortable in her presence, for things can change very quickly.

Eight

Dear Miss Sweetie,

I do not possess the plump curves so in fashion. My arms are like sticks, and I have a barrel for a chest, but wearing a corset makes me red in the face. How shall I ever be beautiful?

> *Miss Broad in the*
> *Middle*

Dear Miss Broad in the Middle,

Puffed sleeves deemphasize a stocky middle, and adornment on the bib adds "treasure" to the chest. Leave the whalebone to the whales; it is healthier for both man and fish. The best way to boost your attractiveness is to accept yourself the way you are, which will free your mind to pursue creativity and joy.

> *Yours truly,*
> *Miss Sweetie*

Noemi takes in my crisp uniform and nods. "Welcome back. Let the fun begin." She hands me a broom.

While she glides around the kitchen assembling Caroline's tray, I sweep up pecan shells.

"Mr. Merritt wants pecan pie for his engagement party." Her cast-iron eyes glare at a wall hook. "Folks who love pecan pie ain't usually the ones making it. Barely finished half, and look." She shows me a constellation of blisters along her palm.

"Mind if I take a crack?" I set down the broom, then take the hammer and begin splitting nuts. The first bang nearly cracks open my thumb. The second leaves a dent in the table.

Noemi bends an eyebrow my direction. "Good. By the time you're done, we might not have pecan pie, but we will have firewood."

I say a silent word of appreciation for Noemi, who had made Caroline's cruelty easier to bear growing up here because she knew firsthand how it felt. Her mother had been Caroline's mammy.

Etta Rae pokes her head in the kitchen. A breeze couldn't enter the house without her knowing it. "Work don't get done on giggles. Noemi, if Solomon comes by, tell him to move the bicycle to the work shed by the crates with the castoffs."

Noemi's eyes become thoughtful. "Yes, ma'am." She hands me a tray of steaming oatmeal, a pitcher of cream, a bowl of brown sugar so fine it glitters, and a pot of coffee. "Better git before the porcupine starts throwing quills."

Climbing the stairs, I manage to keep most of the coffee in the pot, though the tray is as awkward to carry as a live pig. "Miss?" I call through Caroline's door. Keeping an iron grip on the tray, I let myself into the room.

Caroline sits at a mirrored dressing table. The formerly pastel room has been updated with wallpaper featuring peacock feathers, which stare like a hundred eyeballs. Turquoise swags cascade into indulgent puddles on the floor. A potted African violet with a single bud stands its ground among all the eyes. Don't I know how it feels.

I set the tray on a table by the window.

Through her mirror, Caroline casts me a look severe enough to crack the glass. "Oatmeal is hardly robust. Eggs are robust. Bacon is robust. You've wasted my time. Still slow as ever, I see."

I grit my teeth and remind myself it is just a job. One that pays money that I wouldn't have otherwise, money that will become critical if the *Focus* folds. Refusing to acknowledge her mocking expression in the mirror, I heft the tray and carry it back to the door.

"Make sure you bring those eggs sunny-side. I only eat eggs sunny-side."

Perhaps that is because she doesn't have one of her own. "Certainly, miss." I duck out of the room.

I nearly drop the tray on the old farm table. Noemi barely glances up from her spot at the sink where she is washing out the oatmeal pot.

"Miss Caroline would prefer bacon and eggs, sunny-side," I pant, taking over the washing of the pot.

Noemi shakes her head slowly, as if she isn't surprised in the least. She sets a frying pan on the stove and soon the smell of frying grease is making my stomach grumble. Something out the window catches her eye. "Ever ride a bicycle?"

"No." I hang the pot on the wall and edge next to her. Outside, Mr. Payne's butler, Solomon, wheels the bicycle down the carriage track. "I'm not ready to break my legs just yet."

"You know how to ride a horse. A bicycle must be easier than that. It's closer to the ground, and you don't have to train it. See, I get these ideas, and they keep wheeling around in my head. A bicycle means no waiting for streetcars, sometimes packed so tight you can't even breathe. Plus, I could visit my no-account brother in the blights without being pawed at."

Noemi rarely talks about her brother, whom, according to Robby, she's taken to visiting every week to thump Bible-sense into his low and disease-ridden mind. But I don't see that many women riding bicycles, let alone colored women. I heft the tray, now arranged with two perfectly cooked sunny-side eggs nestled against four rectangles of bacon, and a fresh pot of coffee. "A bicycle must cost a fair penny. You think Mrs. Payne would let you have Caroline's castoff? She is planning to give it away."

Noemi adds a tiny saltshaker to the tray, but not the pepper—Caroline is allergic to pepper. Instead of answering me, she pushes me out of her kitchen. "Go before she changes her mind again."

"ARRANGE MY HAIR into a Newport knot," orders Caroline, still in her dressing gown. "Be quick about it. I am late for my ride, no thanks to you."

"Yes, miss."

While I clean her scalp with a rice-root brush, she smooths

cream from a tin of Beetham's Glycerine and Cucumber onto her face. Her skin favors her father's, thick and ruddy, not the moonlight-clear complexion of her mother.

Her eyes catch mine, and a scowl colors her face. *The mirror makes a fickle friend, my lady.* Besides which, as Hammer Foot always said, it is better to look out a window than into a looking glass; otherwise all you see is yourself and what's behind you.

"Don't touch this. It's very expensive." The label on the tin promises to rid the skin of freckles, rendering it "soft, smooth, and white." But Caroline's freckles are still loud as exclamation points.

"Yes, miss." I coil her heavy hair at the crown, and shape her curls about her forehead.

"Noemi has the manners of a cow, but she makes passable eggs, not as good as her mama, of course, but who *can* measure up to one's *dear* mother? You're lucky you don't have one." Her blue eyes goad me in the reflection of her gilded dressing mirror.

It's impressive how deftly she manages to slap three faces— her mother's, Noemi's, and mine—with one glove. But I steel my ears against her petty remarks. She's been singing that tune about my lack of a mother just as long as she's been pushing Noemi off *her* mama's lap. Mrs. Payne's reminder that Caroline and I are not equals almost makes me laugh. As if Caroline would ever let me forget.

She flings commands like stones. "Powder my neck." "Fetch my fan—no, not that one, you cow, can't you see it's broken?" "Button these boots."

Is this to be my life, then? One tedious chore after the next, with intermittent pokes in the eye? Unlike with making hats, there is nothing to show for my work, nothing to be proud of, and certainly no gratitude. I despise it and I haven't even made it past the first day.

I hold her boots while she pours in her ghostly white legs. The boots are fashioned from leather so dark they are almost black, with teardrop-shaped cutouts along the top and the polished sheen of a violin. I bet they were purchased in Italy.

When we emerge from the grand entrance of the Payne Estate, her in an elegant navy riding habit, me in Mrs. Payne's riding breeches, not even the sun, bright as a new penny, can cheer me.

Old Gin is feeding Caroline's horse, Frederick, pecans, while Sweet Potato tries to lick the cap off his head. The mare has grown at least two hands since I worked here last, and the white jag on her forehead has blossomed into a starburst. Her coat, once fuzzy with a nap that ran in every direction, lies smooth as spilled ink over her well-shaped hindquarters.

I scratch the star on Sweet Potato's forehead. "Aren't you the prettiest belle on Peachtree Street? Robby would approve of those teeth. Old Gin, give me a few of those nuts."

Old Gin shakes his head. "No nuts for Sweet Potato. We are on a diet, hm?" He pats her neck.

"Diet? She's shipshape." I stroke her left front leg, which still bears the crook that made her limp as a foal, but it feels strong and pliant. Old Gin's massage and exercises have worked magic.

Once Old Gin helps Caroline into the saddle, Frederick immediately begins to jitter and snort. Old Gin says that to understand your horse is to understand yourself. You cannot get a horse to mind if your own mind is in turmoil, which might explain why Frederick is trying to fling Caroline off like a hot coal.

Frederick finally settles, and Caroline presses a hand to her nose. "I feel my allergies acting up." She has always been reactive in both mind and body.

Old Gin hands Caroline the reins. "At least not too windy today, so hat stays on."

"Well, we wouldn't want Jo to lose that charming scrap of roofing." Caroline smirks at my misfit hat. Her gaze drops to her mother's outfit, which fits me like a glove under a velvet jacket with a nipped-in waist. Quickly, she turns away, but not before I catch her blotchy cheeks puffed out in a scowl.

I swing a leg over my own mount, excitement blooming inside me for the first time today. I haven't been topside of a horse in months. Old Gin's cowboy saddle, bought for a dollar, fits me like water cupped in a palm.

"Giddap!" Caroline calls with a flick of her reins, before my foot has even found the stirrup.

Remembering her mother's caution, I tap my heels, and Sweet Potato sets off. I catch my breath at the lithe athlete she has become, with no hint of a falter remaining in her step. The world is a ball for her alone to kick and bounce along under the afternoon's cool gaze, and we quickly catch up with Caroline traveling north up Peachtree.

My lady's too-erect carriage and lifted chin speak volumes about her regard for who's riding behind her, but I'd take her back to her front any day of the week. At least the back doesn't have a mouth. Caroline doles out nods and greetings to those she deems worthy, including a woman large with child.

Caroline sneezes and then, with two fingers, tugs an embroidered handkerchief from her glove. I bring Sweet Potato alongside her. "Miss, would you like to rest?"

She waves a dismissive hand. "Mrs. Nettles looks like she swallowed a planet. If men truly are the stronger species, why aren't they the ones having the babies?"

"Because it would require them to knit, I suppose."

"Ha!" Moving ahead again, she leaves me to marvel at the miracle of our exchanging words without injury. We pass under the shade of the magnolias and red oaks that sprout everywhere in Atlanta. Trees easily outnumber residents. If you could bottle up the shade and sell it for a nickel, Atlanta would be richer than even New York.

Finally, we stop at a watering trough in an empty lot just before Our Lord's Chapel.

"Oh, pshaw." Caroline twists around on the saddle, casing the ground, while her horse dips his nose.

"Is everything okay, miss?"

"Seems I lost my handkerchief. It can't be far. Find it."

Sweet Potato is lapping thirstily, and so I set off on foot, trying to remember the last time she used her handkerchief. It was at least a block ago. She let out a honk that caused Sweet Potato's ears to twitch. Leaves, cigar butts, miscellaneous wrappers, horse patties . . . aha! I spot it, looking like a crumpled bird in the street fifty feet away. I hurry to collect it before something stomps it, and then hoof back.

Sweet Potato stands alone, shaking her face in the water

and making a mess. It takes me a moment to recover my wits. Caroline has tricked me. The only thing left of her is the oily scent of her deception. Her mother warned me about this, yet I settled into her lie as easily as into a porch swing. I was even fooled into imagining a moment between us. I remount, cursing this job once again.

Beyond the chapel, the mansions along Peachtree thin, and the trees grow denser. I turn down the closest cross street, keeping an eye out for her blond gelding. On my right, an expanse of tall grass leads to Six Paces Meadow. I doubt she would've gone there—too much pollen for her allergies.

After another fifteen minutes of jogging up and down Peachtree and seeing no sign of Caroline or her horse, we re-tread to the watering trough. Somehow, the snake has slithered into a bush. The chapel clock chimes, indicating half past one. Beyond the chapel lies Our Lord's Cemetery, shaded and uninviting.

The cemetery.

"The dead don't tell secrets." I steer Sweet Potato in.

We never set foot in Our Lord's Cemetery, but not because of the ghosts. Many years ago, a Chinese man with "rabid eyes" was rumored to have violated a white woman here. When the caretaker's wife came upon the appalling scene with a shotgun, the Chinese man ran off, and Chinese men everywhere tried their best not to look rabid.

Beyond the paved driveway to the chapel, hoofprints mark the ground, freshly turned dirt the color of a mourner's suit. I pat Sweet Potato's neck. "Guess that wasn't so hard."

The few headstones are haphazardly planted among ferns,

as if the dead were buried where they happened to drop. Dogwood blossoms spot the mossy carpet with an eerie kind of snow, and the air feels cool and wet. Statues of grimacing martyrs and saints with gnarled hands put a hurry in my step. Forget last rest; this is the kind of place that might keep you awake forever.

No wonder Caroline's previous maids did not last.

The ground becomes drier, and the hoofprints become harder to pick out. But soon, a single vault of white stone carved with the name INNOCENTI appears on our right. Two angels guard either side of the structure, which is shaded all around by a dense grove of trees. In the grove, Frederick is tied to a stout trunk, and beside him stands a tall piebald with unusual coloring, white with a black mane.

I have seen that horse before. Its name is Thief, and it belongs to Mr. Quackenbach, Miss Saltworth's beau. Poor Salt. Has he spurned her? Or is he just playing a little petticoat peekaboo?

A voice sounds from inside the vault, followed by Caroline's distinct snort and high giggle.

My nose wrinkles. I bet the occupants of that particular tomb wish they could move house. The guardian angels stare lifelessly ahead, daydreaming on the job.

I tuck the information into a pocket of my mind. Then quietly, I back Sweet Potato away, leaving the sinners to their folly.

Nine

I catch Caroline coming out of the cemetery, a dreamy smile strung on her lips. Even the sight of me, primly waiting in a stone courtyard at the front of the chapel, doesn't dampen her mood. Mr. Q is nowhere in evidence. "Hullo, maid."

"I trust your afternoon was refreshing, miss." If not debauching.

She slits her eyes at me. We ride in silence save the jingling of the harnesses. Only when we reach the water trough does she finally toss out, "I like to take my rides by myself. If you want to keep your job, you won't tell my mother. Just think, you'll have an hour all to yourself to do whatever you want— paid, too. Surely you know a good melon when you thunk it."

I consider my options. The idea of taking daily larks on Sweet Potato is enticing, though I know it is wicked. Fly with the crows, get shot with the crows, as they say. Of course, Mrs. Payne will fire me if she ever finds out. But if I do tell her, Caroline will certainly find new ways to make my life a misery.

It's time to catch the snake under my boot, before her bite

proves fatal. "The way I see it, the cemetery is where one goes to abandon their mortality, not their . . . morality."

Her mingy eyes clench like two fists. "You dirty sneak."

Despite my confident act, my heart squeezes with the thought of my boldness. "I think Miss Saltworth would be very interested in learning who else has been seasoning her roast."

She gasps. Even her back molars blanch. "You know Melly-Lee—? You wouldn't."

"What I want is fairness. I was hired to be a lady's maid, not to suffer your tricks and meanness. Treat me fairly, and you can keep your activities to yourself. Also, I will be wearing my hair however I wish. Agreed?"

Crossing her arms over her chest, she glares down at the leaves floating in the trough, and I wouldn't be surprised if the water started to boil. Frederick whickers and bows his head for another drink. Caroline glances in the direction of Our Lord's Cemetery, and when her eyes return to me, they are laced with malice, but resigned. "Agreed."

WHEN I BRING the horses to the stables, Old Gin is talking over the low hedge surrounding the property with a show pony of a man leaning against a giant curly oak.

My tongue nearly falls out of my mouth. It's Billy Riggs, the fixer, trader of dirty secrets. He's even wearing the same hat he wore for his picture in the *Constitution*, a demi-top with a stingy brim, burgundy to match his suit. Dark auburn curls conspire like weasels in the den of his neck. While his sorrel drifts on the sidewalk, he works a pocketknife over the tree's thick bark with quick slashes.

Sweet Potato whinnies to Old Gin, and the men, standing a hundred feet away, look up at us. Billy stops carving, and his foxlike face sharpens, becoming almost gleeful. His eyes take their time tramping around on my face. "Well, who do we have here?" His words float toward me.

Something in Old Gin's wary expression warns me away, and I make tracks toward the stables.

Acting disinterested, I tie the horses to a hitching post for Old Gin to untack later.

Then I duck into the work shed and double back to the rear, where Caroline's safety keeps company with a pile of crates containing an assortment of objects, from cracked dishes to hats. Must be the Paynes' castoffs. Peering through a crack in the wood slats, I can make out Old Gin and Billy still talking. Billy points his knife at Old Gin, and my breath comes out as a hiss. Old Gin does not react.

With a flick of his wrist, the man folds the knife and tucks it up his sleeve. Then he swings a leg over his sorrel and urges her away.

What would the fixer want with Old Gin? My stand-in father clearly wanted to distance himself from me, though I doubt his ruse succeeded. Anyone familiar with Atlanta would know that two Chinese people in the same place at the same time is more than a coincidence. I shake out the stiffness in my limbs and try to make my breathing effortless again, the way Hammer Foot instructed to get energy flowing.

No doubt there is an explanation. I will simply ask Old Gin later.

That decided, I edge around Caroline's bicycle, and my eyes catch on a hat in the crate of castoffs, a top-shelf camel bonnet with box pleats and a thick tie of rose silk. With its good bones, it must have cost at least eight dollars new, though Mrs. English would've charged eight fifty. Perhaps Mrs. Payne will sell it to me for a discount.

At quitting time, I bring the camel bonnet to Mrs. Payne's study, where she often writes in her Lady's Planner. This room used to be my favorite because of the fairy-tale books she kept on the shelf. Then Caroline locked a litter of kittens inside, who tore through the place like termites in a bag of sawdust, and blamed me for the prank. The books were ruined. When Mrs. Payne believed me over her daughter, Caroline hissed in my ear, "I despise you."

Mrs. Payne looks up from her journal and blinks at the hat in my hands.

"I would like to buy this, ma'am."

A minnow of curiosity darts across her face. "Go ahead, try it on."

I remove my lace cap and fit the bonnet over my head.

She rounds her desk and ties the rose ribbon to one side of my chin, as is the fashion, and then sweeps my simple hair braid to the front. "Please accept it as a gift."

"Wh-what? Oh no, I couldn't. I was thinking you could set it aside for me until I could pay for it—"

"I just lent Noemi Caroline's bicycle. Take the hat. It's fuzzy anyway."

"Thank you, ma'am. You are most generous."

Her gaze falls off me and lands on the rug. A strange moment passes, then she gracefully folds her hands as if warming them around a teacup. Her smile teeters. "We shall see you tomorrow, then."

I WAIT UNTIL Old Gin and I have stepped off the Payne Estate before blurting out, "Why were you talking to Billy Riggs?"

His forehead pinches. "Turtle egg," he growls, a Chinese insult. "He claims one of the Chinese owed his father money."

"Who?"

"Someone who left before you were born." The gray in his brown eyes suddenly looks like iron streaks in ore. "If you see this turtle egg again, stay away from him. We do not need his reek in our nose, hm?"

The streetcar arrives, and we drag our tired bodies aboard, along with other workers. In the streets, a different citizenry moves about. These ride carriages with polished seats, and their eyes roam freely about the scenery.

Old Gin slides in next to me. "On the way home from the baths, I saw twin Shetlands."

He means the Shetlands belonging to the Bells' landlord, who only visits when the rent is late. "That's the third time this year."

He nods. "If Bells evicted, landlord will build a factory."

A factory is more lucrative than a single home. We will have to leave when the place is torn down. The memory of Carcass Alley tightens my belly. Where would we go? Southerners do not like the Chinese living among them, as Lucky Yip could have attested. Shiny pink scars covered half of his body from the fire that ruffians set to his shanty in Mississippi, where he was building railroads. The Chinese who drifted this way lived in shadows, and shadows were not easy to come by.

Old Gin notices me grimacing and tsks his tongue. "Do not worry. I have taken steps to ensure our future, even if that future is not in Atlanta."

His words throw a switch, halting my other thoughts. For all its faults, Atlanta would be a hard city to leave, with its generous sunshine, rolling hills, and ladylike breezes. Seventeen years of living here has mapped its streets and alleyways into my veins. "What steps?"

"Many Chinese in Augusta. Maybe a husband."

Augusta, Georgia, lies over a hundred fifty miles east, its bachelors mostly men who'd come to dig the canal. Something sour rises in my throat. "I have no desire to be someone's wife."

Consternation pulls the wrinkles on Old Gin's face. "Motherhood is a most noble calling. My own mother was only sixteen when she married, but she raised two good sons."

It is hard to argue with that. Unlike the other uncles, Old Gin was not one of the laborers brought to Mississippi during Reconstruction, but hails from a line of scholar-officials in the Qing dynasty. His mother was a gentlewoman who attended her sons with great devotion, and was esteemed among his father's wives.

"What would you do if you did not raise a family? Hats?"

My shoulders droop. Hats had given me a way to put my

fingerprint on the world, but Mrs. English had seen to it that I wouldn't get another apprenticeship here. "Maybe I haven't discovered it yet. But do you remember when you told Hammer Foot that a cricket is happiest when it sings?"

He nods. "Hammer Foot hated digging ditches. He liked performance." Hammer Foot could walk a tightrope blindfolded. I'd seen it with my own eyes. He'd headed north, where he hoped to join P. T. Barnum's Traveling Museum, Menagerie, Caravan, and Hippodrome. "Of course, not always easy to find work you love."

"I know. But you did."

"I told you I have been lucky, hm? Still, a good partner can support you while you discover this purpose. We will find you one with a big nose."

WITH ONE EAR stuck to the wall, I listen hard for clues that Miss Sweetie might be making her debut soon. The rumblings from the printing press obscure the conversation, but Nathan eventually takes a break.

"Striking," he says. "Looks . . . oriental?"

"Yes," comes his mother's voice. "A Chinese girl made it."

Her hat's embellishment. My neck aches from the effort of keeping still.

"You don't say. I ran into a Chinese girl the other day. At least, Bear did."

"What did she look like?"

"Startled."

"As did mine. What else?"

"I don't know, Mother," he says with impatience. "She had two eyes, two legs . . ."

I grit my teeth, remembering the exposure of the legs.

"Oh good, for a minute I thought she might have had three. If we were ever held up, how would you describe the perpetrator to the police? The young woman I saw was pretty, about your age, five foot and some change, with soft brown eyes the color of chestnuts. She had creamy skin—I suppose all hatters are good about keeping out of the sun—and she had a careful way of moving around. She didn't throw herself about like some young people. Stop twitching. So, what do you think?"

"I think, if she ever holds us up, you'd better do the describing."

"We don't see many Chinese around here, especially after the Rabid-Eyes Rapist. Of course, you were too young to remember that."

"I read Father's articles."

I allow myself a breath. They never did catch the Rabid-Eyes Rapist, but they caught another man who looked like him—if you ignored the ten-inch difference in height. The unfortunate soul was eventually cleared, but only after they had hanged him from a stout oak. The Chinese who remained in Atlanta began drifting away after that.

"I suppose that could be who I saw," says Nathan at last.

"I didn't catch her name. Perhaps I will ask Mrs. English tomorrow. I'm curious about her."

I stifle a gasp. Hammer Foot says when people make connections, their energies seek one another out with more frequency as the mind strives to see patterns. That's why Old Gin was so strict with the uncles about following rules. Footprints are not just left on the ground.

Have I stamped another footprint with my Miss Sweetie column? Yes. Perhaps sending the Bells my letter was a very bad idea.

Ten

My muscles protest as I shift around the bench of the streetcar, scanning passengers for copies of the *Focus*, ears attuned to any mention of the word *sweetie*. Though 90 percent of me dreads the Bells' accepting my proposal, the 10 percent of me that wishes for it is a vocal (and regrettably vainglorious) minority. A man in front of me is reading the *Savannah Tribune*, one of the few colored newspapers available in this town. Beside me, a butler unfolds the *Constitution*, clutching it closer to him when I try to get a look. At least the Paynes will have a copy. They subscribe to every newspaper, save the colored and the Jewish ones.

The air is shrouded in droplets, making it feel as if the morning is spitting in my face. Every jostle of the streetcar seems designed to wreak maximum injury on my limbs. Old Gin, though, takes the bumps in stride, serenely chewing on a piece of ginger. Shivering, I slide closer to him, being careful not to muss my new "cheeky clouds" hairstyle with its rolled bundles that peek out from my "borrowed" bonnet.

"I must spend tonight at the Paynes'," says Old Gin, side-stepping my surprised eyes. He's been working late hours recently, but he's never spent the night. "Merritt will be arriving with a new Arabian stallion. Mr. Crycks wants me on hand, just in case."

Merritt has always loved fast horses, just like his sister. An Arabian stallion is sure to cause a stir among the mares who are in heat. "Where will you sleep?"

"There's an extra room besides Mr. Crycks's in the work shed."

"The work shed is always drafty."

"If I'm cold, I'll sleep in the stables."

"The dust will hardly help your cough."

"I'm only a little hoarse, hm?" He begins to laugh at his own joke, but when he becomes short of breath, I fix him with a glare.

"Will they compensate you for your additional work? You should not set a precedent." Of course, that would never happen. Folks like us are just lucky to have jobs.

"There are rewards."

May the rewards from his extra hours be worthy of the loss of his health.

Once at the Paynes', Old Gin opens the kitchen door for me, but leaves before anyone can attempt to feed him. Through the window, I spy Noemi bent over in the garden.

I assemble fist-size cinnamon buns dripping with honey and butter on a doily-thin plate, betting that even my bad-tempered mistress won't refuse this breakfast.

Before I even reach the third floor, I can hear Caroline's

and her mother's voices, the rapid pace telling me how things lie. They must like to get their arguing over with in the morning, sort of like milking the cows. It strikes me that money can alleviate many of the miseries of common folk, but it opens up other avenues of suffering.

I park the tray on a side table and wait outside Caroline's bedchambers for the flames to cool. On the wall hangs a painting of a horse standing atop a knoll, his tail high, ears rigid. A herd of black sheep graze in the valley below it, kept in line by a fierce-looking dog. The painting probably gave the artist a mean hand cramp with all the tiny strokes, but something about the scene puts an itch under my skin.

I hear Old Gin's voice in my head. *Fancy horse like that wouldn't just be strolling around, free as a bird, hm?* Noemi might wonder why the sheep are all black and stuck at the bottom of the hill, a question that four years of bloody battles between the states and twenty-five years of Reconstruction still haven't answered. For me, the piece is simply banal—one of Nathan's favorite words. For once, couldn't the artist show the things people don't pay attention to? Like the wind. Maybe the wind wouldn't be so invisible if people took the time to notice it.

When I detect a lull in the conversation, I shoulder into the room. "Good morning, ma'am. Miss."

Mrs. Payne pulls the African violet away from Caroline, lying in bed, and a trail of soil spills onto the woman's apricot skirts. She dusts them off with a few flicks of her fingers. "Good morning, Jo."

Unlike her mother, Caroline holds her displeasure up for all to see: two hot spots on her cheeks, a scowling mouth, and eyes narrowed to slits. I might have been wrong about the cinnamon buns, which seem to have been frightened into silence and no longer smell. I set the tray on her table and pour the coffee.

Mrs. Payne paints on a bright smile. "Jo, we were just discussing whether common horses can compete alongside pedigreed horses. As Old Gin's daughter, perhaps you are knowledgeable about things like pedigrees."

My gut tells me to demure, but then Caroline pipes up. "She's certainly knowledgeable about being common."

I pass Caroline her mug of coffee, fixing her with a look to remind her of our agreement. I can see the loathing in her eyes, and I can't help wondering if, instead of moving us to a more temperate clime, I've summoned winter forever. She lowers her eyes and takes the coffee.

"With the proper training and advantages, I think any horse can be great. Family name is a burden unique to humans." I pick a cushion off the floor and bring it to the open window to shake out.

Caroline slurps her drink. "You see, Mama, the maid agrees with me. Now you must let Thief race."

Mr. Q's horse, Thief? A *race*horse? I give the pillow I am holding an extra slap. It gives me a stitch in the flank to know I have unwittingly taken Caroline's side.

Her gloating eyes crest the rim of her mug, and I wish I could take back my words. The tricky thing about giving opinions is that sometimes they cost you more than you wanted to spend.

Mrs. Payne sighs. "The sponsors are paying good money

to put their name on a horse. They won't be happy to receive Thief."

Caroline slides languidly off her bed and settles herself at her table. "Maybe the Atlanta Suffragists will win a bid and you can give Thief to them." She holds up a fist and chirps, "Equal votes for all."

Mrs. Payne lets out a ladylike huff. "Heaven forbid they could scrape together enough to qualify." She stiffly crosses to the door. "Your friends will be here soon. Jo, that is a fetching hairstyle. Perhaps you can do the same for Caroline."

Caroline tears a chunk off a bun with her teeth, sugaring her lips. Something tells me the taste is not very sweet.

IN THE DRAWING room where the Paynes receive their visitors, golden curtains pool onto milky carpets. A gilded piano plays catch and throw with the late-morning light streaming in from the windows. This is not the room to be caught smacking your lips or scratching your nits. The simple arrangement of furniture puts every guest on display, the sofas extra plush to encourage lingering while they slowly digest you.

Noemi pours glasses of lemonade for the two ladies seated at a circular table. She moves away, and I recognize two crushed-velvet capotes, hats made by my own hands.

My eyes pop out when I recognize Miss Saltworth and Miss Culpepper, bright as petunias in pink and violet frocks. The sweet scent of Salt's Eau de Lilac perfume mingles with that of the lemon furniture oil and cigar smoke.

Well, if the sun hasn't risen in the west. Old money likes to think it weighs more than new money, and Caroline, at least the Caroline I knew, only associated with girls whose families have carried around their wealth for generations. But perhaps she has dropped her old acquaintances after her years away at school, and is in need of new ones. Funny enough, I don't remember her having many friends.

Salt's round face splits open. "Why, it's Jo! Whatever are you doing here?"

Pepper's dark eyes sweep down my uniform. Unlike the curvy Salt, Pepper's as slim as a fiddle string with a deeper bass of a voice. "Oh! She's a maid."

My reversal of fortune lands like a dead pigeon on the carpet. "It's nice to see you, Miss Saltworth, Miss Culpepper."

"*You're* Caroline's new maid?" Salt was always half a step behind Pepper.

"I'm afraid so," Caroline drawls before I can answer.

Noemi winks at me.

"Caroline!" Pepper folds herself back into a chair. "If I'd known Jo was up for grabs, I would've taken her in a heartbeat." Hope rises in my chest until she adds, "That is, if I didn't already have my Martha."

Salt pulls a blond ringlet with a doughy finger, and then lets it snap back into place. "And if I didn't already have my Lucy, I would've taken her, too. Think of all the hats. Plus, Jo knows the cleverest hairstyles."

Pepper rubs her thin hands together. "I have an idea. Maybe Jo could do Melly-Lee's hair. What do you say, Caroline?"

Caroline, who had refused all hairstyles except for her Newport knot, wrings her mouth into a grim smile. "Of course. Maid, go fetch a brush and pins."

When I return with the items, Mrs. Payne has joined the threesome, the perfect model of poise as she deals the cards. Unlike Caroline, her spine doesn't touch the back of the chair. And unlike Salt, whose knees bounce under her pink gingham skirt like two frogs caught under a picnic blanket, the lady of the house has mastered the art of sitting quietly.

After brushing out Salt's considerable white-blond mane, I begin to weave.

When I was little, Lucky Yip and Hammer Foot let me braid their queues, mostly to keep my fingers out of their games of Chinese chess. Lucky Yip would turn red in the face when he found his hair done up in a "staircase to the heavens," but Hammer Foot always accepted his hairdo with a grateful bow.

I have often wondered if either of them was my father, but quickly dismissed the idea. Hammer Foot had been almost monk-like in his dedication to virtuous and harmonious living, while Lucky Yip was a devoted family man, sending every penny he earned back to China.

Salt wiggles her shoulders, and I lose my grip on her hair. Gritting my teeth, I retrace my work. "If this looks fetching on me," she gushes, "maybe I'll ask Mr. Q to the horse race today."

Caroline trains her cold gaze on a birdcage that contains no bird.

Mrs. Payne tosses down her winning hand. "I wish more ladies had your spirit. Ever since Mrs. Wordsworth forbade her daughters from asking, no one wants to do it. Atlanta Belles can be so stuffy."

Pepper and Salt exchange an uncomfortable glance. Not every branch in Atlanta can be bought, like the premier ladies' society, Atlanta Belles, where membership can only be inherited. Pepper shuffles the deck, all elbows and thumbs. "Miss Sweetie approves, too. Did you see the new advice column in the *Focus*, Caroline?"

The braid goes uneven again, but not because of Salt this time. The Bells published it? My shaking fingers grip the braid tighter, twisting and winding.

"She told women to 'quit their stalling' because their gentlemen may not be available 'furlong.' Isn't she a holler?" Pepper laughs and the deck nearly scatters.

Caroline's mouth puckers, like her lemonade is too sour.

Mrs. Payne discreetly returns a card that has flown into her lap back into Pepper's deck. "Jo, fetch Mr. Payne's copy of the *Focus*."

"Yes, ma'am." I pin Salt's braid to hold my place.

This time, I nearly fly up the staircase.

Eleven

All is quiet on the second floor, where Mr. Payne keeps his office. The man rises earlier than even Etta Rae and stays at the mills past sundown most days of the week. Beyond the family telephone, which used to scare me with its unpredictable shrieking, the door to Mr. Payne's office is closed. I knock once, just in case, but no one answers.

Mr. Payne's quarters haven't changed a bit since the last time I was here. A desk carved from good old Southern red oak anchors one end of the room, along with a matching chair cut extra-large, though the man barely reaches five and a half feet. The somber walls are infused with the scent of tobacco smoke and the ylang-ylang oil Mr. Payne uses to keep his curly hair flat. The smell stirs up memories of my first encounter with him. Old Gin had come here to discuss a matter, and I had tagged along, only four or five at the time.

Smoke from the man's cigar billowed out of his nose and his ears. "Are you a boy or a girl?"

I'd been wearing trousers, and my hair was cut above my ears, so the mistake was understandable. "Girl," I replied. "Are you a man or a dragon?"

His eyes bulged, and I thought he would eat me up. But then he let out a wheezy laugh and jabbed his cigar toward me. "That one has trouble spelled all over her face, mark my words, Old Gin."

I shake myself from the memory and cross to the desk. Several newspapers are piled in a neat stack, with the *Focus* second from the bottom. I unfold the newspaper, and my fingers leave damp spots on the paper. There on the front page in bold type reads:

INAUGURAL ADVICE COLUMN FOR DEAR MISS SWEETIE—SHE ADVISES ALL

Below the title, Nathan had drawn the silhouette of a lady in an old-fashioned hat adorned with cabbage roses, brandishing an ostrich quill. A giggle fizzles out my nose at the cross-hatching that emphasizes a feminine waist, and at the delicate poise of the arms, which are a far cry from these drumsticks. *Well, Nathan, I am not the lady you imagine me to be, but may you never find out.* So much for my misgivings of last night. I bounce on the balls of my feet and squeal. People will be reading my words, *my* words. I hug the paper and circle the desk one way and then the other.

Mrs. English's advertisement for English's Millinery occupies a prime seat next to my byline. May she be enjoying the glacial pace at which her star worker, Lizzie, moves, and the clumsy way she trims, using paste when she should be using stitches.

Below the ad, another catches my eye. Pendergrass's Long-Life Elixir promises to rid one of "anything that ails you, including dyspepsia, cough, liver spots, toothache, lethargia, diarrhea, ingrown toenails, warts, and especially impotence. If we don't fix your problem in three days, we'll refund your fifty cents with no questions asked. Sold at Buxbaum's."

I float back down the stairs, clutching the paper. Would Pendergrass's elixir work for Old Gin's deterioration? Ordinarily, I disregard such snake oils, but Buxbaum's stands behind its products.

By the time I bring the paper to Mrs. Payne, I have composed my face into something resembling a cheese curd, mild and unremarkable. Caroline leans over to read the article, her eyes narrowing as they go.

While she reads, I return to Salt's braid. Salt and Pepper polish off their sandwiches, and Noemi brings around a tray loaded with more. "More egg salad, misses?"

Pepper takes two. "These could use more pepper."

"Yes, miss," Noemi says deferentially.

"I'm allergic to pepper," Caroline snaps, still reading the paper.

"Not everything has to have pepper, Linney." Salt plucks up a sandwich, pulling loose the strand I'm trying to braid by her ear. "Noemi could make a hash out of a block of wood, and I bet it would slide down the gullet."

Noemi dips her head and murmurs, "Thank you, miss."

Mrs. Payne raps the *Focus* with her index finger. "This column is just the thing." She gets up from her seat. "I'm sorry to leave the game, ladies."

"What are you up to, Mama?" Caroline demands.

"I shall buy as many copies of the *Focus* as I can for tonight's meeting of the Atlanta Belles. Melly-Lee, you should definitely ask your Mr. Q today." She glides out of the room.

I tie an extra-loopy ribbon around Salt's braid, feeling a little loopy myself. Perhaps this edition will be a sellout. Long-term subscriptions are what count, but Miss Sweetie is off to a grand start.

I hold a mirror in front of Salt, who tests the limit of her neck, twisting to see every angle of her new hairstyle. With her curls, her hair resembles more a bubbling spring than a waterfall. "Oh, oh!" Salt squeals, pressing her sandwich to her heart.

"Look out, Mr. Q," breathes Pepper.

Caroline's frosty glare is enough to keep the glass of lemonade she is drinking chilled for hours. "If I have to hear another word about Mr. Q, I may need a tincture for headache."

Pepper cuts her green eyes to Salt and shakes her head.

Salt pats Caroline's hand. "Oh, don't be cross with me, Caroline."

Well, that is a horse saddled backward. If Salt knew how Miss P was minding her Q, she wouldn't be simpering like that. The chores seem to fly by while I fantasize about my alter ego as a columnist for the *Focus*. When it's time for our ride, Caroline sets off at a fast clip for Our Lord's Cemetery, and I hardly notice until she is out of sight. Entertaining one's lover's sweetheart must build up a powerful thirst.

Sweet Potato carries the distinguished yet enigmatic advice columnist off for a romp of her own.

Six Paces Meadow got its name from a duel gone wrong, when one of the duelists turned at six paces instead of ten and shot off his opponent's top story. It is said that the ghost of the wronged still haunts this lot, which is why Old Gin liked to bring the "honored sons and daughters" of the stable here—we mostly had the field to ourselves. Old Gin reassured me that a ghost without its head could not see, hear, or smell, so the chances of bumping into it were slim.

"What about the ghost of the head?" I asked, but he didn't have an answer for that.

We clear a grove of trees and an abandoned hansom cab, which hasn't moved in the years since Old Gin used it to boost me onto the horses. "Don't be afraid," he assured me once I got topside. "I am right here beside you, though you might not always see me." The memories forged in this field were sweet and tinged with summer gold.

Thickets of bright sassafras and old man's beard have crept into the meadow, and even clusters of young trees. When I began my women's cycles, the only thing Old Gin said about it was that all meadows, after an awkward stretch as a thicket, eventually ripen into beautiful forests. That left me more con- fused than ever. There were bits about being a mother even Old Gin couldn't replace.

Sweet Potato whinnies. She's been to this playground before, but not with me. Old Gin hadn't started to break her yet when Mrs. Payne dismissed me.

"For my next article, perhaps I will write about what to do

if you're in love with someone else's man. I'll call it, 'Why Buy the Pig If the Sausage Is Free?'" I laugh wickedly, and I swear Sweet Potato snorts. "Or maybe I'll write about the blacklisting of milliner's assistants. 'Watch Your Hat.'" Sweet Potato paws at the ground, probably bored. "All right, enough about me. Show me your legs." With a good tap of my heels, I cry, "Giddap!"

Sweet Potato answers with a neigh like a trumpet, surging forward so fast, I leave my breath behind. A thousand pounds of muscle and bone stretch and collect under me.

"Wahooo!" I bump along like a feather in a top hat, just trying to hang on.

Moments later, I find my rhythm, and the ride goes easier for both of us. We weave through dense strawberry bush, skirting wet slicks as smoothly as a hawk dancing through air currents. The meadow transforms into ribbons of green and yellow streaking past me, and the air plasters my smile to my face.

A shriek splits the air. From out of nowhere, another horse powers up beside us, a bay with a distinctive wedge-shaped head. I nearly tumble off my seat when I recognize the rider as none other than Caroline's brother, Merritt. He snaps a riding crop. "Giddap! C'mon, Jo, to the hansom!"

Mischief dangles from his smile like a feather from a cat's mouth, and the good looks that hail from his mother's side tie my stomach into complicated knots. Of all the people to catch me in a lark, why Merritt Payne?

While I wrestle with my memories, the bay, who must be Merritt's new Arabian, bursts away like a squall. Sweet Potato charges after him. My thighs burn as I struggle to hang on.

Hooves thunder across the meadow, scaring the blackbirds off their bug hunts.

I lean as far forward as my legs will allow, standing slightly with my bum bouncing along the saddle as we try to catch up. I should be running in the other direction, but Merritt has already seen me. I will need to assure myself that he will not tell his mother. The Arabian's ears flick, monitoring us with his keen hearing. As we close in, he surges another length ahead, the cheeky tassel of his tail taunting us.

The heat of battle lights my skin on fire. "You're not going to let that frisky wedge-head sass us, are you?" I dig my heels in deeper, and Sweet Potato lunges, closing the distance once again. "Thatta girl!"

But then a mud slick flashes twenty yards ahead, and we veer to avoid it, losing ground. As we fall behind, the stallion slows, too, ears flicking. Horses are like people. Some work better under pressure. The more hat orders we got at the millinery, the faster I worked, unlike, for example, Lizzie, who crawled at the same snail's pace regardless of whether it rained or shined.

We clear the slick and then charge ahead, the hansom in clear view only a furlong away. As we approach, the stallion—now two lengths away—ups his tempo again.

I crouch low over Sweet Potato's neck. My hat blows away in the heat of battle, and my hair streams behind me like a black banner. "Come on, Sweetie, dig in!" I yell, bracing myself for the final few yards.

We push and grunt, heaving forward as if there were a knife coming down on our back. But Merritt lays on his crop, and the Arabian cruises across the line.

"Thatta boy!" Merritt cries, throwing up his hat.

My breath comes in gulps, and I lean over Sweet Potato's neck as she slows her speed, her tongue tipped out one side of her mouth. Merritt sidles up to us, his oval face one gloating grin as the Arabian dances and skitters under him. In the four years since I saw him last, the Payne heir has puffed out his pie-crust, as Noemi might say. His coat no longer sags upon a too-slim frame; the gray wool skims his muscled shoulders. The mustache that was only a smear at seventeen is now pointed and trim, accenting his upper lip like the hands of a handsome grandfather clock stuck at three forty-five.

He hooks one leg upon his saddle. "It wasn't a fair fight," he says in that animated tone he uses for everything, even something so mundane as "looks like rain." "Girls just don't have enough coal in the box. Still, pretty legs like those would fetch a pretty sum, if Old Gin ever wants to sell."

"Yes, sir," I reply, even though Old Gin would sooner sell his own pretty legs than Sweet Potato's. Perhaps I can tell Merritt Caroline sent me on an errand . . . in the middle of a haunted meadow . . .

"This is Ameer." The Arabian stands a hand taller than Sweet Potato, with a cresty neck and hind legs like birch trunks. Tossing his head, he puffs and struts the way males do when they know the females are watching. Sweet Potato, who is not in season, pulls the heads off a clump of daisies. "His name means 'chief,' and he's faster than a hat in a hurricane. Those other horses will be eating his dust."

"He's on the roster?"

"Yes, ma'am. Even got Johnny Fortune to ride him."

"Johnny Fortune?"

"Best jockey in the States." His blue-gray eyes glint like war medals. "He's like a bird on a fence. You can't topple him. Father isn't happy about it—why play when you can work?—but it's Mama's race."

Mr. Payne is grooming Merritt to take over his mills, but Merritt has always been more interested in pleasure than paper. "Well, good luck with that. I must be on my—"

"I hear you're wrangling my little sister these days."

I brace myself.

"Where is she?" He glances around him with mock concern. "There are no silken divans here on which to rest her mollycoddled posterior."

"Paying her respects."

"I see. To whom?"

"Friends." Dearly departed ones. I cringe as the net closes over me.

"Wonderful. If she were visiting enemies, I fear that would take all month."

I cough. It is no secret that Caroline is the sort of girl many like but few love. Merritt's grin stretches, while I scrape around for a lie.

He wiggles his fingers. "Jo, I don't wish to vex you. Women's pettifogs are the least of my concerns right now."

"What do you mean?"

He sighs. "Father wants me to settle down, gain some respectability, *work*, of all things. I'm supposed to be at the mills. And my bride, Jane Bentley of Boston, is a bore who insists on staying through the horse race, which means I must ferry her around everywhere. It isn't fair. I am only twenty-one, and still have many"—his eyes widen a fraction—"wrong turns left to make." Even as a lad, Merritt was always a rake, catching the neighborhood girls by their pigtails and kissing their cheeks. "If only she had your spunk. You haven't forgotten Chattahoochee?"

My cheeks warm. When I was eleven and Merritt fifteen, he'd gotten it into his head that he would catch dinner. His father had taken him fishing at the Chattahoochee River the week before, but the only thing Merritt had caught was a cold. After he failed to return by late day, Mrs. Payne sent me to look for him.

I found him throwing rocks into a pool at the base of a waterfall. He was drenched. "Forgot to bring hooks."

A trout leaped off the top of the fall. In fact, there were so many trout, the water was a writhing, silvery mass.

"There are other ways to catch a fish."

"I've tried," he lamented. "They're too slippery."

Sweet Potato bugles out a neigh, startling me from my thoughts.

Merritt pushes back the round top of his gambler-style hat, exposing squirrel-brown hair shot with gold. "I was doing it all wrong. Trying to catch a fish with my hands was like trying to wrestle a greased hog. You showed me how to catch it only long enough to sling it onto the riverbank. We caught five." He chuckles.

"That's Old Gin's trick, sir. The fish just need redirection."

"No 'sir.' It's just 'Merritt' between friends." Sea-blue eyes travel around my face.

He got me fired. I have never known the Payne heir to be wicked in the way men with money can be, but a maid cannot be too cautious around her master.

"Well, good day, sirs." Sweet Potato carries us off. When I glance back around, Merritt, still watching, gives me a bow.

Twelve

Dear Miss Sweetie,

My husband chews with his mouth open, despite my asking him to close it for over sixteen years. He tells me that he will close it only if I will stop slurping my soup. But slurping is the best way I know to avoid burnt lips. Please advise before we kill each other.

Most sincerely,
Still Slurping

Dear Still Slurping,

Stir your soup for two minutes before attempting to consume it and not only will you avoid burnt lips, but you will be spared regular updates on the state of your husband's mastication. Since one does not eat soup year-round, you'd make out like a bandit by accepting your husband's proposal.

Yours truly,
Miss Sweetie

I wait a quarter of an hour at the water trough, and Caroline still doesn't appear. Perhaps she didn't hear the bell chime from the chapel at Our Lord's Cemetery. Or perhaps she did hear, but simply does not care to be on time. Or perhaps she was kidnapped by a band of kangaroos, and a ransom note will be punched through the door shortly.

I steer Sweet Potato back toward the cemetery.

Sounds and smells always feel amplified when one walks through a graveyard. It would seem that Death, having visited each of these souls already, has no more business here. But the Chinese believe death simply moves a soul to an ancestral state of existence, and that the dead cause mischief if not properly appeased. So there could be plenty of trouble to be found among these tombstones, and I should watch my step.

The stony angels of the Innocenti vault implore me to relieve them with their pupil-less eyes. Frederick and Thief are still tucked in the wooded area behind the vault, minding their own business. Poor spoony Salt, with no idea that her beloved is dipping his pen in the neighboring inkwell.

Assured that Caroline has not been kidnapped by kangaroos, I'm about to steer Sweet Potato back to the water trough but stop when I hear a voice coming from the vault. "She's warming to the idea of Thief. But you won't be paying much attention to the race anyway, with Miss Saltworth to distract you."

Thief throws back his head, his black mane splashing like a wave. The horse has good bone structure and a well-muscled back end, but does he have the kind of ruthlessness required to cross the finish line?

"She means nothing to me." I expect Mr. Q to have a velvety baritone, but his voice has the soft tenor of a snake charmer, the kind of voice that could coax the gray out of the clouds. "Her father will be moving them to New York soon, and of course she will understand that I cannot go. We shall tell your parents then."

The words are chased by amorous murmurings, and I hastily exit before my ears start to burn.

FRIDAY NIGHT JUST after five o'clock, Mrs. Payne gives me three dollars, which I secure in the waist pocket of my russet dress. Old Gin must stay the weekend at the Payne Estate. Noemi bundles a wedge of cheese and crackers in a handkerchief for me to carry to Old Gin, who neglected to come by for lunch. "This cheese will fatten him up for sure."

I bundle myself into my cloak, then hike to the stables.

In the corral, a whip of a man with ears that stick out like maple pods puts the stallion through his paces. A jockey's cap is pulled nearly to a small hill of his nose. This must be Johnny Fortune, the best jockey in the States. His squinty black eyes track me, his expression landing squarely on disapproving. The two are watched by Merritt and Mr. Crycks, an old cowboy who is all legs, door-knocker mustache, and hat.

Sighting the curly oak where Billy Riggs accosted Old Gin, I squeeze past the low hedge to inspect the trunk. Below eye level, two squares have been carved, one containing four dots, the other, five. They must be dice—maybe lucky numbers. The scratches are small, but it will be hard not to think of them each time I see this tree.

I hurry into the stables, but not finding Old Gin there, I head to the barn next door. Springtime means occasional work helping the caretaker with newborn kids and lambs. In the barn, animals warm the air, their bleating and baaing a peaceful kind of music. I am surprised to find Old Gin, his back to me, in a horse-riding stance. I thought he had given up those strenuous exercises after Hammer Foot left. He holds the stance a full minute before rising. "If you want to sneak up on old men, you should not bring such powerful cheese, hm?"

"I wanted to make sure you ate something." I hold out the food to Old Gin.

He takes it with a sigh. "Thank you, Jo." He unwraps the bundle and offers me some.

I shake my head. "That's for you to eat, and I won't leave until you do."

He sits on a bale of hay and takes a nibble so small, I despair of it making it all the way down the hatch. He catches me glaring at him and pats the space beside him. "Let me tell you a story, hm?"

Reluctantly, I sit.

"A farmer whose crops had not bloomed sent his son to buy a peach to entice the bats of fortune. And so the son found a fruit the color of a setting sun, one so large he could hold it with both hands without the fingers touching." He demonstrates, holding an imaginary ball between his hands.

"On the way home, the son passed a lake. In the lake, a water nymph with golden hair and eyes that looked cut from the lake itself bathed among the lotuses. Noticing the son, the nymph swam to the edge of the lake. She looked at the son with such longing that he felt his heart stir. But it was not the young man she wanted." Old Gin stretches out his skinny arms and makes his voice high. "'I must have that peach. I have wished to taste such a fruit for so long.'"

I bury a giggle.

"'What will you give me in return?' asked the son. 'A kiss,' she said. So his shaking hands passed her the peach.'"

"The fool," I mutter. "Let me guess. She takes the peach, he doesn't get his kiss, the bats don't come, and the father's crops die. Is that the end?"

Old Gin grunts. "For now." He cocks an ear toward me, waiting for me to dig out the hidden meanings.

"Am I the fool or the nymph?"

"You are too sentimental, and so you are the fool. I am the nymph, because I don't need the peach, hm?"

I imagine knock-kneed Old Gin as a nymph, his scraggly beard dripping with water, and burst out laughing. Soon, his own acorn face is split in a grin, and we are rocking back and forth like the time we tried balancing on a cut log for fun. But then Old Gin's laughter sets off a cough, and my happiness drains away.

Ameer screams from somewhere far off, somehow part of this conversation.

Old Gin drinks from his water jug, and then replaces the cork. "You will be okay minding the burrows?" He rubs at his mouth, more as if trying to erase his grimace than dribbled water.

"The burrows will be secure under my watch." I polish up a smile, despite the worries digging around my skull.

Ameer shrieks again, though more half-heartedly, as if he is beginning to tire. "How's the new jockey?"

Old Gin's shoulders stretch the fabric of his coat. "Good at coaxing speed, not so good at coaxing character."

He lowers himself back into a horse-riding stance.

"You forgot the cheese."

"I will eat cheese later. It has already waited a long time."

WHEN I HIKE back up the paved path, Noemi is half riding the safety by the work shed. "This is going to be more fun than a frog race once I get the hang of it. Probably even beats riding a horse." Her bushy eyebrows wiggle.

"I doubt that."

"Only one way to find out. Oh, I forgot." She puts a hand to her cheek. "You ain't ready to break your legs."

The safety *does* look fun, its paint as glossy as a candied apple.

"After a week with the porcupine, maybe I *am* ready to break my legs." Jo Kuan might not have taken such risks, but Miss Sweetie embraces the future, including newfangled machinery. "As long as it doesn't buck, I'm game." I unclasp my cloak and set it on a stump. Then I take one of the handlebars, laying my other hand on the triangle seat. The leather feels smooth, almost slick, and it's attached to the frame with metal coils to take the jounce out of the bounce. A metal plate partly covers the back wheel to prevent one's skirt from being violently "freed" from one's body. I begin to worry that might be the reason for the term *freedom machines*.

"They say you're supposed to coast first, with your feet hiked up to practice balancing." Noemi holds her hands out as if to imitate her feet. "That means we need to face downhill." Both the stables and the house lie at a slight decline from where we are standing.

I face the bicycle toward the stables. If I start flying, I would rather break my legs a little closer to Old Gin so he doesn't have to travel far to rescue me. Noemi holds the seat steady while I climb aboard. The frame curves low, allowing me to pass my leg through to the other side instead of swinging it over as with a horse. I tuck my skirts between my legs so they don't cause trouble.

The bicycle is heavy. Miss Sweetie assures Jo Kuan that means a more stable ride, like how a frigate feels less turbulence than a rowboat. Jo Kuan points out that heavier could also mean deadlier, as an ant might know when a foot comes along. Miss Sweetie ignores her and take a firm grip on the handlebars. A lever is attached to the right one.

"That's the brake," Noemi tells me. "You squeeze it to stop."

I try it out and feel a mild resistance. "What about this button?" I run my finger along a metal piece the size of a doorknob attached to the left handlebar.

"It's a bell. Look." She flips a switch on the doorknob, and a hammer strikes the metal with a satisfying *ding!*

"What for?"

"In case you want to ring for service, obviously."

"But who would come?" Only after my words fall out do I notice the smile riding up her face. She is as sly as the letter *u*, always sneaking in after *q*.

Slowly, I lift one foot, then the other. I wobble to one side and catch myself.

Noemi helps me pull the bicycle back to center. "Steady, August."

"You . . . *named* the safety?"

"A name means respect. If you're going to put your life into someone's hands, best start off on the right foot."

I topple to one side again, and Noemi neatly catches me. "Or the left."

"Ah. You chose August because it means 'respected.'"

"No, I chose it because it's the name of a month, the most powerful month on the calendar. When August comes around, it brings a wrath hot enough to jerky the cows while they're standing in the fields."

"July's not so balmy either."

She lifts an eyebrow so high, I wouldn't be surprised if she could unhook it and throw it like a lightning bolt.

"August, be easy on me." I lift my feet again, and let gravity coax me down the incline. My toes touch down a few times, but soon, I am rolling! "I'm doing it, Noemi! I'm coasting!"

"That's 'cause I'm still holding you, you noodle."

"Well, let go!"

She cuts me loose, and the bicycle picks up speed.

August bobs one direction and then the other, but I keep my grip fused to the horns. A flock of chickens scatters before me with panicked squawks. And then I'm hurling down the road, fast as a spit seed. Before I hit anything, like the pavement, I squeeze the brake, and the contraption comes to a shaky stop.

I set down my anchors, and Noemi comes up behind me. "Did you see that?" I ask breathlessly. "I was flying."

"You barely went ten yards." She brushes a hand toward me, meaning *get off.*

"August, you are hot enough to jerky the cows." I roll the bicycle back to the work shed, and then Noemi climbs aboard. After scooting along with her toes and then coasting a few times, her feet find the pedals, and she's pumping her way back toward the house. She is a natural.

She disappears around a curve. When she doesn't return, I work my way back toward the house after her.

My step slows when I reach the courtyard. Noemi stands with the bicycle forming a fence of sorts between her and the Payne women. Judging by Caroline's white-lipped scowl, August has brought a wrath after all.

Thirteen

The sun cowers in the west, and despite my exertions, the air suddenly feels too brittle against my skin. Mrs. Payne's skirted coat looks hastily shrugged on, judging by how its collar traps her loose hair.

"It was bad enough that you gave my maid my hat, but now you're giving this uppity sass-mouthed nigra my bicycle?" Caroline's face begins to blotch, even though she is the only one not wearing a coat.

"We're only lending the bicycle. Do be reasonable, Caroline. You wanted to give it away."

"If I had known it was going to her, I would never have given it up."

Noemi squeezes the handlebars, her knuckles bunching in her black leather gloves. "I'm sorry, ma'am. I don't wish to make trouble." With her head bowed, it's hard to tell that Noemi is the tallest of the three.

"I said you can have it, and a lady is only as good as her word." Mrs. Payne's blue eyes cock like a pair of pistols.

The moment holds an outraged breath. Caroline's scornful expression has set in her face like a fly in the aspic. Digging it out would only make it worse.

Noemi grinds her gaze into the dirt. "I'd be happy to pay for it."

We all gape at her.

"How much does it cost, miss?" Noemi directs her question to the bow I tied at Caroline's waist.

"My papa bought it for a hundred dollars."

I cough out my shock, and everyone but Noemi looks at me.

"Is there something you wished to say, Jo?" Mrs. Payne asks.

"I'm sorry, ma'am, only that you could buy a horse for a hundred dollars, not a good one, of course, but at least it's got four working legs."

Caroline's outrage pops like a faulty incandescent bulb. "Since when does my domestic's opinion matter? Her soul's even blacker than this nigra's, and I wish you hadn't hired her back."

Mrs. Payne sweeps her hair free from her coat. "That's enough, Caroline. Maybe you will think about the value of things before you cast them aside. Now, the bicycle cost more like eighty dollars, but that was new."

"Ma'am, I'll pay for it," Noemi says without a hint of emotion. "I insist."

I furtively shake my head at Noemi, but she won't meet my eyes.

A smile slithers up Caroline's face. "Half now, half next week." She picks a thread off her sleeve and feeds it to the breeze.

Outrageous. Noemi doesn't have eighty dollars to throw

away. The lengths the haves will go to in order to deprive the have-nots boggles the mind. Even Miss Sweetie has no answer for it.

Noemi clears her throat. "Ma'am, how about you withhold my wages until it's paid?"

Mrs. Payne's gaze passes between Caroline and Noemi and then lands on me. She pulls her coat closed, and suddenly she looks smaller. It's as if battling with Caroline has wrung her out. She twists at her wedding band, an old habit. Mrs. Payne gives Noemi an exasperated smile. "That will be fine. Well, good evening, then." With a shake of her head, she returns to the house.

"Move it back to the work shed for now, you hear?" Caroline wags her finger toward the shed, as if Noemi doesn't know where it's located even after working here all her life. "Only hussies ride bicycles," she hisses as Noemi rolls August away.

NOEMI MARCHES DOWN Peachtree as if the world were depending on her to turn it. Her gloved hands are balled into fists, and the skirt of her brown-checkered dress doesn't dare tangle in her legs. When we reach the streetcar stop, she sails right by. She glances back at me, half walking, half trotting to catch up. "Robby's delivering on the other side of town today, and I feel like walking. You don't have to come."

If Robby's delivering, then he must not have gotten the clerk job after all. I don't mention it—there are more pressing issues to discuss—but this is exactly the kind of injustice Miss Sweetie must speak to. I march doggedly alongside her, trying to catch my breath. "You didn't ask for my opinion, but it's free for the taking."

"Go on."

I'm about to tell her the hazards of spending money she doesn't have for things she doesn't need to spite people she shouldn't spite. But her grim expression blows the words like dust from my mouth. "Never mind."

Noemi sighs. "Mama's been dead for almost ten years, but Caroline still counts the silverware every night."

I was seven when we lost Noemi's mother, Caroline's mammy. At her burial, the world seemed to grow colder and more distant on that dark October day, and the scrape of the shovel sounded like a hawk sharpening its claws. Caroline had insisted on attending, even though the cemetery was for colored only. But when the reverend began eulogizing, she began keening so loud, her father had to take her away.

Twenty yards in front of us, a terrier strains at its leash, its fierce expression at odds with its stubby body. I instinctively shrink away. The dog's owner strolls leisurely behind, chatting with another white lady. Ignoring Noemi, who steps into the busy street, their collective gaze sweeps over me, surprise tinged with distrust. I'm about to follow Noemi into the street when the terrier lunges at me, scaring me there faster.

"Fluffers!" The dog's owner tugs him back with a snap of her ruffled wrist. She hurries after her friend, but the terrier throws an extra snap in my direction.

"Cocky mutt," Noemi mutters. "You okay?"

I nod, though my heart could probably beat Ameer in a

sprint. A carriage barrels toward us, and Noemi pulls me back to the sidewalk.

I'm about to bring up the subject of the bicycle again when Noemi's stout boots stop marching. In the grassy yard of a brick law office, men are hoisting up a statue. Weakening sunlight glints off the bronze figure of a Confederate officer, his chest puffed out like a sail.

"Why would anyone want to build a monument for a war they lost?"

"Because they ain't good at losing. And that's another reason why I want that bicycle. It's bad enough we got the dogs barking us into place, now they're putting up statues to remind us, too. We have to fight for every inch or we'll lose it."

"Every inch of what?"

"When's the last time you saw a colored on a bicycle?"

"About thirty minutes ago."

She bumps me with her arm. "Colored folks don't ride bicycles, but it don't mean we can't. We got to act how we want people to treat us."

The men notice us watching them, and we hurry away.

"But, you're going to make your point with a bicycle? Why not choose something less costly, like not stepping off the sidewalk."

Her eyelids peel back. "You want a gang of white hoods to jump me?"

"Of course not." I interlace my fingers in Old Gin's good-fortune gesture.

Noemi watches me shaking my hands as if I were winding

up to throw dice. "Old Gin does that whenever that old billy goat runs by."

"He doesn't trust things that are white like that goat. Chinese people use white for funerals."

Her cheekbones become knobs. "Ha! We got a lot in common, Old Gin and me. Don't worry about the cost. I'll borrow from my no-account brother if I have to."

Whatever I was going to say dies on my tongue. I always figured her no-account brother had, well, no account.

"Here's the thing. Unlike the sidewalk, there ain't rules yet for bicycles. Means we got to jump in and make the rules." She waggles her eyebrows at me. "Or someone else will make them for us."

WITH THE BASEMENT all mine, I decide to give myself a thorough scrubbing with leftover tea in our kitchen. Nature tells all animals to get clean, and when we don't, some powerful odors build up, not to mention the jibbies. At Mrs. English's, I'd see women ruin their hats scratching to get at the itch underneath, when they could've avoided the problem by simply washing their hair now and then.

I dry mine by passing it over a frying pan I heated on the stove and then braid it into five strands for tomorrow's pagoda hairstyle. Then I pad over to Old Gin's room for paper. The drawer where we keep it sticks, even though Old Gin regularly waxes the wood. I slide open the drawer underneath, which contains scraps of fabric. A length of scarlet silk lies atop the heap.

I pull it out. "What are you doing here?" Old Gin had brought the cloth to the Beautiful Country—America—one of two items that had belonged to his late wife. I open the silk. To my horror, it falls into several irregular pieces. He *cut* it? But why?

I hold up a piece—definitely the beginnings of a sleeve. I measure it against my arm. It's just my length.

My stomach squeezes into a cold knot. He's making something for me. A wedding garment? Chinese women wear red on their wedding day, as it's the color of happiness and luck. Is he planning to give me away so soon? And to whom? He said he had taken steps to assure our future, but it still comes as a shock.

I should be grateful for Old Gin's care all these years. If not for me, he could've returned to China to fetch another wife, who might've given him sons. At sixty now, he is too old to marry. Once I am "taken care of," at least he can put some dust on his soles, as he has always wished to do. For all the time he spends with horses, he never gets to travel far.

Still, the realization that I have been a burden tears something deep inside me. I wipe my eyes with the sleeve and tuck it back in the drawer.

I hope my parents appreciated him for the job he took on. Wherever they are.

Wondering about my parents is a strange kind of agony, an itch that I can't help scratching until it causes pain. Mostly, I think about my mother. There's a good chance my father was a cad—he wouldn't be the first to love and leave a woman. It's harder for a woman to leave her child. Maybe she had a good reason. Odds are, she would've been poor like me and, unless she had people like Old Gin and the Bells in her life, uneducated. Still, I like to think she had a smile in her eyes and a song on her lips. I like to think she smelled of summer peaches.

Back in my room, I stretch out on my bed. There is still time to show Old Gin that I don't need a husband. That I can make my own way, despite my history of dismissals.

Cautiously, I unplug the listening tube. Forbearance woofs, throwing my heart into orbit. I scramble to replug the tube, but then Nathan says, "It's just rats as I told you. We could get a cat . . ."

The barking stops.

Nathan chuckles. "I didn't think so."

Mrs. Bell says something I can't distinguish, hopefully not, *Maybe we should investigate under the house.*

"If they pass that legislation, you can be sure the streetcar companies will jump on it," Nathan replies. "They've wanted to segregate for years."

"We must pray."

It seems to me that praying is a hit-or-miss thing, and when it's answered, it's never quite the way one expects. For a long time, I prayed my parents would come back for me, but they never did. Then I outgrew my need for them, which I suppose was God's way of giving me an answer, albeit a sideways, not to mention protracted, one. I hope God will provide a swift and satisfactory reply to the proposed legislation, which seems as ridiculous as putting robins and blue jays in different trees and expecting them not to share the same sky.

While Nathan works on the Sunday edition, I do my part

ten feet below. I pull out my dictionary, which opens to the *Y* section, where I'd stuck a clipping of "Yea or Neigh?"

Shiny bicycles with red leather seats wheel back and forth across Miss Sweetie's mind. Dare I write about them so soon after the incident with Caroline? If she read it, she might smell a rotting fish, but surely she wouldn't suspect her "slow" maid of penning the column.

My knees bounce, and my eyes find the word *giddy* on the wall, next to *goobers*.

BICYCLES: PEDALING US TOWARD THE FUTURE

To those who are still on the fence over ladies riding bicycles, I say bring on the odorless horse! They don't need feeding on the front end or shoveling on the back end. They don't need exercise, a stall, or blankets, and they won't wander off if you forget to tie them up. Ladies, why should men have all the fun? There is no greater thrill than that which comes from captaining one's own ship through the waters of one's choosing. You can run your errands twice as fast and exercise your limbs while doing it.

And to those who call women who ride bicycles vulgar, may your iron corsets and chastity belts not weigh you down while the rest of us sail the freedom machines into the twentieth century.

Respectfully submitted,
Miss Sweetie

Remembering the wolf-whistling men from when I left the last letter, I fetch the mystery uncle's navy suit and linen shirt from the crates. A lone woman should not travel by herself at night, but a man can go wherever, whenever. It's a wonder more women don't disguise themselves. With a few rolls, tucks, and cinches, I persuade the clothes to keep their grip on me. The Balmorals are missing. Perhaps Old Gin has managed to sell them already. I padlock my face with an old scarf, then top everything off with my misfit hat, which is so confusing in shape, it could be worn by a man or a woman.

The coat of undyed wool crackles when I slip it on. In the inner pocket, I discover a folded paper of good quality that resists my efforts to open it.

尚,

Forgive me.

The Chinese characters are written in penmanship even worse than mine. 尚 means "esteemed" and is also a man's name, pronounced *Shang*. The signature is not a Chinese character I recognize. So Shang must be the mystery uncle. It occurs to me that Old Gin never mentioned his name when I asked. Was that intentional?

Moreover, could Shang be Billy Riggs's debtor? Anything's possible, but I doubt it. Old Gin had carefully screened those who lived with us, refusing all but the most hygienic and trustworthy. Someone who consorted with lowlifes like the Riggses would not have made the cut to be an uncle. If you choose good bricks, Old Gin liked to say, you will not have to worry about your house crumbling.

Well, Shang, whoever you are, we are partners in crime tonight.

Fourteen

Dear Miss Sweetie,

    Hold your horses. What's next? Shall women and men be forced to exchange wardrobes—pants on her and petticoats on him? I think you need to rein in your brazen ideas.

                       Sincerely yours,
                       Mary Steeple

Dear Miss Sweetie,

    Women ask men? A resounding and heartfelt YES from this bachelor! About time women do some of the heavy lifting.

                       Respectfully submitted,
                       RMS

Wearing Shang's clothes transforms me. Miss Sweetie rather likes the loose and swingy fit, and the offense of wearing men's clothes feels strangely right. I swagger down the sidewalk, wishing I had a cane to swing before me. Maybe an eye patch, too.

I giggle, wondering whether my skull has cracked. Miss Sweetie is not a pirate, though she may make waves.

The streets are empty, and I almost feel disappointed no one is around to test out my disguise. Definitely, my skull is cracked.

Both the print shop and the house have gone dark, but the streetlamp coats the path to the door with a wan yellow light. Despite my effort to step as lightly as possible, the stairway groans in triplet as I ascend, then cross to the door in five steps. I give a nod of appreciation to the sloped roof covering the porch, which hides me in shadow. A mail slot is placed at hand level. I lift the brass flap, and the slot practically shrieks at the intrusion. It didn't do that the last time I deposited my letter. I quickly stuff the paper inside.

But the brass flap has trapped the sleeve of my undyed coat! *Goose feathers.* I tug my sleeve this way and that, but the thing has caught me in its jaw. Soon, another jaw begins to bark—Bear. Trying not to panic, I begin to work the fabric loose, but suddenly the door swings open, pulling my arm with it. I give my sleeve a solid yank, and hear it rip.

Bear lunges toward me but doesn't pounce, only circles as if trying to herd me forward.

"Bear!" Nathan slaps his thigh twice. She hastens back to his side and quiets, though her tail thumps like a landed fish. "Pardon me. But it's rather late to be leaving letters." Nathan's gruff voice sounds weighted by weariness. He's still wearing his day clothes, but his shirt is untucked and his sleeves are unbuttoned, as if he were about to undress. Before I can flee, he adjusts the knob of an oil lamp to burn brighter.

I retreat to a spot halfway between the door and the stairs, and turn my back. "I'm sorry to disturb you," I call over my shoulder. My voice comes out too girlishly high, and I clear my throat loudly, trying to find a lower range.

"Miss *Sweetie*, is it?" Nathan's voice perks up. He is holding my letter and reading the envelope where I'd written, To: Mr. Nathan Bell, From: Miss Sweetie.

I shrink farther into the shadows and summon a self-important madam's voice, one that sounds suspiciously like Mrs. English. "Yes. Miss Sweetie, that's me."

"It's a pleasure to meet you face to, er, back."

"As you might recall, I've requested anonymity."

"Don't leave yet," he orders, then belatedly tacks on a *please*. "I was hoping to discuss a matter with you."

"A matter?"

"Your letters of admiration."

"My what?"

"Letters." His shoulders tug with the effort of restraining Bear. "People have been dropping them into our mail slot all day, which is why it's a bit cantankerous. I think the springs have twisted. Sorry about your sleeve."

"What do these letters say?"

"Wait a moment, and I'll fetch them."

Before I can answer, Nathan disappears with Bear.

As much as I want to know about these letters, every moment standing here I risk discovery. Passing as white is a punishable offense whose severity depends on who is duped and to what degree. If it were discovered that a lowly Chinese girl dispensed courtship advice to hundreds, if not thousands of Atlanta women, I would get jail time if I was lucky. If not, I could get an angry mob on my heels, reminding me never to make that mistake again. I have dipped my toe into too deep a pond, and now an alligator must surely be on its way up. Chinese people can't be advice columnists. I thought we could be hatters, but clearly I was wrong about that, too.

While I clutch my sleeves, Nathan reappears holding letters tied with twine. Bear barks another greeting. "I read some of them. I wasn't quite sure if you'd . . . be back. Anyway, not all of it is admiration, but the main thing is that you provoked a discussion, and that's our motto."

I think of the drawing of a microscope that adorns the front page of every issue of the *Focus*, below which is printed, *to feed public discourse that such may achieve an enlightened citizenry.* "I'm pleased at the enthusiasm. Have you received more subscriptions?"

"Forty-two today, and none lost. It's incredible. I suppose we have you to thank."

If the *Focus* needs a hundred subscribers each week until April, or fifty new subscribers for each edition, I will have to do better.

He rubs his arms. "You should come in unless you want to catch a draft. I promise not to . . . look."

"No, it is late."

"How did you get here? Do you have an escort? I don't see anyone." He tries to peer beyond me, though I shift around, blocking his view.

"Yes. He is not far. In fact, there he is now," I lie, searching the empty streets as if I can actually see someone.

"Take the letters. You might get ideas for future columns." He holds out the bundle. The familiar smells of the shop beckon me—printer's ink, lemon oil, the charred hickory used in the fireplace, and other scents I can't identify but that taken together smell like home.

"Toss them here."

He sizes me up, now facing him directly. "Er, will you catch them?"

"No, I shall let them give me a black eye." Then I could definitely wear an eye patch. "Be quick about it."

He tosses the bundle, and I snatch them easily.

"Will you be sending regular posts? Er, not to press a thumb on you. We *are* grateful, in case that wasn't—"

"I will do my best," I interrupt, sure he can see every dot and crease on my face through my hat brim. "I'll send the posts a day or two before publication. Is that acceptable?"

"Yes."

With a joyful bark, Bear breaks away from Nathan and barrels toward me. "No, Bear!" I shrink away.

Before she reaches me, Nathan grabs the dog and wrestles her back inside. "I'm sorry, she's been quite naughty as of late." He throws a stern look at where the dog's eyes would be.

I recover my breath. "Well, it's late. Good night." I begin to descend the staircase.

"Miss Sweetie?"

I pause at the last stair.

"How did you know Bear's name?"

"I, er, I thought that's what you called her." Didn't he? Or did I imagine it?

"Oh. Of course."

My ears burn as the night swallows me up.

THE WEEKEND STARTS off a rinse-water gray, a color that does nothing for fair Atlanta, or as Mrs. English would say, "piles on the ugly." Folks move slower on Saturdays, like they're trying to make it last longer. Even the trains at Union Station move as if they haven't quite woken up yet. I wrap my scarf tighter around my neck, gritting my teeth both against the morning chill and at the stabbing memory of last night's slipup. That shall serve as my warning to limit my interactions with Nathan as much as possible. Miss Sweetie must remain a lady of mystery.

Most businesses, like English's, are closed on the weekends. But not Buxbaum's, whose signage reads, WHEN YOU NEED IT, WE HAVE IT. Abraham Buxbaum himself doesn't work on the Jewish Sabbath but employs a healthy cadre of young men to run the store for him. The two-story brick building spans half a block, with glass windows that showcase furniture, footwear, sewing machines, and even ladies' undergarments, as bold as petunias in a box planter.

I swing open an ornately carved door, ringing the bells. The store's central furnace kisses my frozen cheeks, and I soak up the heat, my face upturned to the flock of light fixtures displayed from the ceiling. Maybe one day I'll have enough money to snag one of those birds, but I'll need to get my own ceiling first.

On one side of the store, the head clerk demonstrates an umbrella for some customers in a hearty voice that carries across the room. I start toward him, but then a familiar figure stacking bottles behind a counter catches my eye. "Robby?"

"Morning, Jo." Robby shines a smile at me. A clerk's apron in practical brown hangs as straight as a cupboard over his pin-striped jacket. "Looks like your scarf ate you for breakfast."

I unwrap my face. "I've got this scarf well-trained. It won't pull the wool over my eyes."

"I suspect not many can do that."

"I thought you were back on the cart."

"Mr. Buxbaum hired another man but caught him snoozing on the job. He asked me to fill in again until he finds a replacement."

"From where I'm standing, that clerk's apron looks just your size."

"It's a shame clerks don't come in the color brown." He squeezes out a smile and bumps a fist against the table. "Guess you heard about our latest purchase."

"It is a fine bicycle," I say half-heartedly. When the situation calls for comfort as opposed to advice, I am remarkably inept. Old Gin would know what to say. The rest of us struggle to find the words, whereas he just plucks the right ones out of the air, like dandelion fluff.

Robby squares a stack of cigar boxes on the counter, and then shines up a brass cash register with a rag, lean arms moving with efficient strokes. "I knew she wanted a baby, I just didn't expect it to come with pneumatic tires. The thing is, Jo, we need Noemi's wages. A deliveryman's income ain't enough for both of us."

He folds his rag into a square. The door opens, letting in

more customers. Robby glances toward them, and then says, "Better give me your shopping list and your bag."

I hand him my shopping bag, which I sewed myself out of a damask curtain. "I need a half gallon of kerosene, soap, matches, a dozen candles, and your cheapest pair of ladies' gloves, size small. Also, what do you know about Pendergrass's Long-Life Elixir?"

"Mr. Buxbaum says we can't keep it on the shelf. Let me check if there are any in the stockroom."

He disappears through a doorway. I study a display case of beaded patches and premade bows. Prefabricated adornment is the rage. The modern woman wants a quick and inexpensive way to deck herself out. A daisy made of chicken feathers sells for three cents. Banditry! All it takes is a little glue and a windy day by your local farm.

The front door opens once more to the ringing of bells, and a chill seeps through the worn spots in my coat. High-heeled boots clap like thunder across the floorboards. The monkeys of mischief have been eavesdropping on my worries.

Billy Riggs saunters toward me.

Fifteen

I feign interest in a length of silk cord, monitoring Billy in a looking glass. He sports a teal cutaway and vest, carrying his twenty-something years with the assurance of someone who has decided the world has nothing more to teach him. Old Gin told me to stay away from this man. But if I leave now, he could simply follow me.

The man stops to finger something at a table marked OPTICS. "The Jew must be rich as rhino fat." He must be talking to me, as the other customers are out of earshot. He has a quick way of snapping his words together without opening his mouth much, the way they do in the mountain areas of north Georgia. "Five whole dollars for this magnifying glass. Of course, one should never confuse cost with value."

He surveys the shop through the glass. "My, my"—the glass stops, and his penny eyes find mine watching him through the mirror—"this place has all sorts of curiosities. A pleasure to see you again, miss." He bows, not the courteous kind that gentlemen do, but a farcical bending of the knees, one heel out, hand stirring the air with the magnifying glass.

A centipede-like shiver crawls down my back, and I withdraw my gaze. Hammer Foot said that not engaging is a victory in itself.

"We don't get a lot of coolies here. Yet the ones that come always end up scratching at my door."

I finally turn around. The man stands a hand taller than me, but mostly on account of the boots. A fire grows in my belly, and some steam wants out. Miss Sweetie lifts her chin. "I wouldn't scratch at your door if it were gilded an inch deep."

His head tilts to one side, and his cocky grin hardens into something more menacing. "I wouldn't be so sure. If anyone can help that old horseman, it's you." He laughs at my stricken expression, but I can scarcely compose myself with all the questions flooding my mind. By "horseman," he couldn't mean Old Gin, could he? But why would Old Gin need help?

My nose floods with the too-sweet scent of Billy's cologne mingled with the metallic stench of corruption.

I wet my lips, which have gone dry. "What do you mean?"

"Information isn't free."

Robby returns with my damask bag, which he sets on the counter. "What can I help you with, Mr. Billy?" He looks directly at the man, and my heart clutches at his boldness. There are unspoken rules in the South that govern how blacks and whites interact, including that blacks do not look whites in the eye. If those rules are ever broken, there are consequences, sometimes unspeakable ones.

Billy's eyes narrow. "So the Jew now trusts the colored

with his treasury. Ain't that like letting a crow guard the night crawlers?" He laughs.

It occurs to me that men are the real sauceboxes, but no one ever calls them sauceboxes because they are allowed to say what they want—at least the white ones. Billy jabs the magnifying glass toward the neatly arranged tonics behind Robby. "I want a bottle of Pendergrass's Long-Life Elixir." He pronounces *elixir* as if he is actually licking the word out of the air.

I cross to the counter and rummage through my bag, more for something to do than to verify the contents. My hand comes across a glass flask with etchings.

"Sorry, but we're out of Pendergrass." Robby shows the space on the shelf where they would be. "Just sold the last one."

I let go of the flask and withdraw my hand from the bag.

"Well, get more." Billy Riggs flourishes his arms, as though for emphasis. He could be a play actor if vice didn't pay so well.

"I'm sorry, sir. Shipment's not due until a week from Tuesday. How about Marbury's Tonic? It's got a good price on it, and also comes with a money-back guarantee."

"Sounds like you got a hearing problem. I said I wanted Pen-der-grass."

The moment turns brittle as frosted glass. Two women who have drifted closer to us trade worried glances and then hurriedly exit the store.

Robby's pliant mouth thins, matching the dark slashes of his eyebrows. "The shipment's not due until a week from Tuesday. And only God can make those trains come faster."

It is hard to argue with that, but Billy's leg has begun to twitch. Hammer Foot says jittery energy needs stabilizing to focus it, like an arrow needs fletching to fly straight. Billy's father, rumored to have been a crook worse than Billy, could hardly have given him the fletching he needed to fly a straight path.

"I don't know about that, Robby. I heard Mr. Thomas Edison's so clever, he could make even a train fly," I drop.

Robby clears his throat, cutting me a warning glance. Billy's leg stops twitching, and he refocuses his sights on me. The *tsk* of his tongue sounds like a match strike.

"Shall I wrap that glass for you?" Robby's casual tone smooths the hackles in the air.

The man's gaze drifts to my damask bag, still lying on the counter next to me, and before I can say "Pendergrass," he has snaked my bag from under my nose. "Well now, what sort of shopping did you do today?"

"Those are mine!" Miss Sweetie's wrathiness overtakes my tongue.

Billy's eyes widen, but then a grin spreads across the crook's face. "I don't see a bill of sale."

Robby's face folds into a grimace. Setting down the magnifying glass, Billy withdraws my items one by one: kerosene, matches, soap, candles, gloves. "Aha!" He grips the flask in a mean fist and brings it into the light. "Teeth rinse?"

Robby crosses his arms, impatience pedaling around on his face. "We have more if you'd like, sir. We could all stand to take better care of our teeth."

Billy sets down the flask so hard, I'm surprised it doesn't shatter. He picks up his magnifying glass again. With flair, he holds up a five-dollar bill and lets it drop onto the counter, where it lies like a dead leaf. "Mind you save me a bottle of that Pendergrass from your next shipment. And, Miss Kuan, come see me sometime. Offers don't last forever."

My spleen curdles. He knows my name, which means he knows I am related to Old Gin. Unless he is bluffing.

We watch him swagger to the exit. Not until he has left the shop do I resume breathing.

Robby carefully wraps each of my items in newspaper. "Whatever he's offering, best leave it on the table."

"Don't worry. If I was a mouse and the world's last hunk of cheese was sitting on his table, I wouldn't be tempted in the least." The memory of Shang's letter unfolds in my mind. Had Shang been one of the Chinese who had scratched on his door?

"Glad to see he didn't take the fizz off you."

"No, sir." My hands shake as I fit my items back into my bag. "You?"

"No, Jo, still bubbly." He grins. "The teeth rinse is on me to celebrate your new job."

"Thank you. My teeth appreciate it."

He fits the last of my items back into my bag. "He was in here the other day, offering to 'influence' the horse race in favor of Mr. Buxbaum's thoroughbred, Sunday Surprise. Of course, Mr. Buxbaum refused."

"So why come back?"

Robby grins, pulling a four-ounce green bottle from his breast pocket. "Maybe because we're the only ones who sell Pendergrass."

I THREAD MY way back to the basement, the memory of Billy Riggs soiling my mind like a dirty fingerprint. I try to wipe it clean, but only spread it around further. Had he followed me to Buxbaum's? He seemed legitimately interested in the Pendergrass, but it could've been an act.

If he'd followed me, presumably it was to try to scare me into believing Old Gin had something to do with the debt. It's the oldest trick in the book. Create a need, and sell the solution. Well, I won't fall for it. Old Gin would never have trucked with the likes of Billy or his father. I would bet all the money in our work boots on it.

I SPEND THE Lord's Day safely indoors, redeeming my holy soul, or rather the holey soles in my stockings.

After three days of toiling under Caroline, it's a wonder my arms can do more than swing. But gamely, they hang in there, like two unsold salamis in the butcher's window. I flex one of the salamis and am pleased to feel the hard ridges of my muscles. Hammer Foot would be happy to know that I am keeping physically active—a strong body means a strong mind, as the Chinese say. I would much prefer my capable arms over Caroline's, which are only expected to lift reins and rotate fans.

Miss Sweetie observes that the higher up on the social ladder one ascends, the less one needs to master the basic skills in life. Perhaps the idea is to free up time for higher pursuits, such as academics or the fine arts, though if Caroline is pursuing those, I have yet to see a sign of it.

When our railroad watch ticks toward seven o'clock in the evening, I fill my mug with barley water before cautiously unplugging the listening tube.

I brace myself for Bear's reaction. But Bear is already barking somewhere near the print shop door, where a muffled conversation is taking place, female, by the sound of it.

"Hanged rats," mutters Nathan. His chair scrapes the floor as he pushes away from the table.

"Come. I'll show you some wool I finished spinning." Mrs. Bell's voice comes into focus from farther away.

"That would be nice," says a woman whose voice I don't recognize.

Two pairs of footsteps cross to the house, and the print shop goes quiet. I rummage under the bed and pull out my writing supplies.

"Er, won't you sit down?" says Nathan. Someone else is there?

"I've missed seeing you on Sundays," a breathy voice floats down the tube. I know that voice.

Nathan coughs. "Oh. Did we see each other on Sundays?"

"Oh, Nathan. I always waved to you from my window."

I fumble my ink and nearly spill it on my flannel nightgown. What is *Lizzie Crump* doing up there?

Sixteen

"Ah. Well, we have a deliveryman who helps us now," Nathan tells Lizzie. "Er, how is your father?"

"He is well," says Lizzie. "He's running a horse-race special to encourage people to spruce up their houses before the race. Buy five gallons of Crump Paint and he'll throw in a brush, free."

"Oh. How civic-minded of him."

"Well, I'll get to the point . . ."

The point must be a few train stops away, judging by the lengthy pause that follows. Bear begins whacking her tail against the wall. Come on, Bear. Put those herding skills to use and drive her out of the paddock.

"I read Miss Sweetie's article about the horse race . . . ," Lizzie says. "And, well, I knew it was a sign."

"A sign?"

"That *I* should ask you to the horse race."

My head nearly knocks against the wall. Sure, Nathan is well-known around town and very eligible, but he's no charm biscuit. And did it have to be Lizzie? I imagine her sleepy blue eyes, the curtsy of her smile, the strawberry-blond ringlets teasing out the blush in her skin. She is as guileless and hard to resist as the cake hats in Mrs. English's windows, while I am a lowly shoe who spends half her life squished up against a wall.

When Nathan doesn't reply, Lizzie pouts and says, "Someone has already asked you."

"No," Nathan replies hastily, maybe now just realizing how unenthusiastic he sounds. "No."

"So it was a sign, because here I am, and there you are."

"Yet . . . if it wasn't a sign, you would still be there, and I would still be here."

I imagine the confusion fanning over Lizzie's face. "So . . . is that a yes, then?"

"It would be my pleasure to accompany you."

My face is stuck in a grimace. I grab my barley water but, in my agitation, misjudge the volume, and the hot liquid sloshes over my fingers. "Agh!" I cry out, dropping the mug. It falls to the concrete floor with a wet crack, along with my heart.

I don't move a muscle, hoping that my extreme silence will somehow rub out the noise.

"Oh! I am looking forward to it," says Lizzie, who seems to have not caught my outburst in her excitement. "I will let you know my colors by next weekend."

Nathan doesn't answer. I run through at least a dozen potential reactions he might be having. Perhaps he has put his finger to his lips, and now the two of them are kneeling by the newly discovered ventilation grill, their faces close as they listen. Or maybe he has taken a screwdriver to the vent, and she is admiring his manly physique and his adroitness with tools.

Being discovered by Nathan would be humiliating enough, but with Lizzie beside him, it would be more than I could bear.

"Your . . . colors?" he says at last, sounding no closer than the last time he spoke.

"So you can choose the right flowers."

"Er, of course."

Dare I hope he didn't hear me?

"Oh, Nathan. You're supposed to bring flowers to the parents of the lady you are courting, reserving one for her to wear on her dress."

"Uh, right."

Courting. That Lizzie is pretty slick for all her guilelessness, slipping in the word in a way that a gentleman could not deny without being rude. The conversation thins. The visit must be ending.

I pick up the broken shards of my mug and sop the spilled tea with a rag. Why should it matter if Nathan goes with Lizzie? It is none of my business. Naturally, I would've preferred not to have played a role in the matchmaking, but how was I to know?

I take a sheet of paper and manage to knock my candle clear off its base. I hastily blow it out before it singes my small rug. I sink to the floor. Miss Sweetie frowns on jealousy, an emotion that, like lye, tends to eat away at its container. He has to date someone, eventually, someone who cannot be me under the great laws of Georgia.

We all must abide by the rules, but some of us must follow more than others. Robby can be a deliveryman but not a clerk. Mrs. English would never have promoted me to milliner, just as Mr. Payne will never promote Old Gin to head groom. Like Sweet Potato and her twisted leg, we have been born with a defect—the defect of not being white. Only, unlike in Sweet Potato's case, there is no correcting it. There is only correcting the vision of those who view it as a defect, though not even a war and Reconstruction have been able to do that.

Miss Sweetie has gone sour.

I stretch my legs, which I can no longer feel. Too much sitting and thinking creates stagnation in the brain, and stagnation leads to despair. I hop on the balls of my feet and make my breathing effortless.

Then I grab my pen.

THE CUSTOM-ARY

Not to be confused with its more common cousin, the yellow-plumed canary, the custom-ary is a species whose characteristics vary from bird to bird. Some knock about in their cages without reason or purpose (such as the custom of knocking wood to ward off bad luck), while others exhibit more sensible patterns of behavior (such as the custom of driving on the right side of the road). A good number of customs cling stubbornly to their withered branches, though they should've been set free of their cages long ago (such as the custom of wearing crinoline slips).

Finally, there are those that are more cuckoo than customary. For example, the custom of women riding sidesaddle when, from an anatomy standpoint, that honor should go to men. Or the custom of not hiring coloreds for clerks and agents when we trust them to manage our households, even to tuck our children into bed. It is time to release these customs into the wild blue yonder before they push the others out of the nest, as cuckoos are known to do.

Readers, what customs would you set free?

Respectfully,

Miss Sweetie

There. Sometimes a point is best made by approaching it from a different angle, like how Merritt and I slung the jumping fish from the river rather than catching them head-on. But will the *Focus* print something so . . . provocative? Definitely not with Mr. Bell at the helm. But Nathan is different from his father. He had pushed his father to print the editorial criticizing streetcar segregation. He's not the kind of man who stands out in a room, but he is the kind who stands up for his beliefs.

My ears perk up at a mention of Miss Sweetie by Mrs. Bell.

"The bicycle article was perfect. Made me wish I were younger. I would like to meet this woman."

I suck in my breath and silently implore Nathan to divest his mother of this notion.

"I don't think that's wise," he says after a considerable pause. "She made it clear she wishes to be anonymous, and if we press her, she might quit, and she's already working for free."

"I suppose you're right. How old did you say she was?"

"I couldn't tell, Mother. Her face was covered."

"Well, what did her voice sound like?"

"Like a regular voice."

I shall need to thrash my voice up a bit, maybe even smoke a few cigarettes like Mrs. English does, chased by some meat pies and plenty of beer.

"Not again, Nathan. You're a reporter. Give me a better description than that."

I press my ear closer and will my heartbeat to pipe down.

"To be honest, it sounded like she was nursing a cold, phlegmy."

"Phlegmy?"

"Yes. Now, that's a word that doesn't care what anyone thinks. All those letters trying to prop up the 'leg' in the middle."

"Nathan."

"Without the cold, I imagine her voice would be clear and forthright like a good ginger ale—the kind of voice that gives good advice."

"So she's bossy."

"I wouldn't—"

"Why do you think she wants to be anonymous? Maybe she has a controlling husband."

I imagine a glint in the woman's gray eyes as she presses a finger to her cheek.

"Or maybe she has chin hairs and nose warts, and she uses a broomstick to get around town," he says.

I slap a hand over my mouth to keep my smile from floating up.

"Oh, Nathan. You needn't be sarcastic. Anyway, we owe her a lot. Forty-nine subscriptions today alone. Advertisers are sure to follow. I hope she stays."

Forty-nine is an improvement, but it's still not enough.

"She got more letters today. *I* hope she has a big broom-stick."

I STEAL UP to the Bells' front door, shivering. The cold seems to have crystallized into a freezing dust. It's as if the winter dragon were salting the earth liberally for its supper. Lucky Yip told me that season dragons can be jealous, producing weather extremes to prevent the next season's dragon from moving in.

Through the arched windows, I can see Nathan running the press, a mesmerizing operation that involves intense hand-eye-foot coordination and reams of paper. Iron blocks hang from the walls, like empty picture frames, and a fire blazes in the hearth. Nathan has pushed up the sleeves of a thick sweater, which obscures most of his collared shirt. His printer's apron is smeared with black ink.

The mail slot has been repaired. Still, I remove my glove and knock. Tonight, I shall be nimble and quick, and avoid jumping over any candlesticks that might end up burning me. The door creaks open, and heat caresses my front, sweetened by the sound of Bear's joyous yelps. The dog paces from side to side, restrained by Nathan's hand around her collar.

"Hello? Is it you again? Er, Miss Sweetie?"

"Yes," I say to the street, though my scarf muffles my voice. I fumble in my coat for my column.

"It's nice to see you're back and, er, your back. Please come in. It is arctic out there. Plus, I have more letters of admiration for you."

"More? Well, I shall keep this short," I bark with annoyance, hoping to pinch more crust into my Mrs. English voice.

A wind so chilly it makes my teeth ache seems to slice right through me. Even Nathan hisses. "How would it look if our advice columnist perished over something as foolish as failing to heed common sense? No one would buy papers for sure."

I loosen the scarf from my mouth and face him. "It's also common sense not to enter the homes of strangers."

"Ah, but there you are mistaken. We are not strangers, and this is not my home, which is over there." He jerks his chin toward the other side of the building. "If it will make you feel better, I will wear a blindfold, though it will be more difficult to fetch you tea."

"I don't need tea. I only wish—"

"Well, if you don't need tea, then it's perfect. I will fetch the blindfold." He disappears with Bear, while I pull lint from my mouth, trying to figure out if he is serious.

The sounds of footsteps and paw scratching draw near again. To my relief, Nathan is not carrying a blindfold but a sack of something bulky, which he sets by the doorway. Bear sits obediently by Nathan's side, though even sitting, she vibrates with energy. "Now then, where were we?"

I clear my throat, off balance by our repartee. Surely, Nathan would not be so cheeky to someone he thought was a respectable madam. I draw myself up to my haughtiest posture, just like Mrs. English when a rival milliner dropped in for a visit. "Here is Thursday's column. The contents are a slight departure from the last two. I shall wait while you read it."

I hold out my letter but shrink back when he moves closer to take it. He stops. "Er, Bear, fetch."

With a *woof*, she springs to life, gamely delivering my letter to her master, only a little wetter than it started out. He unfolds my column and turns to better use the firelight. As he reads, I study his profile, from the stubborn line of his stubbled chin to his deep-set eyes, which take in more than they give away. A rather forgettable nose dips in the middle as if pressed by a finger. As he reads, his usually downturned mouth nudges into a smile, and I feel a strange compulsion to fit my own smile against it.

Despite his grouchiness, there's a sturdiness to Nathan, cultivated by loving parents who, unwittingly or not, blessed him with a humble and principled upbringing. They fletched him right, and he will probably fly far in life.

He refolds the paper, and the smile fades away. His eyebrows clench together, as if he's feeling the edges of his thought before judging its shape. "It is clever. More than clever, it's brilliant." He shifts around in the doorway, as if puzzling out which leg he prefers. "If it were my choice, I would publish it in an instant. But I will need to speak to my mother about this."

"I understand." I hide my disappointment in a brisk and forward manner. "I will bring you an alternative in the next day or two, just in case."

"Thank you. Er, well, there is another thing." He tugs at his collar.

Both Bear and I watch him expectantly, though only one of us is breathing. Perhaps he no longer wants my services now that I've proven myself a rabble-rouser. A tub thumper.

"We insist on paying you. It's not much, a nickel an article. But Mother says if we don't pay you, we would be taking advantage of you."

"I thought I made myself clear," I grumble. "No payment, or I shall not write. If it will make you feel better, donate the money to the orphanage."

"As you wish. 'Pedaling Us toward the Future' was a sell-out. You chose a germane topic."

"I don't know what the Germans have to do with it."

He blinks, and in that fatal instant, I realize I've goosed up. Drat those G-words.

"Not Germans." Half a grin tips his face to one side. "*Germane.* Relevant."

"I know what *germane* means." I grind my voice to give weight to my indignation. "It is rude to correct your elders."

"I only meant to—"

"It is also rude to argue with them. I will have my letters now."

"Er, certainly." He hefts the sack, which is large enough to hold fifteen pounds of grain.

"Giddy goobers."

"Giddy goobers?" He smiles. "I told you there were a lot. May I help you carry them?"

"No. That invites further inspection of my person, of which you have already done enough inspecting for one night. I am used to carrying my own bags. Just set them down and close the door."

"I insist on passing them to you. They are much too heavy to lift."

Before I can protest, Nathan has moved closer and is pushing his cargo toward me. With an exasperated gasp, I reach for the sack, but to my horror, he doesn't let go. We hold the sack from both sides for an excruciating moment, like two farmhands relocating a hive that has started to buzz. He releases the sack at the same time I do, and then we both grab it again.

"I'll take it," I insist, pulling it toward me. But the uneven weight causes me to lose my grip, and I drop it. "Oh! Look what you've done."

I crouch to collect the bundles of letters that have spilled out between us.

"Forgive me," he says, seeming to force the words through his teeth.

The warmth of his energy tugs at mine, and I hastily draw away from him. Bear woofs, dancing around us. "I shall take one bundle. I cannot answer them all." Even if I did manage to drag the sack back to the basement, I could not conceal all the letters from Old Gin.

"Of course not. I simply thought you would like to see how much you are"—something causes him to freeze in place—"admired."

The cold night blows at my lips. My scarf has fallen away, giving Nathan a close look at the territory south of my nose. I quickly curtain my mouth and stand, reining in the pounding hooves of my heartbeat. Still kneeling, he holds out a bundle. My heart catches at the earnestness of his expression, his own mouth half open in disbelief. I'm seized by yet another irresistible urge to fit my lips against his. Instead, I snatch the bundle, and Miss Sweetie makes an exit that is far from nimble, but certainly quick.

Seventeen

Dear Miss Sweetie,

I shunned my dearest friend "Mary" by accepting the invitation of a popular socialite, "Kate," who despises Mary. I had hoped that befriending Kate would open doors for me and, eventually, for Mary. But now Mary will have nothing to do with me, and Kate no longer invites me to her parties. How do I get my real friend back?

Sincerely,
Friend in Mourning

Dear Friend,

As you have learned, better a diamond with a flaw than a pebble without one. Lost trust takes time to rebuild. But with consistency and humility, the diamond can be unearthed again.

Yours sincerely,
Miss Sweetie

Monday muscles in like the first rooster in the ring, talons out, ready to draw blood. With no maid on the weekends, my chores have doubled in size, while Caroline's patience has been reduced by half.

In the library, she scratches out correspondence, her face scrunched in a grimace. I untangle a basket of embroidery thread and work out which lion Miss Sweetie will choose to battle next. So many lions prowl right here in this room. With debutante season starting, this week promises an ever-spinning carousel of social engagements for Caroline, not just whist-playing, but also pressing ferns into scrapbooks and lawn bowling. It all sounds like good fun, but Caroline never seems to enjoy herself with other people, though unlike with the servants, she must put on a good face. Either that or she doesn't care for the conversations, which inevitably turn toward the business of securing a husband.

I can't blame her. The husband business strikes Miss Sweetie as uncannily similar to the scramble that ensues during an Easter egg hunt, where the egg's only hope is to sit as prettily as possible so that it will be picked up before it spoils. Like Caroline, I am in no hurry to be found, though plans are under way.

Dare Miss Sweetie stick her head in the marriage lion's mouth? It is a subject that most women could relate to, especially right now. I bet it would bring in more than fifty subscriptions.

Caroline's wingback chair groans as she fidgets, and if paper could talk, it would probably be whimpering, too, under the weight of her pen. Caroline moves through life with a tight grip on the world, as if she were afraid of being shaken off. Or maybe she's determined to leave a mark on the world, the same reason she grinds her shoes into the earth or scorches the air with her caustic remarks.

"This paper is defective! How did this pass quality control?"

"What do you mean, miss?"

"The fibers caught a speck of something, maybe sand, or an insect." She grimaces. "The nib catches along the watermark."

"What's a watermark?"

I expect her to ignore me, but instead, she holds the paper at eye level, parallel to the floor. "See there?"

I squint at her too-flowery penmanship. At the point that her pen left off, the Payne Mills insignia, *PM*, is pressed into the page, only visible if looked at from an angle.

"I never noticed it before."

"Father puts it on all the premier-line stationery, though if I'd paid an ounce of gold for a half ream of this, I would want my money back. It's that Mr. Foggs. He works the girls too long, till they can't see straight."

"Surely your father can do something about that?"

"Father holds Mr. Foggs in too high estimation." She crumples her paper and lobs it into the fireplace. "Mind you, ask the mail carrier when he calls where my package is. It should've arrived weeks ago. And snuff the fire. The smoke is giving me a headache. No, no, don't open the window. Are you stupid? I shall catch a draft!"

I don't close the window right away, but let the cool air soothe my vexation. Ever since my comment about the bicycle costing as much as a horse, she has begun to rub off the edges of our agreement and my patience.

Mrs. Payne's boots make ladylike taps as she enters the library, elegantly draped in cream-colored wool, and clutching a letter. Noemi follows her, bearing a tray that holds a simple tea service and a small brown package. Still reading her letter, Mrs. Payne lowers herself into an armchair. "How about that? The Atlanta Suffragists put in a bid to sponsor a horse."

"Well, now, did I ever forecast that," Caroline practically sings.

Noemi hands Caroline the package. The sleeves of Caroline's black silk robe flap like the wings on a bird of prey as she tears it open. "At last!" She plucks out a shiny tin of Beetham's Glycerine and Cucumber cream.

Ignoring her, Mrs. Payne reads, " 'Though our offer be meager, we hope you accept, knowing that our sponsorship would be of symbolic importance to all women. We can run the race as well as any man. We only need the opportunity.' " She turns her attention to Noemi, pouring tea. "A hundred dollars puts them in the running. And you know those suffragists will protest if I don't let them put their name on a horse. What to do?"

"Tell them they were outbid." Caroline applies the cream with vigorous strokes to her cheeks and hands.

"They'll figure it out. People talk."

Noemi offers Mrs. Payne a plate of gingersnaps. "Seems to me, you can never go wrong with honesty, ma'am."

Caroline's shiny face splits open. "What has possessed you to think we care for your opinion?"

Noemi drops her head, and Mrs. Payne's face becomes thoughtful. "We have always valued our domestics' opinions."

Caroline's gaze slings to me, as if I were the source of the trouble.

"Honesty *is* the best policy, especially with all eyes on this race," Mrs. Payne continues. "Though, if I give the suffragists a horse, the Atlanta Belles will be in a lather. Fans will go up." With her letter, she mimes drawing open a fan and hiding her face behind it, as the ladies do when they gossip.

Proceeds from the race go to the Society for the Betterment of Women, which supports orphans and widows. But the Atlanta Belles would rather parade about in their petticoats than associate with the loudmouthed suffragists, even though they are working toward the same cause. It is perfectly acceptable to treat women as charity, but perish the thought they should be enabled to help themselves. Another lion growls in Miss Sweetie's face.

I snort a little too loudly, and I fumble the spool I am winding.

Caroline cups her hand to her ear and leans dramatically toward the entryway. "What's that? I believe another unsolicited opinion is knocking down the door."

Mrs. Payne purses her lips into a quick smile. "Jo?"

"I'm sorry, ma'am. I was just remembering the time Mrs. English put two playing cards on her blackjack hat, and the Anti-Gambling League threatened to boycott her. That was the best-selling hat of the season. Controversy boosts sales, and think of all the poor women who would benefit."

Noemi, standing quietly beside Mrs. Payne's chair, nods

thoughtfully. "It's why people pay good money to see Tantrum, the baby-eating spider, at that Barnum's Traveling Museum. If it's just spiders they want, they could stare at their ceilings."

I laugh, and I swear Mrs. Payne does, too. She fans herself with the letter. "I've been curious about the Fiji mermaid myself, half monkey, half fish, though it's all fiddle-faddle, of course. Animals just can't mix like that."

Caroline noisily gets to her feet, maybe having a baby-eating tantrum of her own. "Rather like people," she sneers, sweeping away.

THE EVENING STREETCAR takes its sweet time arriving. A group of ladies cycles past us. Perhaps it's my imagination, but the population of safety bicycles appears to be on the upswing. I smile, remembering the clever picture Nathan drew for Miss Sweetie's column of a woman bicycling past a train. I filed a clipping in the *B* section of my dictionary.

"I am glad to see you smiling," remarks Old Gin, wearing the curious expression he gets when I play an unexpected piece in Chinese chess. "There is something different about you."

"Oh? It must be the rides. Sweet Potato has grown wings on her feet." It's a wonder that Six Paces Meadow is still standing after our searing afternoon rides across it. Thankfully, Merritt's work at the mills has kept him from intruding.

"Seems so."

After today's jag, I allowed the mare to carry me north to where the streetcar tracks bend toward Piedmont Park, the site of the upcoming race. With her nose up and ears forward, it was almost as though the thoroughbred in her were drawn to the sweat of her kinsmen emanating from that oval shrine. If I had not drawn up on the reins, she would've sailed through the stone pillars and past the stands.

"And Miss Caroline, how are her rides?" Old Gin tacks on casually as he watches a jay bully away a titmouse.

But why would he ask me separately about Caroline, as if my first answer had not included her? Surely he couldn't know that we take separate paths unless he had followed us, which he could not possibly do without my noticing. The longer I don't answer, the more I hang myself. "Fine, I expect." Before he can throw me more rope, I pull out the Pendergrass's elixir from my damask bag. "Got this for you. Robby says they can't keep it on the shelf. The instructions say to drink the bottle for three days—you can see they marked the lines—and when you finish, you should feel 'strong as a horse.'" I'd decided not to tell him about Billy Riggs, as he would worry, maybe even feel compelled to do all the shopping himself.

He skims the ingredients.

"Cost fifty cents, but it comes with a money-back guarantee if it doesn't work, so we have nothing to lose and everything to gain."

He fills his lungs, but noting my crossed arms, his protest slips away. With a sigh, he uncorks the bottle and gulps down a mouthful. "Strong as horse, hm?" He smacks his lips. "Please let me know if you see a tail growing."

As the streetcar approaches, Maud Gray hobbles up, still wearing her blue-and-white-striped milkmaid apron. Her cap has gone askew, and her mussed hair puffs out like dandelion fluff from her dark skin.

Old Gin nods to her. "Evening, Mrs. Gray."

"Didn't think I'd make it. Something spooked the cows, and they wouldn't let down till noon."

Sully halts in front of our stop with a single *clang* of his bell. It is an ominous sound, different from the *ka-klank, ka-klank* that the children make with their eager hands, milking the clapper for every last ring. Tonight, everyone seems to sit too rigidly in their seats. No one is talking, not even chatty Mrs. Washington.

Old Gin slips into a middle row with enough space for both of us, while Mrs. Gray moves to the front as usual, in order to warm her old bones by the coal heater.

"There ain't room for you here," says a crabby gardener whom I never liked, with his eternally sunburned face caused by a too-small hat. What kind of a gardener wears a one-inch brim? He shifts his lanky frame, closing off the empty space next to him. "I suggest you set your pins farther back."

A ball of anger gathers in my chest. Old Gin stiffens beside me.

"She always sits there," says someone, though it's hard to tell who.

"Hm." Old Gin's usually musical utterance comes out curt and disapproving. People in the front rows have begun to glare at Maud, who plucks at her shawl with her thin fingers.

Something cold pours through my veins, running all the way to my clammy toes. It occurs to me that all the faces in the front are white. A child in the back whimpers, and his mother squeezes him to her.

Maud stares down at her shoes. "My hands are so stiff. I just wanted to warm them." Her husky voice has lost its bounce.

The gardener flips up the collar of his coat. "Well, warm them in the back from now on."

"Sit down already," Sully throws over his bony shoulder. "I've got a schedule to keep."

"Come sit by me, Maud," says a young maid from the row behind us.

Maud gives the coal heater a longing glance. Then, with a sigh that crumples the stripes of her apron, she scoots in beside the maid.

The streetcar carries us off in our unnatural silence. I sit still as a bottle, attuned to every curbed whisper, every tight glance. Atlanta has always had her rules, but tonight, someone has planted a foot on her back and yanked the stays even tighter. I want to talk to Old Gin, but he looks busy in his own thoughts, his pupils tracking a fence heavy with snowy Cherokee roses.

At the second-to-last stop before ours, Old Gin nudges me and then points his nose to the front, where a man has just unfurled the *Constitution*. The headline reads: RESOLVED: STREETCAR SEGREGATION OK.

Eighteen

"It's not right," I whisper once we have reached the warm shadows of our basement. "The streetcars are for everyone." I set about switching on our lamps while Old Gin boils water.

"There have always been lines drawn. Lines will just get darker."

"When will it be enough?"

Old Gin glances at me holding my elbows, the kerosene lamp I've just lit moving the shadows. "In China, there are many social orders as well."

"China is not a democracy."

He alights on his milking stool and unties his laces. "Sometimes, things must get harder before they can change."

"But why?"

"Pain drives progress, hm?" After removing his shoes, he takes our broom and sweeps the dirt we've tracked in. "When I was a boy, there was a drought in my village that lasted three years. Food was scarce for everyone. I remember seeing a dog wandering the streets, so hungry, he bit into his own leg. It was only after he drew blood that he let go." He works the dirt into a neat pile. "Sometimes, we are so driven by our own needs, we do things that hurt ourselves. But eventually, the dog must let go."

If there aren't enough rows, the colored will have to give way, just as on the sidewalks. And where are Old Gin and I supposed to sit? Somewhere in the middle once again. Old Gin has always steered us away from trouble.

I rouse myself from my frozen state and fetch our rusty dustpan, holding it so Old Gin can sweep in the debris. An itchiness has crept into my soul, and it's as if my insides are full of shifting debris that no broom can hope to sweep away. I wish the water would boil faster. I wish the Pendergrass would work quicker. I wish the dog would release its mangy, flea-bitten leg.

I pour tea, and my eyes catch on Shang's letter, which I had set in the catch-all basket hanging from a wall hook. "Who is Shang?" I set the letter before him.

His glances at the letter, lingering on the loop of the signature. "Where did you get this?"

"It was in the pocket of the coat I found in the rug."

Before speaking, he presses a thumb over a pressure point in his palm, then slowly lets it go. "Shang was a groom, like me. He left in search of silver in Montana, after the tragedy," he says, referring to the hanging of the gentle fieldworker who paid for the Rabid-Eyes Rapist's crime. He sighs, closing himself the way a heron collapses its neck and wings after a long flight.

"Was Shang the man who owed money to Billy Riggs's father?" I can't help asking.

He nods.

"How much did he borrow?"

"Much more than he could afford." Something dark crosses his face, like a crow's shadow as it passes over land.

"Who sent the letter?"

"Many questions. Sometimes it is better not to get involved. The river travels fastest—"

"Around the stones, yes, I know. But the river always feels the stones, no matter how it travels." My voice tightens as wounds open. "And sometimes they are sharp, yet we are to pretend it doesn't hurt, just keep our heads down as always. But how will things ever change if we always act like rabbits, hiding away and being afraid?"

"Jo!" His bright face rebukes me. "We are not rabbits." He refolds the letter and slides it back to me. "Do not speak of this again." His chest rumbles, and he retreats to his corner, removing the cough like a wayward child to its nursery.

I press my sleeves to my face, caging the sob that wants out. The only person who cares for me does not seem to care at all tonight.

THE NEXT MORNING the confusion on the streetcar has only grown. More protests are voiced and silenced; more people shuffle about. Some choose to walk, an avenue not open to the weak or infirm. Old Gin sits beside me in the middle row, his shoulder twitching, which only happens when he's tired. I try to let go of the injuries of last night; however, the mystery of Shang still pulls at me. With Old Gin's refusal to shed light on the matter, the mystery seems to double in size.

When we arrive at the Payne Estate, Noemi's kitchen smells of bacon and . . . sour mash? At the kitchen table, Merritt hunches over a glass of something yellow. Noemi sits across from him, picking gravel from a sack of cornmeal.

"Good morning." She gives me a tight smile. I wonder if the new streetcar rules are on her mind.

"Good morning, Mr. Merritt, Noemi." I get busy assembling a tray.

Merritt claps his hands over his ears. "Quit hollering."

He is the source of the sour-mash stench. Violet crescents hang under his eyes, and his hair leans to one side like wheat in a breeze.

"Hold your nose, and throw it back," says Noemi. "Like you did your daddy's good Scotch last night. I heard you told everyone about the first girl you were sweet on."

Merritt groans. "What?"

Noemi drops an especially large pebble onto her pile, then gets up to stir a pot of oatmeal. "Don't worry, you didn't mention names, only that she had raven hair and pearls for teeth."

Merritt squints at me through bloodshot eyes, then holds up the glass to me. "Well then, here's to first love." He gulps it down with several jerks of his Adam's apple.

Merritt sniffs at his glass. "Smells like a sewer. What's in it?"

"Egg yolks, Worcestershire, and a pinch of white pepper. Pepper is power. It solves a lot of problems you don't expect it to—swelling, bruises, and hangovers."

Merritt coughs, and his empty cup strikes the table with

a thud. His chest heaves, and with one hand clamped over his mouth, he runs out the door to the courtyard.

Noemi shrugs. "Works every time." She spoons oatmeal into a bowl. "Today's oatmeal and peach preserves, and that porcupine can take it or leave it. August was the last straw, especially now with that mess of a streetcar. I needed that bicycle today."

"She will send it back."

Pots clang as she moves them around the stove. She sighs. "Fine. I made a ham. Cut a few slices if you want."

I hop to the task for both of our sakes.

Noemi wipes her fingers on her apron. "I've been thinking about those suffragists."

"What about them?"

"The Fifteenth was supposed to improve our lot, giving our men the vote. But then the *man* started taking it all away. It's like they put a plate of hot biscuits in front of us, but before we get a chance to eat, they say, that'll be five dollars. And if you come up with the five dollars, they say no, no, no. You gotta tell us, if you got sixteen hens and thirty-seven roosters, where is Rutherford B. Hayes buried?"

"I don't know about the poultry, but Rutherford B. Hayes was from Ohio."

"Wrong. It's a trick question. Hayes is still alive. Point is, they make it so hard. Now, if women got the vote, maybe that gives us a second wind. Adds our fists to the fight. Those suffragists say the Fifteenth gives the vote to *all* citizens, not just the men. But we got to insist on it." She gives a pot of chowder a stir. "Imagine, Jo, if women got a say, that could change the whole stew." *Bang* goes her spoon, punctuated by the *clang* of a closing lid. "They're meeting Monday night at Grace Baptist. You could come with me."

I imagine the suffragists, reform-minded women of the middle class, their starched skirts dragging the pavement. Women with whom I have little in common. Those who dwell in shadows get along by not standing out, *not* by raising their fists to the sky. And even if women are given the vote, Chinese will still get left behind.

Noemi steers her hopeful face toward me.

It is one thing to speak under the safety of Miss Sweetie's name. Quite another to take a public stance under Jo Kuan's. "I'll think about it."

Nineteen

Old Gin must stay at the Paynes' the next few nights, citing much work. Though he maintains this work concerns the horse race, I can't help taking it personally. Things have not been the same between us since our skirmish over the letter. Perhaps my stand-in father expects to marry me off soon, so why bother trying to smooth things between us? I hunker down in the middle row of the streetcar, too tired to walk and feeling cowardly for my weakness. The stench of sewage and overworked bodies smells extra foul this evening, locked in by a layer of brown clouds that float like the scum off boiled bones.

Once home, I give myself a thorough scrub with barley water. It is already Wednesday, and Nathan might be wondering whether he scared Miss Sweetie away.

In a fragment of looking glass that Old Gin uses for shaving, I study the lower half of my face, with my pearl lip and rounded chin. Is it possible to identify someone as Chinese based only on a few bits? It *was* dark. Well, Miss Sweetie is not the sort to be intimidated. She is like an old rash that keeps coming back, each time more cranky and twice as determined.

I lift my chin and put my fists on my hips. The face in the mirror loses its injury, though my ache over Old Gin persists on the inside.

Though I want to write about the streetcar rules, the topic is even more controversial than "The Custom-ary."

Only two sheets of paper remain in Old Gin's dresser. I should've picked up more when I was at Buxbaum's. I peek in the fabric drawer, and to my dismay, the silk pieces have conjoined and transformed into a jacket with a breast pocket. The sleeves are still unfinished, though Old Gin has neatly squared the collar. Old Gin does everything with precision. Why should giving away his daughter be any different?

I tuck it away, and my fingers brush a tiny box, the second item that had belonged to Old Gin's wife. I lift the lid, and the sweet scent of cedar fills my nose. A silk padding still holds the shape of the snuff bottle that once lay there. The bottle has been lost, but its top remains, a jade bead with an attached spoon for drawing out the snuff. I once asked to use the box to hold ribbons, but Old Gin shook his head. "A turtle shell may one day hold soup, but not before the turtle has moved out."

In my chambers, a solitary spider builds her web where two walls meet the ceiling. I pull my quilt around my lap, watching the spider connect two strands. She doesn't need a mate. She'll do fine on her own.

Caroline's scowling visage appears in my mind. With her

wealth, every door will open for her. But maybe what she wants is not for doors to open, but for the walls to come down. When one grows up with walls, it is difficult to dream of a world beyond. Who knows what Caroline—what any of us—could accomplish without the constant pressure to get married? Without the walls, we could be like this spider, who can go anywhere she wants.

THE SINGULAR QUESTION:
IS IT SO WRONG NOT TO MARRY?

It seems to me that in the rush to the altar, few who marry give much thought to how they got there until it is too late. And then they are stuck with a lifetime of disappointment, not to mention an exponential growth of laundry. We are all well-schooled in why women supposedly should marry: A husband will take care of her and secure her respectability and prestige; bearing children is every woman's divine privilege and responsibility; without marriage, society would decline into barbarism.

Yet, little thought is paid to the benefits of remaining single, or at least delaying marriage. While some women are spinsters simply because life has not dealt them the marriage card, I submit that many women are single by choice, though it may not be obvious. It is one thing to be single and miserable, and quite another to be single and content. We cluck our tongue at the former and brand the latter as "off her onion."

Sometimes Mrs. English's clients would tell her, "A fine widow like you surely deserves to remarry," to which she would always demur, "Perhaps I shall be so lucky one day," and then turn to me and whisper, "Do I look like I deserve a kick in the teeth?" And then there are women, like Miss Culpepper, who have never seemed to be interested in men.

So what are these benefits to remaining single?

1) *Singlets do not risk a lifetime of being shackled to a bore or, worse, wondering whether she is the bore.*

2) *Singlets are free to pursue whatever activities interest them, and to be industrious without having to share their wealth.*

3) *Singlets grow more robust in constitution than married women, having only to look after their own welfare. Furthermore, with no man to "protect" her, she learns to walk with steel in her spine, and a confident mind lights a dark path.*

Invisible fingers stretch the golden thread of my candle to the ceiling, where the spider has completed her web.

We are all like candles, and whether we are single or joined with another does not affect how brightly we can burn.

Respectfully submitted,
Miss Sweetie

"Miss Sweetie?" Only one sleeve of Nathan's oak-brown sweater is pushed up this time, exposing an ink stain that looks like a paw print. The fireplace casts a halo around his thatch of hair. "Would you like to come in, or are we still strangers?"

The blazing fire in their hearth beckons me forward, but I remain fixed to my spot halfway between the door and the stairs.

"Still strangers," I say crisply, willing my heart to pipe down. Bear is nowhere to be seen. I briskly hand Nathan the column and then step back. "Please pardon the delay. What did your mother think of 'The Custom-ary'?"

"She agreed it was very good. But I am sorry. We are a moderate newspaper. She worries that if we print something too, er, radical, they will call us carpetbaggers. We would go out of business."

"I understand." I hide my disappointment in a brisk and forward manner. "Please tell her not to worry. I am a seasoned professional, not some ingenue who will cry into her handkerchief at the slightest rejection. If one column doesn't serve, I move on to the next." I dust off my gloved hands with two quick movements.

"Delighted to hear it."

"Any new subscriptions?"

"Yes. Ninety-seven!"

I gasp and clap my hands. "Ninety-seven! That is swell!"

"All thanks to you." With a grand sweep of his arms, he bows low to me.

I hear myself giggling and stop immediately. "Ahem. Well, I don't have all night. Does this column serve?"

Nathan, who has started to move his feet back and forth in a lilting gavotte, abruptly straightens. "Oh, er, let me see." When he is done, a smile skims his face. "Very serviceable. Certainly puts the male pressures in perspective."

I shouldn't linger, but when the window is opened, the breeze always floats through. "Which pressures are those, Mr. Bell?" I hug the undyed coat to me, rooted to the spot by the certainty that I am about to learn something very intriguing about Nathan, something I would never hear eavesdropping.

"Well, er, the pressure of providing for a family."

At least that is a nobler concern than that voiced by Merritt Payne. "Your parents have given you a noble profession." A profession that Lizzie Crump has no reservations entertaining.

"Noble, yes." He bends his neck to one side, and a joint pops. "But a printer's life means late hours. Constant soot. Work that wears the fingers to the bone . . ." His eyes drift back toward the print shop. I can't help wondering if he is thinking about his mother.

I adjust my hat, which has scooted so far down on my forehead as to act as a blinder. "Late hours. Constant soot. It sounds dreadful. If it is such a concern for you, you could always prepare a disclaimer, much like the horse breeders do."

His eyes crimp. "That would certainly give new meaning to the word *mare-ried*."

"Yes. 'Here comes the bridle.'"

He tucks his chin, hiding his grin, just as I conceal one under my scarf. But I must shake myself loose of the sticky web that has trapped us both. "Mr. Bell, I seem to have used up all my stationery."

"Say no more. If there's one thing we have, it's paper. Payne Mills supplies ours at a good discount. It's one of the reasons we can afford to stay in business."

"*Payne* Mills?"

"My father and Mr. Payne attended Yale together."

"Oh." I'm not sure which surprises me more, that Mr. Bell knows Mr. Payne or the other way around. He disappears for a moment, and when he returns, he passes me a package whose weight suggests a fifth ream of a hundred sheets, plus a box of envelopes. "There you go. Enough for several letters and maybe a few memoirs while you're at it."

"Is that a comment on my age?" I snap.

"No, only your experience, which of course must be vast." He leans forward, as if to catch a glimpse under my hat.

I recoil so quickly, I give myself a crick in the neck. "Of course it is. Well then, good night."

"Before you leave, I have been doing some thinking. You see, I'd attributed Bear's poor manners to a regression in training. But she also gets excited when she encounters people with whom she has developed an affection. She starts herding them, as if she wants to protect them."

A cold sweat makes me itch to molt my clothes and slither away. But I don't move a muscle.

"Is it possible that we . . . know each other?" The words fly like darts looking for a mark.

It takes me a moment to recover my wits. "There are some people, when you meet them, you feel as if you've known them all your life. And then there are people who live under your nose all your life, yet you don't know them at all. Perhaps the same is true for dogs. I bid you good night."

I leave him to untangle that and stumble away. I can't help feeling that despite the layers, he has somehow managed to see right through me.

Twenty

Salt and Pepper swirl through the front door of the Payne Estate like soap bubbles pushed in by a breeze, their faces glowing.

Salt looks especially fetching in a dress of watermelon pink, her plush smile brimming with pleasantries. She dips side to side as I help her remove her coat. There's a giddy energy about her that makes even her Eau de Lilac perfume bounce around in my nose. "Guess how *we* got here?" Salt asks Caroline, who sashays down the staircase at a regal pace.

"Adam and Eve had too much time on their hands?" Caroline says dryly.

"No. Bicycles!" Salt claps her gloved hands. "Miss Sweetie called them 'freedom machines,' and they are such fun."

The sneeze building in my nose screeches to a halt, like the rest of me. It wasn't just my imagination. More women are trying out the safeties.

Salt runs a hand down each narrow sleeve. "We 'exercised our limbs.'"

I swear Caroline turns a shade of green equal to Pepper's mossy dress. She trudges to the drawing room without even waiting for her guests.

Pepper sheds her coat and hands it to me. "Thank you, Jo. Remember this hat? You made it for me last spring, and it's *still* my favorite."

"Of course, miss. I'm pleased you still like it." The color sets off her eyes, and the pheasant feather is still tight and shiny.

In the drawing room, the ladies arrange themselves around the card table, and Noemi pushes out the tray.

Salt tugs off her riding gloves with delicate plucks of her fingers and tucks them into a fashionable chatelaine bag that hangs from her waist. "It only took us two days to learn the safeties. You should've seen all the looks we got from the boys."

"There's only one boy who should matter," Pepper chastises. "Mr. Q accepted Melly-Lee's invitation to the horse race."

Caroline goes from moss green to shiny eggplant. I pour the lemonade as unobtrusively as possible, certain I hear a gun cocking somewhere.

"Somebody deal the cards while I still have a full deck," Caroline snaps.

Pepper reaches for the cards, while Salt helps herself to an egg salad sandwich from Noemi's tray. "Oh, Noemi, you are a peach. I was hoping you'd make these today." She lifts the sandwich to her mouth, but then her arm knocks her glass. A wet *clunk-crack* freezes everyone in place.

"Oh! Oh, I'm sorry, I'm so clumsy." Grabbing her napkin, Salt dabs at the lemonade splashed on her dress.

Caroline groans, and Pepper pushes away from the table. Noemi alights to the kitchen.

"Are you all right, Miss Saltworth?" I press a dishcloth to the spill and gather glass shards into a pile. Noemi returns with a broom and pan and fresh towels.

"Yes," Salt says shakily. "I'm sorry, I guess I was a bit over-excited. Caroline, may I borrow a dress?"

Caroline flicks her cards on the table. "Jo will show you to my chambers."

"Follow me, miss."

In Caroline's room, I swing open the wardrobe, and the powdery scent of her sachets wages battle with Salt's lilac perfume. Salt selects a simple frock with bows at the wrists. I help her undress. She removes her chatelaine from her wet dress and then hands the dress to me. "Would you mind helping me rinse this out?"

"Of course, miss."

"Caroline is lucky to have you." She glances behind me, and then leans closer. "But should you ever find yourself unemployed again, I do hope you'll let me know." She winks.

How interesting. I'm tempted to take her offer right there and then, but I manage restraint. Though Salt has always treated me kindly, sometimes a known tiger in one's mountain beats an unknown tiger in the mountain next door. At least for now. "Thank you, miss, I will."

For the rest of Salt and Pepper's visit, Caroline curbs her tongue, both in the dishing-out and the dishing-in. By the time she is primping for her afternoon ride, a den of lions has moved into her stomach. "Bring up the leftover sandwiches at once."

"Yes, miss."

When I return to her chambers, Mrs. Payne and Caroline are having a row. Caroline jumps up from her vanity, where she has been applying her skin cream, and helps herself to the egg salad sandwiches, groaning as she eats. "I promised Annie I would visit. Her mama has been feeling poorly."

"Then perhaps Annie should attend her mama instead of receiving you."

"You told me a lady only misses appointments if she is in peril of life or limb." Caroline's chewing slows, and her mouth smacks as if tasting what's in it, though she must have eaten Noemi's egg salad a thousand times.

Mrs. Payne sits very still, probably wanting to put Caroline in peril of her life or limb. I'm reminded of the time I watched the family telephone, certain it was about to ring. Moments later, it did. Well, far be it from me to stand in the way of a good ringing. I grab Caroline's mending basket and begin to leave.

"Why does this sandwich taste . . . peppery?" Without warning, Caroline sneezes into her sleeve, three times.

"Good heavens." Mrs. Payne sniffs at the remaining sandwich. She takes a cautious nibble. "I don't taste pepper."

When Caroline emerges from her sleeve, her face is blotchy. "I feel so hot!" She jumps to her feet and grabs a fan from her dressing table, waving it with such vigor that I feel it from across the room. Mrs. Payne opens a window.

"Shall I fetch cool water?" I ask.

"Ice! Ice!" pants Caroline.

I carry Caroline's tray downstairs and, once in the kitchen, sample the sandwich myself. I don't taste pepper either. But then my eyes fall to the tin of white pepper Noemi used for Merritt's hangover cure, right by the butter crock. *Pepper is power. It solves a lot of problems you don't expect it to.*

Taking a bowl and an ice pick, I make for the cellar, which lies just outside the kitchen door. An uneasiness has begun pecking at my skin. A few hundred feet toward the stables, Noemi's large straw hat moves through the herbs. Noticing me, she salutes me with a carrot. I force a smile and wave.

Sunlight rinses the room when I lift the cellar door. The scent of turnips stirs my stomach. During one unbearably hot day, Noemi joined Caroline and me down here, one of the few times Noemi's mother allowed her to join us. Caroline dared me to eat a raw turnip. Noemi told me not to do it, but I, five years old, didn't listen. The taste put me off turnips forever, but more important, it taught me that Noemi could be trusted, Caroline, not.

I unwrap the blocks of Hudson River ice and chip a few pieces into my bowl.

The water in my pitcher sloshes as I ferry it and the bowl of ice up three flights of stairs, passing Mrs. Payne using the telephone on the second floor.

Etta Rae glances up at me from the breakfast table, where she's fanning Caroline with two peacock fans. "The fire's over here."

"Why did you take so long?" Caroline face is red and swollen, as if she'd stuck it into a beehive. "Oh, it burns! Make it stop!" She fans her face with her hands, which are also inflamed.

I set the bowl on the table and fill it with water. Etta Rae is about to dip a dishcloth into the water when Caroline dunks her entire face into the bowl.

Water spills everywhere. Etta Rae puts her dishcloth to work. "Easy, Miss Caroline."

Caroline reappears, water streaming down her cheeks, turning her silk riding habit from blue to black.

Etta Rae clucks her tongue. "The doctor will be here soon. He'll have an ointment or some such. You'll be fine."

"I certainly will *not* be fine! That nigra ruined my looks. She's ruined me!"

"It's just temporary. Like when you got the poison ivy. Jo, fetch more ice."

Noemi's smiling face appears in my head, and my teeth clench. I clutch at the banister as I hurry downstairs, feeling suddenly unsteady on my feet. It will take more than ice to soothe Caroline's wrath.

Twenty-One

Dear Miss Sweetie,

   I get shucks in the foot from time to time and my freind told me to salt a tomato and wrap it around the shuck and after a day the shuck will pop out, and I wunder if it is true.

> Much oblijed,
> Shuck in the Foot

Dear Shuck in the Foot,

   That seems like a waste of a good tomato, and not much good for a splinter out of season. The simplest solution is already in your cupboard: vinegar. Soak the foot in a bowl of vinegar, and in about twenty minutes, the splinter should have broken through the skin enough to pull out.

> Yours truly,
> Miss Sweetie

   P.S. Do not reuse the vinegar.

The doctor leaves calamine lotion, saying her rash should be gone in a few days. If only there were a salve for her foul temperament, we might all rest more comfortably.

I carry a basket of wet things down the stairs, but stop when I see Etta Rae standing just outside the kitchen holding a vase of bluebells. She puts her finger to her lips as I creep closer, professional eavesdropper that I am, and though she frowns at me, she doesn't shoo me away.

"No, ma'am," Noemi says. "Celery, onion, pickles, mustard, oil, vinegar, lemon juice, and salt. Like always."

"What about the bread?"

"Potato buns ain't got pepper."

A long pause follows, during which Etta Rae and I exchange worried expressions.

"Take tomorrow off," Mrs. Payne says at last. "The weekend, too. Caroline will need rest and quiet, and—"

And she will need to be convinced that Noemi has not tried to poison her.

Etta Rae's usually erect head seems to sink into her thin shoulders.

"I understand, ma'am," Noemi says hoarsely.

The sound of Mrs. Payne's boots straightens our postures. Etta Rae busies herself arranging the flowers on a table. I continue toward the kitchen, sidestepping Mrs. Payne coming out. "Oh, Jo. I'm afraid the sight of Caroline's face will shock her when she wakes up. Find all her looking glasses and put them in my study."

"Yes, ma'am. What about her vanity?"

"Solomon will take care of the vanity. Etta Rae, please call for one of our substitute cooks."

"Yes, ma'am." Etta Rae heads toward the staircase.

I move toward the kitchen again with the wet laundry, wanting to talk to Noemi, but Mrs. Payne blocks the doorway. "Now, Jo."

"Yes, ma'am." With heavy feet, I follow Etta Rae.

IN THE ROW in front of me, the hackle feather of a white woman's flowerpot hat wags like a finger every time the streetcar hits a pothole. The invisible line between the front and the back takes shape with every ride. Only whites sit in rows one and two. Rows three through five vary, depending on the passengers.

"Adelle Jones was arrested yesterday for not getting up fast enough when a mother with child wanted her seat," whispers a woman from behind me.

"Ain't Adelle pregnant, too?" says another woman.

"Yes."

My mind returns to Noemi. Come on, Miss Sweetie, think. Noemi would never have taken such a chance. She has too much to lose and too little to gain. Caroline's rash must have been caused by someone or something else. Spring allergies again? Maybe an insect bit her. Once, a spider stung Lucky Yip on the earlobe, and his ear swelled to the size of his palm.

His palm. Caroline's palms were also inflamed.

Her tin of Beetham's Glycerine and Cucumber cream

appears in my mind. She spread it on her face just before eating. Is she allergic to it? She's used it without problem before, but things can turn on you, like eggs.

The Beetham's had just arrived and must have been fresh. Did someone tamper with it? I can think of few people who wouldn't stick a foot in her path if given the opportunity, including myself.

Salt. The spilt lemonade. Perhaps Caroline tasted pepper not from her sandwich but her face cream. Salt's detachable chatelaine bag surely could've hidden a pinch of pepper. If Salt knows about Caroline and Mr. Q, she'd have every reason to despise Caroline. Maybe, beneath those frothy pink layers, Salt is as cunning as a foldable sunhat.

THE NEXT MORNING, Caroline lies in her bed, orbited by a ring of pillows and holding her potted violet. Her face is no longer swollen, but blisters form peer groups on her skin, including a popular crowd on her forehead.

Mrs. Payne throws open the windows. "A little powder, and no one will even notice."

Moving as unobtrusively as possible, I exchange a bowl of rosemary tincture for Caroline's plant.

With a scowl, she soaks her hands in the herbal remedy. "That witch did this on purpose. She should be locked up, but you send her away for a *few days*. Imagine what she'll do if you take her back? She'll poison me for sure, and then you won't have to worry about whether I marry, as I'll be dead."

Mrs. Payne pops a spoonful of medicine into her mouth.

"Rest easy, dear. Jo, when you get a moment, please come see me in the stables." She breezes away.

Have I done something to displease her? Perhaps I need another reminder about my place in this house.

Caroline scowls. Even her blisters manage to look grumpy.

I hand her a towel. "Noemi didn't do it. But I have a hunch I know who did."

She sits very still. "Pray tell."

"Miss Saltworth. I think she peppered your Beetham's."

Her eyes dart to the empty spot where her vanity used to sit. "Melly-Lee? My Beetham's . . ."

"It is in your vanity, which, as you know, Solomon has placed in storage along with all the other looking glasses. Your mother believes you might shatter one."

For once, she fails to pounce on my innuendo. "How do you know this?"

"It's a hunch. Noemi may not like you, but if she were to even the score, it wouldn't be by peppering your food, which is as subtle as a flying brick. Especially not with a bicycle to pay off." I let that one burrow in her ear before adding, "Not even your mother believes it, which of course is why she hasn't fired her."

Caroline's eyes glaze, as if she is replaying the memory. "That goosey, whey-faced sneak." She clenches her towel into a knobby ball. "If Melly-Lee knows, surely she will break things off with him. I must be ready."

"Yes. She could ruin you."

She snorts. "He would not let that happen."

"A man who cheats is not the most reliable of knights."

"Edward loves me." She wiggles her hands free of the towel. "And anyway, it's none of your business."

"As you say. But now that you see Noemi didn't harm you, you can ask your mother to bring her back."

"Why would I do that?"

"Because it's the right thing to do."

She grimaces. As if that argument ever worked with Caroline Payne.

"And because if you don't, I shall need to tell your mother of my suspicions regarding Miss Saltworth."

"You are pushing the limits of your blackmail."

"I could've kept my thoughts to myself and let Salt take her time brining you."

She purses her lips, which I hope means she concedes the point.

"I suggest you get Noemi back sooner rather than later. Miss Saltworth also enjoys Noemi's cooking. In fact, I bet Noemi could tell Miss Saltworth a lot about you."

She growls. But then I hear a bump. Her head rolls back against the headboard, hair scattered like threshed wheat. The sharpness has left her eyes. "Stay," she murmurs in speech that has begun to thicken.

I scoot beside her and press a cool towel to her face. She blinks sluggishly at me. "Jo, you used to be on my side. Remember the plums?"

When we were children, a traveling salesman with a cart of instruments came upon Caroline and me playing in a wooded area where we had run away for the afternoon. He gave Caroline a clarinet, but when she put it to her lips, he grabbed her from behind, a wet grin upon his face. She shrieked and hit him with the clarinet, while I grabbed a trumpet and clocked him on the knee.

Then we fled back to the house, hand in hand. Caroline would not loosen her grip until Noemi's mother pulled us apart and stuck plums in our palms.

"I remember," I say, but she has already begun to snore.

ASIDE FROM THE apprehensive stutter of my heart, the cogs of the Payne Estate are running smoothly. Nature's groundskeepers—the chickens—scratch and fertilize the grass, while the hired groundskeepers trim branches and repair fences. Squirrels run patrol over their trees.

A group of men that includes Jed Crycks and Merritt watch Johnny Fortune ride the defiant Arabian across an expanse of pasture. The jockey shows Ameer his whip. "This is what you'll get next time you go lazy in the lead," he yells, his voice high and whiny. Ameer snaps at the whip.

In front of the stables, Mrs. Payne leans over the corral fence, where Sweet Potato and a few other horses are kicking around a ball blown from a sheep's bladder. There's a crane-like gracefulness to her slender figure, a breathless hovering as if she might fly away if I approach too quickly. On the other side of the corral, Old Gin oils a saddle with even strokes of his skinny arms.

Mrs. Payne doesn't acknowledge my presence. It's as if her eyes have turned inward, and instead of watching the horses, she's watching another scene evolve in her mind.

When I am two paces away, her gaze finally drifts to mine. In the streaky light filtering through her straw bonnet, she is as hard to read as vapor, unlike Caroline, who hangs her wet feelings around her. "That Sweet Potato sure has legs on her. Old Gin has done an excellent job."

"Yes, ma'am."

She lifts her petal-like cheeks to a cloud, adjusting the rim of her hat to shield her eyes from the glare. "She reminds me of another filly I used to have, Savannah Joy, named for the city in which she was born." She speaks slowly, as if reading the words from a faded page. "She was a beauty, just like her mama. From the sweet curve of her cheek to the nap of her hair, you could see the hand of God in her shaping. Good-natured, too. A good nature can make or break a horse, not just in a race, but in life." The trace of a smile tugs at her face.

"What happened to Savannah Joy?"

"They made me give her up." Her fingers twist her gold ring. "I wept every night for a year."

Why would Mrs. Payne's parents make their only daughter give up a filly with whom she was so smitten, especially when they were in the business of horse breeding? It makes no sense. But then, trying to understand Mrs. Payne is like trying to unfold a wet newspaper, impossible to do without tearing the pages.

We warm in the afternoon sun, watching the horses, and I wonder if the reason Mrs. Payne called me out here was to tell me about her lost filly and nothing more. But then she sweeps a hand in front of her as if clearing away fog and says, "How are your rides with Caroline going?"

"Fine, ma'am."

"You're not letting her out of your sight, are you?"

Merritt pops into my head, the only one who could expose my lie. Has he already said something?

The longer I stand here saying nothing, the more suspicious I become. "No, ma'am, she's stuck with me," I hear myself say. "Your daughter rides as well as the comb on a rooster's head. I expect she gets that from you."

I'm not sure why I lie. I owe Mrs. Payne much more than that crank. Probably because I am not a snitch.

Mrs. Payne dimples prettily. "Yes, perhaps. Well, I'm glad to see you getting along."

Ameer tumbles closer into view, his jockey uttering curses. With a sigh, Mrs. Payne picks her way to them.

Old Gin approaches, smelling of saddle soap and ruddy with the day's efforts. "Notice something different?"

"You're skinnier." He has knocked a new hole in his belt, bunching his canvas trousers at his waist.

He brushes that aside with a wave of his chapped hand. "No more coughing. Even blew up that ball." Sweet Potato tries to step on the sheep's bladder, but it slips out from her hoof. "Seems we don't need that refund."

You could take the smile from my face and hook it for the moon. "We should celebrate. Tomorrow, we could take Sweet Potato to the creek. Find where the quails are nesting? Or if you want to rest, we could play chess—"

"I will need to stay here again this weekend. I am sorry."

"Well then, I shall keep the burrows secure—" I say, but Jed Crycks has already summoned Old Gin away.

Twenty-Two

Solitude is a frequent visitor here, often dragging along her companion loneliness. Tonight, the latter plants herself right in my lap.

How many other lonely souls have taken refuge in this basement, enduring horrors that put my own troubles to shame? I trace a finger along the word *galaxy* on the wall, a word that means all the stars in the heavens. May those who passed here have found their way. Like the stars, may they have claimed their own bit of sky.

My letters of admiration form an uneven pile on the floor. I gather them up and reread them, hoping to ground myself in the inky pleas of others. What is it about a stranger that makes it easy for one to unburden oneself? Perhaps a stranger is less likely to gossip to people you know or judge you based on their knowledge of you. Or perhaps it is simply comforting to feel that a stranger cares to listen.

Most of Miss Sweetie's letters seek advice on love, a topic on which she is apparently an expert. I opine on what to do with a suitor who prefers grunting to conversation (drop him like a hot biscuit), a gold digger (same), and a woman who is a coquette (get thee a cooler biscuit). May I bring a certain wide-eyed candor to the table.

Hungry for biscuits, I come across a letter with no return address, which can only mean the sender hopes for an answer in print.

> *Dear Miss Sweetie,*
> *I hear they have passed a new law requiring my maid to sit in the crowded back rows of the streetcar, even if there is a perfectly empty spot beside me. Your thoughts?*
>
> > *Yours truly,*
> > *Name Withheld*

The flame of my candle flickers, tugged by unseen hands, and I'm caught by the great contradiction of Southern society: No one minds putting colored people in the back of the streetcar, so long as it's not their colored people. Mrs. Payne would certainly have an earful for anyone who forced her to sit apart from Etta Rae—not that Mrs. Payne would ever need to ride a streetcar. But no wonder lines must be drawn. The farther away you stand from someone, the harder it is to like them.

> *Dear Name Withheld,*
> *Do these lawmakers think we are so witless that we cannot make up our minds on the most trivial of decisions, namely, where to place our bottoms?*

Time and money would be better spent on the
problem of how to transport our sewage out of our city,
rather than directing more garbage into it.

Yours sincerely,
Miss Sweetie

It may be more controversial than Nathan wants to print, but let him decide. It is a sincere letter, and if readers are asking, why can't Miss Sweetie answer? Controversy sells, and this is a hot topic. Maybe we'll even reach two thousand subscriptions before April rolls around.

I begin to fetch my disguise, but Shang's letter beckons me from its place in the basket. Even inanimate objects have energy. Old Gin believes that, one day, the positive energy of his wife's snuff bottle will reunite it with its matching top, which is why he wouldn't let me use the box. Similarly, I feel sure the positive energy of the letter attracted me to it, so long hidden in Shang's clothes. The paper seems to huddle now, curled into itself as if it had longed for someone to understand it, this forgotten scrap of memory and pain.

My fingers have gone damp, and I wipe them on my dress. Then I remove the letter.

Forgive me. Why would the sender use English here? "E," as I've come to call the sender, as the loop looks like a lowercase *e*, must not have been Chinese. Then again, Old Gin and I mostly use English. Sometimes, even the uncles would drop English words here and there, especially those with no Chinese equivalent, like *coffee*.

I study the paper more carefully for clues and, remembering Caroline's comment about watermarks, hold the paper up to the lamp.

The letter nearly drops from my hand.

The familiar insignia *PM* runs across the page, like footprints on sand.

Father puts it on all the premier-line stationery. An ounce of gold for half a ream. Whoever sent it lived on the top branch.

It could be anyone. I should leave it alone.

Yet, the mystery pulls at me, soft and sticky as a cobweb. Something Old Gin said nags at me. When I first showed him the clothes, he said they belonged to an uncle. Then when I saw him with Billy Riggs, he said the debtor left before I was born. Which means Shang couldn't have been an uncle.

The inconsistencies rub together like a door and a frame that do not quite fit.

Perhaps Old Gin is trying to protect me from something. But what could possibly concern me about a man I never knew? I cannot help remembering how he purposely did not mention the urn involved with Lucky Yip's trip to a better home. That was an omission meant to protect a child's heart.

But I am no longer a child.

Who was Shang? Someone whose history Old Gin wanted to roll up in a rug.

Was he . . . my father?

My back thuds against the wall, as if my thoughts had just butted me from behind. The lamp swings too loud, each squeak stabbing my ears. I'd stopped asking about my parents long ago, after getting all I could out of Old Gin; I had been left on his doorstep, wrapped in chenille and sucking my finger. After all these years, could I have stumbled upon an answer?

I slide down to the floor, letting the cold concrete catch me and ground me.

My mind wheels back to my skirmish with Old Gin. I had just told him about the stones in the river hurting, but he seemed to not care. Perhaps he did care, more than I knew. Learning that Shang was my father would be a very sharp stone indeed. One he did not want in my path.

A heavy breath parts my lips. Our basement has grown smaller over the years, the brick shrunken and faded, the ceiling lower than I remember. Or perhaps the realities of my life have grown too big and unwieldy for the walls to contain.

I pull on the navy trousers, then slip on the shirt. My fingers mismatch the buttons, and I have to reseed the row. The idea I could be so close to the man I'd spent a lifetime wondering about puts an ache in my heart.

Whoever he was, he left.

I sniff. The scent of damp soil, pungent and earthy, crowds my nose, a reminder that the world will continue to spin, whether or not we are ready. Well, I must get on with it. After all, most underground residents can no longer smell the soil, so what complaints do I have?

I emerge from my hidey-hole and soon alight on the Bells' porch, wearing a grimace that does not require much effort. Bear howls almost immediately. But then the yelps grow fainter. Perhaps Nathan moved her to another part of the house. The door swings open.

He looks different tonight. His hair has been trimmed and smoothed back, bringing out the height of his cheekbones and the rectitude of his forgettable nose. His eyes, usually hidden, shine bright as a full moon, crinkled at the outside corners by years of wry humor. Gone is the slubby sweater as well as the ink-stained apron. His usually crumpled collared shirt hangs straight as a sail, tucked neatly into pressed trousers. The slouch is gone. Instead, he holds himself as stiffly as a choirboy singing a high note.

Miss Sweetie is tongue-tied. Of course, I couldn't be the reason for the faint whiff of spruce needles I detect coming off his freshly shaven face. I suddenly remember that Lizzie Crump said she would let him know her colors by this weekend. Perhaps she visited earlier this evening.

"Nearly a hundred more subscriptions with 'The Singular Question'! A hundred more to two thousand."

"You're nearly there." Too late, I realize my error. He blinks. "I mean, the *Focus* used to have two thousand subscriptions, but I noticed the numbers dropped off."

"Right. Well, as a matter of fact, we have been trying to regain those numbers, so your help has come at a most opportune time."

Before he starts to wonder about the coincidental timing, I pretend to hack up a viscous wad of phlegm in my throat. "Here is my Sunday column, and a few replies to my letters of admiration."

He takes the piles. "My, you are assiduous."

I frown with the effort of remembering what that particular word means.

"*Assiduous*, meaning 'hardworking.'"

"Yes, I know, young man," I snap, wondering how I got caught in the same trap twice. "I've just never been fond of words that are led by an ass."

His face tightens, as if with the effort of trying to hold something back. "Ah. Then I shall assay not to assault your ears." He opens the letter from Name Withheld. His eyebrows knit together as he reads, and when he reaches the end, he refolds the letter and taps it against his chin.

"You are not pleased."

"On the contrary. Your concern for social inequity is admirable. In fact, the recent ordinance has led us to reconsider your article 'The Custom-ary.'"

"Oh?"

He rubs a hand over his cheeks, as if unaccustomed to its smoothness. "The *Focus* has always erred on the side of restraint. But the moment that means siding with injustice, then we have lost *our* focus. You and I will never know how it feels to be judged by our race, yet we both feel a moral urge . . ."

I am hardly listening as the warm ball in my stomach begins to cool. At least now I know the bottom half of my face doesn't give me away as Chinese. I release my knees and elbows from their locked positions, suddenly longing for the basement, which, though lonely, beats the loneliness I feel here.

" . . . a method of subversion," Nathan is saying. "We would be foolish not to use it."

"Speak plainly, young man. Do you want to print 'The Custom-ary' or not?"

"Yes. I imagine you'll get plenty of responses. Personally,

I'd like to rethink the custom of fruitcake. All those nuts and fruits jumbled together gets confusing. What do you think?" A smile dances around his face.

I squeeze my feelings into something very small, like a walnut, and chuck it behind me for some other silly squirrel to find. There are lines that others draw for us, and ones we should draw for ourselves, knowing only disappointment lies on the other side. Interracial marriage is forbidden. Old Gin knew an uncle who took a colored wife, but they moved to a remote community outside of Atlanta, farther from society's relentless gaze. And anyway, haven't I already decided this spider can spin her own silk?

Stuffing my hands deep into my pockets—Shang's pockets—I begin to turn away. But somewhere in my imagination, doorbells clatter. A chill lifts the hairs of my neck. *We don't get a lot of coolies here. Yet the ones that come always end up scratching at my door.* If Shang is my father, that would explain why Billy Riggs is putting the squeeze on Old Gin. *If anyone can help that old horseman, it's you,* Billy's voice rasps in my ear.

A fire roars within me. If he is bullying an old man, Miss Sweetie has a thing or two to say about that. "What do you know of Billy Riggs?"

Twenty-Three

Nathan's face empties of humor. "If you believe the *Constitution*, Billy is a fixer, someone who helps others out of a pickle."

"I take it you disagree?"

He snorts. "What they don't mention is that Billy Riggs is often the one putting them in the barrel. He buys and trades information. He's an opportunistic night crawler, digesting dirt so as to transform it into dirt of a richer nature."

Billy's mean coppery eyes flash before me. "Is he trustworthy in the business sense?"

"As trustworthy as blackmailers come. Why do you ask?"

"I need information that only Mr. Riggs can provide. I have met him and know he is as unsavory as bear-grease pomade. What I need to know is, will I be wasting my time if I attempt to deal with him?"

He scowls and tucks his fists under his arms. All the brightness has left his eyes. "Why would you win a hand to lose the deck?"

"I don't intend to lose the deck. All I require is the barest information."

"It is a slippery slope. He is clever."

"I am clever, too. Where can I find him?"

An exasperated breath gusts out of him, loosening his spine. "My mother would have my head if I sent you into a lion's den."

"No matter, then. I will find out another way. I simply ask for expediency."

He crosses his arms, jaw set in a way that suggests an answer will not be forthcoming.

"Well, then, good night."

He groans. "Billy Riggs receives business at the Church on Saturday evenings."

Tomorrow, then. "Which church?" In Atlanta, there are more churches than blocks. You can change your religion a dozen times just getting to the train station.

"The Church is a tavern on Decatur, just before Butler." Each word comes out bearing a grudge.

"Thank you. And I have never eaten fruitcake."

THE FOLLOWING EVENING, I hike down Decatur Street in a dress that Old Gin helped me pattern out of an old piano shawl. He says the dress makes me look like a fine lampshade, with its fringe on the cuffs, but I think the dress's clean lines give me a schoolmarm's respectability, especially with my borrowed bonnet.

The Church lies farther from the notorious bottom branch of Collins Street than I thought vultures like Billy Riggs would perch. Of course, a racehorse doesn't complain about a dry track. I hurry past Collins, wondering if I am on a fool's errand. But if he is blackmailing my stand-in father, I must know.

Just before Butler, a wet patch of grass connects Decatur to a brick building the size of the Paynes' barn. The stained glass of its arched windows is mostly intact.

Despite having brooded all day over my meeting with Billy, now that the time has come, all my thoughts seem to have boarded the streetcar for home. I stare at the streaked varnish of the front door, its brass push plate blackened with prints. This might be a trap. Billy trades in information, but what if his intentions are more . . . sinister? Who would notice if a poor Chinese girl went missing? Miss Sweetie would advise making tracks for home.

I shiver, trying to shake off some of my dread. It could hardly be good for business to go around assaulting potential customers. I will simply need to keep my wits about me. All I need are a few answers.

The door swings open, and two drunks stumble out, hastened by a kick that is female in origin. "Next time you try to pay with bogus coins, I'll get you booked! Now scram!"

One of the men falls and, seeing me, crooks a dirty finger. "Look, Rufus, we drank our way clear to China."

"Git!" Another push by the woman's rolling-pin arms sends the two on their way. The woman adjusts her wig, which had begun to slide to one side, and cocks a bushy eyebrow at me. "Help you with something?"

The reek of sour mash wafts through the doorway. At the back of the room, a pair of ivory tusks hangs above a bar, where a half dozen men are seated. "Yes. I am told Billy Riggs can be found here?"

"Billy Riggs?" she screeches, quieting the chatter coming from the bar. "If that no-account comes here, I have an elephant gun whose double barrel would fit right up his filthy nostrils." She fists her hands into her hips.

"You mean, he doesn't conduct business here?"

"No, and if you're the sort who conducts business with him, you ain't welcome here neither. Good day." She strides back into her bar and the door swings shut with a *whomp!*

I slouch after the drunks. Was it a mistake, or did Nathan deliberately mislead me?

The sucking sound of the door reopening heralds a loud clamor and a *woof!*

Before I am halfway to the street, something familiar and furry streaks past me, cutting off my path. I stumble, slipping onto the wet grass. A sheepdog pants right by my face, calling up G-words with every pound of her tail.

Gravity.

Grass.

Gullible.

He led me here to deceive me.

"Bear," Nathan says sternly, slapping his thigh twice. Bear returns to his side, bouncing in four directions at once.

Our gaze connects. If looks were sounds, his startled expression would be the braking of a train for a troop of Fiji mermaids swinging through the trees. His gaze falls to my mouth, maybe measuring it against the last peek. A rosy indignation blooms around my neck.

He shakes himself loose of his stare and hands me his hand-kerchief. "I am terribly sorry." He doesn't sound very sorry at all. "Are you okay?"

Woof! The dog settles, now patient as a rook ready to be played.

I wipe dog drool off my face. "I am as well as someone who has been knocked upon grass soaked with the excrement of animals can be, thank you." Even unmasked, Miss Sweetie hangs on.

The warmth of Nathan's hands as he helps me up sends electric pulses through me. I'm astounded by how many thoughts can fit into the space of the second it takes for me to withdraw my hand.

"I apologize. I couldn't send an unaccompanied lady to Billy Riggs."

So he knew all along I had no chaperone. With my cheeks ablaze, I draw myself up as if there were a string attached to my crown pulling me to the sky—Hammer Foot's power stance. "Now that you have seen that I am quite capable, will you not tell me where to find him?" Bear scoops up my hand with her head, asking me to pet her. Nathan combs his hand through her backside.

"On two conditions."

A group of men saunter toward the Church, hats turning at the sight of us, but offering no comment.

"I will come, and you must tell me why."

"Why what?"

"Why *Miss Sweetie*?"

Our petting—me on the engine, him at the caboose—becomes more vigorous. Bear will be bald soon at the rate we are pawing her. Now that I have been revealed, company would be nice. As for the why of things . . .

"Your family"—I begin to say, and then hastily tack on—"*business* has helped me, over the years, understand the world. I wanted to thank you in some way."

He blinks. "How . . . remarkable." The air between us thickens with unexpressed words.

Straightening, he brushes the wrinkles from his coat while I pick grass off my sleeves. "Well then, Miss Sweetie, to Collins Street."

The bottom branch. That sounds more like it. He offers his arm. And though my own legs have done a fair job getting me down the pavement all these years, I take it.

Twenty-Four

Dear Miss Sweetie,
I recently purchased a straw hat off the shelf that is
too small. How do I make it fit?

Hatless in Atlanta

Dear Hatless,
Fire up the teakettle. Aim the steam at the inner
ribbon, rotating the hat so that the steam dampens the
inside brim evenly. Watch your fingers! Once the hat
has cooled enough, carefully fit it over your head. You
will have to wear the hat for at least two hours so the
hat can dry in its new shape.

Yours truly,
Miss Sweetie

"I confess, you are not who I expected," says Nathan after a painful stretch of silence.

"I never am."

Another silence follows, during which we try not to bump

into each other. Bear pads on the other side of me with her tail high, the only one of us at ease.

"I've had so many questions, and now I cannot think of a single one of them."

"Then silence is your best option."

"Who *are* you?"

"If that is how you plan to snare the ladies, you should consider rewiring your trap."

He snorts. "We are well past introductions, yet I still do not know your name."

"Jo Kuan."

We turn a corner, and a dirty carpet of an avenue unrolls before us. Nathan slows to avoid a collision with a drunkard. "Welcome to Collins Street, where you can get your boots dirty and your pockets clean at the same time."

Vice dens huddle as if conspiring, the crooked teeth of an upper and lower jaw. At the end of the street, a church stands like the final molar, so you can swill and then rinse clean in two easy steps. We skirt around a group of men, black and white, throwing dice, and street sellers hawking enhancement oils and sticks of black opium.

"So, where did you grow up, Miss Kuan?"

"Just Jo is fine."

When I don't say more, Nathan's eyebrows become question marks. "Who are your parents?" he tries again.

"Mr. Bell, I realize as a reporter it is in your nature to get to the bottom of things. But you will need to stick to questions of a more general nature."

"Fair enough. Generally, who are your parents?"

I hide a smile and shake my head, trying not to breathe in the stench of stale tobacco, human sweat, and waste.

"What about questions of a highly specific nature. Like, what is your favorite word?"

"*Hullaballoo*," I lie. I would never admit to Nathan that it's actually *besotted*. "I like how it makes your mouth move around. If I guess your favorite word, will you stop moving your mouth around?"

"How could you possibly guess? There are so many words."

"*Quixotic*." After Mr. Bell read the story of Don Quixote to him, Nathan spent a whole year proclaiming everything from the way his bread crumbs stuck to his shirt to the way certain flies don't budge even when you blow at them quixotic.

"How did you—?"

"Mouth is still moving."

He quiets, though his face is still loud with disbelief. I should not arouse suspicion. "It was a guess. I do read the *Focus*, as I told you, and you overuse the word."

He stops before a lavender Victorian. Up close, the paint is peeling, and the gray trim appears to have once been white, a color likely to cause great disappointment in a railroad city.

A leprechaun of a man with a small hill of a nose peels himself off the porch post. He leers, and the cigarette pursed in his lips droops, raining down ash. While we ascend the stairs, he swaggers down with a gait much wider than a man his size should take. "Enjoy that pretty bit of arse," he drops in a rough brogue, and then laughs.

"Enjoy . . . ?" The words catch up to Nathan. He wheels

around, midstep, and begins to storm back down the stairs after the leprechaun, but I grab his arm.

The front door has opened, revealing a middle-aged woman solidly packed into a pin-striped dress. Her white skin is even paler under a thick dusting of powder. "I recognize you," she tells Nathan in a voice that sounds as scratched as old soles. "The ladies loved you last time you came."

Nathan tears his attention from the departing man, and with a flush blooming on his face, he clears his throat. "Good evening, Madam Delilah. May I introduce—"

"Jo Kuan. I am here to see Billy Riggs."

The madam's bloodshot eyes slide up my lampshade dress to my face, and then shrink. "Wait here." She closes the door.

Bear's tail swats at the porch.

"Come here often?" I can't resist asking.

Nathan frowns. "I came here to investigate. Didn't get very far." He refocuses on the door, on which I notice two carved squares, a cleaner version of the carving on the curly oak.

"What do the dice mean?" I ask.

He rolls back on his heels and the floor protests. "That four-five combination is a Jesse James in craps."

"The outlaw?"

Nathan nods. "He was killed by a forty-five caliber pistol. Billy thinks himself a better outlaw than Jesse."

"Better as in more virtuous?" Despite his being a train robber and a violent murderer, some considered Jesse James a folk hero who gave his plunder to the poor.

Nathan snorts. "Jesse James was as virtuous as Satan on a Sunday. 'Better' as in more cunning."

Madam Delilah appears once again. "He will see Miss Kuan only."

"But the lady requires an escort."

"If she is bold enough to seek out Billy Riggs, she can handle herself."

"I will be fine," I pipe up, somewhat relieved at the notion of not having to expose my affairs to Nathan.

He angles himself so the woman cannot see his face, which is clouded with concern. "Miss Kuan—" he says between his teeth.

"Jo, please."

"Jo. The word *imbecilic* comes to mind."

"As does the word *vexatious*. Madam, I am ready."

He shoots me a black look as I enter the house. Before he can follow, she locks the door behind her.

The parlor extends at least twenty paces, with a bar at the end. Dim lamps make it hard to distinguish faces, but it is clear from the slouched postures and raucous laughter that the occupants are not here to play whist.

Madam Delilah leads me down a dark corridor. Maids, mostly colored, in uniforms more revealing than the ones used by the Paynes' staff, deliver trays of food and drink. Their faces are closed, as if used to minding their own business. Velvet wallpaper smooths the walls between doors, tight as a lady's bodice. A laughing woman pulls a man into a room. No doubt, much of Billy's information is collected in these very halls.

The madam stops in front of a door marked with the number 9. She knocks. "Jo Kuan to see you."

The door opens, and I come face-to-face with a man bearing

the dead expression of an undertaker. He's even dressed for death—a black frock coat with gray-and-black-striped trousers.

"Knucks, let her in."

The man steps back, and the dirty pennies of Billy Riggs's eyes appraise me. Billy is not dressed for a funeral, or a wedding, for that matter. He is not dressed at all.

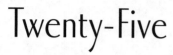

Twenty-Five

Dear Miss Sweetie,

My ten-year-old boy takes after his father, a lazy back-talkin' lout. God rest his black soul. How can I raise him to be a good man?

Worried Mama

Dear Mama,

Make him sweep the porches of the elderly. Caring for others is a gift we give ourselves. Then the only thing left is to teach him how to pick up his own socks.

Best regards,
Miss Sweetie

Billy Riggs is bathing. The pale mountaintops of his scarred knees peek out above gray suds. His auburn hair frames his face in wet noodles. "Well. I guess the gilding on my door was too hard to resist." He smirks, feeding my saucy comment back to me. His gaze cuts to a single chair positioned beside the tub. "Please, sit."

My eyes crawl around the curiosities lining the walls—a

stuffed owl missing its eyes, bottles in different sizes, and several dolls, at least their heads. An expensive-looking vase painted with a grinning Buddha adorns a side table.

Something inside me flares. There is little doubt in my mind that exposing himself this way and in this bizarre setting is meant to intimidate me. I flex my back. If I can handle the two-headed she-devil Caroline Payne, I can handle this bathing freak show. The way out is forward.

I summon Miss Sweetie's most irritated voice. "I prefer to stand." A quick exit might become necessary.

The undertaker henchman positions himself before the door, his hands held in front of him. His left hand sports a tattoo of a horseshoe. At Mrs. English's, women often requested horseshoes on their hats as symbols of luck. He must be superstitious. On his business hand, a metal band around the knuckles gleams in the light of a pulley lamp. No wonder he is called Knucks. Perhaps he hopes the horseshoe on the left hand will restore some of the bad fortune that might follow the harm done with his right.

Billy's scrutiny intensifies. With every passing moment, his eyes pry information from me.

"What do you want with Old Gin?"

"Information costs five dollars per question."

I try to keep the shock out of my eyes. Five dollars is more than a week's wages. "How shall I know if you have information I want to buy?"

He gives me a sly grin. "Life is full of risks. Keeps it interesting." The water makes rhythmic slaps against the sides of the tub.

"Well, I don't have five dollars. But I do have something you might want."

The water stills.

I unsheathe the bottle in my pocket, which I'd filled with barley tea and sealed with wax. "Pendergrass's Long-Life Elixir."

His lips peel open, exposing a small gap between his front teeth. "Where'd you get that?"

"I bought it at Buxbaum's before you showed up."

Billy snorts, and the suds shift alliances, though I try not to look. "That only costs fifty cents a bottle."

"One should never confuse cost with value," I say, an echo of his own words from our last encounter. "As I recall, the next shipment isn't due until Tuesday."

Some of the suds have scaled Billy's face. He makes his finger into a razor and shaves them off. *Fft! Fft!* The moment feels slick and dangerous. Maybe I *have* miscalculated the Pendergrass's value. Knucks's steel eyes lock on to mine, and suddenly he does not appear quite so dead after all.

Someone knocks. "Water."

Knucks unlatches the door, and in steps a maid with a steaming bucket. I consider fleeing while I have the chance. The maid quickly empties her vessel. I force myself to stay the course. I have come this far, and there are answers in this room, just as certain as there are questions.

The maid leaves and Knucks resumes his guard.

"Very well, I will answer your question," Billy announces.

I hand him the Pendergrass and quickly step back.

He winks. "Bottoms up." He works off the cork and swigs. After a thorough swish and swallow, he recorks the bottle and sets it on the side table. His attention lingers a moment on the Buddha vase. "Now, to answer your question, Old Gin needs to pay a debt."

"For what?"

Water drips off his long eyelashes when he blinks. "Questions are five dollars each."

"That is hardly fair. You barely answered my question, and as I told you, I don't have five dollars."

A cunning smile grips his face. "Fortunately for you, I offer several payment plans. If you would like the conversation to continue, you must answer a question for every answer you want from me. Easy, right?"

Easy as a dime pitch, until you discover that dimes bounce. "I want no part of your blackmail scheme."

"*Blackmail* is such an unfortunate term. Personally, I don't discriminate. Black, white, red, yellow, I serve all. If there is a question you don't wish to answer, you can stop at any time, agreed?"

"Fine," I say primly. "What's your question?"

"Who is the most important person in the world to you?"

Why would he want to know that? He must want to know my weaknesses, probably to tuck away for further blackmail.

When I fail to answer, he adds, "Be careful. I will know if you are lying."

My molars grind. He already knows of my concern for Old Gin, so I would not be giving him anything new. "Old Gin. My turn. But I would like to revise my question." I shall need to extract as much information as possible from each question. Old Gin already told me that Shang owes the debt, and Billy just confirmed that Old Gin is covering it for Shang. What I don't know is why. I could ask straight out if Shang is my father. But I don't yet want him to know that I don't know. The information game is tricky as a two-headed snake. "Why did Shang come to your father?"

His eyebrows rise, and he nods, as if approving of my new question. "A loan of twenty-five dollars, which together with interest over the years is now three hundred dollars."

A drop of condensation, or maybe perspiration, slithers down my back.

"Now. You were recently fired from Mrs. English's—"

A shiver picks up the hairs on my arms. "How do you know that?"

"If that's a question, you must wait your turn."

"No, it's not a question. Disregard it." The Buddha appears to be laughing at me.

"I won't warn you again. If I had answered, you would owe me."

My indignation drains from my face, to my soles, and into the floor. I'm reminded of the dice on the front door, advertising Billy's cunning.

He peels back a tin smile. "What scares you the most?"

"Being boxed in," I answer truthfully. Two can play at this game. If he wants a better explanation, he will need to ask me, and that will cost him a question.

His face turns strangely thoughtful, as if he understands what I mean. But what could a cretin like him understand about how it feels to be a pawn on the chessboard, only moving within tightly prescribed rules? Perhaps he has simply mastered the art of not taking the bait.

His mocking grin returns. He shoots me with a finger pistol, crudely indicating my turn.

"What did Shang need the money for?"

"A woman, as I understand."

If Shang is my father, could this woman be my mother? This is as tedious as picking up bread crumbs, one by one.

Billy's grinning face sinks into the horizon of his bath suds, only to emerge dripping but still gleeful. He rubs water from his cheeks. "Does Caroline Payne have a lover?" he casually drops.

"How dare you!" He must be fishing. Undoubtedly, this is the pond in which Billy regularly drops a line. I could sell her out and not lose a moment's sleep over it. But as much as I dislike her, I dislike Billy Riggs more.

He hooks an arm over the tub, and water dribbles off his twitchy fingers onto the floor. "I dare whenever and wherever I like is how. And since I just answered another question for you, you owe me an answer. I warned you."

"But 'how dare you' is not a real question," I sputter.

Knucks stretches his fingers with loud popping sounds and Billy grins. "Knucks doesn't like coolies. Thinks they're bad luck. If you don't know how to follow rules, he'll show you how."

"Fine." I shrink farther into the room away from Knucks. "But . . . I'd like a different question."

"The lady is bold. Well, there is something else you can offer." Abruptly, Billy stands, spilling water onto the floor. There he poses as if he were John the Baptist, just come up from a dunk in the River Jordan. His muscled chest is a matted rug of auburn hair. "I've always wanted to feel a China girl's hair."

I nearly swallow my tongue. My *hair*? Knucks crosses his arms, testing the seams of his jacket. Against the field of black, his lucky horseshoe tattoo and brass knuckles seem to crouch, ready to strike.

Billy steps out of the bath and, God curse my eyes, there in a dripping tangle of auburn, a morel mushroom and two mossy acorns peek through. He takes his time wrapping himself right in front of me. "Just a touch."

I force myself to breathe. If I want to find out if Shang is my father, I must let this sewer rat violate my hair. I could be ruined if it were ever discovered that I allowed such a thing! But ruined for whom? Few in Atlanta would take a Chinese wife, and the chances that the bachelors in Augusta or in Yankee territory will get wind of this are remote. Anyway, hair is dead, a mere accessory. I can always cut it off if I regret my decision. I untie my bonnet. With businesslike efficiency, I unroll my braid and dangle it before Billy Riggs like a noose.

He draws near. Despite the bath, a musky, feral scent clings to him. I force myself to breathe again, visualizing a cool river flowing smoothly down a grassy ravine, where there are no mushrooms.

Someone knocks. "Water," says a woman's husky voice.

"Go away," Billy barks. He reaches out, and then his grubby fingers are dribbling across the bumpy contours of my braid. A moan slinks across his mouth. Curiously, the morel has not sprouted, and it occurs to me what he might be using the Pendergrass for.

I pull away my braid. "That is sufficient!"

But he doesn't let go, and we engage in a close-range tug-of-war. Suddenly, he is too close, his head twisting to one side, his breath hot against my face, his mouth wet and open. Without thinking, I apply the outside edge of my boot to his bare foot, using Hammer Foot's signature move. He lets go with a curse.

Knucks abandons his post, his brass knuckles flashing, the horseshoe tattoo a blur. I snatch the Buddha vase and toss it to him. *Do not engage an adversary; feed it.* The man catches the vase, but fumbles it. A loud and expensive-sounding *crack* tells me it's not so easy to catch pottery while wearing brass knuckles. I shoulder past Knucks and throw open the door, running headlong into . . . Nathan?

With a growl, Bear lunges at Billy. The man recoils, yielding Bear a mouthful of robe. Nathan pulls up on the leash, his face growing grimmer as he takes in the situation. "What's going on here? I shall have you arrested!" Nathan demands in a voice full of thunder and wrath, a flash of fangs behind his curling lip.

"How gallant, newspaper boy. But Miss Kuan sought *me* out," Billy says, seething. A murderous look contorts his face. "Next time, perhaps I shall pay a visit to her charming hideaway."

I hardly hear Bear's barking as the word *hideaway* echoes through me. Surely Billy couldn't know where I live?

Bear tries again and again to pounce, a blur of gray fur.

The noise and the steam and the sight of Billy's obscene

figure churn my innards. I shall be sick if I stay in this room any longer. I stumble toward the hallway, nearly tripping on my hat. My fingers shake as I retrieve it.

"If I learn you have mistreated Miss Kuan, you shall be hearing from me," Nathan's voice cuts across the din. "On the front page."

I edge past maids, the thick carpet grabbing my feet. A woman shoulders past me, her hooded figure reminding me of someone. The reek of hot lilacs fills my nose. I don't catch her face, and I continue toward the exit as fast as my feet can carry me.

Twenty-Six

"I should've sicced Bear on that amphibious scoundrel. Taking a bath? My God, you're as pale as the page."

"I'm quite all right."

I draw a breath of the Collins Street air, which, though putrid, is still fresher than the air inside Billy Riggs's cathouse.

"No, you're not. Did he hurt you? I happen to be good at fisticuffs." He stops and looks back at the Victorian for the fourth time.

"No. I am fine." I hold my stomach and barrel on, remembering the time Nathan broke someone's nose over the spelling of the word *potatoes*.

Nathan matches my brisk pace. "Are you in trouble? Can I do something? Is it money? We know some officials."

I shake my head. I cannot risk Nathan finding out about us living under his house, even if he could persuade an official to care about outsiders like Old Gin and me. Then again, if Billy knows where I live, the game may already be up.

Nathan was right. To win the hand, I have lost the deck.

I kick a cigar stump out of my path, and rein in my catastrophic thoughts. Old Gin always says if there are troubles on the ground, then look up. The changing sky reminds us that our troubles are not here to stay. Tonight's contains a peach of a setting sun floating in a dark lake. I'm reminded of his story about the son who gave the water nymph the fruit meant for the bats of good fortune.

Bear nudges me from the side, herding me away from a broken bottle I didn't notice.

Old Gin said the story hadn't ended yet. I'd guessed the father's crops die without the peach to bring the bats back, but what of the father and the son? Life keeps going, doesn't it? The only real ending is a shovel of dirt in one's face. Until then, you have to keep on planting and sowing, sowing and planting.

I hardly feel Nathan tuck my hand into his arm. We clear Collins and reach Five Points, the center of the Atlanta pie since even before the war, where two Creek Indian trails converged. We merge into the traffic that draws a circle around a seventy-foot-high artesian well, then take the point that shoots us toward the print shop.

"Goddamned fungus! No information can be worth that," Nathan grouses. His voice becomes pleading. "I implore you, tell me how I can help you." The pleading drops away and anger rushes in. "I've been itching to tie that worm into a knot."

Before we reach the print shop, I stop in front of a livery supply smelling of leather and hay. "Mr. Bell—"

"Nathan." His grimace unfolds, and the warm and steady grip of his eyes anchors me in place. "I know a place that makes good beef stew. Soothes the nerves."

"I want to apologize for making you perpetuate a false-hood."

"Actually, it's truly good. Nice chunks of carrots, potatoes—"

"I meant the Miss Sweetie column. I would understand if you no longer want them."

"No." He straightens the notched collar of his loose-fitting sack coat, which I've pulled off kilter. "Of course we want them. As long as you want to keep writing them."

"Yes," I say, a little too quickly. "I—"

"Nathan? *Jo?*"

My eyes pop out. From across the street, Lizzie Crump has emerged from a carriage painted cabbage green, with gold lettering that reads CRUMP'S PAINTS. The carriage driver offers his hand to another woman, who must be Lizzie's mother, judging by her similar coloring and heavy-lidded eyes. Lizzie strides up to us, tailed by the older woman.

On Lizzie's head sits a cunning hat of magenta felt, with a streamlined saucer profile. Just like on my sensible hat, the one I left unfinished in the workroom, a rooster tail of feathers sprouts from the back, pinned by an eternity knot, though the knot is missing a loop. Mrs. English stole the design!

"Hello, Lizzie," I manage to get out.

"Good evening, Mrs. Crump, Lizzie." Nathan turns his astonished eyes to me. "You *know* each other?"

"Jo used to work at Mrs. English's with me. She's a first-rate milliner." Lizzie stretches the toe of one of her pointed boots, a move that strikes me as feline.

"Is that right?" Nathan's eyes drift to my borrowed bonnet, into which I wish I could pull my limbs and disappear, like a turtle.

"Yes," I say weakly. "How about that?"

"I was just coming to tell you my colors for the race, remember?"

"Of course. Your colors. Ah, about that. I realized that I will not make a very good escort, as I will have my hands full reporting on the race. If you wanted to find another escort, I would gladly step aside."

"Oh." Lizzie stops twisting about and bites a finger. I can almost see her thoughts wiggling into place. "Well, I don't want another escort. And anyway, I would love to watch the newsman in action."

"Right." Nathan's gaze drifts toward me, pulling Mrs. Crump's along with it. Her sharp nose sniffs, as if smelling something off, and her false smile withers like an old rind.

"Oh yes, and Mrs. English has a new advertisement for you." Lizzie pulls a slip of paper from her glove and hands it to Nathan. "Business has gone through the roof. She thinks it's because of the popularity of your new agony aunt column, so she created this special number called the Miss Sweetie, for the 'independent woman.'" Lizzie tilts her head, showing off her hat. "She's selling it at the special rate of three dollars."

If there were more irony in this situation, we could build a railroad.

"Do you like it, Jo? I made this one myself."

"*You* made it?"

Her laughter floats on a breeze. "Don't sound so shocked. I pinned it beforehand like you showed me, and that helped tremendously. Mrs. English said I might make a top-shelfer if I keep up the good work."

"That's wonderful." The words drop like lead casings. I should be happy for her success, but my insides feel as mealy and brown as a January apple.

Mrs. Crump rakes her gaze down my fallen braid and then her spine straightens. "But how does this . . . *creature* . . . know you, Mr. Bell?"

"She is a colleague." Nathan removes his Homburg hat, causing tufts of his hair to put his head in quotes, even after he runs a hand through it.

"A colleague?"

Lizzie playfully bats her mother's stiff arm. "Oh, Mama, she *does* speak English."

"I'm afraid I must be on my way," I say with Miss Sweetie's briskness. Not engaging is a victory in itself.

"But we haven't yet finished our . . . meeting," says Nathan. Mrs. Crump's face draws into a point focused around the nose. Her daughter still wears a loose smile from my compliment of her hat. Unlike Caroline, Lizzie is cut from softer jade than her mama.

I dip my head toward Nathan. "We are done, Mr. Bell." I avoid his gaze, stooping to rub Bear's sweet face between my hands. Into her silky ear, I whisper, "Thanks for coming to my rescue." Up close, I finally see her eyes, which are warm as melted candle wax, just like her owner's.

Then I hurry away, smudging myself from Nathan's life like a rubber cube over a pencil mark. I cannot go spoony over Nathan Bell. The line between us is too dark.

Anyway, Lizzie has already laid her claim, and that is how it should be. Maybe my feelings for him are more brotherly than amorous anyway, just like when he was twelve and I ten, and he sang "Turkey in the Straw" so many times, I nearly yelled at him to shoot the hanged turkey already. I focus on those old feelings and not these new ones.

MY FLANNEL GOWN whips around my legs as I wheel around the racetrack of our spool table, going nowhere fast. A twenty-five-dollar loan for a woman that he never paid back. Did this woman write the letter? Was she the reason Shang left? It occurs to me I still don't know for certain that Shang is my father. For all my efforts, I seem to have gotten more questions than answers.

The speaking tube, visible through the open curtain to my corner, taunts me to unplug it. I keep moving. Lately, I've been feeling more like an intruder anyway. When I was a child, the Bells filled in the spaces Old Gin could not, teaching me about the American way of life, making me feel less like an outsider in my own country. But like Old Gin, one day I'll have to let them go, too. Especially Nathan.

Before I carve a moat into our floor, I pull out the cigar box of silk-cord odds and ends I bought from Mrs. English for a penny and then seat myself upon my flowerpot chair. Maybe tying knots will soothe some of my anxiety.

WITH THE WEATHER finally warming, Buxbaum's buzzes with activity. It heartens me to see Robby at a counter, counting out a woman's change. A line of folks, all of them colored, wait to be rung up.

The woman puts her money in her change purse. "You tell me when they invent self-mopping mops, and I'll be the first in line."

"They do have them, Mrs. Weaver. They're called cats." He notices me. "Good morning, Jo. Be right with you."

"Sure thing, Robby." I collect the items I need—barley, crackers, a salve for my roughened hands, a bar of soap, black-eyed peas, and an ax to replace our rusted one. Plus, it won't hurt to have a reliable weapon handy. Heaven forbid I should have to use it.

Robby finishes with his customers, and I bring my items to him. He looks around us—no one is within earshot—and then quietly says, "Those Paynes are as shifty as sand. Would you believe, they asked Noemi back? Etta Rae called Pastor Harkness this morning, who passed us the message in front of the whole congregation."

"I'm glad they did the right thing. Will she return?"

"Does August have thirty-one days? She's still bent on buying that safety. She even took the dollar I was going to place on Sunday Surprise. Can't a man have any fun?"

"That safety's pretty fun."

He throws me a look that could cut glass. "You're in league with her. By the bye, you in the market for a mop? There's a sale today on sweepers and scrubbers."

"Thanks, but no. You're a natural at this."

"Turns out, I'm good for business. Just hope Mr. Buxbaum agrees. He's weighing whether to hire me full-time."

"I am happy to hear that. Maybe I'll get to buy you some teeth rinse soon."

He nods at a colored woman in a butter-yellow bonnet inspecting fabrics. "Nice to see you, Mrs. Thomson." She nods back.

He finishes packing up my items. "That all?"

"Actually, no." I remove from my pocket the knots I tied last night. "I was wondering if you could show these samples to Mr. Buxbaum. They're not like the embellishments you carry, but I hoped—"

"Jo, they're good." He holds one up. "This one looks like a butterfly."

"It's a falcon, and that one is for Noemi. A falcon for farsightedness."

"She's going to like that. How much you charge?"

"Eight cents each, if Mr. Buxbaum doesn't mind supplying the cord."

"Make it ten cents. These are worth it."

"Thanks, Robby."

"You're welcome."

A stack of the Sunday *Focus* occupies a rocking chair near the exit. The sight of "The Custom-ary," all dressed up in type-face, arouses a mother's pride in me. Worry, too. If this one doesn't go over well, people could turn on Miss Sweetie. The whole paper could come tumbling down. Then the part of me that could take a bite out of the world will lose its teeth. Gone like the frost when the spring dragon roars.

Twenty-Seven

Noemi doesn't show up on Monday, and the substitute cook, a German woman, mans the kitchen with a three-beat efficiency—three pinches of salt, three taps of the egg, three bangs of the pot. I hope Noemi returns by tomorrow, before I begin to waltz. I could see her tonight at the suffrage meeting, though I haven't yet decided if I will go. Certain things are simply not worth the humiliation.

The day I turned thirteen and not long before Mrs. Payne dismissed me, I begged for a taste of the new Coca-Colas served at Jacob's Pharmacy that everyone was so fizzed about. We'd seen colored people in the pharmacy before and figured we might have a chance as well. With two whole nickels from our money boot in his pocket, Old Gin held the bar stool steady for me, as I'd just begun wearing my skirts to the floor. But the soda jerk waved a rag in Old Gin's face. "No colas for coolies."

A woman laughed, and then it seemed everyone was laughing at us. My face still burns thinking of that.

While I dress Caroline for her afternoon ride, the first since the pepper incident, I can't help asking, "Did you catch Miss Sweetie's last column, miss?" I have heard no news over how well "The Custom-ary" has been received.

"Why should I waste my time? Miss Sweetie is a know-it-all. The sort I cannot brook."

I must wait and see, even visit Nathan tonight if I have to. I vowed to stop eavesdropping, but a visit by Miss Sweetie—well, Jo Kuan, now that I have been unmasked—would be okay. This is business, after all.

Outside, Old Gin shuffles up between Sweet Potato and Frederick. The horses' necks turn adoringly toward him. My own heart is a sparrow's nest of emotions for the old man: love, annoyance, gratitude, and injury, threaded with worry. He could look in every nook and cranny Atlanta has to offer, but it would take him years to find three hundred dollars' worth of change. His gaze meets mine, his eyes dark like printer's ink, with smudges under the eyes. He needs a rest.

Caroline scratches at a dry patch on her forehead. The red puffiness on her face has mellowed into a flaky pink. "Oh, bother."

"Miss, is everything all right?"

"Obviously not. Wait here." She stomps back into the house, probably to rub more lard into her forehead.

Old Gin holds Sweet Potato steady for me. "Thank you for minding the burrows, daughter. How are you?"

I bite my tongue, which longs to wag about the three-hundred-dollar debt. But it would upset him greatly to know that I went to see Billy Riggs, and in the company of Nathan Bell, too. Once trust is lost, it is a mountain of gravel to reclimb.

On the other hand, what is a mountain of gravel compared to the never-ending hole of debt? What we need is a solution, one that cannot be found right now, with Caroline's footsteps punching the hallway. "I am well. And you?"

"Pretty good." Old Gin tilts his chin toward me, the way he does when he's listening for the unspoken words. I have trouble meeting his gaze, as if doing so might crack the egg of my resolve and all my messy secrets will come spilling out.

Caroline emerges through the front door looking no different from when she entered. Her black hat, maybe to match her mood, comes to a point in the front. Taken with her gunmetal-gray riding habit, her figure puts me in mind of a crow, those most cunning birds known for bullying others twice their size. "Let us be off. I have an appointment to keep," she snipes, as if she wasn't the reason for her own delay.

We have hardly made it off the property when a rider on a black stallion appears.

Caroline pulls up on her rein. "Merritt!"

Ameer chugs merrily toward us, his mane rising like black smoke off a locomotive with every sure step. Unlike the horse, the Payne heir is not in good form. His normally erect shoulders stoop as if trying to touch, and his head crooks to one side. "Good afternoon, ladies. Fine day for a ride, isn't it?" He attempts a devilish smile, but it comes out as strained as the whey through a cheesecloth.

"Why do you look so down in the mouth?" Caroline demands.

"I think I just had my heart flambéed."

Sweet Potato fidgets under me, eager to fly.

"What do you mean?"

"Doused in alcohol and set on fire."

Caroline tosses her eyes to the canopy of the magnolia we're standing under. "By whom?"

"The blue-blooded Jane Bentley of Boston. She broke off our engagement. Apparently she's an admirer of that Miss Sweetie. She told me she'd rather be single than chained to a bore for a lifetime."

I choke on my own saliva and begin to cough. With an impatient huff, Caroline moves Frederick away from me, as if choking were infectious. "Good riddance. She had an apple-juice smell about her and not in a good way. And why is every-one so stuck on this Miss Sweetie?"

Merritt picks up his smile. "Why, sister, are you jealous?"

"You are insufferable." Caroline kicks off.

"I am sorry, sir," I tell him.

"Father will probably disown me."

"He would not want you in an unhappy marriage."

He swats at a cloud of gnats. "My father owns a paper mill. Jane's owns a lumber mill. That is two broken engagements. Miss Sweetie's opinion might work in theory, but it is hardly realistic for people like us. Marriages need not be happy as long as they are mutually advantageous." That's his father speaking. "Plus, she wasn't that bad."

Apparently, the same could not be said of Merritt Payne.

He rolls his wrist and bows.

I set off after Caroline, wondering if a bruised ego feels the same as a broken heart, and if so, does knowing the difference shorten the recovery time? Miss Sweetie doesn't worry about

Merritt. The roses of wealth and good looks tied with the bud of youth open many doors.

Sweet Potato kicks up grass and scatters the crows, bringing us even with my lady in no time. Caroline seems to hardly notice us walking beside her. She keeps playing with her lace collar, folding it up in the demure style, and then flipping it down for a more casual look. Her hat moves from the mansions on our left to a field of long grass on our right, and then into the boughs of a pine. I sense she is looking for Mr. Q. Though, of course, why would he be hiding in a tree?

"Has your Mr. Q inquired after you?"

"Why would he?"

"You missed your"—cough—"*appointments* with him Thursday and Friday. One would think he would be concerned."

"He is too discreet to call upon me."

"I didn't say 'call upon.' But perhaps he sent you a note. Or climbed to your window."

I wasn't serious with that last suggestion, but she seems to consider it for a fraction of a second. "No, he did not. And your frankness is not appropriate, or appreciated."

I listen to the horse hooves play a merry duet for at least five seconds. "Fine. Just seems to me that if one's sham love—Miss Saltworth—pulled a prank on one's true love—you—one would be concerned. Alarmed, even." I am speaking recklessly, but something has loosened my stays. Maybe it is the knowledge that my term here is temporary, just until Old Gin finds me a husband. Or maybe it is Miss Sweetie talking. My voice seems more like hers every day.

"Tie your tongue, or I will do it for you," Caroline hisses.

When we finally arrive at the water trough, while Frederick drinks, she uses the reflection to smooth wayward hairs and pinch her cheeks. And then she is off, treading the thorny path that so many hopeful lovers have tread before.

INSTEAD OF SIX Paces Meadow, I let Sweet Potato hoof back toward Piedmont Park in North Atlanta. May at least one of us go where her heart leads her today. Perhaps we can sneak a look at the action on the track.

The smell of cut grass and freshly turned soil digs up a sweet memory. Not long after the Paynes fired me, Old Gin decided we should try to attend the Piedmont Exposition of 1887, the biggest thing to happen in Atlanta since the war. Since the event was whites-only, except for workers, I put on my gray skirt and black jacket, and Old Gin wore his standard groom's attire. We carried buckets of flowers, as if we actually had somewhere to deliver them. If you walk like you know where you're going, you can fool a lot of people, especially in a place with so many distractions.

Cannons fired, bands played, and exhibit halls showcased Atlanta's best, from animals and farming equipment to motorized sewing machines and phonographs. I even saw President Cleveland's wife, Frances Folsom, buy an eagle carved from local manganese marble. She caught me staring at her, and I plucked out one of my blooms. "May this chrysanthemum bring good luck to your home."

She took the flower. "A China girl who speaks like a Southerner? I guess Atlanta does have it all."

With its witch's-hat shape, the two hundred acres of Piedmont Park, home of the Gentlemen's Driving Club, features long swaths of green cut with pathways, and surprisingly few trees for a city so full of them.

We approach from the west entrance, both because it is closer to the racetrack, and to avoid the buildings at the main entrance where we are likely to be chased away. A carriage approaches from behind, and I sit lower in the shadows of my hat.

Several single-horse carriages sail by, headed toward the grandstand a thousand feet ahead. Beyond that stretches the mile-long track.

Off the groomed path, a colored man in a white collared shirt and grass-stained trousers pushes a lawn mower in an impressively even line. A boy rakes clippings into piles nearby.

The man finishes a line and stops to mop his face with a handkerchief. Seeing us, he tips the brim of his boater hat. "Looking finer every day."

I slow, caught off guard, until I realize he's talking about Sweet Potato.

She whinnies, and I bring her closer. "Good afternoon. Have we met?"

"I'm Leo Porter, and that's my son Joseph."

The boy, who must be ten or eleven, stands at attention, chest puffed out, rake held straight as a bayonet beside him. His cheeks are still full of baby fat, and his cap is straight enough to balance a bottle.

"Always nice to meet another Jo, even if it's a Joseph. I'm Jo Kuan."

"Hello, miss."

"You must be Old Gin's daughter," says the father. There's a slight drift to his right eye, so I focus on the left. "He said you were quite a horsewoman."

"I learned from the best." But what was Old Gin doing here? Maybe he took the horses here for exercise through the extensive driving trails. He would've had to come with Jed Crycks or Mr. Payne, of course. No wonder Sweet Potato is familiar with this route.

"Well, the track's full of practice runs and horse trading today. There's no sneaking in. You'll have to wait till after everyone's gone home this evening, like usual."

Like *usual*. Old Gin has been sneaking in here? The years might've emboldened him, but I suddenly wonder if his attic is getting dusty. Maybe he just came for the joy of the ride. At least the dirt track is smooth, unlike Six Paces, where one could easily lose one's footing at night. He certainly couldn't have come for horse trading, as there is no better horse than Sweet Potato with her good temperament and fast legs.

Pretty legs like those would fetch a pretty sum, if Old Gin ever wants to sell, Merritt's good-natured voice echoes in my mind.

Suddenly, my limbs don't work. Is Old Gin planning to *sell* Sweet Potato? The after-hours trips here and Old Gin's optimism shuffle into place. Maybe he was meeting with potential buyers at the Driving Club, showing her off on the track. She'd certainly command a good sum, maybe even three hundred dollars. He knew I'd protest if he told me. She is part of the family.

Sweet Potato skitters, feeling me gripping her flanks.

The sound of an approaching horse pulls Mr. Porter's gaze behind me. "'He will come like a thief in the night.'"

I gape as the rider tumbles by.

Mr. Porter blows out a low whistle, probably meant for the piebald, but my eyes are drawn to the rider. The tail of Mr. Q's shirt blows freely from the back of his slim-fitting jacket. His sleeves are pushed up, showing the bronzed skin of his arms, which move rhythmically as he trots.

"Must be late for his practice run," says Mr. Porter.

Under Mr. Q's calfskin swashbuckler, as Mrs. English called it, with its dented crown and folded-up sides, a scratch runs down the smooth slope of his cheek. I bet I know whose fingernail made that mark.

"I'm sorry, I have to go."

Twenty-Eight

Caroline is not at the water trough, and so after letting Sweet Potato slake her thirst, we head for the cemetery.

It's not hard to find her. I simply follow the rotten odor of forbidden fruit. That, and the sobs echoing through the Innocenti vault. The angels keep a stiff upper lip, having gotten more than they bargained for when they took this job. Beneath the heavy boughs of a hemlock, Frederick stands as still as a chess piece, only moving when Sweet Potato whinnies. I tie Sweet Potato to the neighboring tree.

Inside the vault, Caroline weeps over her lap on one of two stone benches. Her jacket, hat, and gloves appear hastily thrown on the bench behind her, watched over by her sleek violin boots. On the back wall, melted candles form shapeless blobs in an alcove. At the front, a marble tomb is big enough to house an entire family of skeletons, and could not have made a comfortable bed, at least not on the outside.

Caroline looks up at me, her blotchy skin wet with tears and snot. "Go away."

The stone bench cools my backside along with my temper. I try to drum up my old dislike for her, but it is like sucking on a bone that has lost its flavor. Heaving and moaning, Caroline spends her grief by the dollar, until her purse empties and she's down to nickel hiccups and penny whimpers.

"You are too high a nut for a two-timer like Mr. Q."

She squeezes her arms over her wet blouse, her face tight. "Of course, I know that. The man has scant fortune, and his head is as empty as all his promises. I cannot abide a stupid man even more than a stupid woman."

"Then why spend tears on him?"

"Because." She swings her gaze back to the crypt, her head jutted forward like a vulture. Her bottom lip begins to tremble. "Edward heard a rumor that Mama had an affair." Her voice tightens under the noose of hysteria. "That she had an illicit daughter."

"Who—you?"

"No, Merritt. Of course, me! He said he could never betroth himself to me in light of such a scandal."

"But you don't want to marry him."

"No. But if word gets out, no one else will want to marry me either."

"I thought you didn't want to marry anyone."

"I don't, but what if I decide I do?"

"I say you are better off without those who base marriage on such shallow rock." An image of the milk-livered Mr. Q galloping toward the racetrack after delivering such a shocking blow throws sand even in my face. "Do you think he started the rumor himself?"

She shakes her head. "You give him credit where none is due. He says the information is reliable."

Who would have that kind of information? The memory of a hooded figure brushing past me at the Riggs's cathouse brings all other thoughts to a screeching halt. The woman smelled of lilac. I was too distraught at the time to realize who she was: Melly-Lee Saltworth. As they say, a pinch of salt beats a lick of sugar, and it's true in her case—shrewd gets you farther in life than sweet. Tampering with Caroline's face cream was just the opening shot. Buying information on Caroline was clever, actually, a way to fell the enemy without a public battle, one that Miss Saltworth would surely have lost.

"What if it's true?" Caroline presses two soft fingers into her temples. "If Papa finds out, he will disavow us." Her eyes clamp shut, squeezing out more tears.

"No. Mr. Payne would not leave you to ruin. You are his crown jewel. Remember when he hired the Silver Saddle Militia to make sure no boys showed up to your fourteenth birthday picnic?"

She sniffs. "May as well have asked a bunch of foxes to guard the henhouse."

"I recall it was the hens doing most of the chasing."

A smile wrestles the corners of her mouth, but she shakes it off with an exasperated sigh. "This is a grave situation."

I nod. "Especially for them." I jerk my chin at the crypt.

This time, she snorts, and then the snort slips into a wheeze. Then suddenly we are giggling like our heads are full of soda water.

When we emerge from the tomb, I cannot say I like Caroline Payne any better. Only that my perspective of her has shifted. It's like how climbing up on a horse makes the world look less threatening and gives a clearer view of the road ahead.

I FEEL TROUBLE rumbling down the street before the streetcar arrives. Then again, my visit with Billy Riggs has had me feeling like there's a tiger on every corner. Old Gin discreetly passes his hand around the base of a statue of some dignitary, but not finding any coins, he dusts off his hands. I haven't had a chance to speak in earnest with him in days. I hug my cloak to me, trying to work out how to broach the topic of our debt. "I ran into some friends of yours today on my ride," I begin conversationally. "Leo Porter and his son."

"You went to Piedmont Park?"

"Yes."

He hooks his hands behind his back, and his eyes stop tracking the ground. I blurt out, "You're not trying to sell Sweet Potato, are you?"

"Why would I do that?"

"To pay debts owed."

Silence falls like a stone into water. I'm reminded of our skirmish again and brace myself. "I am not selling Sweet Potato. Please trust me, hm?" The *hm* doesn't assure me as it usually does.

The streetcar arrives with its usual brassy clatter. When it stops before us, the new sign on its flank jars me more than the clanging bell: WHITES ONLY, ROWS 1–5. The words hardly sink in, only buzz like angry bees before my eyes. Old Gin sighs.

"This isn't right." My words drop out.

"*Right* and *wrong* don't have much say in these parts," says someone in the back. "*Will* and *can* are in charge."

Some of the regulars squeeze into the already packed back rows, while others begin walking.

A traveling salesman in the third row shifts his bulk, causing the streetcar to bounce. "Well, the coloreds in Atlanta are sure fresher than the ones out in the country," he says, his voice high and amused. He cracks a sunflower seed with his teeth and spits the shell onto the sidewalk.

I wait for Old Gin to decide where we should sit, but he hasn't budged from the sidewalk, and his face has become pinched in the center.

Sully stands up in his seat and glares at Old Gin, his conductor's cap looking like a squashed fist. "For the love of leeches, Old Gin. Bend your perpendiculars so we can go home."

"There is a problem," says Old Gin. "Rules do not cover Chinese." I stare at him in shock. Old Gin has never spoken up like that before, but there he stands, steady as a lighthouse in a rough sea. "I am brown like a potato, but Jo is white as you, though easier on the eyes, hm?" A few chuckle. "Bad rules create chaos."

Sully looks more red than white right now. "You ain't colored. Hitch your saddle up here, old man."

The moment feels heavy with held breaths and tight with discomfiture. Most people avoid our eyes, but they are all watching with their ears.

Old Gin surveys the roomy first five rows, and then the last, packed close as cigars. He moves up to the third row, empty of all save the traveling salesman and his bag of sunflower seeds.

The salesman stretches a thick hand along the back of his seat. "You ain't colored, but you ain't white neither."

Folks in the first rows have turned around, their faces rigid, some with impatience as they stare at Old Gin and me standing behind him. The crabby gardener who chastised Maud Gray sweeps a leathery hand at us, his eyes jumpy like fleas. "Dogs have no need for streetcars. Git."

The traveling salesman's head draws back. With a sudden jerk, he whuffs out another seed.

Old Gin's hand flies to his face. His thin shoulders cave.

The salesman wheezes out a laugh. "Got him right in the eye, that's how!"

"Why, you grotesque lump of flesh—" I begin to sputter, but Old Gin puts a hand on my arm, leading us back to the sidewalk.

Old Gin lifts his gaze to meet Sully's. I'm reminded of the time Sully's mule started walking crooked, and Old Gin found an abscess in the animal's hoof. The men are not friends, but surely seeing the same person every day for twenty years fixes them in your life in some way.

"This streetcar is not for us," announces Old Gin.

Sully's usually hard face loses its fight. He turns his shoulder, and it is like the closing of a heavy book.

With a *clang* and a *giddap!* the streetcar bumps along and out of our lives.

Anger sparks around inside me, but pride, too. By opting

not to take the streetcar, Old Gin has chosen not to play in a rigged game. The river's path will be harder this way. We will need to wake earlier and arrive home later. Then again, perhaps the path is easiest when the heart is light.

Old Gin walks smoothly beside me, the only sign of agitation the twitching of his pupils, reflecting the thoughts inside. I'm reminded of that day that we tried to get Coca-Colas. While I struggled to hold in my tears, Old Gin led us out of Jacob's Pharmacy with the same quiet dignity of kings of old. His head was not bent low, or held too high, but he moved with a bearing that knew its course, no matter what the world hurled at us.

There's a lit quality to the dusky sky that makes all the angry bits inside me line up. Something powerful surges through me, a feeling that has nothing to do with ambition, and everything to do with principle. "I would like to join Noemi at a suffrage meeting tonight at Grace Baptist," I hear myself say. I watch Old Gin out of the corner of my eye, bracing for disapproval.

"It does not surprise me that Miss Sweetie is a suffragist."

I stop walking. A protest bubbles up, but then fizzes away. Many lies have rolled off my tongue lately, and I can't help wondering how many I can hatch before they start pecking my eyes out. "How long have you known?"

He shrugs. "Jed Crycks is a devoted reader."

I picture the tough, tobacco-chewing cowboy reading my column and nearly choke.

A smile alights on Old Gin's face. "Parent always recognizes child's voice."

Twenty-Nine

Dear Miss Sweetie,
*   My sisters and I wonder, why must women suffer a few days each month?*

*   Sincerely,*
*   Bloated, Crampy,*
*   and Spotty*

Dear Bloated, Crampy, and Spotty,
*   Because the alternative is worse, although they do get to vote.*

*   Sincerely,*
*   Miss Sweetie*

The three-story white brick of Grace Baptist Church does not feature a cross or a bell or any of the standard-issue church symbols. However, a bronze plate on the door tells you that if you are seeking God, you can find Him here. As long as you can read.

A white woman with a knit cap stretched over her bread-loaf bun puts a hand over her heart when she sees me.

"Good evening, ma'am."

"May I help you?" She speaks painfully slow, as if she is not sure I can understand.

"Yes, I'm here for the suffrage meeting."

"You? I'm sorry, but they've already started. We don't admit latecomers." A fingernail of a smile digs at her face. "Too distracting."

The buzz of voices behind her indicates a crowd, but she moves her stout frame from side to side as if to block my view. I can't help thinking that the least distracting part of me is the late part. "I'm supposed to meet a friend here."

"Who?"

"Noemi Withers."

"Never heard of her. I am sorry."

"But—"

"Jo? Is that you?" warbles a familiar voice.

Mrs. Bread Loaf steps aside, revealing Mrs. English, all five feet of her, looking formidable in a slate-gray suit with silver buttons. On her head sits another of the Miss Sweetie hats, this one in mauve with a pink-and-black rooster tail, and an eternity knot tied better than Lizzie's. I can't help admiring not just the color combination—she has always been a fashion maven—but also her business sense. What better way to advertise her product than to wear it at an event filled with her target audience?

"You know this girl?" asks Mrs. Bread Loaf.

"Well, yes. Let her in." Mrs. English pulls me into the church by the elbow. In the reception hall, a few women, all white, mill about tables set with a bowl of punch and spice cake. Conversation pauses while everyone gets a good look at me. "What are you doing here?"

"Votes for women," I announce to everyone, but no one smiles.

"Yes, but—" Noticing all the attention on us, she throws around a mind-your-own-business glare. Conversation resumes, but at a more subdued tone. Her attention resettles on me. "I hear you're back with the Paynes. I am glad you have landed on your feet."

I manage a thin smile, despite the fact it was her hands that tossed me out. "Nice hat," I say.

She has the grace to flush. "I'd been hoping to talk to you. I can't seem to get the knot to lie flat in the back, and I was hoping you could help me."

"It is missing a loop."

"Well, perhaps you can stop by the shop and do a few for me."

"I am rather busy." A doorway of carved wood leads to what I assume is the sanctuary. The ceiling rumbles with the sound of footsteps, and a circle of overhead candles sways.

"Oh, for heaven's sakes, let bygones be bygones. I will pay you for them, let's say, a nickel apiece. Of course, I'd supply the ribbon. I'm desperate. I got eight orders tonight alone."

"Ladies, to your tables, please," says Mrs. Bread Loaf, clucking about like a hen gathering chicks. "We must get our banner done tonight."

Mrs. English still watches me with her hawkish eyes.

"I will think about whether it makes economic sense," I tell her, and an exasperated breath wings out of her.

Women file upstairs to a community hall, where more ladies—about a hundred in all—are sewing. Some embroider squares of marigold fabric at worktables. Others simply whip-stitch strips of the same marigold fabric, creating what look to be sashes. A woman in a mutton-sleeve dress jabs a finger at a sketch pinned on a wall, her face animated as she gives orders. She must be the top hat in this shop. The words VOTES FOR WOMEN—RACING FOR EQUALITY! span the length of the sketch with a racehorse underneath. So, Mrs. Payne accepted their bid after all.

The top hat notices me and her eyes sharpen. She brushes off a woman trying to get her attention and marches over, hands fisted.

Mrs. English does not notice the storm cloud on the horizon. "There's Lizzie." My former coworker sits at the largest table, her tongue sticking out of her mouth as she attempts to thread a needle. "Our table is full, but I'm sure you'll find a place."

"Who is this, Mrs. English?" The top hat has a teapot face, with cheeks that are starting to droop above a doily of a collar, and a nose that tips up at the end. A nervous energy surrounds her, like the teapot is kept at a high simmer.

Mrs. English's vast bosom grows twitchy. "Oh, Mrs. Bullis, may I present Jo Kuan. Jo, Mrs. Bullis is the president of the Atlanta Suffragists."

"How unusual. I didn't know Chinese could even be citizens. Why are you here?"

"Same reason as everyone else, I expect, ma'am."

She sniffs. "There are many who try to pin their causes onto ours, but we are here for one reason only, and that is to advance the cause of *American* women. I find it hard to believe someone who is not an American woman can help in that effort."

My teeth clamp around the retort that springs to my lips. I fold my hands in front of me and plant my feet. "You must be thrilled that your bid to sponsor a horse was accepted for the race."

Her black pupils look like pinpricks. "Yes, of course we are."

"Being matched with a fighting pair, like the Paynes' new Arabian and their New York jockey, would certainly advance your cause, maybe lead to national recognition, wouldn't you say?"

"It is a random draw, but yes, we are hoping for the best pair. Your point is?"

"Neither the jockey nor the racehorse is an American woman."

Her face seems to crack a little at the jawline. Mrs. English dabs a handkerchief to her brow, maybe congratulating herself on ridding herself of me.

Before the teapot begins spouting, I incline my head. "I am only here to help where I may, ma'am."

She huffs and spins around, chasing away the looks that have gathered at her back. "There's a place for you over there." She points to a spot in the corner, where I'm heartened to see Noemi, writing at a table, alongside two other ladies, the only other colored people in the room.

243

Mrs. Bullis sweeps away, and Mrs. English escapes to Lizzie's group.

As I make my way to Noemi's table, I catch snippets of conversation.

"—the custom of wearing black for mourning. It washes out the complexion."

My ears perk, and my feet slow as I try to unravel the conversations.

"—baseball. I can throw better than some of our local Firecrackers."

"—saving one's best gloves for parties."

A young woman with sausage curls pokes the lady beside her. "I would give up my best gloves to find out who this Miss Sweetie is. I think it's Emma Payne."

Her table erupts in gasps and squeals, and a smile blooms on my face. Seems as though "The Custom-ary" has worked its magic for the *Focus*.

Noemi grabs me by the elbows. "You made it." She's pinned the falcon knot I made to her hat.

"Looks good there."

She bends her iron eyes to me. "I named it Farney."

"Why Farney?"

"Because August was already taken. Mr. Buxbaum liked your knots. He says he'll take a hundred at ten cents apiece if it's exclusive. Imagine, Jo, that's some good egg money."

Twice as much as what Mrs. English is offering. Visions of hanging up my own little shingle on Madison Avenue dance across my vision. Would the fine ladies of New York like my knots? Perhaps I can tie and advise at the same time. My sign could read *Jo Kuan, Thoughts and Knots*.

"Come, I'll introduce you." She pulls me toward her table. "You have trouble getting through the door?"

"A little. You?"

She snorts. "I would've, if I hadn't come with Atlanta's best seamstress. Meet Mary Harper. She works for Mrs. Bullis." She throws a glance to the top hat, who is back to barking orders.

"Hello, I'm Jo Kuan."

Mary doesn't smile at me, but nods, her large eyes bright and curious. Her needle whips in and out of a wide swath of marigold cloth, already stitched with trees and flowers. Beside her, a pointy-chinned young woman with a bright handkerchief wrapping her hair gives me a look full of barbed wire. Her skin is more golden than brown, and the only soft thing about her are her full lips.

"And this is Mary's sister-in-law, Rose St. Pierre."

"Nice to meet you."

"Same."

Noemi pushes me into a chair.

"What did I miss?"

"That Mrs. Bullis made a big speech about how women's brains are just as heavy as men's. They done research on that. Then they put us all to work on this banner for the horse race, since Mrs. Payne accepted their bid, and you know who had a hand in that." She winks. "And, oh, did you catch the Miss Sweetie article yesterday?"

"I did," I say, holding my breath.

"We're also supposed to write down the 'Custom-aries' that work against women. Mrs. Bullis says she'll collect the best and send them to the *Focus* on behalf of the Atlanta Suffragists. Why do you look so surprised? You got a good one?"

"No, but I bet you do."

"Almost done adding my bit." Noemi writes on her paper.

"Nice work," I tell Mary, who has sewn an impressive image of the horse's hindquarters on her fabric, and not a single grinning stitch. The other tables have barely started on their squares.

"Thank you."

"Course they got to give us the horse's backside," says Rose. "And why do you think that is?"

"Because that's the half that gets things done, that's why." Noemi sets down her pencil. "We been standing in the back for a long time, but we can change that when we get the vote."

"They don't care about us. Just using us as always." Rose tugs the fabric away from Mary. "Let me add some stitches so I can say I did something."

Noemi hands me the list. "What do you think?"

1. *Lynching.*

2. *Selling some folks eggs with cracks in them even though their money's the same color as everybody else's!*

3. **Not letting us follow the path we wish to tread.**

"I think I know who said what," I say, looking at each face in turn. Rose is watching Mrs. Bullis and Mrs. Bread Loaf draw closer as they pass out marigold sashes from a cardboard box. Without even looking at us, they sweep by.

Noemi quickly gets to her feet. "Excuse me, Mrs. Bullis, ma'am."

"Yes?"

"I was just wondering if we could get some of those sashes, too?"

"These are for wearing at the race." Mrs. Bullis sweeps her restless fingers down the length of a sash, petting it as if it were a cat's tail.

"Yes, ma'am. We'll be there."

The petting stops, and Mrs. Bullis cuts her gaze to Mrs. Bread Loaf, who is squeezing the box to her chest as if it might try to run away.

"Mary works on Saturdays," says Mrs. Bullis.

Mary, who is wrapping an embroidery thread around her finger, glances around her and then back down at her lap. "I was hoping you'd let me have a few hours off, ma'am." Mary's voice is whisper soft. "To support the cause, and all."

"I'm sorry, Mary. The cause doesn't need you."

Rose pauses her work on something resembling a potato and rolls the needle between her fingers. I bet she's thinking about which end of the top hat she'd like to stick it to.

Noemi seems to sway on her feet, an oak enduring a wind. "But you just said in your speech that the woman's hour is at hand. Ain't we, that is, aren't we women? And we're about finished with our part. Even wrote some Custom-aries that need releasing, right here." She holds out her list.

Mrs. Bullis's eyes rake over the list and then she blows out a breath that reminds me of Frederick. "These are not women's concerns, they are colored concerns."

"They're not colored concerns, they're human concerns, and women make up half the humans. If we all work together, we can make some real change. Laws that fix the bad smell. Laws that give us rights to keep our property, instead of letting good-for-nothing husbands gamble it away. You want that, don't you?"

Mrs. Bullis's teapot face blows steam. "How dare you! Mary?"

Mary jerks, eyes wide.

Noemi knots her shawl tight over her solid arms and keeps her gaze fixed on Mrs. Bullis's chin. "Mary didn't tell about your situation, Mrs. Bullis. It's well-known, is all."

Mrs. Bullis reels up her nose as high as it will go, eyes searching out a good place to cast her hook. "You'll have to wait your turn, *all* of you"—she glares at me—"just like we did. Your men got the vote, but most sold it for drinking money. Now it's our turn."

The room has gone silent. You would probably hear the drop of a needle if one were to fall. On the other side of the room, Lizzie's face is stretched long, though Mrs. English is staring through the ceiling, maybe wondering why she is here and not home soaking her feet.

Noemi rocks from side to side, but when she speaks, her voice is even as steel tracks. "If any did sell their votes, they likely did so only because they thought it made no difference how they cast them. A greased pig isn't worth much if you can't hold on to it long enough to make bacon."

"I don't know what you're talking about, and you're verging on impertinence."

Noemi takes her time filling her lungs, her lowered gaze taking in all the eyes cooling on her. "Ma'am, what I'm saying is, we got plenty of good women waiting to cast our ballots and make things right again for everyone. And we're going to keep pulling for ballots, whether you let us or not."

A collective gasp sweeps through the room, and then whispers start up.

Mrs. Bullis's marigold sash whips through the air, a jag of lightning. "I think it's time you leave. You, too, Mary. Go back home and work on the curtains like I asked."

Mary's head is bowed, exposing the bumps of her neck bones.

"Mary, do you hear me?"

Rose bites off thread with her teeth and mutters, "She hears you." She squints hard enough to tangle her lashes, and it's as if she were trying to keep her vexation from seeping out her eyes.

Mary unbends her neck, and I'm reminded of a bird unfolding. She gathers her gray skirts and rises. "I don't want to do the curtains right now, Mrs. Bullis."

"Don't want to do . . . ," Mrs. Bullis echoes, looking wildly around her as if she could be the butt of a joke. "Well, then you . . ." Her eyes fall upon the embroidered half-horse, and she sucks in her sentence. A good seamstress can be hard to find. Especially with so many vultures waiting to swoop in. "All of you, go. Just go!"

Noemi's nostrils flare, and I would not be surprised to see smoke curling out of them. She snatches her list back from Mrs.

Bullis. With her head held not too high, nor too low, she crosses to the exit.

We file behind her, each passing over a creaky floorboard. The shame that warms my cheeks feels more diffuse than it did at age thirteen, and I gather it in my hands and set it in a corner. Maybe self-worth is something we grow into day by day, the way a spine elongates and calcifies. Hammer Foot once said that people don't lack strength, they lack the will. As I follow Noemi and her friends out the door of the Grace Baptist Church, I muse he wasn't talking about these ladies, whose iron wills may not shine, but do ring when hammered.

THE STREETLAMPS FLICKER as we pass by, and a three-quarter moon keeps its eye on us. Rose slips an arm around Mary, who sways a little on her feet. "Well, that was a bust. I didn't even get to finish my stitches."

"Just what were you stitching anyway?" asks Noemi. "A squirrel?"

"Nope." Rose throws a grin back at us.

"A pinecone?" I offer, but she shakes her head.

"Oh no, Rose, you didn't," says Mary.

"I did. They deserve a few patty cakes. Maybe next time, they'll think twice about giving us the back end of the horse."

The night is cool but not cold. Water droplets hang in the air, blowing wet kisses at our cheeks as we walk.

"We should form our own society," Noemi says quietly from beside me.

Rose snorts. "Please, Noemi. Not until I've had a hot bath."

A voice calls after us. "Jo! Wait, Jo?"

We all look around. Lizzie waves.

"You go on," I tell the others. By the time slow-footed Lizzie catches up, they could be home in bed. "I'm just around the corner."

"See you in the kitchen tomorrow." With a wink, Noemi leads the others off.

By the time Lizzie catches up, the women are no more than ripples against the screen of night. "I didn't expect to see you here," she drawls.

"Nor I you."

She throws back a tuft of hair, but it returns, like a terrier wanting to play fetch. "What happened back there was just so"—she wiggles her gloved fingers—"unseemly. I didn't want to be a suffragist, but Mrs. English said it's the right thing to do, and plus it's good for business."

"She's right on both counts."

"Yes, well, Mother wasn't happy. She says politics are too difficult for women to understand and that we should trust the men. She's not a fan of Miss Sweetie."

I feign interest in a passing carriage.

"Not like me." Her blue eyes watch me with an unexpected intensity, and my skin tingles. "I *know*, Jo." She brings her face close enough for me to notice a thin white scar above her eyebrow.

I hardly breathe. "You know what?"

"*You* are Miss Sweetie."

Thirty

Something smug sits back on Lizzie's face.

Did Nathan tell her? I lick my lips, which have suddenly gone dry. "Why would you think I'm Miss Sweetie?"

"You lost your job and then suddenly you're working at the *Focus* the same time as her columns start showing up. Remember that letter from Hatless in Atlanta, asking how to stretch a tight hat? I wrote that letter. I didn't expect you to write back. Steam the inner ribbon, you said. I forgot that you had taught me that trick at English's." She hoists a wide grin like a trophy.

"Oh." My kneecaps bobble. She could unmask me. The *Focus* would lose its credibility, and all the work Miss Sweetie has done will slip loose, like poorly tied knots. "You won't tell, will you? I could get into real trouble if anyone finds out."

"Shoo, why would you say that? We're friends, aren't we?"

"Er, friends, yes. Thank you, Lizzie. I appreciate it. You should get back to the meeting. Mrs. English will be wondering where you're off to."

"No, she won't. She sent me after you to ask you about those knots."

"Please tell her she can order them exclusively through Buxbaum's."

Before reaching the abandoned barn, I conceal myself between a pair of trees, tempted to detour toward the Bells'. However, as far as I can tell, "The Custom-ary" has done its job raising interest and not pitchforks. Surely subscriptions will follow. If I visited Nathan, it would be for personal reasons, and there should be nothing more personal between us.

A rustle in the grass freezes me in place. I strain to see into the field of weeds and brush that stretches out to the street fifty yards behind me. But anything more than a few paces away has been tarred in night. I should've paid more attention, instead of walking so deep in my thoughts.

Crickets chirp, and the breeze hisses, but the sound doesn't come again.

Get ahold of yourself. It's probably just a snake or a rabbit.

With my heart beating a drum in my head, I scamper to the barn.

Even when I'm back safe in my burrows, it is hard to rub the chill from my skin.

WHEN I ENTER the kitchen the next morning, Noemi is hunched over the counter, reading a newspaper to Etta Rae.

"Good morning," I say.

Etta Rae claps me on the shoulder with one of her rug-beater arms. "Morning, Jo."

Noemi straightens. "Good, you're here. There's trouble afoot, and it ain't wearing shoes."

"Is it walking toward us?" Perhaps Caroline has confronted Mrs. Payne with the rumor of her illegitimacy. If so, Mrs. Payne will need to stamp out that fire before the good Payne name goes up in smoke.

"Let's hope not. It all started with Miss Sweetie's article 'The Singular Question.' You seen it?"

"Yes, I've read it."

Etta Rae folds the newspaper and sets it in the letter basket she usually delivers to Mrs. Payne every morning. "I never saw the good in catching a husband, myself. Why would I want another job waiting for me back at home?" She ties on a bonnet. "The chickens are waiting for me. Mind you walk soft today and don't bother Mrs. Payne. She's in one of her melancholies." Out the door she goes.

Noemi takes up a narrow knife and, with smooth strokes of her wrist, slices the meat from a freshly severed lamb shank. "They in a fit over Merritt's broken engagement. Mr. Payne didn't go to the mills today, and seems no one here can talk without slamming a door. According to Solomon, Mr. Payne paid the *Focus* a visit yesterday and demanded they expose Miss Sweetie."

I sag against the counter, not trusting my legs to support me. "What did they say?"

"They showed him the door. Then today, this shows up." She pulls out the newspaper she'd been reading to Etta Rae. It's the *Constitution*, with its distinctively wide pages and dense columns. The leftmost article grabs my attention.

MISS SWEETIE, AGONY AUNT
OR ANT-AGONIST?

Atlanta has been beside herself to discover the identity of the rabble-rouser, whose biweekly column in the Focus has aroused many a heated discussion in our peaceful city. While a few welcome the controversies, many wonder if the Miss Sweetie column is a ploy for attention by a newspaper many consider "too loosely wrapped."

My thumbnail dents the page. Whoever wrote this clearly has not seen my letters of admiration. Where false light falls, a monster grows.

Perhaps those who know Miss Sweetie's identity would do our fair city a favor to expose her for the troublemaker she is.

"You okay? You look a little pale."

I refold the paper and set it back into the basket. "I'm fine." Of all the weeks to stop eavesdropping.

Merritt's breakup must really have put a stone on Mr. Payne's tracks. If he wants to shut down the *Focus*, all he need do is cut off its paper supply. By orchestrating a witch hunt, he exacts a little humiliation to boot. He can't know the kind of public scorn they would face if the truth were known: that a Chinese girl had duped everyone. But of course that won't happen. It can't. Only Lizzie Crump knows the truth, and while she might be slow in the foot and frivolous, she is not cruel.

I fetch a mug. Miss Sweetie will not be intimidated, not after she's come this far. The *Focus* has nearly reached two thousand subscriptions, and once the sponsors see the newspaper's success, surely alternative paper sources could be found.

"You waiting for me to put change in there?" Noemi eyes the empty mug I'm strangling.

I set down the mug and pour the coffee, hoping she does not see the way my hands shake. "That Miss Sweetie's sure stirring up trouble." For herself and everyone around her.

Noemi scrapes away the silver skin encasing her meat. "I like her. In fact, I'm fixing to write her my own letter about those suffragists. We got the same working parts as those other women, but their hate's more important than getting the vote." With a flick of her wrist, Noemi chucks the tough skin into the slop bucket. "Course, that Miss Sweetie is white and probably wouldn't answer me."

"Even if she doesn't write back, I bet she'd agree with you."

"You think?"

"Yes, I do."

I CARRY MY tray up to Caroline's room, noticing the door to Mrs. Payne's study is closed. She rarely closes the door. It is the melancholy at work, no doubt.

Caroline's vanity is back in its corner, but she's staring out her window when I enter her chambers. I wonder if trouble looks less scary when glimpsed through a pane of glass. "Are you well, miss?"

She doesn't answer, but her gaze drops from the window to the floor. There's a restlessness to the way she moves, and the dimple in her cheek seems to have changed overnight into a permanent pinch.

After setting her tray before her, I straighten her bedsheets, having my own frown lines to mind.

"How does it feel to be a nobody?" She taps at the shell of her soft-boiled egg.

My temper flares. "How does it feel to be an overstuffed porcupine?" The words fall before I can catch them. It occurs to me that with Mr. Q out of the picture, I no longer have leverage to demand reasonable treatment. The good news is, I'm pretty sure our agreement made no difference in how Caroline treated me, anyway.

"I don't know why I put up with an ill-bred hussy like yourself," she snaps, though her words lack the heat of true indignation. Sighing, she sets down her spoon. "If the rumor is true, Mama and I might have to move to the country. Perhaps it will be nice to live in anonymity. I won't have to pretend I like anyone, and I can go about as I please. Grandpapa has many horses." Her eyes follow as I arrange her pillows.

"Most nobodies I know don't have horses."

She scoops a spoonful of egg but, instead of eating it, lets the golden treasure drip back into the shell. "I think I would enjoy the simple life. I might even take up drawing. Or horticulture."

She eyes her potted violet. "I raised that one from a seedling. Almost got the bud to bloom, too."

I crisp the corners of her bedsheets. "Most nobodies I know don't have time for horticulture."

"You are drear."

I shake out a petticoat she has left on the floor. "Most nobodies I know are drear."

Her mouth buckles, and then she aims her gaze out the window again. "Would you come with me?"

She holds herself very still, and a cloud draws a shadow on her face.

The memory of how the kittens destroyed her mother's study scratches at me, and my laugh sounds bitter. "You despise me, don't you remember?"

"I despise everyone."

"Why?"

She snorts. "Who knows? I wanted her to myself."

Mrs. Payne left when Caroline was two, too young for her to remember, but maybe the heart remembers what the mind is too young to grasp. Perhaps that is why Caroline hates Noemi so much. Her mammy's own child took priority. But me? I was just a poor orphan to whom Mrs. Payne was occasionally kind. Maybe in her young mind, Caroline considered every nod to someone else a snub to herself.

"Old Gin believes I should take a husband."

"Marriage? But who would marry *you*?"

I bristle. "Someone with exquisite taste, obviously."

"I *mean*, there are no Chinese in Atlanta."

"There are some in Augusta."

"Ugh, no, not those commoners."

Plumping one of her overstuffed pillows, I toss it against the carved headboard, where it makes a satisfying *oomph!* like a gut being punched. "We have a saying. The superior man thinks of virtue, the common man, comfort."

She trills her fingers at me. "Virtue is overrated. Papa worked hard for every dime we have, and says that we . . ." Abruptly, she turns from me and stares out the window again. I can't help wondering if she just remembered her father might not be the man she thinks. "He says that we deserve to live in comfort," she finishes softly. "Take the tray. I'm no longer hungry."

She folds her hands in her lap. With her shoulders rounding forward and her dressing gown wrinkled about her, she reminds me of one of the crumpled newspapers in Etta Rae's basket. I curse myself for feeling pity for her and slide the tray off her table.

Even before I get to the stairs, Mr. Payne's booming voice is making the pictures rattle against the wall. I pull in my stomach and descend. His voice suggests the kind of man who fills the doorframe, the sort with a jaw that could bite through a steel bit or a brow that juts like an overhanging brick. But the truth is, he is nothing remarkable to behold.

I peer through the leaves of a philodendron plant that manages to thrive despite the smoke on this floor. Mr. Payne carries his medium frame with a light clip, pacing as far as the telephone will allow. His head might be hard, but there's a definite sag in his jaw, a melding together of chin and neck like a turkey gullet. A center part splits his dark blond hair into two even shares, slicked against his head with his signature ylang-ylang hair oil.

"Merritt *is* of the highest caliber, that duplicitous Bostonian wench." He pauses as the other person speaks.

"I tell you, it's a conspiracy and it's only going to get worse. Mark my words, that Miss Sweetie is a Yankee sent to infiltrate our ranks. When I smoke out the witch—and I *will* smoke her out—we'll see how loud those Bells ring." His eyes, brown as the butt of a rifle, are suddenly looking at me.

Thirty-One

I step out from behind the philodendron, which feels as paltry as a fig leaf. The muscles of the businessman's face shift ever so slightly as his attention abandons the speaker.

With the breakfast tray dug into my ribs, I stumble out from behind the plant. But instead of making tracks away, someone has poured iron in my boots. Mr. Payne's chin swings to one side, pulling the gullet with it. His gaze rummages my person, one eye squinting more than the other, as if that were the one he uses to judge the world. "Gilford, I will ring you later." He sets the receiver back on its cradle. "Come closer, girl," he orders in the kind of commanding voice that could part the sea. "Set that down. Jo, isn't it?"

"Yes, sir." I rest the tray on a side table and then pick my way across a carpeted runner, stopping when I am two paces away. The cherry scent of a cigar recently smoked perfumes the air, and paintings of long-dead relatives grimace at me.

"How old are you?"

I pinch the sides of my maid's dress, my gaze fixed on his gullet. "Seventeen, sir."

His scrutiny grows heavier, and my breath shorter. I try not to stare at the flesh curtain of his throat. He knows I know something about Miss Sweetie. He can sense it. Maybe the intuition that makes him Atlanta's paper king has heard the panicked flapping of truth, ready to spring from my mouth like a quail from the bush.

"Old Gin tells me he has educated you. And that you like reading newspapers."

I swallow hard. "I—I—"

"Speak up, girl."

I force myself to breathe. "I like to be informed. P. T. Barnum said, 'He who is without a newspaper is cut off from his species.'"

"P. T. might've been a politician, but he was a circus man at heart. I am fond of newspapers myself, but lately, I have found they are full of drivel. Sensationalist slush more likely to raise blood pressure than understanding."

"Yes, sir," I squeak, hoping he will excuse me now.

"Tell me, are you familiar with this Dear Miss Sweetie column?" His voice dribbles with disgust at the name.

"Yes, sir."

"And what do you think of her column 'The Singular Question'?"

"My opinion is of no consequence."

"Nonsense. You are a young woman who reads newspapers, the quarry for whom this woman has sprung her traps. Do you feel this article emboldens women to reject marriage in pursuit of their own interests?"

Here it is. My chance to confess. If I take responsibility, perhaps he'll overlook his grievance with the *Focus* and things can return to the way they were before Miss Sweetie arrived on the page.

My toes curl in my boots, trying to keep myself planted, but the world has begun to spin too fast. Visions of our local jail, with its stone walls that constantly echo the wails from within, grip me with terror. "I think . . ."

He stretches his chin up, his eyes zeroed in on mine.

"I have known your daughter for a long time. She has always been spirited. One day, she shall make a fine wife."

The man's face lights up in a way that should assure Caroline that, even if the rumors of her being illegitimate are true, her father will never deny her.

"Yes, she is my greatest treasure."

"As daughters should be. However, if she finds that no man is worthy of her, would you force her to marry someone anyway?"

"Of course not. But she should be encouraged to keep looking."

"As Old Gin likes to say, not all horses are meant to race, but all horses are meant to run. If Caroline is happy, are you not happy for her? As you know, she cares little for the diversions of other women. She's bright and well-versed in the business of Payne Mills. If she were allowed to do something productive and meaningful there, her temper might be much improved."

I clamp my mouth shut. But my words have already galloped off, and there is no calling them back. I wait for the man to reprimand me for insulting his daughter, but his eyes have lost focus and he is rubbing his shoulder. Perhaps he is imagining his daughter accompanying him to work.

"Miss Sweetie's words are not meant solely for young women like Caroline, but their fathers, mothers, brothers, and anyone who desires for them a happy, useful life."

He makes a guttural noise, probably the prelude to a spouting-off, but then his attention catches on something behind me. "Princess, you're up early."

Caroline steps out from behind the traitorous philodendron, likely placed there to catch eavesdroppers like us. "Good morning, Papa," she says, letting him kiss her cheek.

She casts me a look that is half confusion and half surprise, sugared by wonder. Then she refocuses on her father, clearing his throat with loud rumbles. Maybe he is wondering how much Caroline overheard. Maybe *she* is puzzling out what she missed. I scoop up the tray.

I pick my way down the stairs, hoping I have cleared the path of a few boulders.

For the afternoon ride, Caroline wants to ride solo again, but this time I doubt the cemetery is her destination.

Sweet Potato and I draw up to Six Paces. A familiar horse screams. Not far from the abandoned hansom, Merritt's muscular frame draws a striking figure, impeccably draped in a blue riding coat, his midsize hat dignifying his sweep of brown-blond curls. I edge my mare away, but it is too late.

When he spots us, a rakish grin bends the perfect line of Merritt's mustache. "Hullo, Jo!" He trots Ameer up to us.

"I am glad to see you in good spirits, sir."

"Never been better. Ever since the news broke of my, er, status, I've received, so far, four invitations to Mama's horse race. It's curious how things work out."

It doesn't surprise me. He has always been one of the most eligible bachelors this side of the Mason-Dixon Line. Jane Bentley is a distant memory.

"I rather like being a coquet. It's a good life you ladies have. I don't know why those suffragists are so hell-bent on being men."

Miss Sweetie bristles. "They don't want to be men, only to be allowed to have a say. God wouldn't have given us feet if He didn't want us to walk. By the same token, why give us a brain if He didn't want us to have thoughts?"

He paces Ameer in front of us, his eyes roving my figure. I'm suddenly all too aware of the form-fitting nature of my riding breeches and turn Sweet Potato to block the view.

He laughs. "I'm merely admiring your . . . thoughts."

"The thoughts happen higher up." A warning bell clangs in my head. The most powerful piece in Chinese chess, the chariot, goes where it wants, felling anything in its path, while I am a lowly disposable soldier. Merritt and I might've been friends once, but now that we are older, lines must be drawn. Miss Sweetie would insist on it. "I'm sorry, sir, but your family is my employer. I must be on my way."

Something wistful passes over his face. "Can we not be friends?"

"No, I'm afraid not." My mare ferries us off, and this time, I do not look back.

Thirty-Two

Dear Miss Sweetie,
   An admirer caught me staring at him. Of course,
I quickly looked away, but I am certain he now thinks
I'm a hussy. I want to die of shame.

                    Mortified,
                    Fannie Smith
                    (please don't use my real name)

Dear Mortified,
   An anxious mind makes lions of tumbleweeds. Live
in the present, not in the future.

                    Yours truly,
                    Miss Sweetie

The printer whirs and thrums next to my ear. I am back to listening in on the Bells, if only to assure myself they are still in business.

Old Gin is spending tonight again at the Paynes'. I finish tying a knot from the spools of cord Mr. Buxbaum sent through Noemi.

The printer stops and the soothing tones of Mrs. Bell's voice tumble down, too distant to hear. Nathan's voice follows. "Let him try to shut us down." His voice grips the words. "The more he blows, the weaker his son looks."

"Not if the *Constitution* turns this into a witch hunt for Miss Sweetie. *I* could claim responsibility. It would make sense that the publisher's wife is Miss Sweetie. Probably no one would care after that."

"Exactly. People would stop caring." Something bumps the desk, maybe Nathan's fist. "As much as people want to know who she is, her anonymity is part of her allure. She could be anyone, a sister, a friend, a neighbor. It's what makes her relatable."

"What will your father say?"

"No doubt he'll have a fit. 'Revolution is best taken by the teaspoon, not the glass.'"

I replug the listening tube. The idea that I have created discord in the Bell household stirs an itchy restlessness in me. My socks catch against the uneven concrete floor as I trek to Old Gin's room.

The silk lies in a neatly folded pile. He finished it. My fingers glide over the thick cloth, pausing on the chrysanthemums woven into the silk in gold thread. I lift out the garment. To my surprise, it falls into two pieces. I hold up a long-sleeved blouse, which is more of a jacket that fastens down the middle, and a pair of close-fitting pants that taper at the ankle. Strange.

Stripping down to my cotton underclothes, I step into Old Gin's creation. My feet just fit through the tapered openings, and I cinch the waist tight. The jacket hangs looser. Five button-and-loop closures down the middle resemble gold frogs. Old Gin's knot-tying surpasses even mine.

I consider my outfit. With a cap and from the back, I might pass for Johnny Fortune in riding silks. I strut with my nose in the air, like a puffed-up jock.

Now, who would marry a woman wearing such a peculiar getup?

I freeze so fast, my socks nearly slip out from under me.

Old Gin and I stand the same height, though he bests me in girth by an inch or two.

The outfit is not for me.

The words on the Paynes' flyer parade through my head . . . *Mr. and Mrs. Winston Payne invite all Atlantans to attend an eight-furlong race at Piedmont Park Racetrack, a purse of $300 to be awarded to the winner.*

Three hundred dollars is the same amount Shang owed Billy Riggs.

Coincidence? Coincidence is just destiny unfolding.

Old Gin is planning to run in Mrs. Payne's horse race.

Perhaps that is why Sweet Potato knows her way to the track. It occurs to me that Old Gin's birdlike appetite may not have been due to sickness after all, but discipline. The less weight for Sweet Potato to carry, the faster she will be. I peel off the deceptive outfit, and the glossy weave of the silk catches on a hangnail. I suck on my finger. Even the most beautiful of fabrics has a traitorous side, and so, it seems, does Old Gin.

I OVERSLEEP, OWING to a restless night, and half walk, half jog down Peachtree, frozen hands stuck under my arms. At least the nippy air clears my foggy head. My two fishtail braids whip my backside with every hurried step.

Sixty-year-old men have no business racing horses. Old Gin's knees creak and his back seizes up when the weather is too damp. Not to mention, months of hacking must have crumpled his lungs into paper sacks. A horse race could kill him. Each beast is a thousand-and-a-half-pound engine of muscle and flesh, all stampeding down the same narrow corridor.

I shiver, and not just from the chill. It's cracked.

Preposterous.

Unthinkable.

Yet here I am, still thinking about it.

If anyone knows how to ride a horse, it's Old Gin. Johnny Fortune might be as steady as a bird on a fence, but Old Gin is a bird on a clothesline. He has a natural equine understanding that transcends any learned skill. In fact, it was his ability to calm a steed that had gone wild in the middle of a Shanghai marketplace that caught the eye of a wealthy American businessman. When Winston Payne offered him a job in America, Old Gin, not so old then, accepted.

And Sweet Potato is in her prime. Light on her feet with a competitive spirit. She could get the job done.

Twenty minutes later, the trim lawn of the Payne Estate spreads before me. The paved driveway, the crab apple trees, and the white columns—none appear any different from previous days. Still, the scene appears too orderly, the edges too crisp, the colors too sharp. Or perhaps it simply looks that way in contrast to the messiness of my own thoughts.

Though I am already a quarter of an hour late, I bypass the kitchen and hurry to the stables.

Half the horses are gone, including Sweet Potato, and there is no sign of Old Gin or Mr. Crycks. A stable boy mucks out the stalls, while Solomon scours the rust off a section of an old wheel. I had once thought Solomon a giant, but the years seem to have hollowed out the Paynes' all-around man, who is nearly as old as Old Gin. He looks up from his work, and his neck bones crack. "Why hello, Jo. Looking for Old Gin?"

"Hello, Solomon, yes. Have you seen him?"

"He and Mr. Crycks took some of the horses for exercises. Probably be back in an hour or two. Something the matter?" He rubs a handkerchief over his red-brown skin.

"No, er, it can wait. If you see him, will you let him know I need to speak with him?"

"Sure thing."

Noemi's watering her vegetable garden with rinse water when I return to the house. On her apron strap, she's tied a cluster of bluebells. "Nice of you to show up."

"I overslept. Nice flowers."

"I'm starting my own suffrage society. The Atlanta Bluebells, for the belles of a different color."

"It's a good name. Do you know where Mrs. Payne is?"

"Upstairs in her study, I think. Everything okay?"

"Yes."

I hurry into the kitchen and hastily assemble Caroline's tray. Both the cream and the coffee slosh over the sides of their vessels as I carry the tray upstairs.

Caroline is calculating some figures on her writing table when I set the tray beside her. "Good morning. Excuse me for a moment."

"Excuse you? You just got here."

I ignore her and slip down the hallway. The door to Mrs. Payne's office is like a raised hand, warning me away. She will not like my impertinence. But she alone chose the contestants.

I knock. When no one answers, I knock again.

"Come in," she says, and not in her usual pleasant voice.

Mrs. Payne sits at her desk, writing in her Lady's Planner. I assume it's where she records her deepest feelings, as she never leaves it in plain sight. Maybe she hides it in a boot the way we do our savings. You can tell a lot about what someone values by what they hide.

"Jo, I asked not to be disturbed. Whatever is the matter?"

"I'm sorry, ma'am." My prepared words all fly out of my head. I blurt out, "Is Old Gin racing Sweet Potato in your horse race?"

"Well, yes."

"But why?"

"Because he asked me." She sets down her pen and gets to her feet. Her shawl lies across another chair, and she ties it over her wrinkled housedress.

"He'll be ridiculed. And his sponsor will not be happy.

They'll complain, and you'll probably have to refund their bid. It might cause a scandal. Not to mention, he's sixty!"

"I have thought of those things, of course. There will be no gambling odds on him, as the odds are written for twelve players. The suffragists will be matched to Sweet Potato. They are fortunate to be in the race and won't complain."

So much for a random draw. "Actually, I have met their president, and she is not exactly a shrinking violet."

"I don't require advice on this matter. Old Gin is a grown man. You should respect his decision." There's a warning in her tone. Her black slippers peek out from her dress hem, two arrows pointing to the exit. She crosses her arms, drawing an X over her center.

My eyes fall to her planner, still open on the desk beside us. She seems to be writing a letter of some sort. At the bottom, she has signed it with a loop. A lowercase *e*.

An *e* for Emma.

Mrs. Payne's eyebrows clothespin together, and noticing my interest in her planner, she reaches over and closes the book.

But it is too late. I have already seen.

My mind churns like a loom, drawing threads, weaving connections, finding patterns. "You wrote the letter."

Her face twists in confusion.

"You asked him to forgive you."

She begins to say something but swallows it back down. "You—you've seen this letter?"

"Yes. You wrote his name in Chinese. Shang."

I watch the way hearing the name tears at her face, causes

the delicate planes to tremble. She covers her mouth. Her wedding band draws my eye, a worry bead for her adultery.

Mr. Q was right. She had an illegitimate daughter.

But it was not Caroline.

My head begins to swim, and my knees give way, but Mrs. Payne collapses on the floor, one step ahead of me.

Thirty-Three

The sharp odor of smelling salts rouses me from my deadened state. Etta Rae helps me into a seated position on the floor of the study. "Wh-what happened?"

"You fainted. Both of you did. You were only out for a few minutes. How are you feeling?"

My head throbs, but nothing feels broken. On the outside, at least. Mrs. Payne comes into view, propped up a few feet away with her back against the desk, her hair slipped from its knot. "I'll be okay," I say, not bothering to hide my anger.

Mrs. Payne lifts her gaze to meet mine, but the effort is too great. "It was for the best," she whispers hoarsely. The similarities are undeniable. Our bony fingers, our bumpy shoulders, even our widow's peaks, and the pearl at the center of our upper lips. Apparently, we even faint alike. More pieces tumble together: her yearlong melancholic spell, during which she left to live with her parents in Savannah; the story about the filly she was forced to give up, the one she named Savannah Joy. Jo is a bastardization of Joy. A bastard, like me.

Shakily, I rise, despite Etta Rae's protests. It's not clear to me why the woman's here, only that Etta Rae has always been here. Her lips purse, and a prick of regret dulls her light brown eyes.

Mrs. Payne still doesn't look at me. I sway, pummeled by emotions that leave me breathless. Anger, hurt, shame, each takes its turn on me, bruising me deep in my core. The truth is worse than I imagined. In all my years here, she has been watching me grow with no more regard than for a thickening meadow. Each glance was a denial; every word, a rejection. Her gaze skitters over my pebbled-goat-leather boots, perhaps noticing for the first time how my toes have stretched them to the breaking point.

My mother didn't leave me. She abandoned me. Women like her do not, cannot form affinities with people like me, not if they wish to remain on the top branch. They are knots that slip out easily with the barest of tugs.

Etta Rae pulls over a chair and helps Mrs. Payne into it. Caroline bursts into the study. "Maid, you forgot the utensils. What's going on here? Mama, you look like you've seen a ghost!"

No one answers. Caroline glares at the housekeeper, as if prodding her to explain, but Etta Rae's lips remain closed. Caroline blows out a frustrated breath.

When four winds meet, there is only silence.

Mrs. Payne's eyes plead with me to understand. And though I know well the fences that corral us into our designated squares, I also know there are the chains we are born into, and those we choose to wear.

I take off my apron and set it on Mrs. Payne's desk.

"No." Caroline snatches it back and pushes it toward me,

but when I don't take it, she drops it and grabs my arms. "Don't go. What did you do, Jo? Why is Mama crying?"

Etta Rae glances at Mrs. Payne, who gives her the barest nod. "Let your sister go, child," says Etta Rae.

She knew, too. Shame takes another jab at me. Who else? Has the world conspired against me?

"My sis—" A soft gasp releases from Caroline's mouth. "Oh my God." She gapes, searching my face for the truth, but the truth is in the details we both missed while she was gazing in the mirror and I was looking away.

I descend the staircase for what I know will be the last time. A sob builds in my chest, but I bar it from leaving. Dignity can only be surrendered, and when it is gone, we are like the snail who has lost its shell. All it can do is find the nearest leaf and hope it's not parade day. At least the snail never need care who its parents are.

The front door fights me, and the paved stones of the driveway scheme to trip my feet. The jangle of an approaching carriage pulls my attention. A vehicle painted a distinctive cabbage green with gold lettering sets off an alarm bell in my head. I conceal myself in the shade of a magnolia, watching the carriage swing into the Paynes' driveway. What would Crump's Paints be doing in this neighborhood? The Paynes do not buy discount paints, even if their house needed a touch-up, which it does not.

The passenger pushes aside her curtain, and I catch sight of her heavy-lidded eyes, her thin nose, and the withered rind of her mouth. Something icy chills my stomach.

Mrs. Crump is here because of me. I recall the way the woman looked at me when Nathan suggested Lizzie find another escort, as if I were to blame. Lizzie must have told her my secret, and now she is here to expose me, the troublemaker. She does not know I have nothing to lose now.

If only the same could be said of the *Focus*.

I hurry away, barely noticing Sully's streetcar until it is rolling briskly past me with *clangs* that make my ears ring. The ever-present reek of sewage strangles the scent of the magnolias and overwhelms my sinuses. Too much morning light pours into my eyes. Yet Peachtree rolls along as always, heedless of the pain coursing down its veins.

My thoughts race. Leading the pack is the question of how my parents met. Old Gin said Shang was a groom, too. Maybe he'd even worked at the Payne Estate. Did Shang know about the baby he left behind? I imagine the man, two hands taller than me but not much wider, a shadowy figure shaking dice in his loose fist, a maverick who desired more than his earthly allotment. A bitter fluid burns my throat, and tears fill my eyes. I grip my damask bag to me like it is the only thing that might keep me anchored to this world.

And what about Mr. Payne? How did she hide a pregnancy from her husband? A deep-enough pocket can hide many things, and just as her husband is ruthless, Mrs. Payne is shrewd. And sometimes the eye sees what it wants and skips over what is in plain sight. Mr. Payne had the biggest house on Peachtree Street, the most successful mill in Atlanta, the belle of the ball for a wife, a son, *and* a daughter. Why fix what was not broken?

So many questions. So many lies.

A crow squawks from somewhere nearby, but I hardly hear it. Old Gin knew, that's for certain. Lucky Yip's urn almost dances before me, a child's lie compared to this whopper. Why else would Mrs. Payne allow him, a lowly and aging servant, to ride in her race? Guilt. Was he ever going to tell me? There are many arrows of blame in my bow, and without the proper targets, many are pointed at him. All my life, Old Gin knew exactly who I was. He lied to me for seventeen years, even when I was desperate to know who left me on his doorstep. I hear myself whimper and wonder if I am collapsing into myself.

Bile rises again in my throat, and I force it back down.

Instead of going home, I steer my rudder toward Whitehall. It is still early enough that most shops haven't opened, though the cloth-covered food stalls by Union Station have begun unfolding—one row of white sellers and another row of colored farther down. With few pedestrians out and a sky as clear as glass, there's a crystalline quality about the city that I feel like shattering with a kick of my heel.

When I was seven, Robby's mother, a washerwoman, built a contraption for spinning the water out of laundry using a barrel with a crank. Once, I tried stopping the barrel with my hand—it was going too fast for my eyes to track—and got a scolding that burned more than the raspberry on my palm. "You got no business trying to stop this. Run along and do the things you supposed to be doing."

Maybe the world is like that spinner, and I should stop touching it so much and let it spin.

Buxbaum's brick façade and long display windows stretch before me, its neat appearance somehow anchoring the chaos in my head. Before entering the shop, I attempt to breathe away some of my anger.

Even the sight of Robby folding a bolt of cloth at the far wall only cheers me a little. He is filling in again, which must be a good sign.

"Don't tell me you finished those knots already," he says.

I nod, not trusting my voice. I set down my damask bag, containing a hundred knots, on the waist-high table where Robby has been cutting fabric. "I no longer work for the Paynes," I spill.

His eyes soften. It's funny how one glance of sympathy can trigger an avalanche of self-pity. I worry my finger into a knot in the oak, refusing to give in to my grief.

"I told you not to stand so close to Noemi."

I can't even smile. When we were children, we would joke with each other not to stand so close—him, because I used to swing my braids around, sometimes clipping him in the face; and me, because he had a gangly phase that put my feet in constant jeopardy.

My face must crumple a little, because his own expression wavers. He smooths a bolt of fabric with his hand and sets it on a shelf. "What happened?"

I reach for my handkerchief, grateful there are few customers around, and then unload my grief.

He leans his forearms against the table as he listens, his thick eyelashes blinking now and then. When I am done, my handkerchief is soaked.

From a cabinet, he pulls out a box of thin paper and places it on the table. "Just got these in. Mr. Buxbaum calls them 'disposables.' They're handkerchiefs you can throw away. Go on, help yourself. They're samples."

The disposables feel rough on my nose, but I am grateful they do the job. I stare at the bolts of fabric. Each color occupies a different shelf. "Where would you shelve me?"

Robby's eyes sharpen, and he straightens his cuffs with quick tugs. "Don't you dare let some self-loathing, chicken-livered blueblood make you doubt yourself. You know where you're from, and I know where you're from, and that ain't a shelf or a country or even a place. Sometimes I forget you're even Chinese."

"I don't." I help myself to another disposable.

"That's 'cause you care too much about what the world says. Listen to those who know you best, and you'll be okay."

"It's hard to do that when the person who knew me best was lying to me this whole time."

"If Old Gin did anything wrong, he was doing it for you." His gaze drifts away. "Does seem strange him repaying that debt now, after all these years. Billy Riggs ain't the sort to let a debt go that long. You should've never gone to see him. He's so crooked, I bet his bones won't even lie flat when he's dead in his coffin."

I half listen as my mind returns to the years toiling at the Payne Estate. It's not so much that I minded the mucking and scraping and serving, but did it have to be for that family? My insides roil at the thought of Merritt's—my *brother's*—constant flirting. He had admired me in a way that was ungodly and immoral. Maybe I had admired him a little, too, damn my mother's cold, unfeeling heart. My stomach bucks, and I am thankful for the small mercy of not having eaten today.

"You look a little green. Here, sit." Robby pulls out a stool. "Bring you water?"

I shake my head, knowing I won't be able to keep anything down. Robby sweeps threads into a pile with his hand. "Sometimes things fall apart so better things can come together," he says gently. "When Noemi was sacked, I thought it was going to break her. She spent the whole weekend pulling lint pills off the blankets. Thought we were going to have to reknit them from the piles she was making just to keep warm at night."

I still can't smile.

"But then Mrs. Payne wants her back. And Noemi tells her she'll come back, but only if that bicycle is five dollars, not eighty." A chuckle floats from his mouth. "My point is, a blessing loves a good disguise. And something tells me the Paynes are a stepping-stone for you, not a destination, just like for that woman of mine. Hello, Mr. Buxbaum."

I didn't even notice the shop owner walking up behind me. Trim and quick, he's the kind of man that could slip into a door before it closed and not get his coattails caught. His eyebrows sit high on his forehead, giving him a look of perpetual frankness, which works in his favor when it comes to doing business.

"Slow morning?" he asks.

"Just cleared out. We had a crowd earlier."

The man frowns, pressing wrinkles into his forehead. I hope he does not attribute the slowness to Robby.

His gaze lands on me. "Miss Kuan, your knots are enchanting, and I think you'll see a nice profit given time." He thumps the worktable with his fingers.

"Thank you," I say simply. The thought of making small talk exhausts me.

"Mrs. English dropped off a special order this morning," says Robby. "Selected the cord, too. Let me fetch it." He glides to the register at the back wall.

"I haven't seen Old Gin around lately. Last time I saw him, he had a nasty cough. Is he over it?"

"Yes. That Pendergrass . . . helped." Billy's steamy bathtub seeps into my mind, and I fight back a grimace.

"Wonderful. You know I stand behind my products." Mr. Buxbaum's tan-and-white Balmorals squeak as he stretches high to straighten something on the shelf. His shoes are shinier than Shang's black-and-white ones. I wonder if Shang bought his here. Buxbaum's is one of the few stores that has always welcomed Chinese.

A nervous sort of energy floods through me. "Mr. Buxbaum, did you ever meet a man named Shang?"

The man squints, and his brow furrows like a wet book.

"I'm not sure what he looked like, but he wore a size nine shoe. I am told he moved on about seventeen years ago."

He gives me a strange look. "Of course I met him."

Robby returns, holding a list in one hand and a box of cord in the other. He hands Mr. Buxbaum the list and is about to speak, but notices that I'm about to fall off my stool.

"Er, you were saying, sir?" I prompt.

Robby measures the cord against a yardstick hammered into the table, then cuts it with precise snips.

"Shang is Old Gin's son."

Robby's scissors stop. The room spins around me, and I put

a hand on the table to steady myself. If Shang is Old Gin's son, that makes Old Gin . . . my grandfather.

"They worked at the Payne Estate together," Mr. Buxbaum continues, staring at the overhead fixture. "Nice young man. Liked practicing his English on me, especially the big words like *glockenspiel*." He beams at me.

I lick my lips. "Glockenspiel?" A G-word.

"It's a German xylophone."

Robby ties up my cord in neat bundles, sneaking me sympathetic looks.

"Once, he asked me to order a few things from China to celebrate the Chinese New Year. Wanted to surprise Old Gin." He ticks off his fingers. "Red melon seeds, joss sticks, dried shrimp, and fireworks."

"Fireworks?" says Robby. "What's that?"

"Pasteboard tubes filled with gunpowder that, when lit, produce colorful sparks. Boom!" Mr. Buxbaum throws back his arms. "Looked like the stars exploding."

Robby grins. "I'd like to see that."

"Course, he spent a day in jail for disturbing the peace, but those of us who caught the show have him to thank for a spectacular night."

More shoppers trickle into the store, drawing Mr. Buxbaum's attention. "Old Gin said he'd left to strike it rich on silver in Montana. Surprised Old Gin didn't tell you that himself." He straightens his cravat and sets off toward the newcomers. "Don't get too tied up in your work, Miss Kuan," he calls back over his shoulder.

"Yes, sir," I manage to croak out.

A customer solicits Robby's help, and he finishes wrapping my cord in paper. "Remember what I said about things coming together."

I gulp down the lump in my throat. "Thank you, Robby."

BY THE TIME I slog home, a reluctant sun has begun to coax life back into the streets. I try to hold on to my anger at Old Gin, but it is as slippery as a fish. All this time, I have had family by my side. Memories of Old Gin flood my mind, the years of patient instruction on discarded newspapers and paper cartons. Old Gin wasn't just teaching me out of duty, but devotion. Why would he not tell me that he was my grandfather? Probably he knew I would ask too many questions, making it harder to keep the secret about my parents.

I slip carefully into the tree entrance and close the door behind me. In the basement, I step out of my boots and pull the pins from my hair, which weighs too heavily on my head. With a piece of chalk, I write the word *glockenspiel* on my wall before I forget it and, for comfort, unplug the listening tube.

Hearing nothing, I move to the stove. While I fill the tinderbox with newspaper, a draft from the barn entrance blows at my face. My pulse begins to trot. It is too early for Old Gin to return.

Someone is here.

Thirty-Four

I drop the kindling, scattering branches on the floor. My eyes rummage the room for our new hand ax, trying to shake off my panic.

If trouble's coming through the barn door, I'm not running to meet it. I hurry down the western corridor to the tree exit and am soon gulping in cold Atlanta air.

But now what?

Scaredy-cat. Perhaps it was an animal. Though no animal I know can open a trapdoor, except perhaps a bear, and I've never seen a bear in Atlanta or anywhere.

Well, I'm not staying in this tree. Branches grab me as I dislodge myself less gracefully than usual, then casually walk toward the street. For the first time, I actually hope to see people. A pair of women with baby strollers shriek when they see me and hurry their strollers away. I must look like a demon spat up from hell, unshod, my hair like a monsoon on my head, and wielding an ax, no less. I would run from me, too.

My teeth chatter. I need to get ahold of myself. Hammer Foot would hate to see me this way—afraid, and worse, stirring up fear in people around me. I quickly twist my hair into a knot, and then tuck the ax under my arm. My socks have grown soggy with dew and make sucking sounds as I walk.

After a few more aimless paces, my fear ebbs away. The basement is our home. I might have lost my job today, not to mention my belief in the steadfast nature of motherly love, but I shall not give up my home without a fight.

I shin around to the barn entrance, the sharp gravel picking up my feet.

Hiding behind a snaggle of pine trees, I watch the abandoned barn for movement. The exterior warns people away with its blackened walls, only half standing, and caved-in roof. A margin of thistle provides a further deterrent, if you don't note the spaces to place your feet. Inside the barn, however, the beams are solid and dry, the rotting wood long ago carted away.

Our interloper was probably a drunk making himself at home inside the horse stall, somehow finding the concealed pull that unlocks the trapdoor. Just because it never happened before doesn't mean it couldn't. If I make profits from the knots, I shall buy a real lock. Maybe one day, a home with a real locking door.

Mustering my courage, I tiptoe to the entrance.

A moan breaks through the hush. Blood spatters the earth, like rubies on dirt.

From the stall with our trapdoor, two skinny legs stick out.

One foot is missing a boot, its flannel-reinforced sole twitching like a half-dead fish.

I rush into the barn. "Old Gin!" I cry.

The trapdoor is open, but he could not climb down into it. I bend over his crumpled form. Blood leaks from his mouth, and red bruises puff out on his face. "Who did this to you?"

"The turtle egg," he spits. "His man caught me on walk home."

"Knucks."

Old Gin nods. He glances at an empty green bottle lying a few feet from his head. "He gave me that."

I set down the ax and pick it up. Pendergrass's Long-Life Elixir.

All feeling drains out of me, except guilt, whose sharp points stab me from all angles. Billy figured out that I double-crossed him. All this over a fifty-cent bottle of barley water. I think back to the day he asked me who the most important person in the world to me is. Now I realize why. I bite back angry tears. "Coward. Beating up an old, defenseless man."

Old Gin grimaces. "Not so defenseless. You should see him."

Despite his words, he is panting, and one eye oozes tears and blood.

"It's my fault. I wanted to know more about Shang. I'm sorry."

His good eye dribbles over me and my ax. "When you go to chop wood, please remember shoes, hm?"

"Where does it hurt?"

"Who says it hurts?"

I hiss in exasperation.

"Rib might be cracked," he concedes. "Maybe a few other things." He clicks his tongue at the tears spilling over my cheeks.

Pull it together! Old Gin needs me. I dash back into our basement to fetch clean water for his thirst and rags for his wounds. With cooled barley tea, I make a compress for his injured eye and then pick debris from his wounds. Fresh tears spill out again when I view the state of his torso. Bruises cover every bit of his skin in even patterns of four, marking each blow of Knucks's brass knuckles. Old Gin has grown so thin, his ribs stick out like a pair of open shutters.

I apply more barley-tea compresses to his bruises, wishing we had pepper. Noemi said pepper solves a lot of problems you don't expect it to, including bruises. He winces as I wash his bloodied knuckles. Perhaps he did manage to inflict some damage.

"Mr. Buxbaum told me about Shang. Why didn't you tell me the truth?"

He sighs, an invisible thing more felt than seen, like water. "Some burdens are too heavy for young shoulders."

"Did he know about me?"

"No. That letter was the last he heard from your mother before she left for Savannah." His voice has dropped to a hush. "I'm sorry for bringing you back. I wished for a bond between sisters, one that could outlast parents."

Caroline's shocked expression materializes before me, lit by the faintest glimmer of understanding. Old Gin's eyes flutter closed.

"Grandfather," I call, feeling the cold finger of fear press against my heart. "Wake up."

He doesn't move. I fetch blankets and pillows. Under a folded blanket tucked in one corner of his room, I discover the Balmorals. He never sold them. They are, after all, one of the few remembrances of his son. I return to his side and arrange the bedding around him. Then I hold his hand, a hand that seems to have grown smaller over the years. A hand that has patiently guided me through life.

With a gray blanket tucked around his body, he looks so frail, like an injured fruit bat. My heart floods with love for Old Gin, who did the work of two people, asking nothing in return. I was so mad at him, when he's the one who changed my diapers and soothed me to sleep. When I caught the influenza, he scared off the devil winds, coaxing the fire within me to life with soup and his own gentle humming. He wanted me to have a sister so that when he was gone, I would still have a family.

My chest begins to hiccup and pull. Not wanting Old Gin to see me cry, I duck back into the basement and collapse onto my bed in a sweaty, grimy heap. I take in huge gulps of air and sob and try to think of a plan. How will I get him back into the basement? Trying to lower him down the metal rungs without injuring him further will be as difficult as climbing down a ladder with a barrel of water. I need to find him medical attention. But how? We don't have money for a doctor, even if I could find one that would treat a Chinese man.

He will die in the abandoned barn, of cold or infection or exposure, when he should be resting on the finest feather mattress, with clean sheets and cooling ice for his bruises. I will need to find his boot. The thought of it lying abandoned and alone in the streets somehow makes me cry even harder.

I mop my face on my quilt. My eyes stick on the word *grievous*, "shockingly cruel or brutal," written when Mrs. Bell told Nathan that the combination of whatever he had thrown on was grievous to her eyes.

Grievous is the word that fits our predicament, but I am not grieving yet. There is work to be done. I will bring a warm brick to Old Gin, and then find help. Creakily, I get to my feet, when another sound freezes me in place.

A *woof.*

Thirty-Five

A giant snowball of fur bounces up to me, and I fall back against the bed. "B-B-Bear?"

Woof! Out rolls the pink herald of her tongue.

"H-how did you—?" My eyes fly to the listening tube. In my haste to leave the basement, I forgot to plug it.

I reach for the wool stopper, but Nathan's voice drifts down to me. "Where is she? Must've gone out the window again. It's that new cat across the street, I bet."

I stuff in the plug before Bear woofs again. She looks from the speaking tube to me, and her ears lift, as if she is waiting for an explanation.

"Oh, Bear," I say, my voice shaking. She puts her head on my lap, and I swear that creature knows exactly what I need. I fling my arms around her, and she doesn't move away until my sob is spent.

"Thank you," I tell her at last. "But I must get help. And Nathan will be worried for you. Come."

Old Gin has not moved an inch. Bear circles him, then sits by his feet, and when I make for the exit, she does not follow.

"Bear, come!" I slap my thigh twice the way I've seen Nathan do.

She looks from me to Old Gin.

"Come!"

This time, she lowers her belly to the ground.

Now what? Well, I can't worry about her right now. I must get help for Old Gin. But from who?

Bear lifts her head, watching me from somewhere under that shag.

No. The Bells can't find out our secret. Old Gin had strict rules, rules meant to keep us safe.

Yet, somehow, I don't think he would mind a change in the rules today.

The Bells' front door is already open when I scramble up the porch steps. Nathan emerges, shrugging on his coat. When he sees me, his face loses all its scowl lines. "Jo? What are you doing here? Is everything all right?"

"My grandfather," I cry as a sob amasses in my throat once more. "Billy Riggs hurt him."

His mother appears behind him, wiping her hands on a dishcloth. "Oh, my dear." She shoulders past him and takes my frozen hands in her slightly damp ones.

"Where is he?" asks Nathan. A lock of hair sticks up from his cowlick like a question mark.

"I will show you."

Back to the abandoned barn we go. If they are worried about its dilapidated appearance, they don't show it, following right on my heels. Bear greets Nathan with a *woof!* and bounds to his side.

"Ah." He pats her head. "There's a good girl."

Mrs. Bell crouches next to Old Gin, her eyes grim. If she feels disgust at the sight of Old Gin's bloodied and battered form, she only tsks her tongue. "We must get Dr. Swift. Nathan—"

"I will be back as soon as I can." Bear and I watch him jog away, her tail motoring back and forth. When Nathan disappears from view, the dog plunks herself again at Old Gin's feet, protecting her injured lamb.

I take Old Gin's hand again, placing myself on the side opposite Mrs. Bell. She still carries her dish towel, and there's a streak of flour on her cheek. "Don't worry, Jo." She knows my name. "Dr. Swift is quite skilled and lives up to his name. He'll have your grandfather fixed in no time." She arranges herself in a more comfortable position, knees tucked under her, the hem of her herringbone skirt picking up the dirt of the barn.

"Could I fetch you something to sit on?"

"No, thank you. But, er, how would you do that?"

She follows my gaze to the open trapdoor. A question lodges itself between her eyes.

I take a deep breath. Then I tell her about our life downstairs. She does not flinch at my recounting or recoil or do any of the things one would expect from someone who has just discovered there are more than rats in her basement. Instead, she sits calmly listening, arms knotted into her marigold shawl.

Old Gin's eye has started to bleed again, and I wring out another barley compress, my own head a strange brew of helplessness, gratefulness, and shame. Now that we are discovered, I can't expect the Bells to lie to their landlords. "I am sorry, ma'am."

Her gaze drifts to Old Gin. "Sometimes, I get dyspepsia and have trouble sleeping. I wander through the house, trying to get my stomach to settle. Many years ago, I swore I'd hear a young girl's voice now and then whenever I'd go into the print shop."

I swallow hard, remembering the nights I'd fallen asleep to the lullaby of the printing press. Maybe I talked in my sleep.

A smile forms on her face. "Mr. Bell told me it was probably the indigestion giving me gas. Have you been hearing . . . us?"

I nod guiltily. "But not all the time. Just sometimes, when I need to."

She presses her hands over her crestfallen expression.

"And only in the print shop," I add hastily. "That's where the abolitionists built the speaking tube."

"Abolition—" The word breaks off. She carefully shifts into a cross-legged position. "I wish I had figured it out earlier. I had seen you and your grandfather a few times before, and thought you must have lived around here. When the solicitor's wife told me about the Chinese girl in the hat shop, well, I was curious about you, but I still couldn't work out why you were so familiar to me."

I wipe my leaky eyes on my palm. She reaches over Old Gin and takes my wet hand in her warm one. "And at last, when Nathan told me you were our Miss Sweetie, I thought, well, of course. That girl is destined to be in our lives."

"So, you're not upset?"

"No." There are tears in her eyes. "I am relieved."

The next half hour passes quickly as I answer Mrs. Bell's questions about how Old Gin and I came to be living under her house. I tell her the truth about my relationship with Mrs. Payne. Now that the worst has happened, there is no reason to hide. Either that or I am too tired to think of one.

The sounds of clopping hooves and grinding wheels hasten toward us. Then a bear-size man with a grizzled beard appears in the doorway, smelling of cigars and swinging a large carpet-bag. He takes one look at Mrs. Bell's and my tear-streaked faces and says, "Hope I'm not too late."

Mrs. Bell pushes herself to her feet. "No, Doctor. But please hurry."

Thirty-Six

From the outside, the Bells' two-story house features cheerful curtains in its white-framed windows. Two potted cypresses stand guard on either side of a stout brown door. I always imagined Mrs. Bell kept her house the way she dressed—plain and neat. But while the house is neat, its contents are like a field of wildflowers to my eyes. Knitted throws in whimsical colors like meadow green and tulip pink drape the couch and two fireside chairs. A bucolic landscape pieced from cheerful feed sacks has been stretched onto a wooded frame and hung on the wall. Braided rugs stitched with a stout needle cause each footfall to feel lovingly supported. There's even a tufted cushion on the floor by the fireplace, perfectly sheepdog-size.

After Dr. Swift patched up the worst of the injuries, including Old Gin's eye, Nathan helped him cart Old Gin to the Bells' front door. We did not find the boot; it was probably already picked up by a street urchin. The men carried Old Gin into a spare bedroom on the first story with a view of the street, and laid him upon a mattress made of ticking with sheets that look freshly ironed.

Dr. Swift rolls his sleeves back down. "Elevate his back. It'll make it easier to breathe with that punctured lung. We must pray that infection does not set in."

I help Mrs. Bell tuck pillows behind Old Gin's back and under his knees. "What about his eye?"

"Keep it clean and be thankful the good Lord gave us two."

My toes grip the floor extra hard. Oh God, please save his eye. A sympathetic noise feathers from Mrs. Bell's mouth.

The doctor takes a bottle of antiseptic from his bag and sets it on a dresser, along with a blue vial. "This tincture will help with the pain, though start small—a teaspoon or two. I never gave it to a yellow man before, but I expect he'll tolerate it like the rest of us. He needs two months of rest and good soup. How's he at chess?"

"Chinese or American, if he loses, it's on purpose," I say weakly.

"Really. Well then, maybe it's time for the old horse to learn a new trick."

Maybe it's the way the last of the sunlight falls when Nathan adjusts the shutters, but despite the news about his eye, I swear a smile ghosts around Old Gin's face. I hope he knows he's in the best of hands. Not quite home, but home just the same.

MRS. BELL GIVES me a rice-root brush and then shows me to a washroom on the first floor. "Take your time. I will prepare dinner." She leaves, and soon I hear the *clang* of a pot meeting a stove.

The washroom matches the size of my basement corner and contains a bin of towels, a basin, and a catching tub, meant for the dribbles from washing and rinsing. Another door conveniently leads to the garden, where used water can be deposited, and an outhouse.

I glance into a looking glass, and my own face scares me, my eyes painfully loud, my mouth chewed up with worry.

Nathan brings two buckets of steaming water, which he sets by the catching tub. He edges past me to the doorway, as if he is suddenly conscious of the close quarters.

"I could fill the tub if you don't mind waiting." He takes in my matted hair, maybe wondering if he'll be boiling water all night.

"This is more than enough. Thank you."

"Jo, I just wanted to say, I'm sorry about your grandfather, but I'm glad you're here. I couldn't stand . . ." He grips the doorframe, and his gray eyes are not sure where to land. "Er, I should let you get on with it." He winces and then closes the door.

My limbs ache, but I make every drop of water count, scrubbing my skin with a washcloth until it turns pink. My discovery this morning seems a lifetime ago. Who knew so many moments could happen in the span of one day? I will need to inform the Paynes of what happened, though the thought of going back blows more smoke on my mood.

Did she ever love me?

I never loved her, only the idea of her. I dreamed of having a mother like Mrs. Payne, someone with a smile in her eyes and a song on her lips. Someone who smelled like summer peaches. What a fool she has played me for these seventeen years. I detest the woman. Maybe even more than Billy Riggs.

I take my anger out on my tangled tresses, washing, rinsing, and detangling until the mass gleams like spilled ink over my shoulders. Then I station myself by Old Gin, watching every rise and fall of his bony chest. Mrs. Bell brings me a bowl of stew to eat while I watch him. It is good stew, with silky bits of potato and carrot, but I can only eat a few bites as my stomach knots with worry.

Mrs. Bell pokes her head back in, and I carry my half-finished bowl out of the room to talk with her. "Thank you, ma'am. I will finish the rest later. You must let me take care of the dishes."

"I won't hear of it. Would you like to borrow one of my Mother Hubbards?"

"That is kind of you, but I need to return to the basement for a few things."

Nathan, carrying a stack of newspapers through the house, stops. "Will you let me accompany you?"

The idea of letting him look into the private corners of my life makes my stomach as jumpy as a hundred dried beans being poured on a pie tin. But all my life, haven't I been the one looking in on him? "I would like that."

After he takes the papers to the burn pile, he returns with a kerosene lamp. I shake my head. It's one thing for the Bells to know about our home in their basement, but I wouldn't like others to find out. "I will lead you."

The night is blacker than usual with no moon to light the way. I slip my hand into Nathan's so as to lead him, grateful to the dark for hiding the wildfire blazing across my face. Together, we move quietly to the abandoned barn, which is easier to negotiate than the Virginia cedar. We climb down the rungs, engulfed by that familiar scent of earth and magnolia roots. When I light the kerosene lamp we keep in the western corridor, his breath shushes out of him. I carry the lamp down the corridor, seeing our quarters as if for the first time with him treading breathlessly beside me. When we reach our living area, my chest puffs with pride over the tidy little home Old Gin and I have built here.

I collect my nightgown and underthings while he roams the room, taking in the stove, the spool table, even crouching to inspect the rug. He crosses to my corner. His incredulous eyes rove from my embroidered curtains, to my small bed, to my wooden-crate nightstand supporting a dictionary and a candle. Then to the G-words, growing both more complex and neater in penmanship the higher up the wall extends. Two words catch his eye. "Giddy goobers," he reads.

I pull the wool stopper from the listening tube. Moving slowly, he lowers himself onto my bed, then puts his ear to the hole. No words drop out. No one is in the print shop. "You must have heard quite a bit growing up."

"Well, yes." I cough, struck with the sudden urge to pull the embroidered curtain around me.

His gaze spreads over the room again, and he presses a fist to his chin. "This is your Avalon."

"Avalon?"

"It's what Bear and I call our secret hideaway, named after King Arthur's magical island. There now, seems you didn't know everything about me." His eyes invite me to laugh.

"Your family taught me so many words. If I had lived under, say, a goat herder, I might never have been Miss Sweetie."

"You do an injury to goats. I heard they recite Shakespeare when no one's watching." He puts a hand to his heart and says grandly, "'To bleat or not to bleat, that is the question.'"

I let out a tiny smile and squeeze my bundle of clothes. "Cud you . . . find it in your heart to forgive me?"

He smiles. "Thanks to Miss Sweetie, my heart may never be the same."

It is hard to read him in the dim light. But of course, these are words of admiration, not love, or why else use Miss Sweetie's name? The sentiment ripens like fruit, fruit from a tree I cannot touch. I ignore how the shadows conspire to pull me closer to him. He draws nearer as well, but cautiously, as if afraid to break anything.

"I would like to get some fresh socks for Old Gin's feet," I announce.

"Er, of course."

Nothing like the word *feet* to break a spell.

He clears his throat. "Tomorrow, I would like to file a police report on Old Gin's assault."

"I—I don't think he would like that."

"Why not?" A frown mars his smooth cheeks.

"Because we do not trust certain things."

His face asks more, but it is difficult to explain a lifetime of wariness. Justice and fairness are for other people, umbrellas that open only for certain heads. The Chinese just try to stay out of the rain, and if we are caught in a downpour, we make do, knowing that the rain will not last forever.

"Do you . . . trust me?"

"Yes."

Thirty-Seven

Nathan offers his chambers, but just the thought brings a blush to my cheeks. Anyway, I would rather sleep in the room with Old Gin in case he needs something. Mrs. Bell lays a thick rug and several quilts on the floor, which coax me to sleep sooner than I expect.

I wake with a start to the sound of Old Gin coughing.

The sunlight seems too bright, even filtered through the cracks in the shutters. I rise and bring water to Old Gin's lips. He's wearing a flannel nightshirt I haven't seen before. One of Nathan's? I adjust the pillows around him, wondering if he needs to make water. But he slumps back, somehow managing to look smaller and more injured than yesterday. His wounded eye is now the size of a baby's fist.

Mrs. Bell pokes her head in and I follow her out of the room, closing the door behind me.

"Good morning, Mrs. Bell. I'm sorry to oversleep. Has he had his medicine?"

"Yes, this morning, and then Nathan helped him use the

outhouse." She wipes her hands on an apron embroidered with fruits, her premature white hair neatly whorled into a bun at her neck. "You were sleeping so soundly. We didn't want to disturb you."

"Thank you. Is Nathan—"

"He's delivering one of our jobs."

My eyes fall to today's copy of the *Focus* on the kitchen table. Nathan titled the Miss Sweetie column about the street-cars "I Know How to Sit." He must have been up all night running the press.

"I must go. The Paynes will be wondering where Old Gin is." Troubles are like weeds, and the longer you avoid them, the bigger they grow. Might as well give this one a good yank now before it can do more damage.

THE SPRING DRAGON roars, its breath reeking of cut grass and pollen. I trudge down the gilded corridor of Peachtree, wearing Old Gin's cap and carrying my borrowed bonnet in a gunny-sack. I never thought of Mrs. Payne's hat as mine, and that makes it easier to surrender. Maybe that is how Mrs. Payne felt about me—only borrowed as needed. With rising costs, it is easy to give me back.

My outrage at the woman has mellowed into something duller but somehow more painful, a gnaw versus a bite. Hammer Foot taught us that standing in another's shoes is good for our own postures, but today, I can barely manage to stand in my own.

Old Gin's cap sags over my ears. They will have to bring in

a replacement, though they will never get anyone as capable as Old Gin. A good groom is hard to find, too.

The biscuit Mrs. Bell insisted I eat has cooled in my stomach by the time I turn into the Paynes' driveway. There is a haunting stillness to the property, the same kind that creeps over an old battleground, never quite achieving peace. Since I am no longer employed here, I knock on the front door instead of rounding the courtyard to the kitchen.

Etta Rae answers, her reedlike figure more stooped than yesterday. Her sigh seems to sink through to the floor. She knew, too. Has she pitied me all these years? What other burdens has she carried?

"How long have you known?" I try to keep the bitterness from my voice.

"I carried you to Old Gin's shanty. You were just a peanut."

"You?" I croak. A younger version of the housekeeper moving with purpose toward the row of ramshackle dwellings fills my mind. Was she trying to protect her mistress, or me? Or simply the fragile state of the house she kept tidy for so long?

"It was for the best. Mr. Payne ordered your mama to send you to an orphanage."

"So he knew about"—the shameful words stick—"the affair."

"He knew about the dalliance in the cemetery."

"The cemetery?"

"The papers got wind of it, but Mr. Payne made sure the story didn't mention your mama."

All my blood seems to pool in my stomach. "My father was the Rabid-Eyes Rapist?"

"That's what they called him. But your father was not a rapist. They were foolish, but they were in love."

Poor Shang. He was never fingered for the supposed crime, but another man paid for it with his life. The injustice of it all makes me want to lay waste to the whole of Peachtree Street with one fiery breath. "Does Mr. Payne know I'm her daughter?"

"No. Your mama told him the baby was a boy."

She is clever, that much is undeniable. Something tells me he might have figured it out anyway. Yet, the man had always been decent to me. Maybe that was a chain he chose to wear.

Noemi appears beside Etta Rae. A fresh sprig of bluebells adorns her apron, and she's holding a jar of pickles. "Thought it was you."

It is hard to look into her concerned eyes and keep my composure. She drapes an arm around my shoulders and gives me a sideways squeeze. "Robby told me what happened, and Etta Rae filled in a few other details." Her gaze floats to Old Gin's cap. "Why are you here?"

"I need to talk to her. Old Gin's not well. He won't be coming for a while."

Etta Rae clucks her tongue. "She's in the stable."

Noemi pulls me inside. "I'll walk you there."

The house feels cold and disapproving, each clap of my footfalls a rebuke. I glance up the staircase but see no movement.

Noemi notices. "Caroline went with her father to the mill. How about that?"

"And Merritt?"

"He went, too."

At least I won't have to face him. It is grievous that the

thought of seeing one's brother should make one so ill. The scent of vinegar in the kitchen almost comes as a relief. Jars line the window, filled with an assortment of vegetables.

We set off toward the stables, Noemi's arm looped through mine. Unlike the front of the estate, the back moves with activity, men lifting potted plants off a wagon in the courtyard, trimming trees, and painting fences. Merritt's broken engagement will not stop the post-race merrymaking. Scandal loves a good distraction.

Noemi cuts her gaze to me. "Now, what happened to Old Gin? He never misses work."

"Billy Riggs."

Her arm stiffens. "What about Billy Riggs?"

I tell her, and when I am done, she issues a loud *hmph*.

"This time, I'm really going to hit him with the Book."

"Who?"

"My no-account brother." A worker rolling a wheelbarrow of pinecones tips his hat toward us, but Noemi sees right through him.

"You're going to read him the Bible?"

"No, I'm going to hit him with it. He might not get up for days. What was he thinking, sending that smelly corpse to beat up an old man? He's out of control."

"I—I don't understand. Your brother knows Billy?"

She sighs. "My brother *is* Billy."

Thirty-Eight

My shock falls out. "B-b-b-b—"

"Billy's father stuck Mama with a baby before I came along, but that's a story for another day," Noemi says, not breaking her pace. "When Billy came out fair as a lily, Billy's father stole him from Mama to school in his vile family business. Billy only tolerates my preaching 'cause he knows I got something on him. If people thought he had a little color in him, he'd be rotting in jail right now, not clinking glasses with the mayor." She casts a patch of dandelion a look so grim, I expect the blooms to whiten and blow away right in front of us.

Noemi's mother had been one-quarter colored, though many here considered a single drop of African blood enough to damn a lineage. It's like how Mrs. English would never use an ostrich plume with a gray spot on one of her top-shelf hats, even though the feathers naturally came speckled. And with the push for new segregation laws, now is not a good time to have a gray spot, especially for one who has already made his share of enemies.

The thought that I have something in common with Billy— both of us passing in our own way—makes my teeth ache. "I'm sorry, but even if he is your brother, I can't forgive him. I spent last night plotting out ways to make him suffer."

She nods. "Tonight, we're gonna pay him a visit. I'll hold him down while you give him your best shot."

"Okay."

"As for Mrs. Payne, I own you deserve a lot better than her." A crow lands on the ground in front of us, and Noemi lunges toward it, growling. The crow flaps away with a squawk, and she continues on her way. "But each of our personal roads got crows on them. With every crow we meet, we get better at shooing them away, the filthy flying rats. And guess what's at the end of the road?"

"Pearly gates?"

She tsks her tongue. "Not that road, that's on a different map. Vic-to-ry." She cuts the word into pieces and savors every syllable. "I wasn't too keen to get on that slick-looking August at first. But now that I know how, I'm riding him to the finish line. Victory. Do you understand me?"

"No. What is this victory?"

"It's knowing your worth no matter what the crows tell you. Victory is waiting for us. We have to be bold enough to snatch it."

Her words swirl around my head, white and fuzzy, like the pollen-filled air around me.

The stable is more cluttered than normal, with piles of rope waiting to be wound and gear scattered about the floor. Mr. Crycks fits a headstall over one of the horses. The man knocks his hat back an inch and squints at me, flat mouth working at something. He's not much for words.

Sweet Potato whickers a hello from her stall, head bobbing up and down, telling me to come closer. She wants a taste of Old Gin's hat, no doubt, and I give it to her to chew. She drops it onto the floor. Maybe things that come easy are not as good.

Mrs. Payne emerges from a stall a few spaces down. "Jo?" Her thick shawl covers her poplin dress. No hint of yesterday's emotions remains on her face. She is back to the well-bred lady of the manor I grew up knowing—or not knowing. Perfectly aligned spine, gaze soft but unreadable, hands loosely cupped like magnolia blossoms by her side. "What are you doing here? And where is Old Gin?"

"He is in a bad way after being attacked yesterday on his way home. The doctor has recommended two months of rest."

Mrs. Payne works at her wedding band. "Oh my Lord. Who attacked him?"

"Billy Riggs."

"The fixer?"

"Yes." I wonder if she has any idea of the trouble my father got himself into on her account.

Jed Crycks crosses his arms and spits. "The swine. He should be tarred and feathered."

I make a noise of agreement, though that would be a waste of good chicken feathers.

"I wanted to discuss the matter of Sweet Potato with you," I tell Mrs. Payne.

"Sweet Potato?" she asks distractedly.

Jed leads his horse out of the barn with a click of his tongue.

Mrs. Payne gestures at a nest of rope. "Noemi, wind that before someone trips."

Noemi looks relieved at having something to do. "Certainly, ma'am." She hunkers down on a milking stool and sets to the task.

I hand Mrs. Payne my gunnysack. "Your hat," I inform her before she can wonder whether there's a dead animal inside. "We have paid up through the month of March for Sweet Potato's stable and board. I will need access to your property so that I may take her for exercise. Do I have your permission?"

She seems taken aback by my businesslike tone. "That sounds reasonable." Wearily, she watches me through those watery eyes, which today are not lake blue or river gray or any of the colors I've seen before, but a murky bog of uneven depth. I no longer care to figure her out. I've spent my whole life trying to read those eyes, when all this time, they were a steel fortress intended to keep me out. Perhaps what I've been seeing all this time was my own stubborn reflection.

"Was there anything else?"

"Given Old Gin's condition, he will be unable to race Sweet Potato this Saturday."

"Of course." She frowns. "The suffragists will protest. I might need to bring another horse and rider. That, or hire a militia."

Noemi, who has managed to blend into the scenery, lets her rope go slack. I never told her about Old Gin racing, much less being paired with the suffragists. Her fidgety pupils snap to mine. She makes shoving motions with her hands.

What?

Now she's pretending to ride a horse, lasso and all. She stops riding and stretches up her fists, and then points at me.

Victory is waiting for us. We have to be bold enough to snatch it.

Sweet Potato puts her nose into my hand. An image of Old Gin weaving her through a throng of moving horses sprints through my mind. Despite Billy's savage attack on Old Gin, no doubt he will still press us for the three-hundred-dollar debt, and though the chances of me crossing the finish line first are slim to none, at least it is a chance. Plus, I could show those suffragists who's an American woman. And Mrs. Payne could see for herself what I'm made of, something that goes beyond flesh and blood.

But a nobody like me has no business on the track, let alone in the biggest horse race Atlanta has ever seen. It's probably illegal.

Old Gin believed he could do it. He would believe in me.

Mrs. Payne has opened the gunnysack and smooths the camel felt with her hand. "Well, please give Old Gin our best—"

"Of course, Sweet Potato will still be racing," I hear myself say. My heart begins to squirm around in my chest. Noemi grins and holds her hands tightly in prayer.

Mrs. Payne stops fiddling with the hat. The sunlight sifting through the rafters draws lines like prison bars on her face. "Oh? Who will be her jockey?"

I stamp down a foot and imagine an entire flock of crows scattering before me. "Me."

Thirty-Nine

Dear Miss Sweetie,

My wife ain't talking to me. She talks fine to our children and our dog, so I know she ain't gone mute. What happened is she pruned the trees too early and now they stunted. I told her she should have never fooled with stuff she don't know about. Then she told me I'm the one who's stunted. How can I get her to talk to me again?

Stunted

Dear Stunted,

The two words that will change your life are "thank you." Like a candle that can light a thousand more without shortening its own life, appreciation is a gift that, when given, can set the whole world aglow. Do your part in passing it along.

Yours truly,
Miss Sweetie

Even the horses fall silent at my proclamation. Mrs.

Payne's mouth hangs half open in shock. "You." She shakes herself free of her stupor. "I'm sorry. It wouldn't be proper." Maybe hearing the hypocrisy in her words, she adds, "Not to mention unsafe, not just for you, but the other horses and riders."

I stroke Sweet Potato's sleek nose. "You can avoid a protest."

"Those suffragists will protest regardless."

"Not if I win."

She snorts, and the sound squares my jaw. But she is glaring at a knot in the floor, and I wonder if her reaction is more complicated than I think.

Noemi finishes tying her rope and busily stacks pails. "Remember that baby-eating spider, ma'am," she casually drops. "Controversy sells."

Mrs. Payne straightens a halter hanging askew on a nail. It flops to one side again, and she shakes her head. Before she can refuse me, I put the final feather in the cap. "Plus, I have been told there is horse-riding in my blood."

The statement stamps a hoof before her, daring her to turn away. It is the first acknowledgment of our shared lineage, a final choice between pride and shame. Her choice.

Her chin becomes a small fist. "I will add you to the roster."

"Thank you. And one more thing. I trust there will be no unmasking of Miss Sweetie. Seems she is not the only one wearing a mask."

She coughs. The dust seems to hold its pattern around her, until at last, she nods. "I understand."

I RIDE SWEET Potato through Six Paces, though having my skirts hitched up on the cross saddle hinders my speed. On the turnaround, I nearly tumble off. I will be wearing trousers in the race, but I begin to doubt myself all over again.

There will be professional jockeys in the ring, men who know all the tricks. The only trick I know is the one where you pull up your knees and pivot in the saddle, but that one's not going to speed me to the finish any faster.

Returning to the estate, I kiss Sweet Potato's face and hand her to Mr. Crycks.

Only his door-knocker mustache moves when he talks. "Tell Old Gin to come back before Sweet Potato decides she likes me better."

"Will do, Mr. Crycks. Thank you for watching after her. See you tomorrow."

When I return to the Bells', Old Gin stares dreamily out the open window. There's a slow but steady limp to his breathing. On the nightstand, a half-empty cup of tea weighs down a copy of today's *Focus*. He doesn't seem to notice me, even when I kneel in front of him. Bear sits patiently at attention next to me.

"It's the tincture," whispers Mrs. Bell, pulling a basket from under the bed. "I used it once when my arthritis was bad, and it really sets your mind to sail. But at least he won't be feeling too much pain."

I touch his arm to assure him that I am here. "Sweet Potato says hello, and so does Mr. Crycks, Daylily, Portia, Charlie-Sam, Bullet, and Justice. Pirate, Frederick, Ameer, and Liberty Bell are out working." His good eye wanders to me and then closes.

I follow Mrs. Bell to the parlor, leaving the door to Old Gin's room open in case he wakes. A chambray couch with worn arms cradles us comfortably. She sorts through her basket, which contains knitted caps. Bear noses through the basket, too. "Does Old Gin favor any particular color?"

I'm about to choose a buckskin-brown one. We've always worn only plain colors so we don't stand out. But Old Gin won't be standing out or even standing up anytime soon. I bet he'd like the orange one. Once, a woman gave him an orange as a tip for escorting her jittery horse across the tracks. After we slowly consumed the "noble fruit," he declared it even better than the mandarins he remembered in China. "Orange, please. I've never seen so many beautiful yarns."

"My family are farmers. We own lots of sheep."

Bear woofs, and Mrs. Bell pats her on the head. "Yes, you could've been chasing after those smelly puffballs instead of roughing it with us here in the city."

"Mrs. Bell, you must let me take care of the house chores while we stay here. I can do everything except, well, cook. But even with that, if you could direct me, I'm a quick learner."

"We never noticed smoke from your stove. What did you eat?"

"Black-eyed peas and things that could be steeped. We only used our stove when your fireplace was lit."

"How could you tell?"

"Easy. The exhaust pipe would get warm."

"What about light?" She draws out an orange cap with white stripes, and sets it on a side table.

"Lenses built into the walls. From the outside, they're

hidden by the boxwood. Old Gin cleared them from time to time of leaves and dirt."

Her smile pulls her face into delicate wrinkles. "I would love a proper tour. First, there is someone I would like you to meet." She rises stiffly, then makes for a door in the wall.

The door to the print shop.

Inside, Nathan and Mr. Bell hover over their desk, *the* desk, which looks wonderfully old yet strong, and on whose back hundreds of thousands of words have been written. While the sight of the publisher pours a thrill down my spine, so does simply standing in this room. I inhale the iron-y smell of the press, the ink, and burnt cedar, which all together smell like creativity and progress. The sight of the ventilation in the wall, so cunningly designed as to be barely noticeable, squeezes a gasp from me.

"None of the players will talk to us." Mr. Bell's extra-large voice carries easily to us across the floorboards. "They all signed exclusives with the *Constitution*. If only we had an angle."

"Ah, there she is," says Nathan, straightening.

Mr. Bell stands the same height as his son, though he is thicker in build and more emphatic in expression. A knitted cap hugs his rather lumpy head. He removes the spectacles from the end of his ponderous nose and tucks them into the pocket of his linen coat. In four strides, we are face-to-face, his good ear cocked slightly toward me.

Peering at me through bloodshot brown eyes, he rubs the stubble on his chin, maybe working out what to say. My nerves lick the back of my neck. He must have just arrived on the morning train. "So, Mrs. Payne's illegitimate Chinese daughter has been living under the house all these years." The statement echoes in the room, with its lack of furniture or rugs.

"Sir, I am sorry for all the . . . inconvenience." A more accurate word would be *upheaval*. "My grandfather and I are in your debt. Please be assured we will pay you back as soon as we can."

He makes a brushing motion with his hand, as if shooing my words away. "We are the ones in your debt. Subscriptions have reached—" He glances at Nathan.

"Almost two thousand two hundred," Nathan nearly crows.

My breath falls out of me. And still one week left in March.

"Maybe I should leave more often." He hikes his belt up over his midsection, but it slides back down. "Course, I'm not sure I could keep up with all the houseguests."

"Apologize for that, George."

"I am sorry. You and your grandfather are certainly welcome in our home."

The mail slot opens, and a letter sails through, skidding on the floor until it lands beside a feed sack full of more letters. Nathan retrieves it.

Mr. Bell begins to pace, arms held behind his back. "You don't look like a rabble-rouser. Yet, I understand you've stirred up quite a fizz." He stops pacing and shoves his gaze at me. "Any other surprises I should know about?"

"Well, actually . . ."

The whole room grows ears.

"You wanted an angle on the horse race, and I have one. There is to be a thirteenth contestant. Me."

Nathan and his father respond at the same time. "*You?*"

"It was supposed to be Old Gin on our horse, Sweet Potato."

The letter Nathan is holding crunches in his fist. "This is madness."

His father harrumphs. "Dangerous place, the track. Saw a horse take a bad fall on a sprint a few years back and had to be put down."

"Don't scare the girl." Mrs. Bell puts a warm hand on my arm. "Jo, it's true the racetrack is no place for beginners."

"I know. But Old Gin wouldn't have entered her if he didn't think she was as good as the others."

Nathan's eyebrows tighten. "It's not your . . . Wait, your horse is a *mare*? The deuce—sorry, Mother—it's not your *mare* that we're worried about."

"I can assure you that I am an experienced rider."

"Is it the money you need? Does Billy Riggs have something over you?"

"No."

"George. Now would be a good time to ask her."

"Ask me?"

Mr. Bell hitches up his belt again. "Yes, well, we could use some help here, though pay wouldn't be much to start. Of course, room and board would be included for you and your grandfather, either here in the house or, er, downstairs."

"Though perhaps a few improvements are in order if the latter," says Mrs. Bell.

All the words collect at my door, waiting for it to open. "You, you are offering me a job?"

Nathan holds himself stiffly by the elbows. "Yes. In addition to the Miss Sweetie column, you could assist with typesetting and research."

"But wouldn't we be breaking the law? People would think I was white."

Mr. Bell sweeps up a finger. "I'd wager most of the agony aunts are actually agony uncles. People don't care who it is, as long as the advice is good."

"Maybe one day"—Nathan glances at his father—"you could write columns under your own name." Mr. Bell's jaw loosens, and Nathan quickly adds, "It is clear she is a good writer, not to mention more than a little knowledgeable about what goes on here."

"Let's not get ahead of ourselves. Well, girl, what do you think?"

"I think that's . . ." My throat constricts, siphoning off words. "This is too generous of you." The idea that one day people might read Jo Kuan's thoughts and viewpoints in print whirs the pages of my mind. I never imagined someone like me could be permitted to write using *my* name, but perhaps when you live in a basement, you get used to a low ceiling. The Bells are willing to take a risk on me, so why hesitate?

The mail slot opens again, and a gloved hand stuffs in another letter.

Mrs. Bell presses her hands together. "You would be a help to me in the home as well. With every year, it seems my joints get rustier."

Three pairs of hopeful eyes press into me. Here is the family that I always wanted, wanting me back. I swallow down my emotions before they leak out of my face. "I will need to talk it over with Old Gin."

Mr. Bell nods. "Certainly, your grandfather must be consulted."

"As for the horse race, I'm afraid it is something I have to do." Nathan's eyes pick a fight with me, but I study the tight weave of Mrs. Bell's shawl. A community is like that shawl, and once you are a part of it, you tie your fate to the threads closest to you. Would I be creating a hardship for the Bells if I raced? If something were to happen to me, the Bells would feel obligated to take care of me, just like with Old Gin.

Nathan pins his elbows to his side. His father's face tightens around the mouth, the look of one reining in words. It is Mrs. Bell who lifts her voice. "The path to progress has never been without risk, whether that path be a march for the vote or an eight-furlong stretch. Jo, if you feel you can do this, we are behind you."

Mr. Bell lets out a long breath. "I don't know, Laney, if she were my daughter—"

"If she were your daughter, you would be stitching the number on her saddle pad yourself."

"I don't even know how to sew," he grumbles, but he doesn't dispute her statement. "Well, you've certainly given us an angle. Nathan, maybe you can even draw—wait, where are you going?"

Nathan grabs his coat and his Homburg from the wall hook and then, without glancing back, strides out the shop door.

I bet I know exactly where he's going.

Old Gin has begun to stir, so I feed him some broth. Then I coax Bear from the room, bringing the used bowl to the kitchen, where Mrs. Bell is taking tea. "May I take Bear for a walk?"

"I'm sure she would love that. The leash is by the door."

I tuck my braid under Old Gin's cap, which I've taken to wearing out. Then I attach Bear's leash to her collar. The afternoon sun heats the grass in front of the Bell residence, putting a sour tickle in my nose. Lowering myself to Bear's level, I comb the hair out of her eyes. I might not know where Nathan went, but she does.

"Okay, Bear, take me to Avalon."

Woof. She licks me on the nose. Then with a flick of her head, as if to say let's go, she sets off.

Forty

Bear leads me north along a street full of shotgun houses, long dwellings whose inside doorways line up so you could fire a shot through the front and out the back without hitting any walls. Of course, I don't know why anyone would want to do that, but not everything in Atlanta comes with an explanation.

After a mile of walking, the houses thin and the landscape grows scraggly, gangs of trees edging out the sky. The sound of running water strums along to the honks of passing geese. I begin to wonder whether Bear knows where she's going or whether she's just happy to be on the prowl. "Where's Nathan, Bear? I hope we're going to Avalon because I'm getting bunions on my bunions."

Just as I'm about to call off the search, she dives into a screen of brush so tangled, I couldn't throw a shoe through it without it bouncing back. I push aside the brush and find that it gives easier than it looks. I follow Bear up a small incline.

Below, a rocky stream about forty feet across runs with

clear water. A flattish rock in the shape of a newsboy cap lies midstream. Nathan sits at the lip of the cap, feet dangling over the water, a book open on his lap.

Woof!

Nathan looks up, and his Homburg scans from side to side. He closes the book and gets to his feet. Bear bounds down to the stream and zigzags over a series of rocks to reach him.

"Hello," I call over the water. "So, this is Avalon." With the tree line obscuring the road and the hills beyond, it is hard to recognize this as part of Atlanta. Lacelike ferns brush at my face, and the cool air smells sweet and green.

Nathan embraces his dog and rubs her on the neck. "I don't know whether to be impressed or . . ."

"Depressed."

A reluctant smile peeks out from the shadow of his hat.

I lift my skirts and hop onto the first rock.

"No, stay there, I'll come—"

The second rock is only a fist-size bump, so I quickly step to the third, then fourth, and then—

"No, not that one!"

The last rock wobbles, and my boot begins to slip, but I leap onto Nathan's rock. With a curse, he catches me by the arm.

"I don't fall easily," I tell him.

He doesn't release my arm, and my heart flops around like a landed fish. "I don't fall easily either," he says quietly.

Giddy goobers, suddenly I don't feel so sure-footed at all.

He lets go his grip, but the warmth of it still makes my arm tingle.

"It's not much." He sweeps an arm to the far end of the

rock. "As you can see, the magic apple trees are not yet in season. Care to sit on my couch?"

I carefully lower myself to the lip of the newsboy-cap rock. "The unicorn tapestries are a nice touch."

"Thank you. I do the decorating myself." He points to a depression a few feet from where we are sitting. "There is where Excalibur was forged. Er, that's a sword."

"I know. Your father used Excalibur to slay the headless horseman under your bed. You'd come into the print shop night after night." I smile at the memory, though one look at Nathan's startled face chases my smile away. "I'm sorry."

"Please don't be. I guess I'm still getting used to the idea that you already know me."

Our feet dangle over the water, which breaks in a froth of bubbles around our rock. Bear returns from where she had gone to quench her thirst and plants herself on Nathan's other side. Draping an arm around her, he watches the stream in the same steady way he regards the world, absorbing much, giving away little.

He hooks his long fingers around the edge of our rock, stretching his back. The stream whooshes and clucks. "Well, now that you know so many of my secrets, maybe you can tell me some of yours." His eyes widen a fraction.

"My whole life is a secret."

"It doesn't have to be."

The daylight draws him in sharp lines. For so many years, his face was little more than a fuzzy image, despite him being as familiar as my own cloak. Is it possible to have the kind of life his family offered me? Not just working with them, but living among them, in the spaces that show? Interracial marriage is illegal, but no one can legislate family, friendship, or love.

When I don't answer, he gives me half a smile. "I really just want to know, since you are an experienced hatter, what do you think of my Homburg?" Removing the hat, he flips it back and forth in front of him.

"You mean your humbug? It's like a giant frown on the crown."

"Then I shall continue wearing mine with pride."

"At least put a feather in it. Lizzie will appreciate that."

He sets his hat back on his head, and the brim slumps into an extra-deep frown. "I'm not interested in impressing Lizzie."

My suddenly fidgety hands pick up his book. Faded silver lettering on the leather cover reads *Modern Horse Racing*. "Where did you get this?"

"Used bookshop down the street."

"Are you reading this for her?"

"Yes, I am reading this . . . for her. Not Lizzie." The grumpy set of his jaw has loosened, and his throat moves. "Jo, you've known me all your life. Do you think"—he swallows—"do you think you could ever care for someone like me?"

My skin tingles, and my pulse clamors in my ears. As I watch his eyelashes bow, the messy deck of my emotions squares itself and turns up a heart. I realize I am holding my breath. *"Besotted."*

"Besotted?"

"My favorite word. I lied, before."

The voice I have heard all my life whispers right by my ear. "Jo." And I no longer need to wonder how it would feel to kiss him.

Forty-One

This time, when the portal to Billy's cathouse heaves open, Madam Delilah lets me in without inquiry. Perhaps it is because I'm in the company of Noemi, who, with her lightning-bolt scowl, looks in no mood to suffer fools. After a perfunctory "Good evening, ma'am," Noemi hooks her arm through mine and marches us past the watchful square eyes of the Jesse James dice on the door. Madam Delilah's shocked face seems to droop under the weight of her cosmetic paste, like an old sock that is dangerously close to slipping off.

"Does she know?" I whisper, hearing the woman's boots scrabbling down the hallway after us.

"She thinks the church sends me," Noemi whispers in my ear. "Let me do the talking."

My stomach clenches at the ripe scent of the overly perfumed hallways, and my heartbeat picks up its feet. If the patrons here are curious about our arrival, I don't notice, as anger swells inside me. The only thing that stays me from storming the corridors is Noemi, whose firm hand keeps me by her side.

In room 9, Billy Riggs sits at his desk, a cigar drooping from his mouth as he writes in a ledger. His hat hangs on the wall, and his coppery hair is tied back by a black ribbon. Sleeve garters keep his cuffs from smearing the ink. Four white men stand around the table, their expressions caught between sheepish and surprised. Billy blinks at Noemi. "Is it Sunday already?"

Noemi growls, but before she can speak, Billy closes his ledger. "If you'll excuse me for a moment, gentlemen, Madam Delilah will get you watered, on the house."

Casting us annoyed looks, the men file out and Madam Delilah closes the door behind them. Billy rounds his desk and leans his backside against it. "Let me guess, you're not here to place illegal bets."

Noemi lights in. "I never agreed with your depraved lifestyle. I did my honest best to overlook the perversions in your soul, knowing judgment is not mine to pass. But when you start taking swings at folks I know, *good* folks, you have gone too far. Your creepy clothes-hanger almost done in Old Gin." She pushes up the sleeves of her dress, as if she is getting ready to take a swing herself.

Billy puts up a hand, his open cuff blooming like a lily around his crooked wrist. "What do you mean, 'done in Old Gin'? I only told Knucks to scare him a bit. Then Knucks comes back a bloody mess and bolts the door on his room. Thinks that old man put a curse on him. I might have to hire someone new, and it's not easy to find a good menace, you know?"

I choke on my saliva. Old Gin bested Knucks?

"Serves both you creepy crawlers right," Noemi snaps, clapping me on the back.

"She's the one who double-crossed *me*, giving me that counterfeit elixir." He picks up an already lit cigar from its ashtray. "I run a fair racket here. You can't expect a man to give away his assets for free."

"Assets," I say, seething, waving away the smoke. "If you weren't blackmailing Old Gin, I would never have debased myself by paying you a visit."

His coppery eyes cinch. "I was not blackmailing Old Gin. He came to me."

I nearly choke again. Old Gin would never have truck with a criminal like Billy Riggs. "I don't believe it."

Billy takes a long draw of his tobacco, but Noemi plucks the stick from his fingers. "Explain."

I never thought I'd see Noemi boss around the likes of Billy Riggs, but he is surprisingly tolerant of her. "He wanted to buy back a family heirloom."

My eyes lock on to the empty space on the side table where the Buddha vase sat before I threw it.

Billy laughs at my horrified expression. "You flatter yourself. That was Ming dynasty, worth six hundred dollars if you hadn't broken it." Moving toward his oddities shelf, his twitchy fingers hover before his assortment of bottles. He selects the smallest—a jade snuff bottle—and presents it to me with a mock bow. "Shang pawned it for twenty-five dollars. Of course, over the years, it has accrued interest."

The bottle bears the shape of a peach, its roundness matching the impression in the box I wanted for hair ribbons. Its color is the same green as the screw top with attached spoon. It had belonged to Old Gin's wife. My grandmother. The jade feels warm, like a polished rock left in the sun.

Old Gin's story of the farmer's son and the nymph creeps into my mind. The son gave up the peach for the nymph, a peach meant to attract fortune. The farmer, Old Gin, had taken steps to ensure our future by attempting to buy it back.

Noemi leans against the edge of his bathtub. "You thought an old groom could pay that?"

"Again, *he* came to *me*," Billy says through his teeth. "No one held a gun to his head."

Noemi ties her arms into a knot. "Give her back that bottle. You know what I have on you."

Billy's mouth purses into a petulant knot. "Even if I gave it back, she would *still* owe me for my Ming vase. Besides, you wouldn't rat me out. I just gave an anonymous donation to that Bluebird society of yours."

"Bluebells. Take it back. Your money comes with more strings than a harp."

An argument starts up between them, with Billy protesting the banditry of his favorite bauble, and Noemi making threats that she would likely never carry through. I pull at my braid as my outrage loses its focus. It's Billy's own fault that Ming vase broke. As for the snuff bottle, it is unfair to ask Noemi to spend more of her family currency persuading him to return it when it was Shang's decision to pawn the bottle away.

I clear my throat and the arguing stops. "You are a man who values information, secret information, am I right?"

Noemi's chest expands, as if filling up to fuel all sorts of protests. I avoid her eyes.

"Indeed." Billy's teeth seem to sharpen.

"I have some information about the race that I will trade in exchange for the bottle."

He crosses to the open window and reposes upon the ledge. Dying sunlight bronzes his pale skin. "I very much doubt you could tell me anything I don't already know."

"Life is full of risks," I say, feeding his words back to him. "Keeps it interesting."

Billy blows smoke in my face. "I'm afraid that's not how it works. Tell me what you know, and I will decide its worth. Otherwise, we are at an impasse."

My collar grows sticky, despite the breeze blowing in through the window. How would Mrs. English close the deal? She would butter the biscuit so that it would be impossible not to take a bite. "Unless you have received information in the last eight hours, let me assure you, you do not know my secret, a secret that is sure to cause a stir when made public. Of course, by then, you will have lost a very lucrative business opportunity." The official betting station may not offer odds on Sweet Potato, but an illegal gambling ring certainly can, and Billy Riggs does not run the only racket in town.

Noemi suppresses a smile. She picks up a dried sea sponge that resembles a brain and squeezes it. I can't help thinking she is paying me a very peculiar compliment.

Billy's hair rambles wildly around his head, somehow un-shackled from its ribbon. "Tell you what. I'll buy your information with a hundred-dollar credit toward your father's bauble."

"Not good enough. It would still take me a decade to save two hundred dollars." I toss out the words like dice. He could easily retract his offer, and then I would be out of luck.

Noemi's grip on the sponge tightens even more, and this time, I do not think it is a compliment.

Billy's leg begins to twitch just like that day in Buxbaum's. "Once I am satisfied with your information, I will make you another offer for how you may pay for the remainder."

Noemi gives me the barest nod.

"Fine."

"Now, what is this information?" He cuts an irritated glance at Noemi. "And it better be good."

"Oh, it's good," she says.

"As of this morning, I have been added to the roster."

"You." The news seems to suck Billy's displeasure right out the window. "Well, well. Ain't you a thief's bag, full of all sorts of goodies. But I hardly see how that information helps me."

"There will be no odds taken on my entry. *Official* odds, that is."

A moth of a smile alights on his face. "You ever race before?"

"No, but I know how to ride."

"And your horse. Is he seasoned?"

"*She* has never raced either."

"She." He runs a pointy tongue over his lips, then chuckles. "Well, good." He shoots a few rounds from his finger guns. "People love a long shot. Now, if you'll excuse me, I have some odds in need of refinement." He grabs his hat off the hook and wiggles it onto his head.

"But what's the offer for the rest?"

Billy hardly seems to hear me, smoothing his eyebrows in a looking glass.

Noemi's reflection joins Billy's in the mirror. Now that they are side by side, I can see a family resemblance around the pointed cheekbones and square hairline. The eye sees what it wants. "Make her an offer for the balance, you crook," she says.

"Right." Turning to me again, he straightens his vest so that the pinstripes running down it are no longer lightning jags. His pupils slide to one corner for a moment as he thinks, and then he scowls so hard, his forehead turns white. "A man I hate has a pony in that race. I hate him for the simple fact that God handed him everything, while He made me bow and scrape for every cent I own." With quick tucks, he adjusts his sleeve garters. "By all accounts, he operates on penny promises nowadays—there is some justice in the world. Still, I would like nothing more than to see his horse and jockey bested by a pair of females. In fact, his jockey was a patron here until I had to kick him out for being too rough on the ladies." He straightens his tie, oblivious to the irony in his statement. "You cross the line before them, and you can have your bottle back."

My shoulders pull at my cloak. "I told you, I am a novice. If I make it around the track, it will be a miracle."

He grins. "God and I may not see eye to eye"—in one smooth motion, he slips into a rifle-brown frock coat—"but I do believe in miracles."

I release an effortless exhale. So, I must pull a chestnut from an open fire. At least that horse is not Ameer. God may have handed Merritt everything, but the Payne heir is as wealthy as sin itself. "Who is this horse?"

"His name is Thief."

Forty-Two

The tincture has kept Old Gin in a foggy but hopefully painless state. But before the sun rises on Friday morning,
Old Gin calls out, "Sao Yue."

"Grandfather?" I fly to his side from my makeshift bed. His
eyes are unfocused and wet.

"Sao Yue?"

"No, it's me, Jo."

His face falls, as if disappointed by the answer. I help him
drink. "Who is Sao Yue?" The words, meaning "graceful moon,"
taste sweet on my tongue.

"Your grandmother. Sao Yue gave me a snuff bottle," he
gasps. "A wedding present. Your father pawned it to the turtle
egg, wanting to buy something to impress Mrs. Payne, a hair
comb, I think. He foolishly thought he had a chance with her.
When I found out what he had done, I"—his face crumples a
little—"I raised my hand against him. I told him he had shamed
our family, and he must leave. I said I didn't want to see him

again." His chest collapses, as if the confession has broken something inside, and a thread-y cough starts up.

"Shh, don't talk."

He shakes his head. "I hoped, if I could get that peach back, the bats of good fortune might return. Maybe bring my son back with them." A tear rolls down his cheek, and he turns his face away, as if to hide it.

I pat his cheek with my flannel sleeve. "I will get Grandmother's bottle back for you."

AFTER A RIGOROUS afternoon of drilling at Six Paces, I return Sweet Potato to the Payne Estate, which is now fully festooned for a party. The groundskeepers have cut topiaries in the shape of horses, and shaved the lawn so close it looks like carpet. Balls made of flowers trim the gazebo. Hired domestics are twisting wire around mason jars with candles, which will be hung in the trees. The post-race party will be worthy of a visit from President Harrison himself.

I am straightening Sweet Potato's tack when I feel someone behind me.

Caroline seems to have grown thinner since her episode with the face cream. It's as if the assault had siphoned off the baby fat and left wisdom in her cheeks. Her hair falls in unkempt waves around her shoulders, and her gray dress with a lace bib makes her look mature without being matronly. She carries a cardboard box with a handle, the kind given with purchases at fancier shops.

"You're not with your father today?" I ask, when no words are forthcoming.

She shakes her head. "Mama wanted me to stay with her."

I nod, not wanting an explanation. My heart tears a little, remembering all the years we were at war without understanding why. The grievances I'd held against her have dropped off like shriveled leaves.

"You look—" Her gaze spreads over my damp riding silks and to my pebbled-goat-leather boots with my bulging toes. I brace myself for a jibe. But then she finishes, "Like a winner."

"I thought you were going to say train signal."

She smiles. "That, too." An emotion flits over her face, hard to read in the filtered light of the barn. She takes a measured breath.

"Is everything okay, my lady?"

She winces and the box handle tightens in her grip. Another breath. Her frost-blue eyes seem to melt, expanding in her face. "I am lost."

I'm surprised at the tears forming in my eyes. "Then you should look up. The sky reminds us that troubles are not permanent. Of course, right now, there's just cobwebs."

She attempts a smile, but a tear splashes out. She whisks it away with the back of her hand. "This is for you." She holds up her box. "My riding boots. You will need them for tomorrow."

"Your violin boots? I—I can't."

"They are just boots." She sets them down by my feet. "And besides, I want you to braid my hair." She pulls a comb and pins from her pocket. "If you don't mind."

Tomorrow is the start of the debutante season, and Caroline will be the belle of the ball. I square a stool into the ground. "Your chair, my lady."

I begin to braid, and the soothing scents of hay and leather mingle with wonderment over what could've been. A strange and meditative peace settles over us. We don't speak until I've pinned the last pin and adjusted the curls around her face.

"I've been thinking," says Caroline. "I might buy one of those safeties for myself." A dozen emotions paddle across her face. None find mooring. "Do you think Noemi would show me how to ride?"

"Probably not," I say, though we both know, if Caroline demanded it, Noemi would have to give in.

A flush builds on her cheeks, and she shakes air into her skirts.

I sigh. I may never be friends with Caroline Payne. But maybe the freedom machine will move us all a step forward. "Let's go ask her."

SATURDAY ARRIVES WEARING a cloud shawl over her damp shoulders. I step into Old Gin's room, scarlet silk skimming my figure, my hair braided into two tight buns on my head. Old Gin refused the tincture last night, preferring pain to feeling groggy. His face is a sunset of blue, red, purple, and gray, with more bruises blooming each day. Deeper injuries take longer to surface.

I shake the tincture. "How about half a dose? I'm worried about infection."

He shakes his head. "If I don't feel the hurt, I wonder if I'm alive."

"Then you must feel very alive."

His forehead crimps. "In life, there will be many races. Not all must be run. Sweet Potato will not be disappointed if she misses this one."

Short of using the Paynes' family telephone, I can't imagine how our mare managed to convey that. "As it turns out, Billy has agreed to return the bottle if Sweet Potato can cross the line before Thief."

He makes a noise that's halfway between a grumble and a sigh. To my surprise, he doesn't press me for details. "Thief has good legs." He licks his dry lips. "But it takes a good heart to win a race."

Like his. I give him a wide smile. "So, you really thought Sweet Potato could beat Ameer?"

"Maybe, maybe not. But she told me she had to try." His good eye winks and I resist the urge to hug him. His face goes serious again. "The Bells are good people. But staying will change the direction of the wind here. Winds can be . . . scandalous."

"Are you worried about the *Focus*? I would continue using a pseudonym. No one need know."

"Wasn't talking about pseudonym." His eyes drift toward the door, where the sound of Nathan's casual whistling drifts in.

I sip from his water, suddenly parched myself. He's right. Even if Nathan and I managed to carve a spot for ourselves in Atlanta, it would be a secret isle like Avalon, and if anyone ever found out, the publisher could be ruined.

Old Gin studies the double tents formed by his feet and

then shrugs. "The river travels fastest around the stones. But sometimes, the stones must be faced head-on. Who knows? With enough momentum, a path may clear, hm?"

"Do you think we should accept the Bells' offer?"

"I think you are good at making your own rules."

NATHAN WALKS IN a tight square around the Bells' reception area, where Bear, his mother, and I stand, his *Modern Horse Racing* book open before him. "I would say good luck, but according to the book, jockeys are particular about those things. I could give you a lucky penny or a rock from my collection. Scratch that, I don't have a collection—"

"I know about the collection."

He gives me a sheepish grin. Dressed in a linen jacket, whip-cord trousers, and wingtips, he could easily be one of the young men girding themselves for the battle for the debutantes. Only his insouciant Homburg hat marks him as an outlier. The daisies he wrapped with lace for Lizzie are still sprightly despite the humidity. I feel myself grimacing and force my thoughts to other avenues.

My gaze drifts toward Old Gin's room, where he is dozing. His skin felt too warm when I left, and his eye had begun to bleed again. What if he takes a turn for the worse while I am away? I could never forgive myself.

Mrs. Bell hands me Old Gin's cap, which she washed and brushed clean. "Don't worry. Your grandfather will be in good hands."

"Thank you, ma'am." I square Old Gin's cap on my head and

nod to Nathan. "See you at the race." Then I slip out. Another battle requires my attention.

THE VIOLIN BOOTS put an unfamiliar elegance in my step as I lead Sweet Potato into Piedmont Park. Thanks to Caroline's habit of wearing her shoes hard, the boots are comfortably broken in, and I may never take them off.

It is hard not to stare at all the finely dressed couples in their open-air carriages and pleasure wagons. The hats alone are dizzying. Tall satins with crushed-velvet bows, cake hats with their layers of ribbons, and of course, Miss Sweetie hats in fresh colors like strawberry and lemon. Mrs. English must be pouring herself a tall coca cordial right about now.

There are also a number of black faces in the crowd. The Paynes, not the Gentlemen's Driving Club, make the rules today, and as long as the colored can pay the fee, Mrs. Payne will not turn away donations to her charity.

People line up at an awning painted with the word BETS, parasols open. Nearby, a contingent of women with marigold sashes has drawn the attention of a crowd. "Votes! For! Women!" Mrs. Bullis pumps her fist with each word, shaking her half of the banner. I can't help noticing that the horse's backside looks more professionally stitched than the front half.

"That's our cheering gallery," I tell Sweet Potato, who is nibbling the cap off my head.

The crowd parts, and the sight of another marching group pulls the stuffing right out of me. These marchers wear sashes of violet blue and are singing. A woman on a bicycle leads the charge: Noemi. Behind her, Rose and Mary carry a white banner stitched with the words ATLANTA BLUEBELLS: VOTES FOR ALL WOMEN. Embroidered around the banner are all manner of colorful flowers, not just bluebells.

The Atlanta Suffragists' chant falls off, and Mrs. Bullis's teapot face looks like it's gathering steam.

Noemi pedals up to me and then stands, with August wedged under her. A new basket is strapped to the handlebars, lined with a picnic blanket. On her straw hat, her Farney the Falcon knot pins down a sprig of bluebells.

"I wouldn't be here if it weren't for you."

She grins. "You got a plan for getting around the track?"

After finishing his book on horse racing, Nathan discussed strategy with me, but none of it stuck. "Once the bell rings, go as fast as I can go." I just have to beat one horse today. Perhaps I can keep my seat simply by focusing on Thief. I've never seen the piebald run at full steam, though I imagine he can burn up a track, with every line of his sleek and tapered body suggesting motion.

Noemi laughs, and her eyes drift beyond my shoulder. "Mr. Buxbaum said Robby could stay on as clerk."

I let out a squeal, wondering if "The Custom-ary" had anything to do with his decision. "Give him my congratulations."

"Give them yourself."

Robby strides up, dapper in his Sunday suit of brushed cotton. "Hello, Jo!"

"Hello yourself. I hear I owe you some teeth rinse."

"How about we toast with it after you cross the line? We're real proud of you."

Noemi nods. "Just moving down that road is a victory."

Robby leans in, his laughing eyes glinty. "But bring home the big fish, okay?" He waves a ticket at me. "I got a bet on Sunday Surprise. But I also got one on you." He winks.

The Atlanta Suffragists have again started up their battle cry, drowning out the Bluebells' singing. Mrs. Bullis is frowning at us, and I give her a little wave that she does not return. She hands her part of the banner to another woman and stalks over. "You." She crooks her pinky at Noemi. "Your group is making us into a spectacle. And you." The pinky switches to me. "You arranged this to spite me." She grimaces at the sight of Sweet Potato, drooling on my head.

"I wish I had that much influence, ma'am." I drape my arm around Sweet Potato's neck. "Rest assured, my mare and I will do our best."

"Mare?" Her gaze slides under Sweet Potato. "Oh, good gullywash. We will be laughingstocks!" Her face crumples, and I feel myself softening, curse my wax heart.

"If you believe that females are equal to males, then have faith, ma'am."

Her face unwrinkles, and she gusts out an indignant "Well!" Then she storms back to her suffragists, hissing to the Bluebells as she passes, "Will you please hush?"

The Bluebells break off their song. Noemi sighs. "I better move the troops, before they show us the boot. But first, I made you something to help you get past Thief." From her pocket, she pulls something wrapped in wax paper.

"A cookie?" I reach for it, but she pulls it away.

"Not you." She holds it to Sweet Potato, who snatches

it right up, wax paper and all. "It's got my secret ingredient. Never hurts to try." She grins and all the bluebells on her hat grin along.

"Do you have an extra sash?"

"No, but you can have mine." She whips it off, then watches as I tie it around my waist. Something airy and hopeful wings around her face. "Good luck, sister."

Sprinting races have already begun to warm up the crowd for the main event. A sign with the word CONTESTANTS points toward the stables at the far end of the grandstand. The word chases a chill up and down my spine.

I ignore the stares, as I have done all my life. The noise of the attendees collects in my ears, making my heart pound like Etta Rae is whacking it with her rug-beater hands.

A gray horse barrels past me, tossing its anvil of a head and snapping its jaws. A purple saddle pad emblazoned with the number 4 wraps the horse's middle. Where do I get one of those numbers? Perhaps this is where having a team helps.

The grandstand is beginning to fill. There must be at least five hundred people there already, watching the sprint races, with room for five hundred more. Next to the grandstand, more people amass under a magnolia tree, on which is nailed a sign, COLORED. There are no chairs, but some folks have brought picnic blankets to set on the ground. I picture Old Gin standing under that tree, not weak and battered, but as he used to look, balanced and whole. His shabby clothes still hang neatly, and he faces the world with serenity, as if he had landed right on the spot he was supposed to land. He waves his flag at me, onward.

Behind a line of trees, a double strip of stables is populated by a grunting, noisy mass of men clustered around horses. The gray anvil that passed us earlier rears up on its hindquarters, and its jockey, a man with a weathered face, yells curses. Old Gin never cursed at a horse. Horses only give, never take, and should be treated with respect. Another horse screams, and I recognize it as the voice of a certain Arabian, Ameer. Johnny Fortune rides him into the arena, looking splendid in gold silks, a riding crop under his arm. I do not see Thief.

Sweet Potato and I stride up to an official-looking man with a red bowler to match his bright bulb of a nose. "Good morning, sir. I am Jo Kuan, and this is Sweet Potato. We are here to check in for the race."

"You? There are only twelve animals in this race, and certainly no females." He spits out that last word as if it were a seed that had gotten stuck in his teeth.

"But—could you please check again?" I eye the ledger he clasps to his velvet cutaway. "Mrs. Payne added us to the roster herself." At least, she said she did. *Don't let me down again. Not today.*

"I have the roster memorized. Twelve horses, all checked in already. Now, move along, or I shall call security."

"But I—but we—"

A tailored morning suit struts up on shiny sable boots. "There you are, Miss Kuan. We've been waiting for you. Have you been giving our last jock a hard time, Mr. Thorne?"

Merritt Payne twists one handle of his three-forty-five mustache and looks down his aristocratic nose at the official.

Mr. Thorne flips through the pages of his ledger, nearly dropping it in his agitation. "Er, sorry, Mr. Payne. I was sure I knew all of the contestants. Twelve, I thought it was—"

"Please." Merritt wiggles his fingers. "Now you are wasting our time. Come, Miss Kuan, Sweet Potato. Your stable boy is waiting, and they will be calling for line shortly."

Forty-Three

Dear Miss Sweetie,

I have three small children, and my life is full from sunup to sundown with the care of them. But though I love them dearly, I am being driven to the nuthouse by their quarreling. How do I get them to stop?

Mrs. Nut

Dear Mrs. Nut,

Redirect their energy toward a common goal, like cultivating a garden, which can bear fruit in more than one way. Oxen untethered will trample the field, but yoked together, they can plow it.

Yours truly,
Miss Sweetie

Merritt leads us through the noisy morass of man, beast, sweat, and fear. And the race hasn't even begun. "Thorne is an ass."

"Thank you. I'm not sure what I would've done."

He gives me a tight-lipped smile. "Carried on, as you always do, Jo."

I try to read his face for signs that he knows about our true relationship, but there is only the sunset of his smile, a glassy look to the blue-gray eyes inherited from his mother, and a slight pull to his brow, as if snagged by too many thoughts. I mourn the brother that could've been, somehow feeling a loss that never happened.

I'm surprised to find little Joseph Porter standing in his military stance when Merritt and I walk up, his flat cap extra sharp.

"Joseph will lead your horse to the line when it's time. Good luck, Jo. If races were won on gumption and not speed, you would have my wager." He bows, and Merritt Payne carries himself away.

"Good morning, Joseph. At ease. I didn't expect to see you."

"You neither. Old Gin gave me ten cents to attend him."

"He isn't feeling well. I'm subbing in."

Moving briskly, Joseph leads Sweet Potato to a watering trough. As she slakes her thirst, he unfastens her saddle. He shakes out a satin horse pad, which matches exactly the Suffragists' marigold banner, stitched with the number 13. "Sorry about the number, but if it helps, Mama says thirteen isn't unlucky if you spit on it, and I done that for you." He shows me the wet spot right between the 1 and 3.

"Why, thank you."

"But don't hold your breath, because you'll still have the most distance to cover on the outside lane."

The odds rocket away, and my spine contracts like a

squeezed concertina. I only hope that Thief is number 12. "Anything else I should know?"

"Stay away from Four and Six. Their riders don't have a good look on them. They got hayseed eyes, like they're common and ain't above taking what's not theirs."

Number 4's the anvil horse. Joseph jerks his head toward 6, a chestnut whose checker-sleeved jockey stands with his back partly turned toward me, staring up at a tree. Water begins trickling down the trunk, and I quickly avert my eyes.

I certainly hope he remembers to thank the tree when he's done. Threading through the mass, I size up the competition, though I'm really just looking for the piebald with its distinctive white hull and black fringe and rudder. Men scowl when they see me, or laugh outright, and I'm not sure which is worse. One just turns up his nose, staring right through me. Clearly, I am no threat to them, but perhaps that is an advantage. The biggest threats are the ones we fail to acknowledge.

A familiar chiseled profile in a swashbuckler hat and charcoal cutaway emerges from a stable. I should be focusing on the horse he leads, but Mr. Q commands attention in a way Billy Riggs could never hope to replicate, not even with his showy wardrobe or manners. Mr. Q walks with a handsome gait that seems practiced, shoulders rolled back, head held high for viewing. His olive complexion seems carved from soap, with sideburns that must have been shaped with a ruler. The only flaw is a twist to his pillowy lips that, like a scratch in the mirror, isn't visible from all angles. But once you know it's there, it is hard to forget.

Something sour coats my tongue. We both got here through a personal connection, but mine didn't cost a human heart—specifically, Caroline's. He was just using her to get his horse in the race.

The number 9 is stitched to Thief's saddle blanket. He is not number 12 as I'd hoped, but at least he is not number 1. Any relief I feel evaporates when a runt of a man in green silks takes the horse by the bridle. It's the leprechaun who leered at me from the porch of Billy Riggs's cathouse. His brazen gaze gropes mine, recognizing me, too. So, this is the man Billy ejected for being too rough on women. Mean comes in all sizes, and getting up on a horse doesn't change that one bit.

I hurry back to Joseph and Sweet Potato, my collar feeling sticky. Any confidence I felt when I left Old Gin drains from my violin boots into the dry earth.

Someone calls, "Line!" and the chaos of beast and man begins to slowly organize. Jockeys mount up, and grooms take positions at the bridle. Companion ponies calm nerves on the way to the track. I step up on Sweet Potato, and her solid warmth calms my own bucking heart.

A colored jockey with an easy smile brings his muscular roan up to us. "Ben Abner, and this is Sunday Surprise." He speaks like he has a train to catch. "Mr. Buxbaum told me to say hello. It's a fast track today, but there are a couple sticky parts. Keep those horseshoes on, and don't let them box you in."

"Pleased to meet you, Mr. Abner, and thank you, I will," I respond as if I have any idea what he's talking about.

He tugs the brim of his cap and clicks his tongue.

Joseph watches the pair trot off, his mouth ajar. "Sunday's

the one I'd bet on. He's number two, a good spot. The number-two lane wins most often." Sweet Potato tries to knock off Joseph's cap, but he ducks. "No offense, girl." Taking her by the halter, he leads us to the back of the line. The foul leprechaun swivels on Thief's saddle and shows me an overbite so severe, he could probably slide pecans into his mouth without opening it. I pretend to ignore him.

A big horse like Thief will roll like a boulder off a slope. Once he gets going, there will be no stopping his momentum. We will need to break from the start as fast as possible. Of course, that's easier said than done, especially with no time to train Sweet Potato. Then again, Old Gin has been training her. Perhaps she already knows how to blow from the line.

We emerge from the trees, a parade of bright silks and clinking harnesses. The grandstand seems to vibrate with all the people cheering, waving their flags and hats, despite the oppressive humidity. I shield my eyes against the glare. A clot of clouds traps the sun, and more seem to be rolling in from all sides.

From the colored section, a cheer goes up when Ben Abner passes by, his tightly muscled back flexing with each of his horse's hoofbeats.

Someone yells, "Jo!"

Noemi waves at me, Robby next to her. Life is a chessboard, and if you've played it right, your best pieces will be standing in the right squares when you need them most. On the other side of Noemi, Rose waves, too, almost hitting the man next to her. He opens his hands, and she jabs a finger in my direction, as if that should explain it all.

Sweet Potato walks tall and there is a swing of joy to her hoofbeats. *To understand your horse is to understand yourself.* I remind myself it is a small miracle that I am here at the biggest race of the year with arguably the best view in the house. Whether I win back that bottle or not, something has cleared my view. Millinery gave me a way to be seen; Miss Sweetie gave me a voice to be heard. But maybe what I needed most of all was simply the freedom to walk out from the shadows of my hat. Somehow, Old Gin and I have managed to fit ourselves into a society that, like a newspaper, rarely comes in colors other than black and white. There will always be those who keep their distance. But there will also be those who don't mind riding their safeties in my lane. I spent my whole life worried that the sound of my own voice might give me away, but I was wrong about that. If I hadn't used my voice, I wouldn't be here today.

In a special box several rows up, the Paynes watch the procession with other members of Atlanta's elite. Mr. Payne leans forward against a rail, like the masthead of a ship, his opera glasses fixed to his eyes. He has always been more focused on the future than the present. Next to him stands Merritt, who, for all his invitations, seems not to have accepted a single one of them. His eyes drift from Ameer to me, and he gives me a two-fingered salute.

Mrs. Payne fans herself, her pleasant demeanor on display. She doesn't acknowledge me. But when I pass, her smile wavers like a candle that feels a breath. Next to her, Caroline watches me with a hawk-eyed diligence. The dancing-lion braid I wove into her hair is still lively under a cream saucer hat. Despite falling off Noemi's safety half a dozen times—a fact that has seemed to put a spring in Noemi's step—Caroline declared she hasn't been bested yet. Though it wasn't clear if she was talking about the bicycle or Noemi, the winds have shifted for my former mistress. May she feel the stretch of a new wing.

"Welcome to the Race of the Year, eight furlongs of thunderous action!" calls an announcer.

Members of the press have positioned themselves along the gate that separates the track from the spectators, notebooks out and scribbling furiously. Signs on posts list all the sponsors and their horse numbers and colors. I scan the crowd for Nathan, wishing to see him, but dreading the sight of Lizzie on his arm.

A figure steps onto a box and tips up his Homburg. I sit a little taller, hoping I look like an elegant lady floating along on an ebony swan. Nathan waves his hat. He doesn't have Mr. Q's dreamy looks or Merritt Payne's statuesque physique, but he has the noble bearing of a compass that always points north.

A pair of pink arms asks for a lift, and soon, Lizzie is standing beside him. They are a handsome pair. Nathan would have an easier life with someone like her, someone with whom the law against miscegenation has no bearing. Her Miss Sweetie hat swivels between Nathan and me. Maybe she is thinking the same thing.

Joseph leads us to a chalked line on the outermost position on the track. I shake off the stiffness in my limbs caused by an anxious mind and draw an effortless breath. "Thank you, Joseph."

He hits a brace. Then he follows the grooms to the sidelines.

Twelve beasts grunt and paw at the ground to the left of us, springs loaded and ready to fire. The track strikes me as narrow and flimsy as cardboard. One wrong move, and I could be smashed into a papery pulp, a bit of bark caught under forty-eight pounding pistons.

A few horses down, Thief undulates as if he were made of liquid, with the leprechaun clinging, amphibian-like, on his back. The man is no longer looking at me but muttering at the clouds. Perhaps he is praying. It seems like a good time to get religion.

Scanning the stadium, I finally spot Billy Riggs near the center, blocking the view behind him with a garish plum-colored top hat to match his suit. Our gazes connect, and he stands, sweeps off the top hat, and gives me one of his mocking bows. It occurs to me that just as Old Gin and I have done our best to blend in, Billy makes his way by not blending in. Perhaps his brazen style is meant to draw attention away from his crimes, not the least of which is the crime of having a great-grandparent who was colored. Around Billy, folks chatter, their faces animated, and I wonder what secrets lie in the basement for them. For all of us. My eyes find Mrs. Payne again, holding out a gloved hand for a guest to kiss. Her hands may be clean, but she's as slippery as a hundred bathing Billys.

Before the field begins to lose the line, the man with the red bowler raises a gun. "Ready?"

I grip the stirrups and lean forward.

"Set?"

I imagine myself as the wind, light and strong, and not invisible.

Bang!

Forty-Four

I kick my heels hard, screaming, "Giddap!" as loud as I can. Sweet Potato charges!

In the span of two seconds, several things happen. Something spooks horse number 1, and he sets off in the wrong direction. Jockeys 4 and 6 with their hayseed eyes jerk their horses sideways, knocking off 3 and 5, whose horses almost go to their knees.

Just as Joseph suspected, 4 and 6 are up to no good, and it is hard to predict what they plan next.

We pass Noemi and the Bluebells, who are shrieking wildly and jumping up and down. In the stands, the Suffragists are all up on their feet, yelling just as loud, and it strikes me that the collective roar is louder than the sum of its parts. Mrs. Bullis clutches her face, eyes levered as far as they can go.

Coming up on the first curve, Sweet Potato and I are far from the lead, but at least Thief is behind us. Ameer and 11 lead the pack, tailed by 4 at the rail, and Sunday Surprise behind him. I move Sweet Potato into position behind Sunday Surprise, hoping Buxbaum's champ will clear the road ahead, clinching our tenuous lead over Thief. Number 4 drifts right, leaving an opening that Sunday surges to thread. But then 4 veers back to the rail, forcing Sunday to dodge right. Number 6 closes in, boxing in Sunday, and we all bunch up behind them. So that's what Ben Abner was talking about!

From my spot behind Sunday, it's clear that 4 and 6 are working together, but to whose benefit? There can be only one winner.

Out of the corner of my eye, a flash of green circles wide around the curve, avoiding the traffic, and then dashes ahead. It's the leprechaun on Thief! Somehow, Mr. Q has rigged Thief up for the win. But how was he able to buy off not just one, but two contestants? Surely, credit only goes so far.

I think back to that day at Buxbaum's. Robby said Billy had offered to "influence" the race in favor of Mr. Buxbaum's horse, Sunday Surprise. Billy has enough money to influence the race. He wasn't successful with Mr. Buxbaum, but for every road that runs straight, a dozen go crooked, especially a road who would name his fine horse for a petty criminal. It occurs to me that Thief's number 9 is the sum total of Billy's lucky dice, 4 and 5, same as the number on his "office" door. I have been outfoxed. Billy would never have let his favorite bauble go so easily.

Predictably, jockeys 4 and 6 have expended their horses' energies and begin to fall behind. But the damage is done, and though Sunday is doing his best to keep up, all the dodging about has cost him his legs, too. Ahead, 11 stalls on a sticky spot, long enough for Thief to shorten the gap between them, with the bulk of the contestants two lengths behind him.

Lightning puts cracks in the sky, and moments later, thunder shatters the clouds. A buckskin gelding in the front rears up at the noise, then takes off in the wrong direction. Rain pours down in sheets, drenching us in seconds. More horses fumble, but not Sweet Potato, bless her steady legs, legs that Old Gin kneaded and trained with his own hands. He didn't give up on her, and I bet she will not so easily give up on me.

I claw at the rain blinding me, my heart lurching as I slip around in the saddle. Mud flies all around. The ground looms dangerously close, becoming slicker and stickier with every passing moment. Beside us, a horse stumbles, causing the one behind it to career into the rail in a blur of hair and muscle. Sweet Potato jerks right, throwing me off balance again.

Somehow, I manage to keep my seat. It strikes me that the cloudbuster that just knocked out several of my opponents could spell the end of me, too. Thief has managed to stay ahead of our stampede, with Ameer and number 11 still going strong beyond him.

Taking advantage of the straightaway, I stick out my tailbone, leaning as much as I can into Sweet Potato's neck to help power her forward. Every hit of her legs rattles into my bones, but I hang on, feeling more like a saddlebag than a passenger. Ameer clears the next turn just ahead with the drenched Johnny Fortune still easy as a blink upon him.

Somehow, Sweet Potato closes the distance behind Thief to one length. His tail whips about like a pirate's flag as we come upon the turn, and now it's a two-horse battle for the rail. Here's our chance to get ahead! The leprechaun clinches Thief to the inside path, with the wooden rail only four feet to his left. Four feet is the width of a stall—wide enough for a horse with nerve to pass, though at a gallop, few will dare. But my horse is smaller, and she will dare.

"Ready, girl? Giddap!" I tap Sweet Potato with my heels, and she surges ahead, slipping through the space between Thief and the rail as satiny smooth as a black ribbon around the neck. We come up alongside Thief, and the sour smell of the horse clears my nostrils.

"Whore!" spits the leprechaun as we pass him. He raises his arm and then brings down his crop against my leg, so sharply I think he's sliced it right off. I would scream, but my lungs are empty of air and all that emerges is a wheezy cry. The pain is like no other I have felt and makes me bite down so hard, I swear I must break teeth. My posture crumples away, undoing all the advantage we have just gained.

Sweet Potato shudders, and I think it is over.

But as we come out of the turn, she shrieks out all the rage I feel inside. When the leprechaun draws up beside us, my big-hearted mare snaps her teeth, trying to take a bite of him, her brown eyes rolling and the froth off her mouth slinging like venom. It's not his hat she wants to taste, but blood.

The leprechaun dodges her blow with a yell, and Thief stumbles, his eyes glassy with panic. I clamber back over Sweet Potato's neck. As we correct our course, I do not look back. *Attagirl!*

At the head of the stretch, number 11 has fallen back,

tripped by the mud, and within moments, we pass him. Ameer, four lengths ahead, slows as he always does when he no longer feels chased. "Lazy in the lead," Johnny Fortune had called it.

Just cross the line, girl, and we will win back Old Gin's bottle.

Or perhaps we can do more.

Bright blood soaks the scarlet of my pants, and my front is caked with mud. There is only one G-word left to speak, one that left me shaken at thirteen but now directs my path.

Go.

The grandstand appears in view again, but the cries of the frenzied crowd dull in my ears. In the final stretch, it's not the crowd I see, but the family who raised me, waving their flags. I raise a glass of appreciation to each.

To Noemi and Robby, for friendship.

To the Bells, for words.

To Lucky Yip, for skill.

To Hammer Foot, for protection.

And most of all to you, Old Gin, for hearing the faint cries of someone who needed you and not turning away.

Mrs. Payne lifts her teary eyes to me, and the splinter of her betrayal works itself free of my heart. A Chinese baby, out of wedlock, no less, there was no easy answer for her. But unlike my mother, I do not live in a gilded cage, and like Sweet Potato, whose mother also rejected her, somehow I will find a way to thrive.

We hang back as we did at Six Paces, waiting for Ameer to loosen his pace even more. And when he does, we charge up the straightaway, powered by love and maybe a pinch of pepper, the secret ingredient. His jaunty tail teases us. Three lengths become two, and then one, and then a streak of white sand barely visible in the mud.

Sweet Potato throws her heart to the sky. With a sob, we sail past Ameer across the line.

Forty-Five

"Tie!" announces the man in the red bowler hat.

The cloudbuster shuts off as fast as it let down, and the ground steams at its departure. Ameer trots beside us, panting and, for the first time, looking chastened. Johnny Fortune grinds his black eyes into mine and spits. He knows he was bested. Still, he holds up his fists in victory, and cheers explode all around us. The eye sees what it wants, and they would never have let us win, anyway.

Billy Riggs also knows he was bested. His wet clothes have darkened to a shade that must match his mood, and he sits with his palm smashed up against his cheek. The sight of his misery lessens the throbbing cut in my thigh, and a horseshoe of a grin edges up on my face. *We are even now, you scoundrel.* Noticing me floating in my saddle, he uncrumples himself and rises. I expect one of his mocking bows. But instead, a grudging smile unfurls on his face and he begins to clap. I know the next time I pass through the doors with the Jesse James dice, I will not leave empty-handed.

The fanfare passes in a blur, the victory lap around the track with Johnny Fortune and Ameer, the handshaking and occasional claps on the back, the tearful hugs from Mrs. Bullis, and the photograph of me, the Atlanta Suffragists, and the Bluebells—well, at least Noemi—taken by a man with an accordion-style camera. While Sweet Potato tries to eat her wreath of carnations, Nathan embraces me longer than he should. "Where is Lizzie?" I ask.

"She said it wouldn't work out for us and took a coach home."

I'd like to think Lizzie did not know about her mother's attempt to unmask me. She was never the bad sort. I expect this will be the last I see of her, though a part of me wishes things could've been different between us.

As soon as I can escape, I steer Sweet Potato back to the print shop. There is only one face I wish to see.

My feet go cold when I spot Dr. Swift's wagon parked next to the Bells' house.

Without even tying up Sweet Potato, I rush into the house, past Mr. and Mrs. Bell's surprised faces, and into Old Gin's room. *Please no, don't take Old Gin.*

Bear greets me with a *woof!* To my surprise, Dr. Swift has pulled a chair up beside Old Gin, and between them is a Western chessboard.

"Grandfather," I cry, knees wobbling under me. "I thought—I thought . . ."

Dr. Swift's eyes glint with amusement under his thick brows. "You thought I might've beaten your grandfather in chess? Don't worry, he's checked me three times already, and I only arrived ten minutes ago."

Old Gin lifts his face to me. With his new orange striped cap, his eye bandage, and a beard beginning to icicle down his chin, he looks like a stringy old pirate who, despite a few rocky seas, still has a few more voyages left in him. "You had a nice ride, hm?" His dry words float out, understated as always.

I let out a half sob, half laugh. "The bats of good fortune have returned. We won."

He works his jaw, but nothing comes out. Tears troop down my face, but he stops them with his bandaged hand. "I think the bats have been here with us this whole time." His broken face smiles, and I'm reminded of a gentle boost onto my first horse in a meadow full of light.

Epilogue

Three months later.

The curtain with the horses now decorates the basement wall, opening up our former kitchen. An old desk has replaced my bed in the corner, and one of Mrs. Bell's whimsical rugs softens the back half of the room, more luxurious than the old speckled rug under my toes. At the spool table, my fingers work a silk cord into a horse knot. Mr. Buxbaum says he can't keep them on the shelf. Anything with horses has been a hot seller since the race.

The sight of Old Gin's milking stool warms my heart. He's out with Sweet Potato. Daily rides have done much for his health.

Graceful Moon's snuff bottle occupies a prime spot atop our new wall shelf, next to my winner's medal, a twin to Johnny Fortune's. With half the winnings from the race, we can afford to house Sweet Potato at the livery down the street, plus save for the future, whenever that decides to get here.

I wind the cord three times around my finger and weave the end through the loops. Silk cord innately has value, but it takes a patient hand to shape it into something better. What is the job of a parent but to teach a child that she has worth so that one day she can transform herself into whatever she wants. Old Gin was that parent to me, mother and father, teacher and friend. One day—hopefully far into the future—he and Graceful Moon will ride the heavens together, faces no longer turned up to the sky, but part of it.

As for Shang, I hope he found what he was looking for, whether that be silver or self-worth. Wherever his journey takes him, as long as the earth is round, may his path lead home one day.

"Ahoy there." Nathan's voice tumbles down the listening tube, which is now also a speaking tube.

Bear woofs.

I cross to the desk. "Ahoy."

"Would you like some tea or a chocolate? Bear is also offering her bone."

"No, thank you. I am leaving for Buxbaum's shortly. May I get you anything from there? Quills? Candles? Giddy goobers?"

"I like my goobers relaxed. Makes them go down easier. Are you sure you don't want company?"

"I shall be fine. Please tell your mother I shall be back in an hour to help her roast the chicken."

"I look forward to that."

"Roast chicken?"

"No. You being back."

Dear Miss Sweetie,

    Ever since that China girl ran that race, my daughter wants to race horses, too. I thought it was just

a phase, but she and her friends have started their own
"Fillies Only" riding club. I even caught her sewing a
pair of riding breeches. How do I convince her that the
China girl just had a lucky strike?

Sincerely,

Wits' End

Dear Wits' End,

A great man once told me that Luck rides a
workhorse named Joy. Let your daughter ride.

Sincerely,

Miss Sweetie

Author's Note

————

WERE YOU SURPRISED to learn that planters shipped Chinese people to the South to replace the field slaves during Reconstruction? I was. Plantation owners envisioned an improved system of coerced labor, as Chinese workers were lauded as "fine specimens, bright and intelligent" (*New Orleans Times,* June 3, 1870). They were dismayed, however, when the Chinese behaved no differently from formerly enslaved blacks. The new workers were unwilling to withstand the terrible conditions and ran away to the cities, and sometimes vanished from the South altogether.

After passage of the Chinese Exclusion Act in 1882—a federal law that prohibited the immigration of Chinese laborers until 1943—the Chinese already in the United States could no longer bring their families from China. Isolated and living in the margins of a country that only saw in black and white, they eventually found livelihoods outside the plantations.

I envisioned the "uncles" in this story arriving this way after the Civil War, and later sojourning through the major cities of the South in search of work. Many of them intermingled with local populations, yet these diverse histories were not captured by U.S. Census records. That a Chinese laborer like Shang might've found love in the arms of someone above his class wasn't hard for me to imagine. Sometimes, as Miss Sweetie notes, love just stumbles into you, out of the blue.

One of the things I love about writing historical fiction is how much the research process affects the creative process. *The Downstairs Girl* takes place during the period in America known as the "Gilded Age," coined by Mark Twain to describe an era of high profits and merrymaking that belied serious social problems. The more I explored these social problems, the more the character of Noemi took shape. The year 1890 marked the beginning of Jim Crow laws, like those segregating the streetcars. (Though, note that the law segregating Atlanta's streetcars was actually passed in 1891, one year after the events in this story.) Before that, with federal troops to safeguard their new civil liberties, including enfranchisement for black men, African Americans had experienced relative freedom of movement in the late 1860s and early 1870s, with some African American men even winning elections to state governments and Congress. But by the late 1870s, as white Southerners turned to violence to protest this new interracial democracy, public support for Reconstruction began to wane. White supremacist groups such as the Ku Klux Klan began to gain a foothold. In a final blow to Reconstruction, Republican candidate for president Rutherford B. Hayes agreed to return the South to "home rule" in exchange for Democrats certifying his contested election in a deal known as the Compromise of 1876. After that, civil rights for African Americans would gradually be stripped away until the civil rights movement of the 1960s.

Black women suffered greatly with the failure of Reconstruction, victims of both racism and sexism. Suffrage leaders who had worked toward the idea of universal suffrage antebellum began turning their backs on their black sisters to court the support of white Southern suffragists, whose interest in restoring white supremacy eclipsed their interest in enfranchising women. White Southern women's overt racism was used to justify the discriminatory policies of national suffrage organizations, and black women were expected to understand that it was for the greater good. Nevertheless, African American women played an active role in the suffrage movement leading up to the passage of the Nineteenth Amendment in 1920, though they themselves wouldn't be fully enfranchised until the Civil Rights Act of 1965.

ACKNOWLEDGMENTS

APPRECIATION IS A gift that, when given, can set the whole world aglow. I would like to light a few candles here.

Thank you to Kristin Nelson, my agent, and the folks at Nelson Literary Agency for being my tireless advocates. I'm lucky to have you on my side! Thank you to Angie Hodapp for your incredible insight and feedback. Thank you as well to my team at G. P. Putnam's Sons and Penguin Random House, in particular, my editor, Stephanie Pitts, for her deep and thoughtful notes and dedication to my book (and for thinking up the title!); Lily Yengle, my publicist; Anne Heausler, my copyeditor; and Samira Iravani and Theresa Evangelista, who designed the gorgeous cover.

I have always been intrigued by the Southern United States, and thanks to this book, I was able to visit there and immerse myself in the history of the region and its impact on the development of our nation. Thank you to all of the institutions whose experts, docents, and volunteers guided me in my journey to understand the South, including the Atlanta

History Center, in particular David Roane, who shared his fascinating family history with me; Piedmont Park Conservancy, especially Ginny, who took me on a private tour of the park and refused my tips; Spelman College; the APEX Museum; Atlanta Preservation Center; the Center for Civil and Human Rights Museum; and the Auburn Avenue Research Library on African American Culture and History. Thank you to Wayne Merritt of the JKL Museum of Telephony. Thank you to the librarians at both Stanford University and my local Santa Clara City Library for helping me uncover obscure documents in my research for this book. Many thanks to Herb Boyd for his contributions to the study of African American history, and for his sage advice.

I am also eternally grateful to my community of writers for their support, including Abigail Hing Wen, Jeanne Schriel, Mónica Bustamante Wagner, Parker Peevyhouse, Kelly Loy Gilbert, Sabaa Tahir, Ilene W. Gregorio, Evelyn Skye, Anna Shinoda, Amie Kaufman, Eric Elfman, Ida Olson, and especially to my fellow mermaid, Stephanie Garber.

Thank you to Ariele Wildwind, Susan Repo, Angela Hum, Karen Ng, Bijal Vakil, Ana Inglis, Kristen Good, Adlai Coronel, and Yuki Romero, for your love and support. Thank you to Melissa Lee, for lending your beautiful name.

A final thank-you to the top-shelf hats in my life, my vibrant and eternally curious parents, Evelyn and Carl Leong, and in-laws, Dolores and Wai Lee; my big-hearted sisters, Laura Ly and Alyssa Cheng; my supportive husband, Jonathan; my whip-smart daughter, Avalon; and my giver of warm hugs, Bennett. To all of you, I am your biggest fan.

Read on for more from Stacey Lee

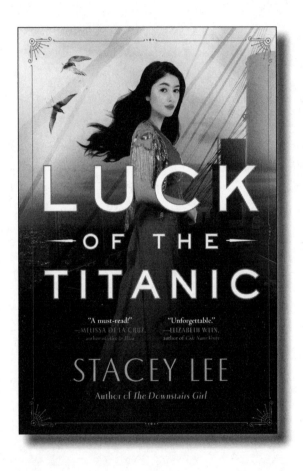

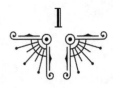

When my twin, Jamie, left, he vowed it wouldn't be forever. Only a week before Halley's Comet brushed the London skies, he kissed my cheek and set off. One comet in, one comet out. But two years away is more than enough time to clear his head, even in the coal-thickened air at the bottom of a steamship. Since he hasn't come home, it is time to chase down the comet's tail.

I try not to fidget while I wait my turn on the first-class gangway of White Star Line's newest ocean liner. A roofed corridor—to spare the nobs the inconvenience of sunshine—leads directly from the "boat train" depot to this highest crossing. At least we are far from the rats on Southampton dock below, which is crawling with them.

Of course, some up here might consider me a rat.

The couple ahead of me eyes me warily, even though I am dressed in one of Mrs. Sloane's smartest traveling suits—shark grey to match her usual temper, with a swath of black bee-swarm lace pinned from shoulder to shoulder. A lifetime of those dodgy looks teaches you to ignore them. Haven't I already survived the journey from London? A half a day's travel, packed into a smoky railcar, next to a man who stank of sardines. And here I am, so close to the finish line, I can nearly smell Jamie—like trampled ryegrass and the milk biscuits he is so fond of eating.

An ocean breeze cools my cheeks. Several stories below in either direction, onlookers crowd the dock, staring up at the ship rising six stories before them. Its hull gleams, a wall of liquid black with a quartet of smokestacks so wide you could drive a train through them. Stately letters march across its side: "TITANIC." On the third-class gangway a hundred feet to my left, passengers sport a variety of costume: headscarves, patterned kaftans, fringed shawls of botany wool, tasseled caps, and plain dungarees and straw hats. I don't see a single Chinese face among them. Has Jamie boarded already? With this crowd, I may have missed him.

Then again, he isn't traveling alone, but with seven other Chinese men from his company. All are being transported to Cuba for a new route after coal strikes here berthed their steamship.

Something cold unspools in my belly. I received his last letter a month ago. Time enough for things to change. What if Jamie's company decided to send them somewhere other than Cuba, maybe a new route in Asia or Africa?

The line shifts. Only a few more passengers ahead of me.

Jamie! I call in my mind, a game I often played growing up. He doesn't always hear, but I like to think he does when it matters.

In China, a dragon-phoenix pair of boy and girl twins is considered auspicious, and so Ba bought two suckling pigs to celebrate our birth, roasted side by side to show their common lot. Some may think that macabre, but to the Chinese, death is just a continuation of life on a higher plane with our ancestors.

Jamie, your sister is here. Look for me.

Won't he be surprised to see me? Shocked may be more accurate—Jamie has never handled surprise well—but I will get him to see that it is time for him, for *us*, to move on to bigger and better things, just as our father hoped.

I think back to the telegram I sent him when Ba passed five months ago.

```
Ba hit his head on post and died. Please come home.
Ever your Val.
```

Jamie wrote back:

```
Rec'd news and hope you are bearing up okay. Very
sorry, but I have eight months left on my contract
and cannot get away. Write me details. Your Jamie.
```

Jamie would have known that Ba had been drunk when he hit his head, and I knew he wouldn't mourn like I had. When you live with someone whose mistress is the bottle, you say your goodbyes long before they depart.

Someone behind me clears her throat. A woman in a pinstriped "menswear" suit that fits her slender figure like stripes on a zebra watches me, an ironic smile wrapped around her cigarette. I put her in her early twenties. Somehow dressing in men's clothing seems to heighten her femininity, with her creamy skin and dark hair that swings to her delicate chin. She lifts that chin toward the entrance, where a severe-looking officer stands like a box nail, a puzzled look on his face.

I bound forward on the balls of my feet, muscled from years of tightrope practice. Ba started training Jamie and me in the acrobatic arts as soon as we could walk. Sometimes, our acts were the only thing putting food on the table.

The severe officer watches me pull my ticket from my velvet handbag.

Mrs. Sloane, my employer, secretly purchased tickets for the two of us with her dragon's hoard of money. She didn't tell her son or his wife about the trip, or that she might stay in America indefinitely to get away from their money-grubbing fists and greedy stares. After her unexpected demise, I couldn't just let the tickets go to waste.

"Afternoon, sir. I am Valora Luck."

The officer glances at the name written on my ticket, then back at me, his steep cheekbones sharp enough for a bird to land on. His navy visor with its distinctive company logo—a gold wreath circling a red flag with a white star—levers as he inspects me. "Destination?"

"New York, same as the rest." Is that a trick question?

"New York, huh. Documentation?"

"You're holding it right there, sir," I say brightly, feeling the gangway shift uncomfortably.

He exchanges a guarded look with the crewman holding the passenger log. "Luck?"

"Yes." In Cantonese, our surname sounds more like

"Luke," but the British like to pronounce it "luck." Ba had decided to embrace good fortune and spell it that way, too. He'd intended the lofty-sounding name "Valor" for Jamie, and "Virtue" for me—after a sea shanty about a pair of boots—but my British mum put the brakes on that. Instead, she named my brother James, and I got Valora. It's a toss-up as to which of us is more relieved.

"You're Chinese, right?"

"Half of me." Mum married Ba against the wishes of her father, a vicar in the local parish.

"Then at least half of you needs documentation. Ain't you heard of the Chinese Exclusion Act? You can't go to America without papers. That's just how it is."

"Wh-what?" A pang of fear slices through me. The Chinese *Exclusion* Act. What madness is this? They don't like us here in England, but clearly, they *really* don't like us in America. "But my brother's on this ship, too, with the members of the Atlantic Steam Company. They're all Chinese. Did they get on?"

"I don't keep the third-class register. You'll need to get off my gangway."

"B-but my lady will be expecting me."

"Where is she?"

I was prepared for this question. "Mrs. Sloane wanted me to board first to make sure her room was ready." Of course, she had already pushed off on a different ship, one that wouldn't be making a return journey, causing me great inconvenience. "We had her trunk forwarded here a week ago. I must lay out her things." Mum's Bible is in that trunk, within its pages my only picture of her and Ba. At last, my family will be reunited, even if it is just with a photo of our parents.

"Well, you're not getting on this ship without the proper documentation." He waves the ticket. "I'll keep this for her for when she boards. Next!"

Waiting passengers begin to grumble behind me, but I ignore them. "No, please! I must board! I must—"

"Robert, escort this girl off."

The crewman beside the severe officer grabs my arm.

I shake him off, trying to muster a bit of respect. "I will see myself off."

The woman in the menswear suit behind me steps aside to allow others to go before her, her amber eyes curiously assessing me. "I saw a group of Chinese men enter the ship early this morning," she says in the no-nonsense tone Americans use. "Maybe your brother was one of them."

"Thank you," I say, grateful for the unexpected charity.

A family pushes past me, and I lose the woman in a flurry of people, parcels, and hats. I find myself being squeezed back into the train depot, like a piece of indigestible meat. Mrs. Sloane would've never stood for this outrage. Probably a rich lady like her would have persuaded them to let me on. But there is no one to speak for me now. I descend the staircase, then exit the depot onto the quay. The glare from the overcast sky cuts my eyes.

I figured the hardest part of this endeavor would be getting on without Mrs. Sloane. Never could I have foreseen this complication. What now? I need to be on that ship, or it could be months, maybe years, before I see Jamie again.

Something skirts over my boot and I recoil. A rat. They are certainly bold here, called by the peanut peddlers and meat pie hawkers. I shrink away from a pile of crates, where the rodents are making short work of a melon rind. The river slaps a rhythm against the *Titanic*'s hull, and my heart beats double time with the slosh.

Taking the American's advice, I make tracks for the third-class entrance farther down the quay toward the bow. Unlike in the first class, passengers crowd the gangway, tightening the queue as I near. I straighten my jacket. "I'm sorry, I just need to check if my brother made it through. Please, let me pass."

A man with a dark mustache chastises me in a foreign tongue, then jerks his head toward the end of the line. Heads nod, cutting me suspicious glares, and people move to block me. Seems wearing first-class clothes will not gain me any advantage here.

Perhaps things would be different if I looked less like Ba and more like Mum. I exhale my frustration, a wind heated by a lifetime of being turned away for no good cause. Then I continue farther along the quay to the end of the line, passing dockworkers manhandling ropes and a navy uniform shining a torch into people's eyeballs. They don't check the first class for disease.

Beyond the nose of the ship, a couple of tugboats line up, ready to tow the *Titanic* from her mooring. Voices rise as people look up to a massive crane on the bow lowering a hoisting platform onto the quay ten paces away. A horn honks, and the queue shifts, making way for a sleek, cinnamon-red Renault motorcar. It stops right before the hoisting platform.

It could take an hour to reach the gangway from here. But even if Jamie has boarded, they still won't let me on that ship without papers. Then the *Titanic* will leave, and he will be lost to me, possibly forever. His letters to me will be undeliverable at the Sloanes', and I will have no way of knowing which new route he was assigned. Jamie is the only family I have left. I won't let him idle his time on a steamship when he is destined for better things. Great things.

A woman with large nostrils glances at me, then pulls her son closer, spilling some of the peanuts from his paper cone. A rat slithers out from behind a crate and quietly feasts. "Stay away from that one. I've heard they eat dogs."

Barely glancing at me, the boy returns his attention to the Renault.

A crewman gestures at the dockworkers positioned on either side of the car. "Easy now. Load her on."

I am getting on that ship, by hook or by crook. Jamie is there, and I won't let him leave without me. As for the Chinese Exclusion Act, put out the fire on your trousers before worrying about the one down the street. But how will I board?

The hoisting platform sways on its hook, the stage just big enough to hold the motorcar. A crewman reaches up and guides it the last few feet to the quay.

By *hook*.

I bounce on the balls of my feet, my muscles twitching. There are more ways onto the *Titanic* than the gangways.

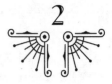

I shade my eyes. The ride up stretches a couple hundred feet, with no walls and no safety net in case something should slide off the platform. I will have to stow away before the platform begins to rise. The car makes a poor hiding spot with its open design, but I can slide underneath and hope no one looks.

It'll be like the times Jamie and I snuck rides aboard the drays about town, slipping on and off without being seen. London is full of distractions. Of course, we usually only needed to distract the driver. The ship with its many portholes suddenly looms like a wall of prying eyes. More pressing are the hundreds of eyes right here on the quay.

I look wildly about for a ruse to distract everyone. Maybe someone is carrying a firearm and I can somehow get him to fire it into the sky. Right. And then maybe a flock of flamingoes will fly in from Africa and a marching band will appear.

Another rat sniffs around my boot, its tail worming behind it. I begin to kick it away but stop. I don't like rats, but they don't give me hysterical fits like they do Mrs. Sloane's daughter-in-law, who boxed my ears when she found one in the pantry. Of course, after this, they might.

Retreating to the train depot a few paces away, I put my back to the wall and tie the ribbons on my black hat tight. Mrs. Sloane gave the hat to me, saying its short brim made her look like a garden hoe. I pull a tin of milk biscuits from my handbag and set the handbag on the ground, wishing the joy of its contents—mostly traveling supplies—to the beggar who finds it. I empty the tin along the wall, crushing the biscuits with my foot.

The dockworkers push the car in place, and the crewman waves his arms. "Stop. Set the brake! Lash it now. Smartly!"

Come on, biscuits, work your buttery charms soon.

The men work quickly, lashing the wheels to the platform.

Of course, when you need a rat, there is none to be found.

Panic jabs at my heart. I abandon my post, searching the dark corners of the quay for the loathsome creatures. After several minutes of scurrying around, I spot a couple of rats feasting on a sausage—at least I hope it's a sausage. Something sour rises in my throat. I've done more repulsive things, but for the life of me, I can't think of a single one.

Slowly, I lower myself, flexing my fingers. Before any more doubts seep in, I snatch a fat one by its scruff. "Got you."

It wiggles and hisses, red eyes glaring, probably oozing poison and disease. Grimly, I hang on, my lips peeled back in disgust. I hurry back toward the hoisting platform, casing the dock for a mark. I'll have to find someone with an open purse or a large pocket. A woman with pin curls stares openmouthed at the foremast staking the ship's bow, the hood of her old-fashioned cloak pulled back from her short neck.

Forgive me, ma'am, for what I'm about to do, and know that it is for a good cause.

I duck behind a bunch of men with long beards and burgundy caps heading her way. My rat jerks in my grasp. With light steps, I sneak up to the woman, and while saying a prayer, I release the rat into her open hood.

In four strides, I return to the platform, which has already started to rise.

"Stand back, folks." The crewman walks the perimeter of the platform, enforcing a two-yard margin. If my rat doesn't do his ratty thing soon, it will rise too high for me to scale.

The woman doesn't scream. Have I chosen that one-in-a-million mark who isn't scared by a rat down her back? Should I take a chance and climb on anyway, hoping to God that everyone blinks at the same time?

A scream that could separate the soul from one's body tears through the crowd.

At last!

The crewman glances toward the woman and the commotion forming around her.

I rush forward and hook my hands over the edge of the platform, which has lifted to waist level. I haul myself onto it from the side closest to the water and scoop up my skirts, praying my added weight won't topple the whole thing. I imagine myself light as a bird, the way I do when we walk the rope.

I flatten myself and roll under the car. But something is wrong. Something has caught me. My jacket! The back of my sleeve has snagged on a nail. With a sharp yank of my shoulder, I flip myself over, hearing the fabric rip. Then I scoot under the car, trying my best to melt into the rough wood.

The platform sways, and seagulls caw as they fly by. I heave in air. The scents of motor oil and my own fear fill my nose. At any moment, I expect the platform to stop. I listen for exclamations, or constables blowing whistles.

But the platform continues its ascent. So far, no one is yelling, except for my unfortunate victim. God save her from the plague. I press my cheek to the wood. From what I can see, no one is looking at me.

Then I see her. A child around five years old with stringy yellow hair and eyes as wide as planets is pointing at me.

I'm just an illusion, kid. Forget what you saw.

The steady pull of the crane snatches her from my view. New worries flood my mind as the platform swings over the *Titanic*'s well deck, ready for its descent into the cargo hatch. What if the shaft to the *Titanic*'s belly does not feature a wall ladder on which I can escape? I'll need to exit before reaching the storage area in the bowels of the ship, where surely men will be waiting to unload the car.

The platform slows as it nears the hatch, and my stomach turns loops. Glimpsing a crewman, I shrink back. He could see me if he thought to look under the car.

His face glistens with sweat and wonder as he walks the length of the platform, taking in the vehicle. "She's a looker. The French know how to make 'em. Thirty-five miles an hour—can you believe it?"

I close my eyes and hold my breath, as if that could hide me from view. Even my blood stops pumping.

He completes his circuit. "Bring her down."

The grinding of a motor and the clink of a chain unspooling herald my descent into the jaws of destiny. Sounds echo off the shaft closing around me, and the light changes.

Rolling out from under the car, I scramble to the edge of the platform and look wildly around for a ladder. It's on the *other* side. My wet fingers slip against the glossy car frame as I swing myself into the seat and scoot across. To my horror, before I can grab a rung, the wall ends.

The platform descends at a walking pace past a room with benches and tables filled with passengers—third class, by the looks of them. Some stare at me dropping from the ceiling, still clinging to the car seat. Nearby, a uniformed crewman chats with a woman, his back to me. Can't get off here. I hold my breath and wait for the platform to pass from view.

At the next level, the shaft becomes enclosed once again. I step up onto the seat, then grab the center chain. Clenching my boots around the chain, I use my legs to propel myself up, trying to climb faster than my stage is falling. The crane brakes, giving me a few precious seconds to scale higher, the chain digging into my hands. Then on it goes, rumbling to life again. I inch up, cursing my skirt for impeding my progress. Sweat blinds me. My limbs scream in anguish. I pass the large room. If anyone notices me, no one protests.

At last, the ladder appears and I hoist myself high enough to place my foot on a rung. Grabbing the ladder, my skirt tears, but at least I'm no longer headed down. I rest, catching my breath.

Then I climb, rung by rung, until sunlight kisses my face.

I peek over the framed opening. Forty feet away by the base of the crane, the sweaty crewman who had admired the Renault has pulled back his navy beret and is looking up at a seagull. No one else is on the well deck. I imagine myself as invisible as the breeze, then hook a leg over the edge. As quietly as possible, I roll onto the pine deck.

With a loud caw, the seagull swoops in my direction, and the crewman wheels about.

Sod off, you screechy tattletale.

The crewman places a hand on the crane base to steady himself, then draws closer, his bloodshot eyes nearly pouring from their sockets. "Wh-where did you come from?"

I scramble to my feet, feeling a breeze through the tear in my skirt. The sleeve of my jacket collects around my elbow. I must look a fright.

Behind the crewman, the superstructure stacks up like the layers of a cake, at the top of which stands a man with a white beard and a proud bearing, the gold braids on his navy sleeves gleaming like bracelets. Even from fifty feet away, I recognize the face in all the brochures: Captain Smith, the king of this floating palace. He spreads his fingers against the rail and bends his gaze in our direction.

I squeeze a toe down on my panic, which, like a tissue-thin handkerchief in a strong wind, is in danger of cutting loose.

The crewman's nostrils put me in mind of the double barrel of a gun. "I said, where did you come from?"

As the Chinese proverb goes, the hand that strikes also blocks. Straightening my hat, I put on the haughty look Mrs. Sloane used with inferiors, eyes hooded, nose tipped up like a seal's. After months of assisting the tough old nut, I could do Mrs. Sloane better than she could. "My mother's loins. And you?"

Someone utters a short laugh. Behind me, leaning against a staircase up to the forecastle, I recognize the slender American woman from the first-class gangway. A fresh cigarette dangles from her red mouth.

The crewman's eyes narrow into slits. He points a thick finger at the cargo shaft. "No. I saw you come from the hatch. Else why's your jacket torn like that?"

"Are you suggesting *I* climbed out from *there*?" I snort loudly. "I can't even walk on this slippery deck without falling. Look, I have ripped my jacket." I crook a finger at his bulbous nose. "You're lucky I didn't break my neck."

Lookouts stationed in the crow's nest halfway up the foremast peer down at us. I half expect them to start clanging the warning bell from their washtub-like perch. But then an officer emerges from a doorway under the forecastle, his boots jabbing the deck, and I forget all about the lookouts.

A noose of a tie hangs from a severe white collar, and a jury of eight brass buttons judge me from a humorless field of navy. A uniform like that could have me thrown off this boat for a final baptism. "Something the matter here?"

The crewman mops some of the sweat off his face with his sleeve. "Officer Merry. She climbed out of the hatch."

Officer Merry folds a clipboard into his chest and glares at me. Shapeless eyebrows overhang a dour expression, perhaps caused by the pressure of living up to a name like Merry.

With my hand to my chest, I laugh, but in my nervousness, it sounds more like the honk of passing geese. "Of course I did. Right after I dropped in from my flying balloon."

"Who are you?" asks the officer.

He will ask for papers. The ruse is up. My leg shakes, but I clamp down on it, forcing it into stillness.

"Should I call the Master-at-Arms?" asks the crewman.

"For goodness' sake, I saw the whole thing." The American with the cigarette sashays up from behind me, her suit as fitted as if it were sewn around her. I'd nearly forgotten about her. "She was just taking some air, same as me, and the poor thing stumbled but caught herself on the lip of that hatch. Lucky for you, she has good reflexes. An accident right before launch could hardly be good press."

I try not to gape at her.

"Miss Hart. How nice to see you." Officer Merry affects an air of pleasant surprise, which is as effective as trying to spruce up a plate of spoiled meat with a sprig of parsley.

Miss Hart begins pacing, moving as regally as the queen's cat. "I must say, the layout of this ship is quite confusing. It's a wonder you don't have more people falling into the hatch. Obviously, you didn't get a woman's opinion on the design."

Officer Merry stares, caught in the fluttering trap of her

glamorous eyelashes. He clears his throat. "It was designed this way so that honored passengers such as yourself could enjoy their luxurious facilities without being disturbed." He glances up at the navigating bridge and, noticing Captain Smith, throws him a quick salute. The captain nods and turns away. "We would not want people to get confused about where they should be."

"So your answer is to confuse them further if they stray," she says brightly. "Interesting."

"You should be relaxing on the Promenade Deck, not down here with the third class. They are serving champagne. It's a good time to meet your fellow passengers. We have several notable guests traveling with us."

My ears get bigger. I learned from Mrs. Sloane's list of "distinguished passengers" that Mr. Albert Ankeny Stewart, part owner of the Ringling Brothers Circus, would be among those guests. When I received Jamie's letter announcing that his crew was being transferred via the *Titanic*, I knew it was a sign that it was time for me to finally get our family back together. We'd dreamed of going "big-time" in a real circus ever since Ba showed us a poster of P. T. Barnum and Co.'s Greatest Show on Earth. We'd even choreographed an audition routine that we called the Jumbo, after the great circus elephant. Somehow, I aim to show Mr. Stewart that routine.

"Mother doesn't care for my smoking." Miss Hart taps her finger against her cigarette holder, and ashes drop. "But I am ready to return to my luxurious facilities. I trust you know a more direct route back to B-Deck." She takes his arm, nodding toward a small staircase that leads to the superstructure. I can't help wondering if she actually does know her way around.

"Pull the gangway," barks a voice from somewhere in the distance, lighting a fire in me. I make a hasty exit toward the forecastle.

At last, it's anchors aweigh.

Officer Merry's gaze follows me, heavy as a boot on my back.

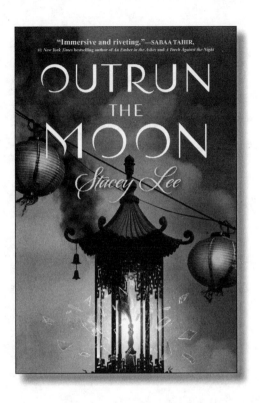

**WINNER OF THE PEN CENTER USA LITERARY AWARD
FOR YOUNG ADULT FICTION**

WINNER OF THE ASIAN/PACIFIC AMERICAN AWARD FOR LITERATURE

"Immersive and riveting. Mercy Wong had my heart from page one."
—Sabaa Tahir, *New York Times* bestselling author
of *An Ember in the Ashes*

"A fantastic read! Emotional, entertaining, and bewitching."
—Cynthia Kadohata, author of the Newbery Award–winning
Kira-Kira and the National Book Award–winning
The Thing About Luck

★ "Powerful, evocative, and thought-provoking."
—*Kirkus Reviews*, starred review

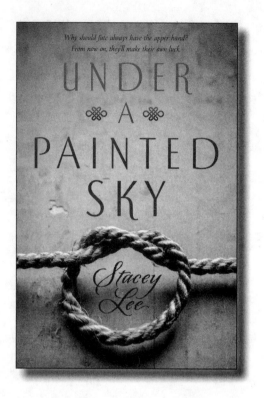

Why should fate always have the upper hand?
From now on, they'll make their own luck.

UNDER
❖ A ❖
PAINTED
SKY

Stacey Lee

"Get ready to fall in love with this one." —*Bustle*

"Utterly refreshing and exciting. Buy this book. It's out-
standing YA." —*Book Riot*

"Stacey Lee successfully rides onto the range with this
sweeping, warmhearted tale." —*Chicago Tribune*

"This moving novel will captivate you." —*BuzzFeed*

★ "Will keep readers on the very edges of their seats."
—*Kirkus Reviews*, starred review

★ "A vivid, nontraditional Western."
—*Publishers Weekly*, starred review